THE WITCH'S PROGRESS OMNIBUS

LEAH R CUTTER

KNOTTED ROAD PRESS

The Witch's Progress Omnibus
Copyright © 2020 Leah Cutter
All rights reserved
Published by Knotted Road Press
www.KnottedRoadPress.com

ISBN: 978-1-64470-153-9

Cover and interior design copyright © 2020 Knotted Road Press http://www.KnottedRoadPress.com

Reviews

It's true. Reviews help me sell more books. If you've enjoyed this story, please consider leaving a review of it on your favorite site.

Come someplace new…

Are you a traveler? Do you enjoy exploring strange new worlds, new cultures, new people?

Journey into the various lands envisioned by Leah Cutter.

Sign up for my newsletter and I'll start you on your travels with a free copy of my book, *The Island Sampler*.

I will never spam you or use your email for nefarious purposes. You can also unsubscribe at any time.

http://www.LeahCutter.com/newsletter/

The Troll-Human War

The Troll-Troll War

The Shadow Wars Trilogy

The Raven and the Dancing Tiger

The Guardian Hound

War Among the Crocodiles

The Clockwork Fairy Kingdom

The Clockwork Fairy Kingdom

The Maker, the Teacher, and the Monster

The Dwarven Wars

The Chronicles of Franklin

Franklin Versus The Popcorn Thief

Franklin Versus The Soul Thief

Franklin Versus The Child Thief

Huli Intergalactic - Science/Space Fantasy

Origins

The Strawberry Girl

Contemporary Fantasy

Siren's Call

The Immortals' War

THE CIRCLES OF WITCHCRAFT

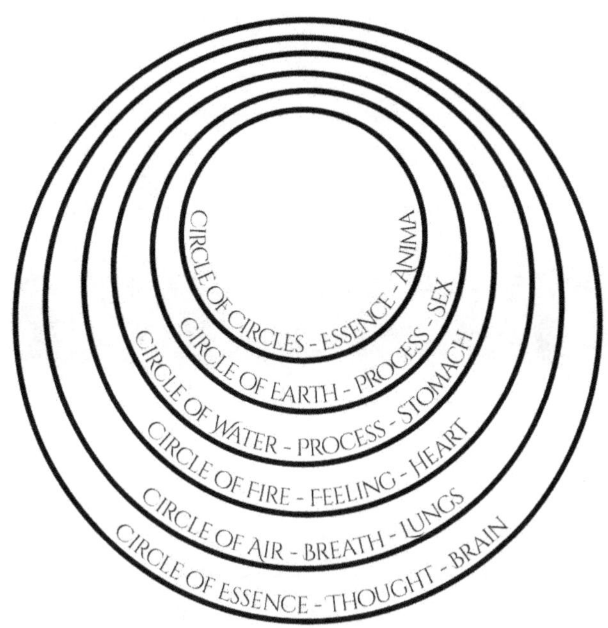

CIRCLE OF AIR

ONE

The smell of rotten wood and wet plaster permeates the streets of Portland now that the flood waters have receded. Mold, too, covers every surface that had been underwater, black inky lines that look like a child gone mad with charcoal. More bloated bodies have been discovered in the first floor rooms of some of the buildings. The cost of lives, livestock, and goods is absolutely astonishing. Though I objected to being brought in to build the next bridge so early, my superiors at the Pacific Bridge Company were correct: I needed to see this damage so I fully understood what the consequences of failure might bring.

Wilson Evermore, Civil Engineer, 1894

TARA WATCHED, delighted, as the bright green hummingbird flitted around the feeder she'd set up earlier that week. The blue glass feeder swayed slightly on the metal stand jutting up from the cold iron handrail of the balcony. The hummingbird—one of the local Annas—

rested after circling a few more times, dipping his head into the bright red-glass flower and sipping the nectar contained inside.

She hadn't been certain that she'd get any birds. The apartment she rented was close to the train station in downtown Portland, not in one of the neighborhoods that was full of greenery and parks. While the waterfront below her held a lot of blackberry bramble, there weren't a lot of trees.

Underneath the feeder, pressed up against the low balcony wall, stood a long bench covered in her potted plants: rosemary, English lavender, spearmint, variegated marjoram, basil (three varieties), curly-leaf parsley, purple sage, borage, French sorrel, to name just a few. Tara kept the plants well-trimmed or they would have spilled over the sides of the bench, then tried to take over the rest of the balcony.

She needed the herbs not just for her salads and teas but for her magical potions as well, so none of the leaves she clipped ever went to waste.

The balcony of her shared apartment faced northeast. Below, she could see the Willamette River. It was the main reason she'd agreed to rent this place, so that she could be on the river. (Well, both the view and the big balcony.) Tara had always tried to live close to the water ever since she'd moved to Portland fourteen years before, when she'd just gotten out of college and foolishly followed her college sweetheart across country, moving from Wisconsin to Oregon.

If Tara could afford it, she'd buy herself a house on a riverbank. But she already had to work two jobs in order to pay her share of the rent of the two bedroom apartment. And she expected the rent to go up again in about a month's time, when their current contract finished.

That Friday, Tara had the afternoon shift at the shop, so she got to sit on the balcony and enjoy the peaceful morning air while sipping her tea. Today, she'd used a beautiful black Assam for the base, to which she'd added cocoa nibs, some dried apple bits, a splash of vanilla, and two freshly picked apple mint leaves. It was one of the smoother teas she'd created, and a regular favorite.

It wasn't that quiet, as usual—too much city traffic seeped up from the busy streets behind her, the constant hum of cars across the Steel

Bridge almost soothing. As summer had yet to take a solid hold, the air was chilly, and Tara wore a soft, gray cotton work shirt over her T-shirt and jeans.

Tara didn't wear any makeup—she considered herself pretty enough with wide-spaced blue eyes, soft brown hair that fell to just below her shoulder blades, and clear white skin that would freckle in the summer sun. Yes, she carried more weight than what was considered popular these days, primarily around her middle, but being almost six feet tall, she carried it well. Plus, a lot of that weight was actually muscle from swimming and yoga.

"Ewww. What's that thing?" said Sharon, stepping out onto the balcony and chasing away the tiny bird. "It's not going to shit all over everything, is it?"

"No, it won't," Tara said with a sigh. She picked up her tea mug from the wrought iron table beside her. Damn it. Empty already.

At least that gave her an excuse to leave and get out of Sharon's way, despite the fact that Tara loved spending her mornings out here and would sit on the hard iron chairs all day, watching the river and the traffic going up and down it.

The hummingbird buzzed by the feeder. He made a loud thrumming noise as he passed.

"Get away!" Sharon said, shaking her hands frantically in front of her face.

"He isn't about to attack you," Tara said mildly.

"How do you know?" Sharon said, glaring over at Tara. "Those things are vicious."

"It's more scared of you than you are of it," Tara said, not wanting to point out that the tiny bird wouldn't even take up a third of Sharon's meaty palm.

"You don't know how scared I can get," Sharon said stubbornly.

Tara just shrugged. That was true, actually. Tara didn't know how frightened Sharon could get, though Tara suspected that if she tried, she could brew up a concoction for Sharon that would cause Sharon to be utterly terrified.

Just for a moment, Tara let herself imagine what that might look like. Sharon had blonde hair straight out of a bottle that she wore poofed up around her face, a modern take on a 1950s bouffant. Her gray-green eyes looked tired that morning, and the makeup on her pale white skin did a poor job of hiding the dark circles—staying up too late reading or watching TV, probably. Sharon wore her typical work outfit, a nice, lightweight black jacket over a short-sleeved white blouse and black slacks—office wear for the wannabe manager. Sharon worked as a technical writer and so didn't need to dress so formally; however, she had her sights set on her boss's job.

Could Tara rig up a potion that would make Sharon's hair stand on end? Like one of those cartoon figures who'd just touched an electric wire? The fear would make Sharon's face grow ashen and no amount of makeup would bring color to her cheeks. How huge would her eyes get, if she was truly frightened? How wide would her mouth stretch with screams?

Tara shook her head, banishing the image. She wasn't like that. Wasn't that type of witch, though she'd originally trained under exactly that sort of witch when she'd first discovered her powers here in Portland.

The hummingbird buzzed the small balcony again.

"You see!" Sharon said. "Mean, nasty thing. It's going to keep me from enjoying the balcony this summer."

"No, it won't," Tara said, though now she wasn't sure. Maybe the hummingbird had the good taste to dislike Sharon and would try to chase her away.

"Fine," Sharon said. "But you're the one who will have to clean all the bird shit off the chairs."

Tara nodded rather than say something, as she wasn't certain she could stay polite.

Sharon stomped off, slamming the sliding glass door leading to the living room of the apartment behind her.

The hummingbird very politely flitted by the feeder again, landing delicately on the stand, cocking his head from one side to the other while looking at Tara, making a *click-click-click* sound.

Huh. Maybe he really didn't like Sharon as he was no longer dive-bombing the balcony.

"I don't care much for her either," Tara told the bird softly. "But she has the largest bedroom, with her own bathroom, and so pays the majority of the rent. I can't live here without her."

The hummingbird clicked at her again before going to feed, as if he was an old aunt, *tsking* at her bad fortune.

It might not be Tara's problem for too much longer, if the rent really did get raised an astronomical amount next month.

She'd just have to find another place to live, close enough to see the water. But with housing prices rising so fast, leaping higher than her wages, that might become impossible.

The buzzing of her phone brought her out of her morning meditation. It was Patricia.

One of the advantages to living so close to downtown was that Tara didn't own a car and could walk to work.

The disadvantage was that anytime something went wrong, Patricia, the owner, tended to call Tara first.

"Tara, darling, I'm so sorry to bother you! I hope I'm not waking you," came Patricia's breezy tone.

"Am awake. Mostly," Tara said truthfully. It would be another hour or so before she was fully "there." Tara enjoyed what she called a slow roll in the mornings rather than jolting herself up and having to run at full speed.

"You know that normally I wouldn't ask, but Han Su just called and asked if she could have part of the morning off," Patricia said. "Something about registration and paperwork."

Tara sighed. While she adored the sly humor of her co-worker, Han Su tended to not understand deadlines. Those were for other people, not free spirits like her.

"I can come in early," Tara said slowly. "But—"

"Thank you! Thank you!" Patricia said. "I knew you'd come to the rescue. I'd work the shift myself but I already have so many things scheduled!"

"Patricia!" Tara said loudly before her boss could hang up.

"Yes?" Patricia asked with just a hint of impatience in her voice, as if Tara was the one calling for a favor now.

"That will put my hours into overtime for the week," Tara said.

A quiet sigh came across the line. "You could just not work next week…"

"We've tried that before and it's never worked out like that," Tara reminded her.

"Fine, I'll authorize the overtime," Patricia said.

Tara could tell that Patricia really wanted to say something more, or even warn Tara to not let it happen again. However, it wasn't Tara's fault that she'd ended up working so many hours this week. Between Han Su and inventory, there wasn't much else that Tara could do.

Plus, she needed the money.

"See you later," Tara said breezily, cutting the connection before she could hear Patricia complain.

It wasn't as if Patricia couldn't afford it. She wasn't dependent on the shop's income. Patricia was independently wealthy and lived in one of the mansions in south Portland with her two long-haired ragdoll cats.

The hummingbird came back to the feeder again, choosing a different red flower to sip from before flitting off to do its business.

Tara rose to her feet and stretched her arms over her head before leaning over and brushing her fingers against the cool concrete floor. The backs of her legs were still a little sore from the yoga class she'd taken the day before.

She didn't like to think how much more effort it took to stay in shape now that she was thirty-eight. Maybe she'd have to take up bike riding or something.

She shuddered at the image. Of course, she'd tried it, more than once. She lived in Portland, after all. But it had never suited her, not even as a kid.

Swimming though—she could stay in the water all day long. She'd actually planned on heading down to the Y and taking a swim later that morning. Then maybe spending some time studying, memorizing the Latin names of plants, as well as their traditional medicinal, culinary, utilitarian, and magical properties.

Tara was a witch of the first circle, the circle of thought. She had a lot to learn before she could pass within, to the next circle, the circle of breath, also sometimes called the circle of air.

However, all her plans had just flown away, as quickly as the hummingbird who had just taken off. Now she had to call her coworker Han Su, find out when she needed to come to the shop, then probably pack both a lunch as well as a dinner.

Maybe the store would be quiet and she could spend more time studying…

But Tara doubted that her luck would be that good. Particularly on a Friday afternoon at the start of the summer. Tourist season was just getting started. The store would be incredibly busy from now through the end of October.

Tara nodded to the hummingbird who'd returned for just one more sip before heading inside to start her day.

"Ye Olde Magick Shoppe" was a popular tourist destination in the heart of the Pearl District in downtown Portland. It was a storefront that had been built into a converted warehouse, so the walls were new but the floor was the original scratched up and scarred wood. The ceilings were eighteen feet high, giving the room an airy feeling. Though no direct sunlight could shine into the tall front windows, they still let in an incredible amount of ambient light, even during the rainy winter months.

The front of the shop wasn't that big, about twenty by sixteen, with the counter smack in the center of the room. Shelves lined the walls and contained a variety of "magical" items, such as sparkly wands for kids, "blessed" candles in every color and scent, books about the ghosts and haunted places in Portland, crystals and geodes, wooden pyramids, and copper-lined bracelets.

Many wannabe witches dropped by, exclaiming that the shop had a good feel to it, a presence—frequently stating that they'd been drawn there. They would tell Tara stories about the charms they were creating, the spells they'd cast, even the sightings they'd had of ghosts, UFOs, and various other things.

While Tara tried to be sympathetic, her co-worker Han Su was shameless. She'd speak to tourists in a heavy Asian accent with broken syntax, then hand sell one of the most expensive geodes or crystal balls to the customer, going on and on about her Chinese ancestors.

Never mind that Han Su was actually Vietnamese, third generation, raised in Portland, and spoke perfectly good English.

The tourists paid good money for trinkets then were on their way, a constant stream of knickknacks flowing out and money flowing in.

However, the front of the store was literally just that, a front, for the actual magic shop in the back.

In the far right corner of the back wall stood an open door to the second room. Patricia called it "hiding in plain sight." Most of the tourists who came in never even poked their head in the room.

Those who found the room had power, whether they knew it or not.

The back of the shop resembled a modern apothecary, or maybe even an expensive tea shop. Dark wooden shelves stuck out from the bright white walls. Precisely placed cream-colored porcelain containers lined the shelves—the kind generally used to hold coffee beans. Handwritten signs listed the various dried herbs, roots, and spices.

A long counter ran the length of the room, in front of the shelves, at the perfect height for Tara to work at (while Han Su complained about it being too high all the time, as she was just over five feet tall). An old-fashioned balance scale dominated a corner of the counter, used for precisely measuring out quantities of dried herbs. It had a large scoop on one side of the balance and a flat metal disc on the other. Underneath the scale, a pyramid-shaped case held all the various weights.

Two large stainless steel refrigerators hummed against the wall to the right, containing all the fresh herbs.

And today, Tara's lunch, as well as her dinner.

Tara carefully slid the large stalks of basil and lemongrass to the side as she placed her lunch and dinner on the top shelf. Han Su was still standing behind her, thanking her profusely for taking the remainder of her shift.

"I don't know what I was thinking!" Han Su said again. "I really thought the deadline for signing up for summer classes was next week, not this week."

"It's okay," Tara said. She shrugged and gave the other woman a conspiratorial grin. "I need the overtime."

"Ooooh, you got overtime this week?" Han Su said.

Though Han Su was twenty-four, it was easy for Tara to see the old Asian grandmother that Han Su would eventually turn into. Han Su kept her long hair primly tied back into a neat bun at the back of her head. She wore an old-fashioned apron while she worked in the store, one made out of beige duck cloth, meant to help convey the image that she wasn't fully American. Under that, she had on a modest peach-colored short-sleeved shirt and gray slacks.

"I earned that overtime," Tara gently reminded Han Su.

"I suppose," Han Su said, nodding. "You work too much."

Tara snorted. "I don't live with my family," she pointed out. She had to work more than just at the shop in order to pay her rent.

"It's tradition!" Han Su protested.

Tara opened her mouth then shut it again. She'd met Han Su's parents. They'd both been born in America and were effortlessly chic. Probably the only reason why they'd agree for their bohemian daughter to continue living at home while trying to complete her fifth (sixth?) attempt at a college degree was so that they would continue to have the opportunity to tame her.

Good luck with that.

"Why are you taking summer classes anyway?" Tara asked as they moved to the front of the store. Only three customers browsed the shelves at that point, but Tara was expecting a complete rush in about an hour, right around noon, when one of the local Portland tour buses disgorged their passengers half a block away.

Despite her high society leanings, Patricia was a sharp shopkeeper. She stayed on top of the inventory and always seemed to understand the trends before they began, stocking the latest gimmick just before it was discovered by the masses. (She'd stocked a whole collection of notebooks with birds on them one week before the show about "put a bird on it" aired.) Plus, she'd chosen the perfect location for the store in terms of walk-by customers.

"Don't tell anyone," Han Su said, staying on the customer side of the counter and leaning over while Tara took her place behind it, "but there's a new playwriting class that I'm taking."

Tara tried not to roll her eyes. Han Su really wanted to be a writer (as did Sharon, her flatmate). They frequently got into long debates about the virtues of outlining versus writing into the dark, what various markets were hot at the time and writing for them, as well as sharing tidbits about their very different writing styles.

However, Han Su tended to take class after class instead of actually sitting down and writing. Sharon wrote more, or at least pretended to, as she was on her social media feeds most of the time when she was supposed to be writing.

Tara had no desire whatsoever to be a writer. Writing up descriptions of the stock always fell to Han Su or Patricia, as Tara tended to just look at the thing and then baldly describe it. ("It's a candle and it smells pretty.") It was Han Su who came up with the various notes around the store describing the merchandise, talking about the primeval power of the pyramids, the healing abilities of the cooper lined bracelets, the mystical enchantments of the crystals.

"Go sign up for your classes," Tara said, shooing Han Su out of the shop as a customer approached the counter.

"I'll see you at the party tonight, right?" Han Su said as she untied the back of her apron.

Tara nearly groaned. She'd forgotten that the "party"—basically, a meeting of the coven—was tonight. "I can make an appearance," Tara said. "I won't be able to stay late."

Han Su pouted. "You never stay late. You work too much."

Tara merely raised a single eyebrow at Han Su, silently pointing out that Tara wasn't even supposed to be working at this time.

"Okay! Bye! See you later!" Han Su said brightly, waving as she left.

"How can I help you?" Tara said, smiling as she turned to the customer waiting patiently.

The rest of the afternoon passed quickly, a steady stream of customers and questions, with barely enough time for her to sneak in drinks of the homemade smoothie she'd brought for lunch.

Fortunately, it was really tasty, so she kept going back for more. Today, it had fresh golden raspberries, spinach, kale, bok choy, cucumber and celery for the veggies part, along with homemade coconut milk yogurt as well as coconut milk, vanilla, and protein powder.

Right around six o'clock came the usual dinner lull, and Tara was able to dig into the mason jar salad she'd brought. She'd cut up just a few leaves of the variegated marjoram and mixed those in, along with some basil, borage, and French sorrel. They gave a nice tang to the various lettuces and cabbage. Plus bacon, of course, and hard boiled eggs.

After the dinner lull many of the local witches stopped by for supplies for the weekend and for the solstice next week. Tara spent at least half her time in the back, measuring out ingredients and bagging them for her customers. A dozen internet orders came in as well that Tara was able to box up, ready to drop off at the post office in the morning. Kyle came by early in the evening, then promised to return later to give Tara a lift to the coven meeting.

Just as Tara was getting ready to close up shop, an older gentleman showed up. Tara was surprised—she hadn't heard the bell ring when the front door opened. She just looked up, and there he was, in the backroom with her.

She tried to get a good look at him; however, it seemed as though he stood in shadows which made his expression and features indistinct. She had the impression that he was shorter and rounder than she was, but not soft, no, he gave off a feeling of granite. She assumed he was white, as his face did appear fairly pale. He wore not only a fancy brown wool suit coat, but a vest and pants as well. His white shirt was the brightest thing about him, held tightly together at the collar with a string tie. He doffed his bowler-like hat to her as he stepped closer to the counter.

"Can I help you?" Tara asked, blinking and trying to see his face. It wavered as if it was underwater. Then again, he also smelled of the sea, of kelp and salt.

"Maybe," the man said, cocking his head to the side. "Tell me, do you have any dried purple heather? *Calluna vulgaris?*"

"We do," Tara said. She reached for the jar on the shelf behind her.

Opening the jar filled the room with the scent of a warm summer hillside.

"Tell me, what are the properties of heather?" the man asked.

Tara suddenly felt as though she stood in front of her first teacher, Miss Lucy.

"Protection, luck, and peace," Tara replied. "Carry it in a sachet to protect against violence. Hang it from the ceiling in the northeast corner of the house to promote peace. Tie it together with dried clover for luck."

"It also brings rain," the man reminded her.

"Yes, yes of course," Tara said. "Burn it with sword ferns to cause it to rain."

"And what are the real properties?" the man asked.

"I…I don't understand," Tara said purposefully. As part of her lore learning, she'd had to memorize both parts of every herb, the traditional, old-fashioned magick as well as the true magical properties. Sometimes they overlapped, often they didn't.

However, Tara didn't want to start listing off the hidden, secret parts of her learning. She didn't know this man. She was certain he was human, as the hairs on the back of her neck didn't stand and warn her of some sort of *other*.

Yet, there was something off with him, and she didn't know him.

"Heather is used by the head, to clear the thoughts of the practitioners before the start of a prayer circle," the man admonished her.

"Yes," Tara said slowly. "And by the lungs, to promote deeper breathing," she added, wanting to show that she wasn't completely stupid.

"Exactly!" the man said with a nod. "Six paths to the light," he said. "Six circles to pass through. Head, lungs, heart, stomach, and sex, until finally, anima."

Tara nodded. He used the older terms for the tenants of witchcraft, but he knew the true path, where the real magic lay.

However, instead of making her more comfortable, possibly

acknowledging that he was a witch like her, it just made her more wary.

She didn't trust this creature, and more and more he was starting to change from man into other, though physically he retained his human-like form.

If only she could see his face clearly!

Silence held the pair of them taut, staring at each other.

What did he want? He seemed to be searching for her soul.

Tara tried to look away from his piercing eyes, but she couldn't. Suddenly, she found herself immobile, held like an insect in a spider's web.

Cold air whipped around Tara, blowing like a storm across an ice-laden river. The man in front of her grew darker. The strong smell of wet sisal rope filled the space.

Tara jumped when the bell over the door of the shop rang, the weird binding that had held her abruptly breaking.

"Excuse me," she said, slipping out from behind the counter and practically racing into the other room.

It wasn't another customer, but merely Kyle, who had returned for he like he'd said he would.

"I'll be just a minute," Tara assured him, though a part of her wanted to go and throw her arms around him.

He wouldn't have taken that well, however. Kyle was uncomfortable with any physical contact, even handshakes.

Tara turned back to room full of herbs, bracing herself before stepping back inside.

The room was empty. The container for the heather was back on the shelf.

Tara quickly turned around. No one besides Kyle stood in the shop. How had the man slipped out?

"Did you see anyone else here in the shop?" Tara asked.

"Not a soul," Kyle said seriously. Then again, he was usually serious. Only a few people, and Tara felt herself lucky enough to be included in that group, knew that Kyle could be a goofball as well, his white teeth practically shining in his black face. He kept his head shaved smooth, and regularly oiled it, giving him a regal appearance. He was taller than she was, a six-foot-three wall of walking muscle. Over his plain T-shirt and jeans he frequently wore a funky vest. Tonight, it was a red-and-white bold print that had its roots in Afrofuturism.

Kyle had a timeless quality to him. He could have been as young as twenty or as old as fifty. Tara had only recently learned that he was actually forty-four.

"There was a man in here, when you came into the shop," Tara said as she stepped into the backroom. She still smelled the river in there, could still feel the wet ropes and hear the cawing of seagulls.

"There's no one here," Kyle pointed out. "And no one came by me."

"And the jar he'd asked about is back on the shelf," Tara mused. She went and opened the heather, the fresh scent banishing her impressions of the river.

Though instead of just bringing the scent of sunshine, an undercurrent of rain was mingled with it.

Tara shook her head, but the scent of rain remained.

While Tara might be many things, overly imaginative wasn't one of them. She closed up the jar and thought for a moment before looking back to Kyle.

"I don't know if he was here or not," Tara admitted. "But something just happened."

"Maybe you fell asleep and dreamed about him," Kyle said. "Do I need to be jealous of your dream man?"

Tara snorted. "More like a nightmare man," she assured Kyle. "No need for jealousy." It wasn't that the pair of them were a couple—far from it, as Kyle preferred men. However, Kyle had stood in as Tara's beard at least on a couple of occasions, and their pretend dates had always gone well.

"I will protect you," Kyle said gallantly, taking a heroic stance, as if he wore a cape or something.

Tara rolled her eyes. "Goof," she said. "Come on. Or we'll be late."

Still, she checked the stockroom before she left as well, making sure that they were truly alone, before she closed the shop and locked the door.

Whoever that man was, whatever he was, she hoped she'd seen the last of him.

She feared, though, that this was just their first encounter.

TWO

The task ahead of me is quite daunting. The combined waters of the Willamette and the Columbia rivers, swollen with runoff from the mountains, regularly flood the region. The old timers recollect floods coming through every three to five years. My superiors want me to ensure that the next generation of bridges will never be washed away. I've developed stronger footings, as well as designs that lift the spans high into the heavens. Still, I fear this won't be enough. The true task is to prevent the floods from striking the bridges in the first place. To that effect, I've applied for funding for an expedition to travel further upstream, to see if it's possible to deal with the problem long before it reaches the fair city of Portland.

Wilson Evermore, Civil Engineer, 1896

THE COVEN WAS MEETING at Gilmore's house, up in Arlington Heights. It was an old craftsman house that was in beautiful shape but hadn't been "modernized," so it still had a separate formal living room, dining room, and kitchen (instead of the open floor plan that was so popular and had ruined many beautiful old houses, at least in Tara's opinion.)

Parking was a bitch, as always, but Kyle managed to squeeze his Mini-Cooper in front of a van. It always amazed Tara how Kyle was able to fold himself into his car, but the Cooper had a surprising amount of headroom, particularly for people as tall as them.

The night was softer out here, away from downtown. Crickets and cicadas sang over the sound of traffic. Tara was glad for her work shirt, as the temperature had dropped with the setting sun. She walked to the house next to Kyle, neither of them saying anything, as was their habit. Kyle was one of the few individuals that Tara could share that kind of silent communion with, enjoying each other's company without saying a word.

Gilmore's house sat on three quarters of an acre, practically unheard of in the city. The backyard was built on a gentle slope, with three tiers. The top layer held an artificial mound that hid a modern pump for the water fountain that merrily splashed up there.

Tara took a deep breath as she stepped into the green space and the sounds of the outside world, the traffic and the planes, all faded. She knew it wasn't an enchantment—it was practically impossible to create magical artifacts, despite what all the myths proclaimed. However, all she could hear was the tinkling of the water.

The first tier up from the house contained a small meditation maze. It was made out of found stones. Instead of being circular, the maze was oval in order to fit the space. The stones led the walker along a winding path inward toward a small circular bowl in the center. Six circles made up the maze, one for each circle of power.

Tara had been allowed to walk the maze for the first time two years ago, during summer solstice. While walking, she'd had to focus her own thoughts and banish the illusions that the coven set for her, to stay true to the path before her and arrive at the center gazing pond without misstep.

It had been her final test, a practicum exam, as it were. Tara hadn't at first known if she'd passed when she reached the inner circle unscathed. The gazing pond had held nothing but dark water for her.

Usually, it showed images to the initiate when they finished walking the maze, either the past or the future.

However, the pond wasn't the final arbiter of whether or not Tara had passed the test. Sheila had declared that Tara was now to be recognized as a full initiate of the first circle, the circle of thought (or brain, as the man had called it).

Since then, Tara had been studying for the next circle, the circle of breath (or lungs). The other circles that lay before her were feeling (heart), then process (stomach), roots (sex), and finally, if she lived long enough, anima, or the animating force that surrounded everything else.

Very few witches reached the sixth circle. It was why most covens were made up of either six or eleven witches, or even sixteen: one or more practitioner of each of the outer circles, with a single anima initiate.

Tara had taken over five years to move from merely practicing to the full first circle, while most who came to their power later in life only took a year or so. In part, that was because Tara had switched covens.

Tara's first teacher—Miss Lucy—for all her power, wasn't focused on bringing light to the world, just drawing more power to herself and those she protected, no matter the cost.

Miss Lucy's teachings had never sat well with Tara. She blamed her long association with that coven on her inexperience, not knowing there was another way. However, in her heart of hearts, Tara had known all along that she'd fallen in with a bad crowd, and then had done nothing to extricate herself.

Come winter solstice, Tara figured she'd be able to move from the circle of thought to the circle of air. It involved a lot of study on her part, to learn the herbs, oils, and concoctions traditionally associated with the new level, as well as building the strength to put those ingredients to use and perform real magic.

"You okay?" Kyle asked after a bit, while Tara still stood at the bottom of Gilmore's backyard.

"Yeah," Tara said. She shook her head and took a deep breath, allowing the peace of the garden to seep into her soul.

She didn't like that she still smelled rain in the air, though no rain was predicted for days, possibly weeks.

"You need to banish that man of your nightmares," Kyle said sternly.

Tara glanced at him, smiling to herself at the stern picture the tall black man presented. He was almost intimidating. Or maybe he would be to anyone who hadn't spent a night the previous week watching bad 1970s teen-dramas and laughing themselves silly.

"That guy is already gone," Tara said, lying. Then she paused and asked, "Should I mention him to Sheila? I'm not sure I want to bother the head of the coven."

Kyle thought about Tara's question for a moment before he shook his head. "Only if he returns," he said.

"Deal," Tara said, nodding. She didn't want to bother Sheila with just a bad dream, though Tara didn't usually have bad dreams, or any dreams at all.

Together, Tara and Kyle climbed the hill to the second tier, where most of the others in the coven were waiting. The area was flat and grassy. Sometimes they had a small fire in the center, that the witches could dance around as they brought in the new year on the solstice.

Almost everyone else was there already. Only Bernie was missing, and he was constantly late. Tara would think that a practitioner of process would understand how to be on time.

The coven only had three males out of eleven, Kyle, Bernie and Gilmore. Traditionally, witches were female, not male. However, Portland was a progressive town and made allowances. Thinking about it, it was one of the things that had surprised Tara, that her old-fashioned visitor was male.

Had he been a witch? Or something else? Tara was aware that there were other beings—spirits, ghosts, as well as the true *other*. However, as she was still only of the first circle, she didn't know anything about them.

Tara shook her head, banishing all thought of him.

He'd just been in her imagination, despite the fact that Tara was more practical than anything else and never indulged herself in such fanciful dreams.

"WE COME TOGETHER to celebrate the goddess Brigid, defender of the earth, the god Samil, warrior for the people, along with the fullness of the season and the blessings of the moon," Sheila intoned, bringing the attention of everyone to her.

Sheila was the head of the coven, their anima initiate, a short Mexican woman. While Sheila had the appearance of someone half her age, she was actually in her sixties. She carefully bleached her hair, hiding the gray by lightening it from its natural black to a ginger color. She hid the faded brown of her eyes with dark-colored contacts. Her face was remarkably free of wrinkles, which Tara believed to be natural, though possibly Sheila had had some work done. Her hands were what gave away her true age, the blue veins displayed across the back, the fingers boney, with age spots still showing.

She stood in the center of the circle, wearing a long flowing dress made out of a bright green cotton, with colorful yellow and red flowers embroidered across the yoke and around the hem. The short sleeves revealed powerful, muscular arms. She kept her ginger hair tied back in a tight bun that sat high on the back of her head.

Tara stood with Kyle on the one side and Han Su on the other. Both were more advanced than she was. Han Su had recently moved to the circle of feeling, while Kyle was still in the circle of process.

Tara wondered if Kyle would stay in the circle of process and never move beyond, to the root, or, as the gentleman that evening had reminded her, sex. One of the reasons for Kyle's aversion to touch was because he'd been gang-raped as a young man. Though it had been over two decades before, Kyle still bore the psychic wounds. Tara knew that her friendship with the tall black man had helped him recover, particularly having someone who accepted him as he was and never asked for more.

Han Su had started with the coven after Tara, then had advanced more quickly. Not because Han Su was a more powerful witch than Tara, but primarily because she hadn't had to unlearn the teachings that Tara had had to.

Shelia had originally been hesitant to take Tara on because of her initial training. Patricia had finally intervened for her, calling in some unknown favor between the two covens.

It was one of the reasons why Tara kept working for Patricia, despite how the other woman treated her sometimes.

Tara participated in the litany with the others, calling on the moon to bless them, sending out prayers and healing into the world. They didn't perform any magic that night: tonight was their usual midmonth gathering. They'd meet again on the solstice in five days' time, to celebrate the length of the light, the shortest night, and to draw from their powers in order to perform a deep healing.

The world needed it right now. Tara felt helpless sometimes, despite how she worked with the others to heal the deadly wounds being inflicted on their society at the present.

Tara briefly held hands with the others at the end of their ritual. It was one of the reasons why Kyle always stood beside her: it wasn't that he tolerated her touch better, but that she understood and would lock only pinkies with him, not insisting that they fully clasp hands palm to palm.

As the circle broke, Tara felt lighter, as usual. The air seemed more clear and crisp, though that might have also been the falling temperature.

Kyle had moved over to talk with Bernie about something, though he'd promised Tara a ride home soon. The rest of the coven would meet and talk far into the night, possibly even practice some magic, prepare a potion or two, everyone gathered together in the large kitchen, laughing and talking. Tara had to work most of the next day —an early shift at the store, then babysitting that evening—so she couldn't stay up late. Not if she expected to be able to function tomorrow.

Aaloka, Sheila's second in command and a long time fifth circle practitioner, came up to talk with Tara as the group was breaking up. Aaloka had no desire to ever move on to the final circle, which made her a perfect companion for Sheila.

"Blessed be," Aaloka said as she put her palms together in front of her chest and bowed her head low to Tara.

"Blessed be," Tara responded, echoing Aaloka's movements.

Though witches didn't normally greet each other that way, Aaloka's family came from New Delhi. She only wore a sari on nights of performance and celebration. Tonight she wore a casual blue-denim shirt tucked into a pair of skinny black jeans.

Tara always felt like an Amazon standing next to Aaloka. The woman was tiny, barely reaching Tara's chest, and bird thin. While Sheila was short, she felt solid to Tara, a tough mountain that would never blow over. Aaloka was more like a willow—not about to be uprooted or broken; however, Tara always had to wonder if Aaloka would sway in a strong enough wind.

"How do your studies go?" Aaloka asked as she usually did. She was the one who administered the oral part of the test for the circles.

"They're going well," Tara said. She wasn't really lying. She'd put in the hours studying and memorizing lists of herbs. She needed to add more practice to her curriculum, though. It was difficult, particularly given her flatmate.

And whenever Tara did make a mistake, the results were more disastrous as she learned to call winds and make them dance around her. Just learning thoughts and control had been a more internal art. Air was external. The circles were purposefully structured that way, an internal art followed by an external, then back to internal, and so on.

"How is your garden growing?" Aaloka asked.

Tara blinked in surprise. Generally, Aaloka inquired more about where Tara was in terms of her studies. Asking about her garden was completely new.

"Really well," Tara said. "The spearmint would like to take over the entire bench, of course. However, the sage has heard the spearmint's bid and would like to raise it. The thyme, too, might be a contender before the end of the summer. And I'm not even going to talk about the oregano."

Aaloka grinned. "That's always the way. First one thing decides to take over the world, then the next. You are staying on top of them though, yes?"

Tara wasn't really sure what Aaloka was asking. "I make the plants behave, keep their runners to themselves."

"Good," Aaloka said, though from her tone, it was obvious that Tara was missing the point.

"Oh!" Tara said, not sure why it was important but deciding that maybe it was. "And I had a hummingbird—an Anna—at the feeder this morning."

"That's wonderful news," Aaloka said, nodding and smiling as if Tara had actually gotten the quiz right. "The hummingbird is a representation of the great Hayvu, the goddess of the western winds. You must be making great progress to draw one of her birds to you."

"Or it could be the feeder," Tara pointed out. That was one of the problems she had with Aaloka. Everything wasn't necessarily the fault of a god or goddess. Sometimes the responsibility lay in the actions of people, usually when they didn't listen to their hearts.

Aaloka cocked her head to one side and looked quizzically at Tara. "Because you live in such a green area and there are always so many birds to contend with, right? Besides the pigeons at the train station."

Tara opened her mouth then shut it again. Perhaps Aaloka was right this time. Tara had been thinking the exact same things that morning.

"Is there something special I should do for my visitor?" Tara asked.

Aaloka gave Tara a wide grin. "Nope. Just keep feeding it. Hummingbirds are very particular about their nectar. You will need to change it frequently, as well as carefully wash out the feeder every time. You know not to use soap though, right?"

"Of course!" Tara said, though she hadn't known at all. What, did soap kill birds?

"If you use soap, you need to just make sure that you rinse away every trace of it," Aaloka explained. "Even the smallest amount, particularly in those tiny birds, can do a lot of damage."

"I'll make sure everything's completely clean," Tara promised. Maybe she should take the feeder down and clean it tomorrow, just in case…

"Is there any chance you'll be able to walk the maze next week? Progress to the next circle?" Aaloka asked, trying to sound casual.

"No," Tara said immediately. "I'm not ready yet."

Aaloka's stare bore into Tara, as if trying to touch her soul. "You're more ready than you realize," Aaloka said firmly. "You don't have to have every spell perfectly memorized before you attempt the next step."

"But I don't want to fail," Tara admitted. "That would just be a waste of your time as well as mine. And the coven's."

Aaloka sighed visibly. "I thought that was the problem," she said. "Nothing is ever a waste. Not even failing to move from one circle to the next. I think you should try it. You would learn what you need to focus on if you do fail. And if you don't?" She shrugged and gave Tara a small smile. "You'll have succeeded. But you can't succeed unless you try."

"I'll think about it," Tara said, though she really didn't feel as though she was ready. Could she cram for the test? When would she have time? The knowledge for each circle built on the previous one. She would have to learn more qualities for all the herbs she already knew, qualities for air as well as thought. Then she'd have to learn even more, adding qualities for feeling on top of everything else.

"Truly, I think you are ready," Aaloka said quietly. "The main thing holding you back is yourself."

Tara didn't know what to say in response to that. She wasn't holding herself back, not as far as she knew. Although she did like to have everything planned out ahead of time. She tended to be very controlled and not very spontaneous.

It was one of her personal challenges moving into the circle of wind, where storms could just blow up out of nowhere and derail her carefully formulated plans.

"Think about it," Aaloka said. "You have the power." Then she took a step back, making Tara realize just how closely they'd moved together, talking as intimately as lovers. "I see your ride is waiting for you," Aaloka said, gesturing with her head and pointing with her chin toward Kyle. "I will see you next week. Blessed be."

"Blessed be," Tara said, bowing her head low to her teacher.

All the ride home through the comfortable silence and dark, Tara thought about what Aaloka had said to her.

Could she move forward a rank? Was she holding herself back? She just didn't know.

But maybe, on Monday, her day off, she could try a few more advanced spells. See if she could loosen up and let the winds come pouring in.

For the rest of the weekend, she was going to be far too busy between the shop and the kids.

TARA PAUSED outside the shop Saturday morning. Weekends during the summer, particularly during nice weather, were the busiest for them with all the walk-by traffic. Combine that with the solstice next week, and the internet portion of the business was also crazy busy.

Trees dotted the street, set along the sidewalk like precise pins. They gave a little shade, which didn't help much with the heat. Cars raced along the one-way street, rushing between stoplights. Both sides of the street were already full of parked cars, narrowing the passage for those trying to go about their important business. Tourists streamed by the shop, usually carrying a coffee cup or more frequently now, a cold drink.

One of the older homeless guys—Bill—had already set up a few doors down from the shop. His tanned skin looked like leather. He had a pot belly despite how skinny he looked, the ribs standing out on the sides of his naked chest. His white-and-black scraggly beard hung down just past his neck. Only tufts remained of his hair on his head, as it had receded and left an island in the center of his forehead and not much else.

For now, Bill sat quietly on the edge of the busy sidewalk with a cup out and a sign. All his worldly possessions were tightly packed around him.

Tara would have to remember to bring Bill some water later, as well as to keep an eye out for when he started ranting, usually about 1 PM. As it almost always happened at the same time every day, she figured it was when the drugs or alcohol wore off. She'd only had to call the police on him once. She hadn't wanted to, but he'd been yelling so loudly and aggressively stomping forward to challenge anyone who dared to walk on that side of the sidewalk.

Fortunately, the homeless left the magic shop alone. They didn't have a public restroom—Tara and the others had to leave the shop and use the restroom in the warehouse building that was only accessible with a key. While it would have been easy to shoplift things from the shelves, Patricia regularly strengthened the protection spells so merchandise rarely went missing.

For a moment, Tara thought she caught a scent of the river, that watery reed smell. Then the wind changed and all she could smell was urine and sour homeless guy.

Was she finally growing an imagination? She snorted at herself. Not very likely.

She banished all thoughts of her "nightmare" man and entered the already busy shop.

Han Su was serving someone. Patricia, too, was in the store, talking with a group of three customers while a dozen others browsed. Tara knew that Patricia would work the backroom once Tara got settled into the front.

For most of the summer the three of them would work every weekend, at least for a few hours. The shop was closed on Mondays. Patricia handled the store by herself on Tuesdays, so both Han Su and Tara got two days off in a row.

Except for this past week with inventory, making sure they had enough supplies for solstice, so Tara had worked Monday as well.

Tara slipped her tiny backpack purse behind the counter, then brightly asked the room, "Can I help someone? Does anyone have any questions?"

The rest of the day flew by working with one person after another.

By the time four o'clock rolled around, Tara was dead on her feet, as usual. The crowds had been particularly heavy that day and she'd barely had time to gulp down the smoothie that Han Su had bought for her.

However, Tara's day was far from over. After saying goodbye, Tara raced along the crowded sidewalk, heading toward the train stop. Bill was still sitting on the edge of the sidewalk, slumped over. Maybe the meds had worked all day, as she hadn't heard him ranting when she'd brought him a bottle of water, earlier.

Or maybe it was the heat. The shop had good air flow, magically enhanced. Even on the hottest days it felt cool in there. Tara hadn't realized how hot it had actually gotten outside. Earlier in the day there'd been a lovely breeze that had kept it cooler, but that had disappeared as the sun had gained strength.

Tara remembered when Portland had had more temperate summers. The last couple of years had just gotten hotter and hotter.

Her coven poured blessings and healing into the earth, but there was only so much they could do.

Half a dozen street kids lounged near the train stop, leaning up against the brick building on the shady side of the street. One had a guitar and was strumming to himself, not really playing. They had a couple of dogs with them, of course. At least in Portland, the street kids knew to take care of their animals. She'd heard that wasn't the case in all cities.

"Got a spare pass?" one of them asked as she walked by.

Tara just shook her head. She wanted to feel sorry for all the homeless people in the streets. However, there were just so many of them. It had gotten really bad in downtown for a while. Tara always set up protection spells before she left her apartment, and had also bought a spray can of mace.

The new construction and gentrification had forced a lot of the homeless people out. There were still huge camps of them in most every park, near the train station, anyplace they could go.

And they rode the train. The smell of urine was so strong in the car that Tara boarded that she ended up walking to the next one just to escape it.

When Tara had been a brand new witch, she'd tried to banish such scents, trying to make wherever she was into a better place.

Wasn't that the root of all witchcraft? Or at least the modern varieties? To connect with one's location and to work to make where you lived a better place? To enrich and enliven the earth?

The problem was that despite how long people spent using public transportation, like the trains and the busses, they weren't really anyone's home. Cleaning a train car or a bus took all of Tara's strength and energy, then tied her to the location so she kept being drained.

It was a good way to burn up extra power, like after a moon ritual when she felt overly full.

But after working all day, Tara needed to recover instead of expend.

At least the train cars were air conditioned. She collapsed into her hard plastic seat and closed her eyes for a brief moment.

The smell of the river made her open her eyes again.

Just a few feet away from her, standing in front of the door, was the gentleman from last night.

He wore the same old-fashioned outfit—brown wool jacket, pants, and vest, with a bowler hat, white shirt, and string tie. His face was slightly clearer, and Tara could see that he was clean shaven. His round cheeks definitely made him look younger, maybe only in his late twenties. He had a perfectly normal nose, though she might have labeled his chin as weak.

She still couldn't see his eyes, couldn't tell what color they were. Were they the gray of summer storms? The blue of winter skies? Or the brown of the swollen spring waters?

He stared straight ahead, looking out the door of the train, watching the traffic and world go by.

The smell of the river rolled over Tara, as if a strong breeze had just blown off the water. Her arms suddenly felt heavy, weighed down with wet ropes. She gulped the air, struggling to take a full deep breath. Her vision grew hazy.

Just as suddenly, everything grew clear.

Dread rooted Tara to the spot. She wanted to flee, but found she couldn't move her arms or legs. She could look around, wildly glancing this way and that, seeking a way to escape.

As the train drew slowly to a stop, the man turned to look at her. His face wavered more, as though he peered up at her from under the water.

She knew, somehow, that he smiled directly at her as he tipped his hat, just before he stepped off the train.

Tara still wanted to run away when she felt as though she was back in control of her limbs, despite the fact that the man had already gotten off the train. It made no sense for her to get off and follow him.

She stayed where she was, the fear sliding off of her as the train pulled away from the station.

Was he just in her imagination? She still wasn't sure. She'd never heard of a ghost haunting a person and not a building or a cemetery. Despite her terror, she couldn't help but think he was human, or mostly human.

Her friend Dave would say that he presented as human, and that had to be good enough.

Why had he appeared on the train that way? Was it just to scare the crap out of her? What did he want?

And most importantly, why her?

Tara didn't know, and she suspected that she wouldn't like the answers when she did find them.

THE QUIET CLACKAMAS neighborhood always reminded Tara of just how different the various parts of Portland were, from the high energy streets of downtown, to the quirky, hip parts of Aurora, to the quieter, richer suburbs.

At least she could easily get to her second job on the train. It took a long while, about forty-five minutes each way. But it was cheaper to take transport than to own a car. Parking would be impossible as well where she currently lived, and yet another expense.

It took her a brisk five-minute walk from the station to get to the house. The Martins had two boys, ages four and six, and needed her to come stay with them overnight most every Saturday.

Both Mr. and Mrs. Martin—Tim and Veronica—were witches. Their coven met on Saturday nights. Tara had first been recommended for the regular job from her first family, the Johnsons. When Tara had moved out of the apartment she'd shared with her then boyfriend, she'd needed a cheap place to stay. The Johnsons had taken her on as an *au pair* for their twin girls.

What Tara hadn't realized for a couple of years was that the main reason the Johnsons had hired her was because she had power. She'd stumbled into it after a couple of years, meeting Miss Lucy at one of the Johnsons' parties.

While Tara still considered the Johnsons friends, and she regularly got both birthday and solstice cards from the girls, she wasn't necessarily friendly with them. First of all, their economic status set them far apart from Tara, who still struggled to make ends meet. In addition, they weren't the same sort of witch that she was. She wouldn't say that they practiced black magic, but it wasn't white either. More like tainted.

The Martins weren't in the same coven as the Johnsons, and they practiced a more clean magic. The two families knew each other from their various day jobs, not their covens.

So Tara came to stay overnight every Saturday night, fixing the boys dinner and babysitting them, then fixing breakfast for the entire family Sunday morning before taking the long train ride back into the city and starting at noon at the shop again. The Martins paid very well and in cash. They didn't have to give her so much money; however, they felt as though they were paying it forward, helping a struggling new witch make ends meet.

Vicky Martin was ready by the time Tara came in the back door. Tim was the one who was always late. She wore a typical soccer mom outfit, a blue polo shirt over a jeans skirt, her dark brown hair tied up into a cute ponytail, with bangs over her forehead. Her white skin was always tanned, no matter what time of year.

"I'm so glad you're here!" Vicky exclaimed as she walked forward and took both of Tara's hands, squeezing them gently. "Davie has a fever. I'm sure it's nothing. But I'd like for you to prepare a healing soup for him."

"Of course," Tara said brightly, though she groaned inside. Davie was the younger boy, only four, while Carl was six. They would normally ignore Tara all evening, coming out of their rooms for dinner, and then disappearing back to the games they played. (It was part of the deal they had with their parents—online games only when the parents were gone for the night, which meant every Saturday.)

If Davie wasn't feeling well, he'd want to spend all evening with her, curled up on the couch beside her. It also meant he'd dictate whatever they watched on the big-screen TV, then complain when she changed the channel, even though he'd been asleep for the past hour.

Then again, Davie had started feeling "sick" at least once a month or so since January. Tara suspected that Davie just liked hanging out with her, but he couldn't admit that, certainly not to his parents or his brother. Girls were kind of icky, and likely to remain so for a while.

"Don't know what time we'll be home," Vickie said. "Don't worry about staying up."

Vickie always said that. Tara had only stayed up the one time, and that was because she felt as though she'd needed to talk to the boys' parents right when they got home. Carl had started a fire and Tara hadn't been sure if he'd actually used matches or not.

The boys had never shown any other indication of power, however. It was too early for any magic to manifest, though Tim had confessed that he'd had some indications when he'd been a pre-teen.

"And can you make a little extra soup?" Vickie asked as she turned away. "It's always so good."

Tara smiled. One of her strengths, both before and after she came into power, was knowing how to make food taste good with whatever spices she had at hand. She'd started cooking at a young age, mainly in self-defense because her mother hadn't been a very good cook.

Then again, her mother considered garlic an exotic spice.

"Anything else?" Tara asked as she followed Vickie out of the kitchen and into the rest of the house.

The front hallway had a large door on the left, which people rarely used, and a grand staircase that wound around to the right. Just past that was the living room. A huge, electric fireplace stood just to the right, with the big flat-screen TV hanging over the empty mantle.

A long, black microfiber couch ran across most of the room. It folded out into Tara's bed when she stayed over. Behind the couch, tall windows showed a small strip of green and a wooden fence. The air smelled of the lavender and peppermint sachet that sat in a basket on a corner of the fireplace, the heart of the home.

Davie was already curled up in a soft, beige blanket on the couch. He did look sweaty, his white skin pale, his brown eyes large in his face. Dark hair fell over his forehead and stuck up at the back of his head. He wore a green camouflage T-shirt, as well as flannel pajama pants covered in trains.

"Hi," he said softly, pushing himself up to seated.

Tara went and sat next to him on the couch, bringing the back of her hand to his forehead.

"You're a bit warm, aren't you, sweetie?" she said to Davie. He wasn't running a high fever, but he was undoubtedly sick.

At least she rarely caught any bugs from anyone these days. Her own natural defenses kept her safe. Plus, if she ever did start to sniffle, she knew exactly which herbs to take in order to heal herself.

"You lay back down," Tara told Davie as she stood up. "Can I talk to you for a second?" she asked Vickie.

Vickie nodded and led the way into the formal dining room that was just off the living room. The kitchen was just around the corner, the downstairs set up as one large circle.

"What's wrong?" Vickie asked as she stopped and leaned against the long, dark wood serving hutch.

"There's been a man—or at least I think he's a man. He's been haunting me," Tara said. "He isn't a ghost."

Both Vickie and Tim were fourth level witches. They knew more than she did about the arcane arts and the various creatures who inhabited all the planes.

"Haunting you?" Vickie asked.

Tara told of her two run-ins with the man. She didn't like how he'd made her feel. She knew she hadn't imagined him.

Vickie listened to Tara's story carefully, nodding in sympathy. "I've never heard of anyone like that before," she said, her eyes wide. "I'll ask Tamia, our anima, if you'd like."

"Please," Tara said, nodding, relief settling across her shoulders.

"Do you think he'll show up here?" Vickie asked.

"I hadn't thought of that," Tina admitted, suddenly horrified. "You know I would never knowingly put the boys in danger, right?"

"I'll add extra protection to the house tonight, before we go," Vickie said firmly. "You'll be safe here."

"Thank you," Tara said. She wasn't sure exactly what she was going to do if this man/creature kept haunting her.

First, she needed to figure out what he was, exactly. Through knowledge came power. While a witch might have some level of wild magic, he or she could never tap into their full potential without a lot of learning and training. Or at least that was what the current schools of witchcraft believed.

Davie didn't get off the couch until after his parents had left. Tara was already in the kitchen, starting the soup. The chicken was already in the pressure cooker, cooking, while she chopped up the herbs and vegetables she'd add next.

"Smells good," he said, pulling up a tall stool to sit on the counter next to her. "What's in it?"

Tara had started with a good bone broth that Vickie regularly made and kept in the freezer. "This and that," Tara teased the boy.

Davie rolled his eyes almost as well as a teenager. "What's that?" he said, pointing to her cutting board.

The large, two-inch-thick butcher block was already covered in chopped up piles of herbs. It rested over the two-basin sink on a piece of plywood that had been specifically made for just that purpose. While the rest of the house was huge, the kitchen was quite small, with very limited counter space.

"So that's lemon verbena," Tara said, pointing to the small pile in the far corner, and not what Davie was pointing at.

He merely rolled his eyes at her again. "Uh huh," he said. "And?"

Tara smiled and went through the rest of the chopped up ingredients, pleased that Davie wanted to learn.

"Thyme, rosemary, sage—those always go well with chicken," she said. Then she finally talked about the herb he was pointing to. "That's lovage," she said, handing him a small leaf. "What does that remind you of?"

He sniffed it, then took a small bite. "Celery!" he said, surprised.

"That's right," she said. "Then I have a little marjoram and some turmeric."

"That's the stuff that turns your fingers yellow," Davie complained.

"And your tongue, too," Tara told him. "You'll have to go check after dinner."

"Cool," Davie said. He watched her chop up the carrots, turnips, and butternut squash. He rested his head on his arms on the counter.

Poor boy was really sick that evening. He normally would have a bunch more questions for her and would want to help. She wasn't used to seeing him so still and quiet.

"You want to go and lay down for a while?" she asked, checking the timer on the pressure cooker. The chicken would be finished in four minutes, and she'd have to let it sit for ten more minutes, slow releasing the pressure, before she could cook the veggies.

Davie shook his head though he didn't bother to raise it.

After a bit, Tara realized that Davie was humming something. She couldn't quite figure out what it was. It seemed familiar, but not.

"Whatcha singing?" Tara asked after a bit.

"The *real* London Bridges," Davie said proudly. "Not the silly one that the other kids know."

"I don't know the real London Bridges," Tara said. "Can you teach me?"

"Sure!" Davie said. He got up off his stool, then pushed it to the side so he had a bit more room.

> *"London Bridge is broken down,*
> *Dance over my Lady Lay,*
> *London Bridge is broken down,*
> *With a gray lady.*
>
> *How shall we build it up again?*
> *Dance over my Lady Lay,*
> *How shall we build it up again?*
> *With a gray lady.*
>
> *Silver and gold will be stolen away,*
> *Dance over my Lady Lay.*
> *Wood and clay will wash away,*
> *With a gray lady.*
>
> *Iron and steel will bow and bend,*

Dance over my Lady Lay.
Steel and iron will be the end,
Of a gray lady.

Build it up with stone so strong,
Dance over the dead lady.
With a heart it will last so long
From a gray lady."

Davie danced in place while he sang, circling, and sometimes lifting his arms up as children did when singing the song.

Tara turned to look at him as he ended. "Where did you learn that?" she asked. "I've never heard that version before."

Davie grinned at her. "Some of the boys at the daycare," he told her proudly. Then he looked worried. "They said we weren't supposed to tell our parents, that the song was just for kids. But you're not my parent. Right?"

"That's right," Tara said. "Did those boys tell you any other secrets?" she asked, wanting to make sure that Davie wasn't getting into something over his head.

"No," Davie said, his eyes wide as he shook his head.

Tara could tell he was lying. The timer beeped at her, telling her that she should quick release the steam on the pressure cooker now.

"Thank you for singing that for me," she said. "Now, are you ready for a loud noise?"

Davie stuck his fingers in his ears and nodded.

Tara pushed the release valve, making sure that her hand wasn't in the way of the blowing steam. "Dinner will be in about fifteen minutes," she told Davie.

"Yay!" Davie said. He looked up at her. "I'm hungry," he said, as if this was something new.

"That's good. Maybe you're getting better."

Davie came over and wrapped his arms around Tara's legs, giving her a quick hug. "That's because you're here," he said. "You make me better."

"Thank you, sweetie," Tara said, patting his head. She slipped her hand down over his forehead. He seemed less warm now. "Why don't you set the table and then go get your brother?"

"Okay!" Davie said.

While the boy noisily clanked around the silverware drawer and got out bowls, Tara thought about the song he'd been singing.

It made sense to her that a song about bridges falling down would be popular with kids here—Portland had a number of bridges going across the river, plus a lot more which traversed the railroad.

Still, the song and its talk about a gray lady, a dead lady, disturbed her.

The kids didn't really understand about magic. No one would talk with them about magic unless one of them displayed that they had power.

But the term "a gray lady" was often used when describing a witch.

Was there some history in the song that Tara didn't know? And why was the song just for kids, and not for adults?

THREE

I thought I was hardened to wilderness. I'd been born in the western territories, and have only spent the last decade in the civilized cities of the west coast. The Oregon wilderness seems different, however. Huge pines fill the forests, each so big that it would take ten men with hands outstretched to reach around a single trunk. Stands of wild rose, salmon berry, and prickly Oregon grape regularly force us from our path with their dense thorns and sharp leaves. The native I hired knows the territory, though, and keeps us on track. I hear him whispering at night to some heathen river god. I still asked him politely to teach me about the river and his beliefs. He may yet find me worthy of his confidence and his lore.

Wilson Evermore, Civil Engineer and Explorer, 1897

Tara was disappointed, but not surprised, when Vickie Martin told her in the morning that no one had ever heard of the sort of man/creature that was haunting her. However, Tara left the house in the morning with a more potent protection spell, and she carried a new sachet full of protective herbs, like heather, verbena, and tansy.

The man didn't show up at the shop either. Tara told both Patricia as well as Han Su about him, making sure that they would be prepared if he should appear.

Patricia promised to do more investigation about him. Though there were many myths about ghosts hanging around downtown Portland, particularly after the floods of the 1800s, in truth, the ghosts were very few, and none of them, at least not the real ones that Tara knew about, had died in the flood.

Still, it made sense to Tara that given the man's old-fashioned clothing, his watery nature, as well as his expressed interest in heather and bringing the rains, that he might have something to do with the floods that had plagued Portland over the decades.

When Tara got home from her long weekend of work, she still made herself take the time to strengthen all the protection spells around the condo before collapsing on her bed.

Unsurprisingly, since the man had been so much in her thoughts, he came to her in her dreams that night.

Tara found herself standing on a huge boulder. The man stood below her. She recognized him from the bowler hat still sitting on his head, though the rest of him was bare. His body no longer looked human at all. Instead, he was built out of rocks haphazardly piled together, giving a hunchback shape his shoulders and making his legs bulge and move strangely.

It was still difficult for her to see his face clearly because they were both underwater, though it took her a moment to recognize that, as she had no trouble breathing. She wore a simple shift dress, reminding her of a nightgown she'd had as a child, instead of the T-shirt she'd gone to bed in.

Despite being underwater, Tara felt comfortably warm, not too hot and not too cold.

When Tara tried to step away, off the rocks, she discovered that her hands were tied behind her back. Looking around, she realized that she stood on boulders piled up around one of the piers for the Burnside Bridge, the part of the bridge that traversed from the upper part of the bridge itself, under the water, and ended buried deep beneath the river bed. She was tied to the pier. She recognized where she was from the news and the reports about the bridge repairs.

The man in front of her nodded once, then started chanting. His voice hummed low in the water, like a tug slowly making its way up the river. The chanted words echoed strangely. Sometimes they sounded clear and Tara could understand what he was saying, though the meaning slipped away as soon as she thought she grasped it. Then, other times, he made sounds like rain or like rushing water. He even echoed the cawing of seagulls and the low thump of waves on an empty hull.

Tara knew she had to escape before the man finished his circle around the footing. She struggled with the wet ropes that held her arms behind her back. She slipped, almost losing her balance. Her bare feet couldn't get a solid hold on the slimy rocks, so she couldn't kick away.

As the man continued, the smell of the water filled her nose, a spring river smell that rode high in the back of her throat, bringing back memories of cold wet winter days, when the river was swollen, pressing against its banks, threatening to overflow.

"Let me go!" Tara exclaimed, surprised that she found she could talk. She struggled again with the ropes holding her, feeling them give an inch. Maybe she could slip her hands out.

She started praying loudly to Brigid, the protector of the earth, to give her the strength she needed to free herself. She asked Hayvu the goddess of the western wind, to carry her away on strong winds, as well as Bonana, goddess of the water, to help free her.

A strong current rushed by her at the mention of the water goddess. Tara would have been bowled over if she hadn't been held there by the ropes.

Was that the river trying to carry her away to safety? She shivered from how cold the temperature had gotten, as if the water was now trying to freeze her.

Stubbornly, Tara prayed louder to Bonana, seeking the goddess's uplifting spirit. The water around her grew colder and darker.

Maybe praying to Bonana wasn't such a good idea.

The odd man still chanted. She heard glee in his tone. He was less than three feet from completing his circle.

Tara thanked the goddesses for listening, then started her own struggles anew. Yes, the ropes were slipping from her wrists. She couldn't quite free one hand yet, but she was close. The rope abraded her skin, and she could smell the copper of her blood, see it blooming in the water behind her back.

What could she do? She wasn't going to escape in time.

Tara remembered an old prayer about sharpening the clarity of her thoughts, bringing them to a knife point to cut away the illusions of others. The prayer was recited while making sachets of sage, lemon balm, and yes, purple heather. It had been one of the prayers that Miss Lucy had taught her.

Miss Lucy had always said that the older magick was more powerful and potent, while Sheila had insisted that the new ways were better and more reliable.

Tara had found comfort in the gentler prayers that Sheila and the others had taught her. She'd also found more power as well, or at least, her powers were more consistent following Shelia's teachings.

Still, Tara started chanting the old prayer. It didn't ask for help from any god or goddess, but merely to find the strength within to withstand the illusion, to parry away falsehoods, to see clearly with her own thoughts.

The ropes loosened a touch more. Tara yanked her left hand out, then turned, took a moment to catch her balance, then started to desperately push on the rope still bound to her right.

She didn't allow herself to giggle at the thought of chewing her own hand off in order to escape. The mania might have taken over and she'd never be able to stop laughing. The echoes of her laughter in her head made her shiver.

Instead, she pushed, then pulled, folding her hand in on itself, wishing she had a real knife to cut herself free. The fingernails of her left hand broke off as she clawed at the rope. Her skin grew raw from being scratched by it, and more blood bloomed around her wrist.

She heard the man's chanting voice draw nearer. He was almost there, almost even with her, his trap complete.

With a final shove, she freed her hand. She tried to push off against the rock strongly, but her foot slipped. Still, after frantically pulling with her arms, she managed to start rising, drawing herself slowly up through the water.

She felt the moment the man completed his circle. The metal in the footing behind her rang like a dull bell, the waves echoing out, shoving her out into the darker waters.

Away from the bridge footing, the water grew so chilly Tara's teeth started chattering. Black currents raced by her, attempting to sweep her out to sea. The smell of stale water and rotten fish filled her nostrils. The water itself no longer felt clean against her bare arms and legs. Instead, it felt as slimy as rotten lettuce.

Tara wouldn't allow herself to panic. She reminded herself that she was an excellent swimmer. She stopped fighting the current and instead aimed herself upward. How she knew which direction was up she had no idea, but she trusted her instinct. With strong strokes, she broke free of the current that had ahold of her and aimed for the spreading light that appeared above her.

As Tara's head broke the surface, she heard the man calling her name.

"Tara. Tara! You're still mine," he gloated.

With a start, Tara woke in her own room. She still shivered from the remembered cold of the water. Her wrists ached, though the skin was whole and not torn and bleeding. Her fingernails weren't broken off, though she could still feel her rapid heartbeat pulsing in the tips of her fingers, the ghost of the pain still haunting her.

Tara reached down to pull up another blanket, then realized that she was never going to sleep again, not like this. May as well make herself some tea before she tried.

Luckily, tomorrow was her day off. She would be able to sleep in.

Tara pulled her thick green bathrobe out of the closet, the one that was soft and ratty and felt like it gave her a hug her every time she pulled it on. She padded silently into the kitchen—wouldn't do to wake Sharon up, who did have to work in the morning.

Without thinking, Tara reached for the herbs that would warm and soothe her, wintergreen and rose hips. As the tea steeped, she leaned over the mug and breathed in the warm humid air.

What had the dream meant? She looked again at her wrist under the light of the stove. They appeared slightly bruised. As did her fingertips, which still beat with pain.

Had she escaped from the creature? She had gotten herself untied, but she hadn't gotten away very far when he'd finished his spell. She'd still been close to the footing of the bridge.

What was he? Who was he?

Thinking about the dream, she started to remember some of the chant that the man had been saying. Each word came to her slowly as it rose out of the watery depths.

He was the Riprap man. And he would claim her soul when the light first turned to dark.

Tara slept heavily the rest of the night, then had difficulty waking up the next morning. Still, she dragged herself out to the balcony with her tea as soon as she was able.

The day was going to be another hot one, though a cool breeze did blow in from across the river, helping her to wake up. Her plants were all doing well and would need a good watering that morning. She'd cleaned and refilled the hummingbird feeder after Aaloka had told her not to use soap, not that it appeared to matter in the least to her little friends, as more than one hummingbird—both male and female Annas—came to visit her that morning.

Finally, when Tara felt warm all the way through to her bones, she pulled out her tablet and started doing some research. She wasn't surprised to learn that riprap was a bridge term. It referred to the large boulders and rocks placed around the footings of bridges to protect them.

She'd been standing on the riprap for the Burnside Bridge in her dream.

While there was a lot of old lore on the internet about the bridges, she couldn't find anything about the Riprap man. She did learn that the London Bridges song was ancient as well as widespread. Versions of it appeared all across Europe, in French, German, as well as Russian, though the words didn't always involve the London Bridge, just some bridge.

There were also theories about children being sacrificed to protect the bases of the bridges, or other guardians.

Just because there was no archaeological evidence—no bodies or bones had been found at the base of the London Bridge—didn't mean it hadn't happened. There were other ways of binding a soul. You didn't need to bury the body in the same place.

Tara couldn't find a direct mention of witches being sacrificed. However, had that been the true meaning of the song that Davie had been taught? Tara really wanted to know what else the boys at Davie's daycare had said, the other things he'd been taught.

Was there a song about the Riprap man?

There was just too much that Tara didn't know. After a few moments, consideration, she sent off an email to Richard, asking about the Riprap man and the London Bridges song. Tara and Richard had gone on a couple of dates a few years ago, before they'd both decided that they would be better off as just friends.

A big part of their problem had been because Tara was a witch and Richard was completely mundane. There were just too many things that Tara couldn't tell him about. Miss Lucy had compared it to marrying someone from a completely different religion, which was accurate, as Tara had different gods and goddesses she prayed to.

Plus, Richard was a research librarian. He was far too interested in any myth she mentioned, always wanting to look up things, find out more. His curiosity and his mundane nature had made it too difficult to be intimate. Tara had felt that she was lying to him all the time, even though frequently they were just lies of omission.

But Tara had held onto Richard as a friend. Almost everyone else she knew were witches or somehow involved in the community. Richard was a good reminder for Tara of the world outside, of the fact that though she mostly associated with witches and their ilk, the majority of people were mundane and without actual magic.

She checked the time. It was still before nine A.M., and a while before she could call anyone with questions. She sighed. While she really wanted to spend the next few hours sitting and communing with the river and her plants, she knew she had to start studying, even though it was technically her day off.

Though no one might know who this Riprap man was, Tara had no doubt that he was coming for her soul the day after the solstice, when the light began to diminish. She needed as much knowledge as she could gather before then.

"Hello, Sheila?" Tara said, surprised that her call was actually answered right away. Sheila worked as a regional manager for one of the health food grocery stores and was usually too busy to answer the phone. Tara had been prepared to leave a long voicemail.

"Hi, Tara," Sheila said. "I only have a few moments between meetings. What's up?"

"There's been a man, or a creature, haunting me," Tara said. "The Riprap man. Do you know anything about him?"

"Oh, don't worry about him. He's harmless," Sheila assured her. "He'll bluster around you a bunch. He does that with the novices sometimes. But he'll fade after the solstice. You don't have anything to worry about."

"Really?" Tara asked, surprised. "He seemed pretty dangerous." She shivered in the warm morning air, remembering the dream from the night before.

"He is an odd ghost," Sheila said. "But he's just a ghost. He can't harm you."

"Wow. Are you sure?" Tara said.

"We can talk more about him at the solstice. Blessed be!" Sheila said, her end of the line going dead.

Tara sat for a moment with her phone in her hand.

Huh.

Tara wanted to feel relieved. She really wanted to believe that it had all been just a bad dream.

However, she couldn't shake the feeling that the head of her coven had just lied to her.

<hr>

TARA WASN'T sure who to talk with next. She'd already told Patricia about the Riprap man, and she'd never heard of him. Neither had Vickie Martin, who'd asked around her coven about him as well.

Feeling guilty, Tara decided to put in a call to Aaloka and ask her. Tara didn't want to bother her teacher, but something about Sheila's response had just felt off to her.

"Blessed be," Aaloka said when she picked up. She sounded very happy to be talking with Tara. "How is my favorite soon-to-be graduated student?"

"Studying hard," Tara lied. She dragged her tablet over to her so that she could open it up to her notes as soon as she got off the phone. "Uhmmm, I hate to bother you, but I've been having some weird encounters lately."

"Really?" Aaloka said. "Like what?"

"There's been this old-fashioned man who's been haunting me," Tara said. "And I had a dream about him last night. Called himself the Riprap man."

"I've never heard of anyone like that," Aaloka said.

"Are you sure?" Tara persisted. "Sheila said he comes and bothers the novices sometimes."

"Oh, that's right. Him," Aaloka said.

Tara waited for Aaloka to go on. When she didn't add anything more, Tara asked, "What can you tell me about him?" She didn't want to mention that Sheila had already told her that he was harmless. She wanted to hear it from Aaloka herself.

"Just that he appears sometimes, generally to novices. Did you talk to Sheila about him?"

"I did," Tara said. She wasn't about to lie to her teacher.

"What did Sheila tell you?" Aaloka said.

"She said that he was just a ghost, albeit an odd, threatening one," Tara admitted.

"See? He's just a ghost," Aaloka said. "You should listen to Sheila."

Tara could hear the deep sigh Aaloka took.

"But you also really need to pass to the next circle on the solstice," Aaloka said. "It's important."

"Why?" Tara asked. She felt the hairs on the back of her neck start to stand, as if a cold wind had just blown across the balcony.

"Just—trust me. It's important," Aaloka repeated. "You know I can't explain all the mysteries. Not until you're ready."

"Okay," Tara said slowly. That was a typical response—there was a lot of knowledge that remained hidden until the practitioner was ready for it. "Does passing to the next circle have anything to do with the Riprap man?"

Aaloka's tinkling laughter came across the line, sounding forced. "Of course not!" she said. "It's just important for you, for your journey."

"All right," Tara said. "I'll walk the circle of breath on the solstice." The weight of all the work she'd have to do between now and then fell heavy across her shoulders, making her bow her head.

"Good!" Aaloka said. "Then I'll let you get back to your studies. Blessed be!"

Tara hung up with her mentor and tried to straighten herself back up.

Had Aaloka also lied to her about the Riprap man? Tara had the weird sensation that her teacher had wanted to say more, but couldn't. As though Aaloka was bound by some covenant made to the coven, or to Sheila.

Tara did believe, however, that Aaloka really wanted Tara to pass to the next circle on the solstice.

Would mastering breath help Tara fight a water creature? Maybe.

Tara pushed her misgivings to the side and started her studies again, trying to memorize as much as she could, unsure if any of it would help.

TARA TURNED OFF HER TABLET, then stretched her arms over her head and bent forward in her chair. Her brain felt overly full. Her fingers felt swollen with heat. She'd made herself an Italian soda earlier, out of chilled sparkling water, heavy cream, and pure vanilla, but it was long gone.

Even the hummingbirds who kept returning to her feeder made her weary, not delighted. The problem was that the tiny birds were very territorial, and would shoo away any other bird who dared come to feed. She'd grown tired of their constant bickering.

Nothing felt comfortable that morning, not the sleeveless shirt she wore, not her shorts, not even the ponytail she kept her hair tied up in. It pulled at odd times, tightening across her scalp like unseen fingers tugged on it.

Her mind kept circling back to what Sheila had said about the Riprap man, that he was just an odd ghost. Tara couldn't believe that. The dream had felt so real. When she recalled it, she could still feel the waterlogged ropes wrapped around her wrists, the slimy rock under her bare feet, how cold the waters had grown.

Normally, Tara would go for a swim to help clear her head. She wasn't afraid of the water, but she wondered if it would be a wise idea to voluntarily go someplace where she could possibly be distracted and drown.

She needed to get the truth from someone about this Riprap man. She wasn't going to ask anyone else in her coven. There was some sort of coverup happening there, starting at the highest level. She believed that Vickie Martin, when she'd asked her coven, had been told nothing. The leaders of the dozen or so covens in Portland all knew each other. If Sheila would lie to her, so would all the others.

Who else could Tara talk with? Where else could she look?

The name that came on the winds surprised her.

With a deep sigh, Tara nodded. She would listen to her wiser self, her intuition, though she didn't want to.

Miss Lucy had never lied to Tara, at least as far as she knew. Tara had found her abrasively honest most of the time.

It was time to see if her old mentor would at least tell her the truth, if no one else would.

AFTER CALLING AND MAKING AN APPOINTMENT, Tara splurged on an Uber to get her to Miss Lucy's house. The neighborhood was in the northern part of Portland, where huge houses took up each lot with immaculate yards out front and the street full of expensive cars. Old trees lined the sidewalk, gracefully leaning over to greet their partners, providing a shaded archway along the boulevard.

Miss Lucy's house was an old craftsman, though bigger than most, and beautifully maintained. It had two stories plus an attic, as well as a finished basement and a root cellar. Miss Lucy constantly entertained there, both witches as well as politicians.

The left corner of the house was a round tower, complete with a witch's hat peaked roof. Tara had always thought it was delightfully ironic, as none of the witches she knew actually wore hats. The right corner was square, with tall, skinny windows on both floors, always making the rooms inside seem airy and filled with light. Gables jutted out from the attic, though Tara knew from experience that it was a dark, cobweb filled space, and that she could barely stand upright except at the very center.

Tara walked up the familiar concrete stairs from the street to the front yard. Wild roses grew in abundance across the front of the house, stretching from the walkway to the corners. Their heady scent filled the area and their sharp thorns defended the house. Miss Lucy had woven them into her protection spells.

Gray wooden stairs led from the walkway up to the front door. Tara's footsteps sounded hollow as she walked up, as if she was walking across the deck of an empty boat. Brown wicker chairs and tables filled the front porch to the left. Miss Lucy had added a swing since the last time Tara had been here. She knew that Miss Lucy liked to spend her evenings out on the porch, sipping sweet tea as the world grew quiet.

Before Tara could knock on the door, it opened. Miss Lucy herself stood there.

Tara hadn't been certain what to expect. Though she hadn't fought with her former mentor, she'd walked away with bad feelings.

But Miss Lucy stood with a sly smile on her face and greeted Tara warmly. "Darling dear, it's lovely to see you." Miss Lucy wore dashiki shirt, made out of yellow cloth with a pattern of white, red, and black embroidered around the collar and down the front. Miss Lucy's skin coloring was a light brown, and she always wore a hat and long sleeves when she went outside so she wouldn't get any darker. She'd straightened her hair recently, wearing it short and slightly curled near her shoulders.

Miss Lucy's appearance hadn't changed much over the last few years. While she was in her sixties, she gave the impression of vibrant power, even though wrinkles lined the edges of her face and her brown eyes had faded.

"It's good to see you too," Tara said. And she wasn't lying. Miss Lucy had been such a key figure in her development as a witch. Though Tara didn't think that Miss Lucy was following the right path, Tara still had to appreciate how much Miss Lucy had taught her.

They didn't touch, didn't hug or even air kiss. Miss Lucy had never encouraged that sort of intimacy with her students. Miss Lucy always said that she'd been raised formal, and had complained of the Victorian manners her parents had fostered on her.

"Please, come in," Miss Lucy said, stepping back to let Tara into the house. It felt cooler in here, as always. Light-colored wood covered the floor, while the walls had been painted a cheery yellow. The front entranceway opened up to the large living room on the right, a spacious area where Miss Lucy entertained. Behind the closed door on the left, in the round room, was Miss Lucy's study, a comfortable place, the walls full of specially built bookcases that fit the walls perfectly.

"I was just about to make myself some tea," Miss Lucy said. A small hallway led directly from the outside door, past a small bathroom and the stairs leading to the basement, then into the kitchen. "May I offer you some?"

"Yes, please," Tara said, following her former mentor. She paused in the doorway of the kitchen. "You've done a lot of work here!"

Miss Lucy gave her a grin. "You don't know the half of it. And I'm so glad it's finally finished! I didn't have a working kitchen for four solid months."

Tara nodded in sympathy. She remembered her last move and how awful everything had been until she'd finally gotten her dishes, pots, and pans unpacked so she could finally cook again.

The kitchen had been expanded greatly. Before, there had been a sunporch just behind it. Now, the wall had been taken out and the rooms merged together. A small cooking island took up the center of the room, the entire top of it a butcher's block. Tara was already jealous of having that much space for chopping up herbs and things. Two stools were pushed up against the far side of it, allowing it to double as a cozy table.

To the left, the tiny sink had been replaced with a huge farm sink made of black slate. Would it always stay cool, even when the rest of the kitchen had warmed up? All the solid cupboard doors had been replaced with glass, making the room seem even bigger. Plus, it gave Miss Lucy the opportunity to show off her china and her crystal stemware.

The new stove was twice as large, with six burners, two on each side, and a grill set in the center. Miss Lucy loved to cook and have guests over, so the large stove made sense. A huge steel hood was set above it, venting all the cooking smells outside. Tara wasn't sure how she felt about that. A kitchen should always smell of food, of garlic and steak, maybe of vinegar and fresh berries.

Miss Lucy put a bright blue enameled kettle on the stove, then selected a small white teapot with red hibiscus flowers decorating the sides. She hummed as she put various herbs into the strainer. Tara caught the scent of chamomile, lavender, and green apple. She didn't bother to ask, however. Miss Lucy would frequently make a tea, serve it to her students, then have them identify the ingredients based on taste.

When Miss Lucy had finished, she went to sit on one of the stools next to the cooking island, pulling the other out for Tara to sit on.

"Thanks," Tara said. "And thank you for agreeing to see me so quickly."

Miss Lucy nodded. "You wouldn't have called unless you were scared. Or desperate. Or both."

Tara blinked, surprised. Was she that scared? Desperate?

Or just deeply, *deeply* unnerved? As though her entire world had shifted under her feet? The last time she'd been this unsettled had been when she'd discovered that there were other paths to power, other schools of magic.

"Someone's been haunting me," Tara said. "The Riprap man."

She carefully watched her old mentor's face when she said the name. She figured talking with Miss Lucy in person was the best way to tell whether she was being lied to.

But Miss Lucy didn't try to hide her surprise, or her dismay. "That's not good," she said, shaking her head.

"What is he? Who is he?" Tara asked. Maybe she could finally get some answers.

"What have you learned so far about him?" Miss Lucy countered.

"Sheila, the head of my coven, said he was an odd ghost, but just a ghost. He'd haunt me until the solstice, then disappear," Tara admitted. "She said he was harmless."

"You don't believe her, though," Miss Lucy said. She gave Tara a smug smile.

Tara gave a sigh. She hated feeling like a toy that Sheila and Miss Lucy both had a hold of. She'd had dreams where the various factions had actually torn her in two.

"I'm not sure if I believe her or not," Tara said stubbornly. She didn't want to go against the head of her coven, but something had been off in her conversation with Sheila. Something that had pinged hard on Tara's bullshit meter, though she couldn't say exactly what.

The kettle started whistling. Miss Lucy got up and walked to the stove. With her back deliberately turned toward Tara, Miss Lucy said, "Sheila's lying to you."

"Are you?" Tara challenged.

Miss Lucy gave Tara a sly smile over her shoulder. She shrugged. "The Riprap man isn't harmless," she said, turning serious, still showing Tara her face. "If he has targeted you, your life is in danger."

Tara swallowed against the sudden lump in her throat. She was glad that she finally had confirmation that the Riprap man was more than just a ghost.

But the fact that Sheila had lied to her…Tara didn't know what to do about that.

Miss Lucy gave Tara a few moments to sit with her thoughts while she poured the hot water into the teapot and set a small tomato timer sitting on the counter. Only then did Miss Lucy turn to face Tara again, leaning against the kitchen counter beside the stove. "There isn't much I can tell you about him," she said slowly. "But I will tell you all I know."

Tara nodded, eager to learn more.

Miss Lucy checked the clock over the stove, checking to see exactly what time it was. Then she seemed to fall into deep contemplation for a few moments.

"What is it?" Tara asked warily. She had the feeling that she wasn't going to like whatever it was that Miss Lucy was thinking about.

"There was a novice, first circle, like you, back when I was just learning the circles," Miss Lucy said slowly. "She claimed the Riprap man was haunting her. The lead witch of our coven turned her back on the poor girl. As made the rest of us do the same."

"But why?" Tara said, bewildered. Why would her sisters and brothers turn away from a witch in need?

"Bad luck," Miss Lucy said earnestly. "As it was explained to me and the others, if we'd helped the girl, it would have brought disease, death, and destruction to all the circles. And our families as well."

"From the Riprap man?" Tara asked, confused.

Miss Lucy nodded. "Yes, as well as Mulinohana, the river god."

Was that why the waters had grown so cold when she'd started praying to Bonana in her dream?

The timer went off and Miss Lucy pulled the strainer out of the teapot, then poured them both tea in glass cups that showed off the golden, steaming liquid.

"I can't tell you much more about him," Miss Lucy said as she seated herself back on the stool beside Tara. "There are a few stories, but the living don't know much about him."

Tara picked up the cup and wrapped her cool fingers around its warmth. The scent of lemongrass and mint filled her senses. There was something warm and earthy underneath it, maybe chrysanthemum.

She took a cautious sip, letting the delightful warmth seep all way into her bones.

After a moment of quiet comfort, Tara made herself ask the question that she knew Miss Lucy would want her former apprentice to ask.

"You said the living don't know much about him," Tara said. "Does that mean that there are spirits of the dead who do know more?"

Miss Lucy beamed at her former student, giving Tara the feeling that she'd just won a prize.

"Not merely dead spirits, my dear," Miss Lucy said slyly. "Dead witches."

FOUR

One by one, my companions keep falling. Old Wilkerson had to be left behind at the last village with a broken leg. The two scouts, Peter and Davis, both came down with such bad dysentery that we had to bid them farewell also. Jacob hadn't even made it much beyond Portland before a sudden cold had carried him off. Our expedition isn't cursed, despite what that old woman in the last village said to me. My native guide, Robin Goodfellow, doesn't think much about going back. He seems as determined as I am to reach our goal, following the path of the river up toward its source. He's introduced me to Mulinohana, the river god, and finally seems eager to initiate me in the mysteries now that it's just the pair of us, alone against the wilderness. I pray quietly to God that I may find the strength to continue, as Robin leads me along deeper and darker paths, so that I might succeed in finally taming the river.

Wilson Evermore, Explorer and Initiate, 1897

TARA DID NOT MISS the burning "kiss" of the stinging nettle, the sunbaked sour smell of foxglove, the way the poisonous sumac berries stained her fingers red. She did, however, take comfort in working beside Miss Lucy once again.

The pair of them were in Miss Lucy's studio, a small protected shack in the backyard. The shack itself had been a kit, but Miss Lucy had hired workmen to line the walls with warm maple flooring, put in cool white marble tile for the floor, and set galaxies of glowing stars across the ceiling, bright enough to light the room at night.

A long wooden workbench took up the center of the shack. Set into the center of it was a black, cast-iron cauldron, hanging over a bright blue gas burner (an electric heating source just wouldn't do for most potions—fire was a necessary element.)

Though the top of the workbench was a solid butcherblock, Tara still used the various chopping blocks that were hanging on the wall behind her, so that the ingredients didn't contaminate each other.

While Tara chopped and added items in the order specified by Miss Lucy, her mentor stood still, chanting and stirring, redirecting the toxins and poison of the plants into powerful magic.

Miss Lucy had laid out all the ingredients on the right side of the table, in the order that they needed to be prepared. Tara would pick them up one at a time, always circling the workbench counterclockwise, then choosing the next chopping board. She cleaned her knife between as well, using a towel that she kept slung across her shoulder.

By the time Tara reached the last ingredient—wild oregano—the smell of the concoction had shifted: instead of smelling wild and green, the air now carried the scent of a hint of summer thunderstorms and dark earth.

Tara stripped the leaves off the tall stems before she set about chopping, the sharp scent of the herb reminding her that it was getting on toward dinner time. She paused for a moment, taking a sip of water, before she continued. They couldn't stop now—the potion had to be drunk while it was still hot. If it rested, the magic would leak out.

When the leaves had been reduced to fine pieces, Tara held up the chopping board for Miss Lucy to see. She nodded, and Tara scraped the chopped up herb into the pot.

She was slightly disappointed that nothing appeared to happen when the last ingredient was added, no dramatic cloud of steam, no sudden hissing or popping.

Miss Lucy grinned at Tara's questioning look. "The oregano's just to make the potion taste better," she admitted.

"Oh!" Tara said. She was surprised. Miss Lucy generally didn't care about such niceties.

"Here," Miss Lucy said, handing the spoon to Tara.

Tara switched places with Miss Lucy, who immediately picked up her chant and started circling the table as Tara began to stir the pot. The heat had been turned down and the concoction bubbled slowly, the herbs as thick as seaweed in the river after a drought. The smell of earth intensified, though Tara still felt a lighter scent tickling the back of her throat, like rain on a summer's day.

Miss Lucy called on the familiar gods, like Brigid and Samil, along with Eural the god of the eastern wind, and Areebin, the protector of souls. It had originally surprised Tara that both sects of witches prayed to the same gods, except they asked for different things. Brigid was still a protector of the earth, but Miss Lucy also asked her for permission to seek answers underground.

Tara couldn't say exactly how she knew that the spell was finished, the potion complete. Something changed in the composition of the air, though perhaps just the sense of anticipation tripled. The smell stayed the same—thickly dark with the sense of imminent storms.

Miss Lucy completed her circle and turned to Tara. "You're going to have to hurry," she said as she lifted up the caldron.

"What—I don't understand," Tara said as she watched Miss Lucy pour the brew into a waiting green metal thermos.

"Spirits don't come to your call, willy nilly. You know that," Miss Lucy admonished as she sealed the thermos and shook it lightly once. "You need to start at the place where they are."

Tara blinked. She had known that, but she'd forgotten. It wasn't as if she was in the habit of calling up spirits. While it was possible to call a spirit or a ghost to you, the most successful rituals took place where the bodies were buried, in graveyards and watery tombs.

"Aren't you coming with me?" Tara asked as she accepted the thermos from Miss Lucy. The metal felt surprisingly cold, given how hot the mixture inside was. It also felt heavier than it should, as if the liquid inside was actually solid.

"No, I don't think I should," Miss Lucy said. She shrugged. "Bad luck."

The words stung more than the nettles had earlier. "Do you think I'll bring you bad luck? The coven?" Tara said, trying to cover her hurt.

Miss Lucy stared hard at Tara for a moment, choosing her words carefully. "If I didn't think you might have a chance, I wouldn't have helped you," she said. "But there's only so much I can do. The rest— and whether or not you survive the coming trials—is up to you."

Tara swallowed down her hurt. At least Miss Lucy probably wasn't lying to her. The coven and all the witches who were familiar with the Riprap man would consider her bad luck and wouldn't associate with her. She'd heard witches talk about the concept of luck before, but it had always been theoretical for her.

"Where do I need to go?" Tara asked as she followed Miss Lucy out of the shack. Instead of going back into the house, Miss Lucy let Tara around the side of the house, out the gate and straight out to the front.

"The bridges, of course," Miss Lucy said.

"Which bridge?" Tara asked. There were over half a dozen bridges in downtown Portland.

Miss Lucy paused at that. "Morrison," she said after a moment. "That's the oldest bridge. Go to one of the bases, close to where the bridge lifts from the ground into the air. Drink the potion there and cast for the ghost of the witch who guards the bridge."

"What?" Tara said. Witches worked as protectors, yes, of local areas. But as living beings, not as ghosts or spirits.

"Quickly, now," Miss Lucy said. "You need to go. While the potion is still potent."

Tara pulled out her phone and called up an Uber. One would be there in just three minutes.

"Thank you," Tara said as she turned to say goodbye to Miss Lucy. Then, because there needed to be honesty between them, she added, "I think."

Miss Lucy gave her a quick grin, unsettling and sharp. "I hope to see you after solstice," she said, setting her limits and her terms firmly. "May the spirits guide and protect you, wherever your path takes you," she added before she turned away.

A car pulled up to the house before Tara could call her former mentor back. Not that Miss Lucy would come.

Tara was on her own.

TARA DIRECTED the driver to the east side of the bridge, at Mill Ends Park, down near the waterfront. A small carnival had been set up with kiddy rides and tents for adult beverages. It was Monday night and the faire wasn't very crowded. The smell of mini donuts and spilled beer followed her as she walked past the rides, up toward the base of the bridge. Tinkling sounds of the rides swept around her.

At least the sun had finally relinquished its heat and cool breezes tickled her hair. Tara wished she'd brought a jacket with her. Then again, there might be a lot of things that she wished that night.

Standing directly under the steel girders, Tara looked up. The noise of the fast-moving cars above was loud and constant. The underside of the bridge was filled with solid metal and concrete. She thought she saw the bridge sway slightly, not quickly, but in time with the traffic.

Almost like a heartbeat.

The few people visiting the faire crossed behind Tara as she faced the water. She heard them fade into the distance as she sent a quick prayer, asking for invisibility.

Her stomach turned over unpleasantly as she opened the thermos. The smell of the potion hadn't grown magically sweeter. If anything, the scent of the liquid mingled with the smell of the dirt under her feet and the scent of stale water in front of her.

Would Miss Lucy poison her? Tara doubted it. First off, if Miss

Lucy was angry with Tara, she wouldn't hide it, she'd speak her rage to the person directly.

Of course, there were always accidents, with potions not precisely measured out, ingredients being substituted or not the highest quality, the proper prayers not being applied.

And sometimes it was just the will of the gods.

Tara took a deep breath through her mouth, trying to calm her twisting stomach. But no relief came.

Closing her eyes and asking again for blessings, Tara lifted the potion to her mouth.

The first mouthful was like warm sludge. It tasted like dirt—no, compost. Dirt that at one point had been shit. Then the bitterness spiked through her, awful and insistent, coating the top of her mouth. And that was after Miss Lucy had added the wild oregano to make it taste better?

Tara forced herself to swallow. She gave an entire body shudder. She did *not* want to drink any more of the vile potion.

She had no choice.

Lifting the thermos again, Tara opened her mouth and took another swallow. This one was both better and worse. It still tasted like dirt, but now, instead of bitterness came the slime of rotten cabbage. Tara made herself swallow, feeling as though worms now crawled down her throat.

Tara gritted her teeth and sucked in air, willing herself not to vomit. Her head pounded with sudden heat. Her hands grew clammy at the same time. She swayed, but she would not stop.

Her hand raised the flask. It took effort for Tara to unlock her jaw. Just one more swallow was all she had to manage. Then she could start her call.

The oregano rode on the top of the vile substance this time, like a savory coating on a rotting piece of meat. Tara couldn't help but start hacking even as she forced the liquid down. Her eyes watered and she couldn't breathe for a few moments. She found herself bent over, one hand on her knees while the other still cradled the precious potion.

Finally, Tara recovered enough of herself to seal the thermos back up. The smell remained. It had transferred to her throat, her hair, her hands. Even her tears.

It took two tries for Tara to clear her throat enough to utter the first words of the calling, entreating Brigid to welcome her into the embrace of the earth, to guide her to those who lived there, to protect her steps and lead her back to the light.

Tara's heart pounded more and more slowly. She felt herself falling into a trance. She couldn't help but sway where she stood. She knew the people passing behind her, those who could actually see her, probably thought she was drunk.

Dark spots formed on the ground before Tara. She blinked, trying to clear her vision.

It took her a few moments to realize that the dark spots were growing, solidifying into a single great maw.

Tara bit back her screams as she felt herself falling forward, a terrifying dark mass yanking her off her feet.

Down.

And into the very earth itself.

TARA HAD ASSUMED that calling a witch's spirit would be similar to calling a regular spirit. That despite the drama of the dark hole and the horrible potion, that a ghost would appear beside Tara underneath the bridge.

It never occurred to her that the ghost would draw Tara's spirit down to its residence instead.

The room was sparsely furnished. A red couch pushed against the wall, with gold cushions, looking like a comfortable place to curl up with a good book. A tall fireplace with a roaring fire stood opposite the couch, the old-fashioned mantle made from river rock, all nubby. The fire burned with bright blue flames and gave off no heat, as though it was merely an illusion. The gray walls looked like rock carved with a melon baller, scooped out one foot at a time, with hard ridges at the edge of every hollow. She would have to remember to never rest her hand or brush against them—they looked uncomfortably sharp. A large braided rug covered much of the floor, but it couldn't hide the fact that the floor was still plain, beaten dirt everywhere.

To the left of the couch stood a closed wooden door. Before Tara could call out, the door opened.

"What do you want?" said the woman who came steaming out. She looked so perfectly put together that Tara wondered if she was a model.

Her black hair was done in a poodle cut, a 1950s style, with tight curls in the front and pulled back along the sides with glittering ruby-encrusted pins. Dark pencil emphasized her almond-shaped eyes, which were a brilliant emerald color. A slight bit of rouge pinked-up her white cheeks and pale lips, making her look young and fresh. Her face was heart-shaped, with a broad forehead, slightly thinner cheeks, leading down to a pointed chin. Though she had a tiny nose, Tara would bet that the woman constantly was sticking it into other people's business.

The woman wore a light blue shirt dress with a white collar, also very 1950s, white cuffs around the short sleeves, and tiny white buttons down the front. It looked both comfortable and stylish. A tight black belt showed off her tiny waist. She had on black pointed shoes with kitten heels, as well as nylons. Only the shoes looked out of date—or perhaps they just hadn't come back into style yet.

"Who are you?" the woman asked, pulling up sharply when she saw Tara.

"My name's Tara," she said. "I called on the spirit of the witch who guards the Morrison Bridge."

The woman nodded. "I am she. Dorothy Parkerson. Welcome to my prison, or as I like to call it, cell sweet cell. Why are you here?"

Tara paused, at a loss. "I am being hunted by the Riprap man," she confessed.

"How did you have the power to come down here?" Dorothy said. Her perfectly plucked eyebrows scrunched together across her forehead, showing her complete puzzlement.

Though Tara was still learning to see, she could sometimes catch a glimpse of another's power and be able to gauge their strength. She assumed that Dorothy could read her, and had realized that Tara didn't have the power to make it down to the "cell sweet cell" on her own.

"My former mentor gave me a potion," Tara said. She looked down. The thermos was nowhere to be seen. Though she was still wearing the same T-shirt and shorts, and she felt solid enough when she reached over with one hand to squeeze her other, she doubted she was actually there, in the flesh. Her body was probably still somewhere else, either in a daze or passed out. As she'd been in a public space, she really didn't have much time before someone called 911.

Dorothy reached out and tried to touch Tara. Her hand passed uncomfortably through Tara's arm, casting spikes of cold through Tara's bones.

"Sorry," Dorothy said.

"It's all right," Tara told her. "What can you tell me about the Riprap man?"

"He caught me," Dorothy said, her thin lips pressed together into a pretty scowl. "Same as he's caught all of us."

"Us?" Tara asked. "There are more of you?"

"One for each bridge," Dorothy said, nodding. "We've formed our own coven," she added. "I'd thought you were the Burnside Bridge witch, coming to complain about the construction again." She paused, then added, "Tell me, what level are you?"

"First level initiate," Tara said. "I'm in the first circle—head, or thought."

"How close are you to the second?" Dorothy asked.

Tara shrugged. "My teacher wants me to try for the second level on the solstice, in two days' time."

"You have to make it," Dorothy told her fiercely. "We—all of us—were only first level initiates when the Riprap man came calling for us. I don't know if a second level practitioner could escape him or not, but she might be able to."

"Thank you," Tara said. For the first time in a day, she felt a touch of relief overcoming her constant sense of dread. Maybe she could pull herself out of his grasp.

"What else can you tell me about him? Who is he?" Tara asked. A wave of dizziness washed over her. Her body was demanding her spirit's return.

"You know what riprap is, yes? The boulders piled around the pier of a bridge?" Dorothy said.

"Yes," Tara said.

"Riprap protects the bridges from waters and flood. The Riprap man captures witches as well, drowning us in the river, sacrificing us on the riprap. Then he binds each soul to a bridge."

"How?" Tara asked. She spread her fingers wide, then made claws of her hands, trying to keep herself in Dorothy's living room for just a few moments longer.

"Dark magic. Black magic. Old magic," Dorothy said. "The Riprap man works for the ancient god of the river, who doesn't like witches. Some old feud that no one suspected or remembered."

"Why is he coming for me?" Tara said. The room wavered, but she grit her teeth and consciously remembered the awful potion that she'd drunk, just to get here.

Dorothy sighed. "The Burnside Bridge is being repaired, isn't it?"

Tara nodded. She'd been keeping track of the progress on the website. There was structural damage, steel inside the concrete footings that needed to be replaced.

"The Riprap man always needs a new witch when there's work being done. I'm the third Morrison bridge witch. The others have passed."

Tara shook her head. Not only would the Riprap man drown her in the river and then bind her to a bridge, the existing witch would be snuffed out of existence. It wasn't necessarily a good or nice existence, but still.

"He'll come for you at midnight, the day after the solstice, when the dark starts to retake the light," Dorothy warned. Her voice grew faint. "Move to the second level. That may save you when the Riprap man comes calling."

"Thank you," Tara whispered. "Blessings on you," she added, though she didn't know if Dorothy heard her or not.

Tara rose rapidly through the earth, her spirit returning to her body, causing an upheaval. She bent in half and heaved, throwing up the potion. It splashed at her feet, vile and green. Long worms—or maybe just living bits of herbs, twisted together—squirmed in the vomit before sinking back down into the earth.

No one seemed to have noticed her momentary lapse. How long had she been absent? Maybe five minutes, not much more. At least she'd been able to stay on her feet and hadn't fallen over.

A couple of men passed by as Tara wrapped her arms around her stomach, holding herself. She could tell from their sharp looks that they were assessing whether or not she was worth the effort—was she out of it enough that she wouldn't put up too much of a fight? Or was she too much work? Would she keep vomiting instead?

With a shaky hand, Tara reached down and picked up the mostly empty thermos. Then she stood up straight and stared at the men. Hard, her "don't fuck with me" face firmly set.

The two men wisely moved on, though Tara hoped they wouldn't find a target.

With shaky legs, Tara started to make her way back out to the street. Her mouth tasted like she'd been on a three-day bender. She couldn't wait to get back to her apartment and brush her teeth. Maybe even twice.

Then, Tara was going to have to make herself a large pot of caffeinated tea. Strong enough to keep her awake through the night. And into the next day as well.

She had to spend every hour that she could studying over the next couple of days so that she might pass into the next circle, out of reach of the Riprap man.

Tara rubbed and blinked her eyes, trying to clear the crud from them. She gazed blearily at her alarm clock. She'd been up past two A.M., trying to cram in as much knowledge as she could. The alarm told her that it was now seven.

She could survive on four hours of sleep, right?

Shaking her head, Tara pushed herself up to sitting. She yawned and stretched her arms over her head, trying to wake up. She'd never been much of a morning person. It took her a couple of hours to get herself moving after she woke up.

But she had no choice. One last day of studying and practicing before tomorrow, the solstice. The coven wouldn't meet until after dark; however, Tara had to work all day. She might be able to get Han Su to cover for her, except that she'd already asked for the afternoon off on Wednesdays due to her new class schedule. And Patricia would be too busy with her own coven and preparing for solstice.

Tara padded off to take a shower, turning the water extremely warm, hoping it would help wake her up. She didn't stay under the spray for as long as she would have liked: something about how hypnotic the falling water was had her swaying on her feet.

She cursed the Riprap man once again. Water was Tara's element. She loved swimming, boating, fishing, anything to do with the water. She'd chosen this apartment specifically because it was so close to the river.

Now, she was looking at all things connected with water with a cautious eye.

She couldn't wait for this to be over so that she could get on with her life. In some sense or another.

After she'd made her tea—a green tea with marigold flowers, lavender, hyssop, and a touch of cinnamon—Tara sat on her balcony and breathed in the morning. She heard Sharon rummaging around behind her, making her usual English muffin with fake butter and artificially sweetened jam.

If only the rent wasn't so expensive here! Tara loved this apartment. But she needed someone like Sharon who could pay for more than half of the rent.

The little Anna came thrumming by, circling to make sure no rival was near before he—no, she, as there was practically no red on the head or chest—settled down to take a few sips.

"I hate those things," Sharon said as she walked out onto the balcony, clunking down her plate and cup.

"Hate?" Tara had to ask.

"It's unnatural how they move," Sharon said. "They flit around so fast, then just hover. And they're aggressive. They dive-bomb me every time I come out here."

"Maybe they just don't like you in return," Tara said. She blinked, then swallowed. She was too tired for polite conversation just then, and was going to get herself into trouble with Sharon by speaking her mind.

"Like you," Sharon said, looking out over the edge of the balcony. "You don't like me much, either."

Tara didn't know what to say. This was the worst time for her to be trying to have this sort of heart-to-heart conversation with her flatmate.

"It's okay," Sharon said. "We don't really fit well together. We're like oil and water."

"Yeah, we kind of are," Tara said with a sigh. She knew what was coming.

"Our lease will be up at the end of next month. If you want to stay here, and I think you love this place so much more than I do, you're going to need to find a new flatmate," Sharon said. "I'll be moving out."

The blow hit Tara hard in the center of her chest. For a moment she couldn't take a deep breath. Finally, she swallowed down her disappointment and said, "Thank you for giving me so much notice."

"I'm not an asshole," Sharon said, glaring at Tara.

Tara was glad that she was able to keep her lips pressed together and not reply.

Though possibly she didn't do as good of a job of keeping her thoughts to herself as Sharon added, "No matter how much you might consider me one."

"I'm sorry," Tara said immediately.

Sharon shook her head. "As I said, we just don't get along. I don't think it's either you or me." She paused, then added, "And it's true that you probably bring out the worst in me. Just like I bring out the worst in you."

"I'm not going to deny it," Tara said after a moment, as this appeared to be a morning of truths. "I really wish you the best," she said.

"And I wish you the best with all your studies and everything else," Sharon said.

Tara had given Sharon the lie that she was taking an online course, hoping to become a registered herbalist.

They spent the rest of the time before Sharon got up to leave in a more or less comfortable silence, watching the river flow beneath them, changing but not changing as always.

AFTER SHARON HAD GONE to work for the day, Tara checked her email, pleased to find a note from Richard, her friend, the research librarian.

In it, he gave her a long, scholarly text about London Bridges, which she merely scanned. No mention of the gray lady in anything he could find.

What caught her attention was that he'd found a fragment of a child's song that did mention the Riprap man.

Oh, the Riprap man will build it tall
Start out small
Oh, the Riprap man will build it tall
Start out small

Roll the boulders like balls
Start out small
Roll the boulders like balls
Start out small

Lift them up like a great wall
Start out small
Lift them up like a great wall
Start out small

Oh gray lady can you resist the call
Start out small

*Oh gray lady can you resist the call
Start out small*

Richard had included both a recording played on a flute as well as the sheet music. It had a simple tune, like London Bridges. He theorized that it came with a game, like London Bridges, with children squatting down every time they sang the chorus of "Start out small."

Instead of replying, Tara picked up the phone to call Richard.

"Good morning," Richard said, answering the phone.

His warm voice made her smile. It really was a shame that they just weren't compatible. Plus, Richard had recently started dating a very nice woman who Tara approved of. She wanted him to be happy.

"Good morning," Tara said. "Thank you so much for the work you did."

"My pleasure," Richard said. "Seriously. If there's ever anything you need for me to look up, just let me know. It's summer, and I have a lot of time on my hands."

"I may," Tara said slowly. "I'm actually looking into an ancestor," she lied. Well, sort of. All witches were family in one way or another, right? "Her name was Dorothy Parkerson. She disappeared in the late '50s, like 1957, 1958, sometime around then."

Tara didn't want to give the specific date, as she wasn't sure if Dorothy would have been sacrificed before the bridge was complete or afterward.

Just as the Riprap man was coming for her before the Burnside bridge construction was finished.

"You got it," Richard said. "I'll see what I can find. I supposed you're going to a big party tomorrow night, right?"

"Yes," Tara said warily.

Richard laughed. "It's okay. You tend to celebrate the solstices, as well as the equinoxes."

"Oh. Right," Tara said. She guessed that was obvious.

"How are your studies going?" Richard asked.

"Fine," Tara said. "But speaking of such…"

"Okay, okay, I can take a hint. Lots on your plate right now. Give me a call after the solstice, all right?"

"I will," Tara promised. She hesitated. How much could she tell Richard? What could she tell him? "You've always been such a good friend," she added. "I have always appreciated you. Thank you."

"You're welcome," Richard said. "I appreciate you as a friend too. And…well, I'd like to talk with my friend about Lisa, soon."

Tara blinked, taking a few moments before she remembered that Lisa was the woman Richard was currently dating. "Getting serious?" she asked.

"It is," Richard said. "It's really weird and wonderful and exciting and it isn't scary, which is the weird part."

"I can't wait to hear all about it," Tara told him sincerely. "I'm happy for you."

"Thank you," Richard said. "You don't know how rare that is, for a friend to be supportive of another friend's good luck."

"You got the wrong friends, then," Tara said. Damn it! She really needed to not actually talk with anyone while she was so tired.

But Richard just laughed. "Yup," he said. "Which is why I appreciate you so much."

"Thank you," Tara said. It was good to know that at least someone in her life wasn't lying to her.

"I'll send you any information I can find on Dorothy," Richard added. "Talk with you soon."

"Thanks, bye," Tara said.

She sat for a while, bemused at how her life seemed to be turning out.

The witches she'd known and trusted, her teachers and her mentors, were possibly not as good as she'd once believed. And the other people in her life, the mundanes, were turning out to be better.

TARA FOCUSED all her energy between her hands and the whirling ball of winds contained there. It was a more advanced spell, to control and capture the winds, rather than just call on them and direct them to blow here or there.

Now, she just had to push her hands out, away from her chest. It felt as though she carried a heavy medicine ball, like what they had at the gym. Except that this challenged both her physical as well as her mental powers, the ball growing heavier as she pushed it away from the center of her being.

The next part was to be able to stand with the ball. Tara tightened the muscles in her thighs, preparing herself to slowly rise from her chair.

She was doing it! Rising up! It took so much concentration to be able to do two things at once, such as carry on a spell and walk. Much harder than patting your head while rubbing your stomach. More like performing a handstand on a unicycle and reaching down with one hand to spin the pedals while at the same time juggling fireballs with your feet.

A shrill bell rang. Damn it! Tara had forgotten to mute her phone. Her concentration broke. The ball blew apart, the winds rushing away from her. A couple tried to push through her out of spite, angry that they'd been contained even for a little while.

Tara sat back down, her legs and arms shaking.

The phone continued to ring. Tara slid it over towards her, then sighed.

It was her mom. Time for their weekly mother-daughter chat.

"Hey, Mom," Tara said as she answered.

"Hello," Mom replied. "What are you up to?"

"Studying," Tara said honestly. "Got a big test tomorrow." All of which was factually true. "How are you? What are you and Dad up to this week?"

Tara had grown up in Menomonee, Wisconsin. It was situated about halfway between two large cities, the Minneapolis/St. Paul twin cities to the west, and Madison to the east and south. Tara had never felt as though she'd belonged there. There wasn't much there to start with, as Menomonee wasn't that big of a town. Plus, she'd grown up pretty close to the freeway, and always felt as though she needed to go, to travel, caught between two big magnets, never sure which direction was right.

It was one of the reasons why she'd followed Sean out to the coast. A part of her had known exactly how irresponsible it was for her to move halfway across country just to be with a boy. However, she'd needed the excuse to get out of Wisconsin and go somewhere else.

When Sean had broken up with her, it had been devastating at first. Tara hadn't known anyone, hadn't found a job yet, didn't have any money. She'd been looking at either having to live in the street or return home with her tail between her legs. Both options had about the same appeal.

Then she'd answered an ad for an *au pair* job that would give her both food as well as a place to stay. Though she didn't have any experience beyond taking care of her two younger siblings, the Andersons had hired her right away.

Tara hadn't learned until years later that the Andersons had recognized that Tara had a spark of power. It had taken Tara five years to realize what she had and to start working with it. Which had led to Miss Lucy and everything else.

Tara's mom and dad, as well as her younger sister and brother, had all stayed in Wisconsin. Tara tried to make it back for Christmas every year, frequently traveling on the actual holiday, as she'd had her own celebration on the solstice with her newly acquired family just before.

Tara's parents had started raising their family late, and so were now retired. They'd bought a hobby farm north of town, a fixer-upper. It had surprised Tara how much both of her parents had bloomed in the country, taking classes and watching YouTube videos about home repair, doing much of the work themselves now.

"We're working on the pumphouse," Mom said. "The roof started leaking this winter, probably the weight of all the snow on it. So we're having to replace that."

"What does that entail?" Tara asked. She was endlessly curious about all the handy things that her parents now did, things they would have hired someone to do when she'd been growing up.

"First, we have to remove all the shingles and tarpaper covering the roof," her mom explained. "Then remove the deck—the actual plywood making up the roof itself. Replace it, put some good tar on it to seal it fully, then put back on tarpaper and shingles."

"Wow," Tara said. "Sounds like a lot of work. You be careful on those ladders, you hear?" That was the last thing that Tara needed right now, for one of her elderly parents to fall off the roof.

Mom laughed, a warm sound. "That's exactly what I've been telling Henry," she said. "I'll be sure to let him know that his daughter is worried as well."

"Good," Tara said. "But you be careful, too."

"Oh, I am. Trust me," Mom said. "And the fact that if Henry falls, I get six months of *I told you so*, is a true caution for him."

Tara smiled. Her parents made bargains and bets with each other all the time. The payment was frequently limited bragging rights, for a day up to six months, but no longer than that. Sometimes the payoff would be dishwashing duties, doing the laundry, washing floors, general clean up, and so on.

"I'm glad to hear that you're both being cautious," Tara said. It would be difficult to do a long-distance healing, but she'd try if either of her parents were injured.

"So tell me what you've learned this week," Mom said. She was also interested in plants and wildlife, particularly since moving to the farm. She was even learning a little herbal lore and had started drying berries and herbs to make her own teas.

"I learned about London Bridges," Tara said instead of sharing more about herbs. "How the children's song spread all the way across Europe."

"Interesting!" Mom said. "Was that because Portland has so many bridges?"

"Exactly," Tara said. A lump suddenly formed in Tara's throat. "Mom, you know that I love you and Dad and the brat and Timmy, right?"

"We do," Mom said. "Why? What's wrong?"

"I just…it's everything," Tara confessed. She blinked her eyes, trying to keep back the tears. "Some of my friends—they're not who I thought they were." Particularly Sheila, the head of her coven, who had lied to her about the Riprap man, who hadn't tried to help her.

Mom's sigh echoed in Tara's ear. "I'm sorry," she said. "Is there anything we can do to help?"

"No," Tara said, shaking her head. "I wish there was."

Tara heard yelling in the background.

Her mom obviously put her hand over the phone, trying to muffle her shout of, "I'll be right there!" Then she returned to Tara. "Henry says that break's over," her mom said, the amusement apparent. "I keep telling him that we don't have to finish this in one day, but he still thinks he's eighteen or something."

That seemed exactly like her dad, always convinced that he was invincible.

"Tell him that I love him too," Tara said. Damn it. How could she say goodbye to her mom without raising all her motherly instincts and suspicions?

"I will. You want me to call tomorrow?" Mom asked.

"Maybe?" Tara said, hating how her voice quavered.

"I will, then," Mom said. "I'll write it down in my calendar."

More shouting occurred in the background.

"I know, you have to go," Tara said before her mom could say anything else. "I'll talk with you tomorrow, okay?"

"Okay. Love you bye," Mom said, hanging up.

"Love you bye."

Tara slowly lowered the phone back to the table. She couldn't say much more to her parents about what was going on. How badly would it destroy them if she was killed? They'd be devastated.

But she couldn't prepare them for that.

All she could do was to study even harder so that she didn't end up disappointing them by dying.

FIVE

I would never have believed it if I hadn't seen it for myself. I've always been a man of science, an engineer. Magic was only for old wives' tales and uncultured natives. How little did I know! I castigate myself daily for my ignorance. How much more could I have done, how great would be my bridges if I had used magic! However, I understand the caution that Robin employs. Too much of this power in the wrong hands could be disastrous. He's shown me, himself, what happens when a witch's coven meets, the harm they cause to the land as well as to their fellow man. It isn't our place to stop them, however. We are close to the river's source, the power all around us. When we get there, we will call forth the gods to see if we can strike a bargain with them, to protect the eggshell fragile towns and cities strung along the water like pearls.

Wilson Evermore, Initiate and Beginning Magician, 1898

TARA DRAGGED herself to "Ye Olde Magick Shoppe" Wednesday

morning, the day of the solstice. Her head felt overly full of knowledge, her bones creaked with suppressed magic, ice dragged itself through her blood, and the winds still whispered in her ears.

For all her focus on air and wind, Tara had tried not to forget that the essence of this circle was actually breath. Not just the winds and the breath of the world, but the breath of the body as well. She knew that she hadn't studied as much of the internal art as she probably should have. Hopefully the shop would be quiet that day and she'd have a chance to meditate and work on her breathing.

However, there were already a couple of people standing outside the shop when Tara arrived, fifteen minutes before the door was supposed to be open. "I'll let you in at ten," she promised the two women as she unlocked the door.

"Take your time, hon," the one said, with a wave of her hand. "It's nice enough out here this morning."

Her friend looked askance, but Tara didn't ask.

"Thank you," she said, slipping inside the shop and locking the door behind her.

At least everything looked normal enough.

She didn't care for the smell of the river that rose up as soon as she stepped into the backroom, sliding her lunch and dinner into one of the refrigerators there.

Quickly, Tara went back into the main room. She counted the money in the register as fast as she could, totaling the bills up, making sure that it agreed with the count from the night before, then she opened up the door to customers five minutes before the store was officially supposed to open.

Tara tried to focus and study the few times the shop had a lull. However, every time she was alone, her sense of dread overwhelmed her. The smell of the river kept haunting her.

Damn it! She kept trying to remind herself that she loved the water, loved living on the river. Now, she wondered if she'd ever be able to look at it the same.

The shop closed up early that night, as it was considered one of the major holidays. When Tara texted Kyle, he agreed to come and fetch her for the meeting that night.

"So, how's your nightmare man?" Kyle asked as Tara started closing up the shop. He wore a gray T-shirt with a beige vest and blue jeans, looking very stylish.

"Don't think you want to know," Tara said. She wasn't sure if she wanted to tell Kyle anything about the Riprap man.

"Why is that?" Kyle asked, the surprise at her answer masking what was sure to be some hurt.

"Honestly? It's so that you have deniability," Tara said. "I don't want to bring you trouble. And you may have some, if I told you anything." Tara really didn't want Sheila or the others declaring Kyle bad luck. He needed the coven, needed a family he could declare his own.

Kyle stood in the center of the shop, mulling over what she'd just said. Finally, he turned and walked over to the door of the shop, planting himself just in front of it, arms crossed over his chest. He went so still he looked like a guardian carved out of black marble.

"I think you're wrong," Kyle said solemnly. "Now, you know that I've gone through some bad shit," he said after a few moments. "The only way I got through that was with the help of some very good friends. So this not telling me for my own good bullshit? Is just that. Bullshit. Tell me."

"Kyle, I—"

"Tell me. Now," Kyle said. "Or I'll make sure you miss this meeting."

Tara blinked, surprised. She wasn't sure where exactly this was coming from.

"This nightmare man got you spooked," Kyle said. "He's been chasing after you. You need help. I don't leave my friends, and particularly not my good friends, to go hang in the wind."

"It really isn't smart—"

"Don't care," Kyle said. He lifted his chin, looking even more stubborn than he had. "Tell me."

"Sheila and the others will deny what I tell you," Tara said, stalling. "And they might decide that you're bad luck as well."

"If it weren't for bad luck, I wouldn't have no luck at all," Kyle said with a ghost of a smile. "Tell me."

So Tara told Kyle everything she knew about the Riprap man, how he'd been haunting her, why he was probably coming for her. About visiting Miss Lucy to get the potion, as well as Dorothy.

Kyle didn't move until Tara was finished.

"All right then," Kyle said. "We got a plan. You need to pass your test tonight."

"Yes," Tara said. "So can we get going?"

Kyle gave her a sheepish grin. "Sure, sure. But I'm going to grill you all the way out. And tell you about what happened to me passing the circles."

"Will that help?" Tara asked. As far as she knew, though witches all passed through the same circles, each initiation was different.

Kyle shrugged. "Won't hurt to know a bit more about the process before you start. Now, you ready finally?"

Tara rolled her eyes at him. "Yes, I am."

"Then let's get you out to the meeting. And get you past that test."

<hr>

AALOKA WAITED for Tara inside the house, in the pantry next to the kitchen. Candles rested on every surface, giving the room a warm glow. The pantry was square at the back end but sloped to a point at the front, where a window box had been built, the shelves full of herbs. Tara smiled at the greenery. Even in the dim light, she recognized most of them: basil, sage, coriander, sorrel, oregano, and hyssop, to name a few.

"I passed forward your application to move between the circles tonight," Aaloka said. She held out her hands, drawing Tara closer. "I must admit, I was surprised at the resistance I got from Sheila."

Tara swallowed hard against a suddenly dry throat. "Did she refuse to let me walk the maze?" Tara hadn't even considered that the head of her order might block her that way.

Then again, Sheila had lied to Tara about the Riprap man.

What would happen to the coven if the Riprap man didn't claim his sacrifice? Would they start to have "bad luck" as Miss Lucy had described?

"She pushed back, but there were several of us who spoke up on your behalf," Aaloka said. "So you will be walking the maze, passing from the circle of thought to the circle of breath."

"Thank you," Tara said, squeezing Aaloka's hands briefly. Her head was suddenly light. The candles seemed much brighter now. She made herself take a deep breath, widening her stance to steady herself.

"What do I need to do?" Tara asked. She'd had to pass an oral exam as part of her test when she'd passed fully into the first circle, then the "practicum" of walking the meditation maze. Kyle had said that had been his experience as well. Tara still thought she should ask.

"It will be much the same as the first circle," Aaloka told her. "First, an oral exam, which I'm sure you'll pass. Then, the walk." Aaloka sighed. "Just keep your head on straight, your thoughts clear, and I'm sure you'll make it."

"Thank you," Tara said. "What else can you tell me—"

"Tara?" One of the existing initiates of breath, a fair-haired, willowy woman named June, poked her head into the pantry. "It's time for you to be prepared."

"Blessed be," Aaloka said, bringing her palms together and bowing her head to Tara.

Tara returned the gesture, then followed June out of the pantry, through the house and into the sunroom at the back, overlooking the garden. The other initiate of breath, Wren, was already standing there.

The room itself was comfortable, longer than it was wide, with couches on the long walls and overstuffed chairs on the shorter ones. Windows filled three of the walls, the fourth being the actual outside wall of the house. The sunroom had obviously been added to the house later, probably in the 1970s.

Just outside of the room stood Sheila and the others who were in the upper circles. They stood motionless, holding candles, obviously there to judge her performance.

Tara felt her back stiffen and her chin come up. She could do this.

"You need to be purified for the ceremony," June said. "You'll have to first change clothes."

It was only then that Tara realized that both June and Wren were dressed in long white gowns, lightweight and gauzy.

Tara looked at the pair of them, refusing to glance at the observers. The pair standing in front of her obviously expected her to strip bare here and now.

That was different than the first time, or than what Kyle told her. Then again, Kyle was a man with a badly abused psyche. They might not have insisted that he strip nude in front of everyone.

But Tara slipped her T-shirt over her head, kicked off her sandals, jeans, then her bra and panties. She stood before everyone with her head held tall, not trying to cover up her body. She might have a little extra weight than she was officially supposed to have according to society, and had a soft belly, but she also had curves, hips, and great tits.

"Good," June told her with a smile. "You keep your head up."

Was this part of the test? If Tara had balked, would she have failed before she'd even started?

June and Wren rubbed scented oils into Tara's skin, starting at her neck and working their way down. It smelled sweet, of myrrh and lavender. Her head started buzzing as they finished. She took a deep breath. Was it just caffeine? Or was it magic? She couldn't tell.

"Put this on," Wren said, handing Tara a robe. It was white with green leaves embroidered down the front of it as well as around the collar and the cuffs. "You'll take this off when it's time to walk the maze," Wren added.

"Thank you for beginning my initiation," Tara said, nodding to both of them. "Blessed be."

"Blessed be," they intoned in unison. "Now, you need to stay here for a bit while your teacher comes to test you."

Tara nodded and widened her stance, prepared to stand for the entire ordeal.

"Glad to see you're prepared," June said with a smile. "I look forward to welcoming you to our circle."

Tara puzzled over the looks and expectations that the two initiates of the circle of breath had seemed to already have. Had someone "warned" them about Tara? How she might not actually be ready?

Aaloka came into the sunroom next. She'd changed clothes as well, and now wore a midnight blue sari with a glittering starburst pattern woven into the cloth. Her black hair was tied back into its usual bun, and a sprig of jasmine was pinned to the top of it. A sparkling red jewel had been pasted to the center of Aaloka's forehead, and her red lipstick matched.

"Though you are my student, I will not go easy on you," Aaloka warned as she rested the book she was carrying on the closest end table. "Tell me, what are the medicinal properties for *rhamnus purshiana*?"

Tara smiled. Kyle had been drilling her the exact same way during the drive out.

This part, she knew. Though her brain might feel overly full from everything she'd tried to cram into it the last couple of days, Tara knew that she could remember the important parts concerning herbs and lore.

It was the practicum that concerned her. Particularly since she'd have to overcome the magic of some of the others.

Would Sheila be casting illusions as well? Tara wasn't strong enough to take on the head of the coven.

However, Tara was determined to successfully walk the circle tonight.

It was her only chance at staying alive.

<hr>

Whatever oil that June and Wren had rubbed into Tara had long since been sweated out. Aaloka hadn't gone easy on her. Tara's lower back hurt from having to stand so long. Her eyes burned even in the dim light. Her mouth felt dry, and she would have loved a sip of water between recitations.

But Aaloka kept barking out the names of herbs and medicinal plants, and Tara continued to recite her learnings back. Mistletoe. *Artemisia vulgaris*. Cow parsnips. *Monarda didyma*.

Tara refused to give up, or give in, or sit before the other woman did. She knew this material. She was damned if she would fail this part of the test.

Finally, Aaloka picked up her book one final time and nodded at

Tara over the edge of it, giving her a big smile. "You did it!" she said. "Congratulations!"

Tara paused, waiting for the next plant to be named. "I did?" she asked. Now, she felt stupid, her head drained of all the knowledge that she'd crammed in.

"You did!" Aaloka said proudly. She leaned closer to Tara and spoke in a very soft voice, quiet enough that those standing beyond the glass outside couldn't hear. "Not everyone in the coven felt that you could pass this part. I had to give you the toughest test, covering almost all the material. But you proved that you're a worthy candidate for the circle of breath."

Tara nodded, the relief making her sway where she stood. Kyle hadn't said anything about such a long verbal exam. Then again, he hadn't had parts of his coven actively working against him.

Could Tara continue in this coven? If she passed into the circle of breath? She couldn't go back and join Miss Lucy's. Would any of the covens in Portland take her? Or would she always be considered bad luck?

Tara bowed her head low to her teacher, then turned and bowed to the silent observers just outside the window. She used her tiredness to keep her pride at bay, keeping her smile and her stance humble.

In some ways, the oral test would be the easiest part for Tara. She had an organized mind. Despite what Aaloka said about Tara getting in her own way, she knew that she'd passed this part through strict discipline. (And a lot of cramming.)

However, to be a truly powerful witch, you needed not only discipline but imagination. Tara had never once been accused of being too imaginative, not even as a child. Even when she'd started coming into her powers, she'd spent very little time believing that she was imagining things and instead starting to test out what her limits were.

Miss Lucy had said at the time that it was a sign that Tara was destined to become a powerful witch, since she'd been so accepting of her powers.

Tara could only pray that Miss Lucy was right, as all of Tara's powers were about to be put to the test.

THE NIGHT HAD TURNED COOL, causing goosebumps down the back of Tara's neck. Even with the city lights, Tara could see a few stars peeking out at her, encouraging her. No breezes lifted her hair and the smell of roses and jasmine lay heavy in the air.

The coven of witches formed a circle on the first tier of the backyard, twenty one of them that evening. Sheila stood in the middle, leading the prayer, celebrating the journey of the light, reminding them that light flowed into darkness and then back into light, the continuous cycle of life, death, and rebirth.

Tara tried to pay attention, to be present in the moment, to focus on welcoming the light, how good it felt to stand with her sisters and brothers in prayer, sending blessings out into the world.

However, her mind couldn't help but flit away, thinking about her upcoming ordeal. She was certain that Sheila would "cheat" and throw things at her that weren't normal or necessary for someone at her level to overcome. She'd asked Kyle about what to expect, but there hadn't been enough time for him to truly prepare her.

She should have reached out for help earlier. She had a network of friends who would have done what they could. Instead, she'd relied too much on herself and not on her community.

If she was ever in this sort of situation again, Tara vowed to reach out for help and support sooner. And to keep her reach broad as well, as Richard had been the one who'd come up with some of the more useful information Tara needed.

She finally wrangled her thoughts back into the here and now when Sheila started talking about the sister passing within, how Tara had to face passing from the internal world of thought to the external yet still internal world of breath.

"Blessed be," chanted the rest of the coven as they let go of one another's hands, stepping back.

"Come face me," Sheila intoned, beckoning Tara to walk forward.

Wren appeared at Tara's side, tugging on her sleeve.

Tara nodded and quickly stripped off the external cover. The air had grown cooler, but Tara didn't allow herself the privilege of feeling it. Instead, she stood tall and proud before the head of her coven. Tara called on her power, to strengthen her and give her grace. Her blood warmed, setting her skin tingling. The night grew brighter and her sight, clearer.

Sheila kept her face neutral, though Tara could tell the other woman didn't approve of something.

But Tara had nothing to be ashamed of, either the desire to advance herself or her completely naked state.

"To pass from the circle of thought to the circle of breath, you must walk the entire meditation maze unaided," Sheila said. "Save for your own powers and the blessings of Brigid and Samil."

"I am ready," Tara said, nodding her head once.

"If you fail to enter into the heart of the maze and reach the gazing pond in the center, you may try again in six months, during the winter solstice," Sheila continued.

There was a falseness to Sheila's words. She obviously didn't expect Tara to pass, but also, that she assumed that Tara wouldn't be around in six months.

Did any of the others hear if? Tara wouldn't break her gaze with Sheila in order to check. But she heard a shifting, as if some of the witches just shuffled their feet, uneasy.

"I understand," Tara said. "Thank you for the opportunity," she added.

Could the others also hear the unspoken *bitch* at the end of her statement?

No matter the outcome tonight, Tara was certain of one thing. She could no longer stay in this coven that had been the home of her heart for so long.

***

TARA STOOD at the start of the meditation maze with her head bowed. It had been so much easier to defy Sheila with words. Tara had truly believed that she'd be able to walk the maze clear through to the center.

It was a completely different thing to be standing there at the entrance, faced with a cold, shifting fog that hid the stones just one step beyond. Weird noises came from the maze, sounding like the moans of the dead mingled with the whimpers of a wounded beast. They sent shivers down Tara's spine and cascades of goosebumps all across her shoulders.

She clenched her hands into fists, then opened them.

She could do this.

She took a deep breath of the clear night air outside the maze, ignoring the scent of rotten cabbage that blew toward her. Her power swelled, vibrating just under her skin like a second rapid heartbeat. She flexed her toes, feeling the solid cool earth beneath her.

After keeping her head bowed in prayer for another long moment, Tara finally lifted it and stepped into the maze.

The fog reluctantly crept away in front of her, like a cat slinking away from a larger predator. Tara felt the strength of the magic she faced, as prickly as blackberry bramble and as tough as old leather.

She kept her thoughts sharp as a knife, cutting through the tangle in front of her before she took more steps. Though she understood that it was better to walk straight through the maze, Tara was determined to take her time.

Most practitioners didn't have to face off against the head of their coven when passing into merely the second circle. That sort of strength wasn't generally called for until the final circle.

The next few steps felt lighter. Tara actually reached the first curve before the next attack came. It was subtle at first. She felt herself suddenly start to question her right to be there, to doubt her own abilities. For the first time, the thought came unbidden that she'd only made it this far through sheer luck.

Who did she think she was, believing that she could proceed?

Before she reached the end of the curve, Tara recognized that the thoughts were not her own. She'd actually faced similar doubts when she'd walked the maze the first time.

Tara had studied hard enough and knew the reality of her abilities, so she was able to banish the doubts. She had every right to be there, same as any of the witches standing nearby. She had power, she had lore, and she was learning the wisdom to know when to apply them.

By the time Tara made it around the corner, the doubts had vanished. She could do this, though she recognized that if she hadn't been prepared, those thoughts might have derailed her.

The next few steps brought fear. Icy cold fingers walked down Tara's spine, reminding her that she was naked and didn't have even the slight barrier of clothes to protect her. She felt her breath suddenly coming in gulps, as if the air was no longer thick enough to support her. Her stomach knotted, the muscles drawing in tightly. Her hands shook.

Tara stopped and shook her head. This fear wasn't real. What was she afraid of?

She snorted when she realized that whoever had started off with this spell had chosen the wrong fear.

Fear of failure? Come on. If she failed, she died.

The realization broke the spell almost instantly. Tara walked forward with confidence, reaching the far curve easily and starting to turn back toward the start.

She couldn't help the sense of triumph washing over her when she passed the entrance of the maze. She'd made it through the first circle. From here on, all the spells thrown against her were going to be from the second circle. No longer internal or thought, but external—breath and wind.

The first breeze tickled Tara's hair, which lay heavily against the back of her neck. Then it tugged harder. Tara tried to keep going, but it felt as though an invisible hand had grabbed ahold of her hair and wouldn't let go. Her head jerked back with her next step.

Ouch.

Tara panicked for a moment. What spell should she use to get the wind to release her? Did she know a spell? She faltered, her thoughts racing madly.

Then she made herself stop and take a deep breath, willing the knowledge to rise up from inside of her.

Ah. That one.

Tara quickly called up a smoothing spell, one that would uncurl leaves and straighten vines. She held the scents of the three herbs she would use to perform such a spell—lemon balm, rosemary, and catnip.

The wind let go. Tara had the strangest sensation that the wind had formed a hand to hold onto her hair, then, as the hand let go, it combed her hair through its fingers, a soothing feeling.

Perhaps that spell had been cast by someone who liked her, and who wanted her to succeed.

She wouldn't always be so lucky, though.

Tara made her way through the next few winds easily enough, either deflecting them when they tried to push against her and blow her off course, or by pushing them upward so she could merely bend over and pass below.

As Tara rounded the corner and was about to pass by the start of the maze again, she suddenly felt herself out of breath. It was as if all the air had been sucked out of the area. She strengthened her own breathing, but that just made her pant harder. Her vision started to grow cloudy as she gasped.

How did she make her own air? She realized this might be the most important spell for her to remember that night, particularly if she didn't pass the test and the Riprap man came after her.

The answer came from the tears that squeezed out of her eyes. Water had air molecules in it. While the air itself might be thin, there was still water in it.

Remembering the purple heather, Tara brought forth the rain. Not a lot—just a light mist blessing her skin.

From the water, Tara drew the air she needed and took the next steps forward, into her third circle around the maze.

The third circle was the heart, feelings, and fire. Hot winds caressed her cheeks. Fear gripped Tara again, but this time, it was the fear of the unknown. Black smoke rose up in front of her, hiding the untamed blaze in front of her.

This wasn't fair. She was only a witch of the first level, trying for the second circle. Not the third.

But Tara had known that this wouldn't be easy. She forged ahead.

These were just illusions. Nothing that would permanently damage her.

Right?

The black smoke cleared and Tara faced the heart of the flames. There was no way to walk around it or even leap over it: the fire raged at least ten feet on a side, and far above her head.

It was just an illusion, though the heat felt real. Her lungs started to complain again about the smoke and the lack of clean air.

Kyle had told her about this spell, as he'd had to pass by when he'd moved into the third circle. She couldn't banish the fire. It would drain her completely if she tried. She couldn't get around it either. She had to pass through it, using the right spells to protect herself.

Again, Tara called up the soft rains, just enough to drench her skin with moisture. Then she added tarragon to the concoction she was blending in her mind, and soaproot, to help her glide past. Finally, she added the last important herb, tansy, to make her invisible, so the flames wouldn't notice her passing.

Thus armed, Tara forced herself to step forward.

The intense heat nearly made her lose her footing, but she made herself take another step.

Then another.

Though Tara wanted to race through the flames as fast as she could, she knew that would be a mistake. The fire would just chase her. Instead, she paused in the heart of the fire, marveling at the different colors, at how the flames whispered to her of ancient knowledge, how their nature was divided and their hidden god actually two-faced, one for destruction and the other for protection.

Tara felt blessed when she stepped beyond the fire, as if her pool of lore had just deepened significantly.

Whoever had devised that spell for her hadn't anticipated her not only facing the fire and stepping through it, but learning from it.

Tara didn't have the time to speculate on how this knowledge felt different. It was a well-accepted tenant that all lore was passed down from one witch to the next.

How much could Tara learn from the elements themselves?

Boosted with the confidence and the knowledge of the fire itself, she quickly passed through the rest of the tests of the third circle, ignoring the way her physical heart slowed as if it was threatening to go on strike and stop, as well as the building rage that came from outside of her, and the grief that struck her over her losses, both in the past as well as the present.

The next circle was stomach. Process. Water. Tara knew that she could pass through this circle easily enough. It was her element. She also recognized that she was more organized than others. Process was also her friend.

What Tara hadn't anticipated was the chaos of a raging river.

The banks weren't that far apart. Could she just step across?

No, that was a trap. She could tell by how wavy the air was on the far side. If she tried to leap across, she'd land outside the circle. If she didn't carefully stay within the stone markers of each circle of the meditation maze, she'd instantly fail the test.

Could she walk through the water? Pass through it as she had the fire?

Except these waters were never the same. They were less stable than the flames. Each drop was separate, and it would be nearly impossible to bind them together to let her pass.

Tara snorted at herself when she considered the aspect of a bridge. That would help her pass from one bank to the other. She suspected that the waters wouldn't allow it. She would get halfway across and they'd swamp the bridge deck, sweeping her away.

No, she had to stop the flow. Part the waters, like Moses had parted the Red Sea.

Tara started building a potion up in her mind. First, she'd need sandalwood and geranium oils to soothe the waters. Then she added a touch of ginseng to waken the senses. The sound of the water was too hypnotic for her. She was grateful for that knowledge, another thing to arm herself with.

For a moment more, Tara paused. Then she figured, why not?

Taking a deep calming breath, Tara called up the flames she'd met earlier.

Was that a gasp she'd heard from her unseen audience? Tara wasn't certain.

The flames came easily to her outstretched hands. She directed them down, toward the water. It parted easily, its mortal enemy driving it back.

Tara soothed the fires in her hands, sending out joy and playful thoughts. Fire was a dancer, pure and simple. The flames leapt forward, hissing at the water and sparking with the winds. Tara welcomed the smell of smoke and the warmth.

As she stepped onto the river bank, the mud oozed between her toes, cool against the warmth of her fire-heated skin. The smell of good earth rose up, comforting Tara. She could smell the herbs in the garden suddenly, the fresh rosemary, the spicy borage, even the sweet strawberries hidden in the corner.

Tara recognized the trap after just another step. The earth and its scents, brought to her on the singing waters, were there to distract her.

The fire in her hands would either leap away, unhappy at being contained, or turn around to burn through their container. The waters, in the meanwhile, would angrily swamp her as soon as she looked away.

Tara focused her thoughts back to the present. The flames grew resentful at the continued fight with the water, spitting out sparks that burned the backs of her hands. The water, too, surged forward, angry at her bringing their enemy so close.

Instead of taking her time passing through the river bank, as she had when she'd walked through the flames, Tara started to hurry, taking small, quick steps.

At the far edge, when Tara lifted one foot off the riverbed and onto the dry ground, the waters came surging back.

Tara recognized her mistake immediately. She should have backed out of the water. She tightened all the muscles in her legs, holding herself still, one leg in the water, the other on solid ground, not letting herself be bowled over.

First, she released the flames. She thanked them for their help, whispering the name of their hidden, protector god. Then, after taking another deep breath, she slowly pulled her leg out of the waters.

The river didn't have hold of her like the wind had earlier. Still, for all its rushing, it felt as though the waters were made out of solid, thick mud. Cold and clammy, sucking at her, trying to pull her back down.

Tara got all but her foot free. The mud grabbed hold of her, tightening its grip. It was like sunbaked clay now, the smell of dry earth filling her senses.

No. This was all an illusion, though Tara still felt the stinging "kisses" the flames had left on the backs of her hands.

Tara tried to call up the wisdom from her studies, the spells she'd learned.

The thoughts that arose surprised her. Would it work? Or was it another trap?

Tara couldn't tell the difference. Her own powers were waning. She knew that she'd be a basket case for the next few days after this trial, her physical and mental strength exhausted.

Still, it was all that Tara could think of at this point.

She called the waters back.

The raging river answered her call. The loudness of the waters startled Tara, setting her heart to beating more quickly. Cold spiked through the bones of her leg, making her toes curls and her ankles ache.

But she didn't have to hold her awkward position for long, one foot on dry ground and the other stuck behind her. The waters did what she'd hoped they'd do, and they melted the mud holding her.

With a sucking, popping noise, Tara freed her leg.

For a moment, she balanced on a single foot. She wavered from side to side, almost tipping over.

If someone had been cruel, at that very time, they could have sent the slightest wind and Tara would have fallen over, stepping outside of the carefully laid out stones.

Instead, after a few moments of a flailing, half-moon yoga pose, Tara composed herself and brought her legs together, bringing her hands into prayer pose over her chest, her head bent and her eyes closed.

She thanked the goddess Bonana for the water, the hidden gods of the fire, the god of the earth and the goddess of the air.

She had made it through most of the circles, though. Learned and grown through levels one through four. She only had two left to pass through. She was so close to finishing.

Though her strength was low and her arms and legs were shaky, Tara raised her head defiantly and stepped forward again.

Bring it.

TARA WASN'T sure what the next circle, sex, roots, or earth, would bring. Kyle hadn't yet passed through that circle. His initiation to the inner circles had been nothing like hers, however. He hadn't been tested as hard as she had been.

Was she stronger than she'd originally believed? Aaloka had hinted at that. Miss Lucy, as well. Tara had ignored them. She was just a late bloomer, and the magic came easier to her because she knew herself better than a twenty year old did, that was for certain.

And so much about power and witchcraft came from knowledge, not just lore but of self as well.

Still, how many witches learned from the elements themselves? Listened to their quiet whispers?

Tara had often felt that the plants spoke to her, telling her the best way to use them for a particular spell or oil. Sometimes the properties were similar to what she'd been taught. Sometimes, though, they were different.

Tara had resisted listening to the plants for their knowledge. It wasn't that she believed that she hadn't heard them. She knew that she had. But that lore was unknown and she didn't know if she could trust it.

Now, she knew she could.

As she rounded the curve and stepped into the circle of roots, a loud cacophony of voices struck her. She shook her head, surprised. Where was that noise coming from? She stopped for a moment and looked around, trying to determine the source.

It finally occurred to her that she could now hear every single plant in the backyard. Each of them were calling her name, demanding her attention. They wanted to tell her all their secrets, sharing the gossip they'd heard from the bees, complain about their roots being cramped, how they needed more water, or less, or how their neighbors were crowding them.

This had to be an illusion. All these voices would drive Tara mad. The plants couldn't talk with her, not really.

She banished the voices, shutting off her special hearing, diminishing her power, bringing it back to just herself.

She took a step forward, then another, then had to pause again.

When the voices had vanished, the ground beneath her had died.

She could no longer hear mother earth, herself.

Crap.

This was a test of balance. She had to find that fine line between too much power and not enough. Had to figure out how to allow herself to feel the world around her, while at the same time, not be overwhelmed by it.

Grounding herself didn't appear to help. That just dragged her feet under the earth, making her as immobile as a tree. She needed to be more like a vine, traipsing along.

But that didn't work either. The first, initial root took hold and held her in place, stretching her and her awareness out until she thinned so much she was afraid she'd snap in two.

How could she move forward, allowing some part of the voices in? How could she be grounded yet still inching forward? Plants put forth runners, dropped seeds, or blew in the wind. They didn't pick themselves up and move.

Tara felt stymied. Her anger at being tested with such difficult assignments came back. She felt herself flare in anger, the fire she'd befriended earlier heating her skin.

She knew that she didn't burst into flames, though she wanted to, in protest of her treatment.

Instead, she calmed the fire inside of her, banking it into a warm glow, adding some water and wind to it so she wasn't stuck there either, constantly angry and bickering.

Tara opened herself up to the voices again, holding onto her own core tightly. The plants couldn't overwhelm the fire burning at her center. The scent of the roses and cool grass washed over her, all the herbs in the garden taking their turn to greet her, turn her fingers green, wind around her ankles before leaving again.

Finally, a single voice rose above the others. It was the old oak tree that provided shade across the bottom of the garden. He spoke slowly, but with authority. He had no use for those flashy maples who colored their leaves in the fall, then discarded them without a care. He held onto his old, brown leaves, proud of how they crinkled with age. He didn't release them until the spring, when his children would need the nutrients to grow.

Tara lumbered forward, heavy with the weight of the tree growing inside of her. She still had need for motion.

After a few dragging steps, she was able to pose her question for the oak: did he move through his children? Was that the secret of this level?

The amusement of the oak came in the quiet rustling of his leaves. No. That was not how he moved along.

His children had only slight awareness. It would take years for them to grow into themselves.

No, the way he moved along was by finally dying. He would fall over in place, his long trunk shattering as it struck the ground, the core of him finally releasing as he died.

In the spring, all his children would have a touch more awareness and strength. They would carry forward, each and every one of them, passing what they could onto their children until they, too, died.

It was the circle of life. The ultimate passage that the oak had to teach Tara. How to live fully each spring, falling back in the winter, living, dying, and being reborn. That was the only way to move along this circle.

Tara stopped her halting progress. She wasn't like the oak. She couldn't die just to be reborn. She had no children to pass her awareness to. How could she move through this circle?

Yet, Tara knew that the oak was right. Sex and procreation were the ultimate form of immortality.

Tara let her consciousness fall into the earth. This time, instead of halting her progress or deadening the voices of the plants above her,

Tara felt and heard everything. Their roots tickled her back as she inched along, undulating across her consciousness like an earthworm. She felt the world around her dying as winter storms struck, the cold frost sinking deep fingers into the earth, slowing her progress.

Tara felt herself die as the winter continued. All thought ceased. Her breathing slowed to nothing. Her heart stopped its relentless beating. The fire at her core dimmed as the waters rushed around her, the winter rains blessing her skin.

Warmth came from an unexpected source: the very earth itself. Tara felt herself cradled in the embrace of the ground, the very world singing to her, calming her fears, lulling her to sleep.

The light in the core of her being never went completely out, supported by the waters there.

Then spring arrived.

Tara's consciousness rose back to the surface, inch by slow inch. The sun had returned. The rains felt warm, now, not the stinging ice of the fall and winter. Her body felt full of promise and the rest of the plants sang to her.

Finally, Tara rose the full way back up. It didn't surprise her to see that she was almost at the end of the circle.

She'd followed the complete path, from living, through death, and finally, to rebirth. That cycle had moved her along the circle, her feet numbly following as she dreamed the big dreams, sang lullabies with the earth.

Humbled, Tara finished the cycle of roots. She was such a tiny part in a much larger world. She wordlessly thanked the oak for his wisdom, the water and fires that had kept her alive, and the earth herself.

Never had Tara felt so connected to where she stood. The present beat loudly in her ears. She knew that she had to progress beyond this moment, but she stood unmoving for a few long moments, drinking in the world around her.

Bowing her head one last time, Tara stepped forward again. She only had a half-circle to complete, before the maze circled around to the center gazing pond. She was so close.

She no longer felt as defiant as she had at the start. Her teachers had tested her further than most, demanding more knowledge than she'd been taught. Anger still burned at her core over the unfairness. However, if she was to fight the Riprap man, she needed all the knowledge she'd gained over the course of the evening.

How long had it taken her to pass through the circles? When she let herself think about it, she felt completely drained, as if she didn't want to take a single step forward. Her hands had a tremor to them that she couldn't stop. Power now passed straight through her: she had none of her own to call on. Her heart labored, beating despite how she just wanted to stop.

Still, Tara took the next step, into the final circle. She'd come this far. Just a little ways further. She could make it. She could be recognized as a witch of the second circle, though she felt as though she'd passed through all the circles that evening.

Tara looked around, seeking the next test. Where would the final threat come from? What sort of trial would the final circle entail?

Yet, Tara felt nothing. The night had cleared. She saw her onlookers gathered in a line at the back of the second tier of the backyard. Some looked angry. Were they upset with her passing? Or at the severity of her tests?

She couldn't puzzle that out now. She just had to survive the last one.

Step after step, the path remained clear. Tara was almost to the final curve. She could see the dark gazing pond, brimming with clear water, at the center, just to her left. Just a few more steps…

Ropes appeared out of nowhere. Heavy, twisted sisal, the kind used on the big boats, as big around as her forearm.

These were the ropes that the Riprap man would use to bind her.

They slithered on the path in front of her, blocking her way. They made a rustling noise as they moved across the earth. The smell of the river washed over Tara, filling her with dread.

Where was this coming from? Had Sheila saved up the scariest illusion for last?

Or had Tara herself provided the illusion, manifesting her worst fear?

Tara stood rooted to the path for a moment too long, not seeing the trap until it was too late.

The ropes had gotten behind her. With a sudden strike, as painful and shocking as a cobra bite, a rope thwacked against the back of her right calf.

Tara couldn't help but take a stumbling step forward.

Directly off the path, stepping across the stones and into the previous circle.

A sigh went through the night, the wind blowing the sound of mourning past Tara.

She'd failed.

Regret clenched her stomach. Her mouth filled with sour bile. She'd come so close.

Then the burning rage rose up. It was unfair!

Tara raised her head and stared hard at Sheila, the head of the coven.

The old woman glared at her.

She had no regrets.

Aaloka and Kyle strode over to where Sheila stood. Tara knew they were arguing with her, expressing their anger at how Tara had been tested. She couldn't hear the words, her own heartbeat pounding too loudly through her whole head, her temples throbbing.

Tara had passed through all the other circles. She knew that she could have made it through to the inner circle.

Sheila had cheated. The last test hadn't been merely an illusion. Sheila had physically manifested those enchanted ropes. Tara couldn't have avoided them.

It wasn't a true test of anima.

The ropes still lay curled at her feet, the life having drained out of them now that they'd struck their target.

The smell of the river encased Tara again. She shivered in its cold embrace. Gulls mournfully cried. The rushing of the waters blocked out all other sounds. Icy fingers pulled at her hair, pinched her skin.

You are mine.

The wind carried the words to Tara. She bowed her head again. The sense of death filled her. Only this wasn't a peaceful passing, unlike the oak. No, this was a death full of anger and pain, that sought to tear her soul from her flesh.

After taking another deep breath, Tara looked up again, defiantly.

The Riprap man was coming for her.

She was going to fight him with every ounce of her being. She had no choice.

SIX

The river holds an angry god. It isn't that he hates just the newcomers, no, he despises all the life around him. He will not be tamed with mere words or simple deeds. He demands sacrifice. Something great enough to satisfy his appetite, at least for a little while. Unfortunately, the river won't accept my companion Robin, something that I didn't learn until much too late. However, Robin and I passed a coven of witches two days earlier, a heathen group who spoil the sweetness of everything just to further their own selfish desires. Robin and I had talked about kidnapping one of their kind as a sacrifice. I'd thought to save time by using Robin instead. The river god dislikes the witches. Something about how they'd soothed him when he wanted to rage. So I will make a pact with the river god: I will give him witches as sacrifice, and he will hold back his anger against the bridges of the great city of Portland.

Wilson Evermore, magician and creator of the pact, 1899

TARA WOKE FEELING BRUISED. Every limb ached. Her toes and

fingers felt swollen—hell, were swollen, so much that she barely had any wrinkles across the backs of her joints.

There were very few other physical reminders of her great battle. Her hands didn't hold any scars from where the fire had kissed her. Her head didn't hurt from where the wind had grabbed it and tugged on it.

The only other reminder was a five inch circular bruise across the back of her right calf, where the rope had struck her.

Kyle had explained as he'd driven her home that Sheila had gone too far. The rope had been real. All of them could see that.

However, Sheila had also defended herself by claiming that Tara was bad luck.

Aaloka and a few of the others had stepped back after that, had stopped trying to defend Tara.

Tara didn't blame them. For the good of the coven, she was the one chosen to be sacrificed.

There had to be another way.

Groaning, Tara pushed herself up out of her comforting bed. She'd already called into work sick that day. She couldn't face the shop, or to waste her last day by working.

She had to prepare. How, and by doing what, she had no idea.

But she'd think of something. After she woke up.

It was already ten AM. It had taken Tara over an hour to pass through all the circles, much longer than most. Then again, she'd had harder trials.

Tara took a long, hot shower. She was damned if she was going to be frightened of the water. It was her natural element. She could tame it if she had to. She was not about to let some asshole take away that simple enjoyment.

Still, Tara wouldn't let her guard completely down, even as she stood under the pounding hot water, soaping up her skin and washing the last of the oil away from the previous evening. She kept her wits around her, not letting her mind wander away. The fire inside her matched the heat outside, warming her all the way through and soothing away some of her aches and pains.

After Tara finished her shower, she slipped on her ratty robe and padded out to the living room.

Then stopped, stifling her scream at the last moment.

"Kyle? What the hell are you doing here?" Tara asked the man calmly sitting on her couch, reading something on his phone. He'd changed clothes, and now wore a faded T-shirt with a quote about killing all the lawyers being a good start. (Which was funny, as Kyle clerked for the federal court downtown, having decided early in his career that he never wanted to be a full lawyer.)

"Taking care of you for the day," Kyle said slowly, as if explaining something to someone who was really slow. Which, okay, maybe Tara was feeling like that a little this morning.

"Did we talk about this last night?" Tara said. She had to admit that her memory was slightly fuzzy.

"We did," Kyle said. "You said I shouldn't. I disagreed. You told me to leave. I didn't. You need someone here to look after you this morning. And through the rest of the day, and into the night, as well."

"Thank you," Tara said. Stupid tears welled up. She was just overly emotional because she was so tired. She pressed her palms against her eyes, pushing out the moisture. After sniffing a couple of time, Tara finally felt ready to ask, "Can I make you some tea?"

Kyle gave her a big grin. "I'd love some."

Tara made him one of her special combinations. She started with a base of the salal leaves that she'd dried that fall, as Kyle didn't do caffeine. (Weirdo.) The salal gave the drink a green-tea taste, light and bright, with a hint of citrus. She used fresh leaves from her hyssop plant on the balcony, as well as a cutting of spearmint. Then she added a few of the strawberry leaves to smooth it out.

Kyle shook his head after she'd finished his concoction. "You know that some of the members of the coven are now referring to you as a hedgewitch, right?"

Tara shook her head. "Not sure what that means."

"A hedgewitch is a witch who's naturally trained, who doesn't study the lore. She's a common witch, the kind you'd find in the back country with a huge garden, who folks pay in milk and eggs. The hedgewitches are quite looked down on, you know, by us city witches."

"Okay," Tara said. "But I do have some lore."

"You have much more than that. You're a powerful witch," Kyle said.

Tara had been thinking about that since the trial. "No, I'm not," she said firmly.

Kyle raised both his eyebrows at her, looking dubious.

"I'm really not," Tara insisted. She sighed, trying to put what she'd experienced into words, force her tired brain to work. "I didn't pass because I was so strong or so special. I passed because I was able to listen and learn from the elements around me."

"Hedgewitch," Kyle said.

"Exactly!" Tara replied. "Anyone could do what I've been able to do so far. They just have to listen."

Kyle nodded, but didn't reply. Not until they were both sitting out on the balcony, enjoying their tea. The day had already started to grow hotter. Both boat traffic and car traffic noises floated up to them. The hummingbird thrummed past the balcony a couple times before he finally settled in for a long drink.

"I don't think that just anyone could do what you're able to do," Kyle said. "Hear me out."

Tara nodded, listening.

"You see these plants?" Kyle asked, indicating the long row of pots in front of them.

"Yes," Tara said. Almost every witch she knew of grew plants. It was the basis of their magic, the herbs and concoctions that they put together.

"How well do you think your plants are growing? Compared, say, to Patricia or someone like that?" Kyle said.

Tara snorted. "Not a fair comparison. Patricia has people for doing that sort of gardening."

"Exactly," Kyle said. "Kind of my point. But maybe Han Su. Or me."

"You can all grow stuff," Tara said.

"Not in abundance. Not like you do," Kyle insisted.

"It isn't that I do that much," Tara pointed out.

"I believe you believe that," Kyle said. "And it might be that you don't do much. However, you care. You take the time. You listen and check in with your plants, trying to give them what they need. Am I right?"

"Yes," Tara said slowly. "They matter to me. I'd feel like a bad parent or something if I didn't try my best with them."

"Do they tell you what they need?" Kyle asked.

Tara rocked her head from one side to the other. "Not really. It isn't as if they talk to me."

Then she pressed her lips together, remembering all the voices of the plants the night before.

None of those voices had been foreign or strange to her. No, she was quite familiar with all of them. She'd just never really thought about it before.

Kyle sat there, expectant.

"All right. Fine. Maybe the plants do talk to me. But it isn't because I'm special," Tara insisted, circling back to her earlier point. "They'll talk to anyone who will listen."

"And that's my point," Kyle said. "All witches, all of those people who have power, can hear. How many bother to listen? Then act on what they hear?"

Tara took a deep breath. She let Kyle's words settle into her skin. What Kyle was saying was true. "It was the only way I survived last night," Tara admitted. "I had to listen to what the fire had to say. And the plants. And the water."

"Exactly," Kyle said. "Hedgewitch. It isn't that you don't have lore. It's that you also have native lore, from the elements themselves."

"But how is that going to save me?" Tara asked bluntly. "I still don't know how to fight the Riprap man. And what will happen if I do get away from him? I don't want to bring bad luck to everyone else in the coven, even if they have turned their backs on me. Or even to Portland."

Since this had started, Tara had looked up a couple of articles on the floods in Portland. While the area was less prone to floods than it once had been, given the sea wall and the other engineering feats that man had done to change the landscape, that didn't mean that it was impossible to flood the area.

Tara remembered a documentary on the floods in New Orleans, how it had ruined so many neighborhoods and lives. And the flooding that had been occurred all along the east coast.

No, there had to be a way to stop the Riprap man and prevent the next big flood from swamping the region.

Kyle stayed still in the morning air. "Would you say that your greatest power is the ability to listen?" he asked after a bit.

"Possibly," Tara said. She'd never thought of it as her superpower before. But Kyle was probably right. She thought about how she listened to customers in the store and was able to match their needs, their true needs, with merchandise, no matter what words they used.

"So now we just have to figure out who you should listen to," Kyle said. "And how to give them what they want."

RICHARD CALLED Tara right around noon. She'd been planning on calling him later that afternoon if she hadn't heard from him.

Tara and Kyle still sat out on the balcony, though Tara had changed out of her ratty bathrobe and into jeans and one of her favorite T-shirts, a pretty tie-dyed shirt covered in a random pattern of pink and blue splotches. Kyle was drinking a glass of homemade lemonade with a twist of mint in it, while Tara was on her second cup of black tea. Her brain still felt slightly fuzzy from the ordeal the night before.

"Hi, Richard!" Tara said brightly. "Got any good news for me?"

Richard gave a puzzled, "Hrmm? You were asking me to find out about the death of a relative."

"Yeah. What can you tell me?" Tara asked. "I don't really know much about Dorothy Parkerson's death."

Now Kyle gave Tara a puzzled look. She knew she'd told him about visiting the witch guarding the Morrison Bridge. Had she forgotten to tell him about Richard looking into it?

She put the phone onto speaker and set it on the table, so that Kyle could hear what Richard had to say first hand and Tara wouldn't have to repeat it.

"It turns out that your relative was a small-time actress, here in Portland," Richard said. "So it was actually pretty easy to find information about her. Her death was officially declared a suicide, but there were a lot of questions about it."

"Like what?" Tara asked.

Kyle nodded, as if he was finally remembering what she'd told him the day before.

"According to the articles I read, rumors were that she'd just gotten a call from Hollywood. If she was just about to make the big time, why would she kill herself?" Richard said. "That was one of the big questions. But there were others."

"Okay," Tara said. "Tell me."

"Dorothy committed suicide by jumping off the Morrison Bridge," Richard said.

Tara couldn't contain her gasp. Luckily, Richard didn't hear it and just continued on.

"But the people who'd seen her that day all commented on how out of it she seemed. As if she'd drunk an entire case of bourbon, at least according to one of the eye witnesses. Her eyes were described as 'lifeless' before she climbed over the bridge wall," Richard continued.

"So was she drugged?" Tara asked.

"They didn't perform an autopsy," Richard said. "It wasn't required in those days. People knew she'd jumped off a bridge. There was some outcry after that as well, as people kept saying that there were fishy circumstances around her death. But the case was considered closed."

"That's really helpful," Tara told Richard. "Thank you."

"And there's something else," Richard said. "Now, I know you didn't ask for this. However, reading about this case reminded me of something else I'd read. In 1966, the Marquam bridge was completed. The day before the dedication ceremony, a woman committed suicide by jumping off of that bridge."

Chills walked across Tara's shoulders, sending cascades of goosebumps down her back. Her throat went abruptly dry. She took a swig of suddenly bitter tea before she answered. "That's really good to know," Tara said.

"If I go looking, I'll find a woman who committed suicide just about the time every bridge went under repair or was completed," Richard continued. "Won't I?"

"What do you mean?" Tara asked, caution overtaking her.

Damn it! That had always been part of her problem with Richard. The man was a completist. He always wanted to research every angle of something, willfully going down every rabbit hole he ran across.

"There are always women's deaths involved with the building or repair of every bridge," Richard said. "No one else has spotted the pattern, because it didn't always happen the day of the opening or dedication. Sometimes it's months apart. But there's always, *always*, the death of a woman by suicide as a bridge is being repaired or built when it crosses the Willamette River."

"I didn't know that," Tara said. Technically, she was speaking the truth. She'd known that there would always be the death of a woman, but she hadn't known that they'd all committed suicide. At least according to those investigating the deaths.

"You aren't feeling particularly suicidal, are you?" Richard asked bluntly. "Because the other thing that I didn't mention was that these always happened just after the solstice in the summer."

"Trust me," Tara said. "I am not about to kill myself. If I do die in the near future, no matter what it looks like, I didn't kill myself."

Kyle raised his eyebrows at her, but Tara stubbornly lifted her head, sticking out her chin at him. Richard was a dear friend and deserved to know.

"Okay," Richard said slowly. "What can I do to help?"

Tara smiled. "There isn't anything you can do," she said softly. "But thank you. Your friendship has always been important to me."

Richard sighed. "This has to do with the witchcraft, doesn't it?"

"What do you mean?" Tara asked, alarmed. She'd never told Richard that she was a witch. He was completely mundane. She couldn't tell him.

"I know you never told me about it, but I'm a research librarian, and you left too many tantalizing clues over the years," Richard said honestly. "You don't have to admit it or to say anything about it. Just know that I'm here, and I support you, no matter what weird religion you may follow."

Tara rolled her eyes. "And how is being Catholic not a weird religion? I mean, come on, blood and body of Christ?" Though Richard was no longer practicing, he'd been raised Catholic.

"Hey! At least my religion doesn't support suicide," Richard said. "Does yours?"

Tara gave a great sigh. "No, it doesn't. Look, I have to go. But I will call you if I need any help, or anything looked up. Agreed?"

"All right," Richard said. "Look, your friendship is important to me as well. And I love you dearly. The world would be a much colder, and less weird place without you."

"And I hope that you can tell me that in person on Friday, when I get to meet your new girl," Tara said firmly.

"I hope that too," Richard said softly. "Goodbye, my friend."

"Love you too. Goodbye," Tara said all in a hurry before she swiped off the phone. Then she looked over at Kyle, who was giving her the stink eye. "What?" she asked hotly. "I did *not* tell him anything."

"You left clues," Kyle said.

"I didn't mean to!" Tara replied. "He's just—he's like a dog with a bone. Won't give up. Which was why I stopped dating him years ago."

"But you're still friends," Kyle pointed out.

"I have a lot of friends!" Tara said. "Both inside the covens and outside of them." She was not about to comment on how few of her friends inside the coven had turned out to be true.

Kyle sat and thought for a while contemplating his fingers tapping together. "Can he be trusted?" he finally asked. "If you did tell Richard the truth?"

Now it was Tara's turn to sit and think for a while.

"Maybe," she said finally slowly. "If I could convince him that it was really important, that the other witches might come after him if he started talking about them."

Kyle nodded. "Then you may want to consider telling him at some point. *After* tomorrow."

"What? Why?" Tara asked, completely confused. Kyle was one who always stuck to the rules. It was one of the reasons why they got along so well.

"Because you can't stay with Sheila's coven," Kyle said softly. "And I doubt there's another one that will take you. You're going to need to start your own."

All the blood left Tara's head, leaving her feeling dizzy. "I can't bring mundanes into a coven circle!" Such a thing was completely unheard of.

Kyle merely shrugged. "You're a hedgewitch. You can do whatever the fuck you want."

Kyle's statement, as much as the obscenity, struck Tara hard. He didn't normally swear. He'd used it for great effect, getting her to really listen.

"All right," Tara said after a moment. "I'll consider what you just said. *After* I survive the Riprap man."

Kyle gave her a bright smile. "You will. Now, let me tell you what else I've learned about Mulinohana, the river god."

Tara nodded, shoving her potential future aside for the moment. She could think about what it meant to be a hedgewitch, to be educated by the elements themselves instead of strictly through the lore of witchcraft, later.

First, she had another ordeal to survive.

TARA CALLED A MIDAFTERNOON BREAK, insisting that they leave the apartment and go walk around the block. She needed movement, not just studying. She longed to go for a long swim, though she doubted that was a good idea.

"So what do you think happened to the other witches who were sacrificed?" Tara asked Kyle as they started down the Riverwalk. A big tug was slowly making its way upriver, while a speedboat pulling a surfer made its way downriver. A nice breeze had started, cooling off the hotness of the day. The smell of the river turned Tara's stomach— she still remembered the feeling of the wet rope binding her wrists, how she struggled in her nightmare and couldn't get away.

"Now, you're saying that the souls of the witches lie underneath the bridges, right?" Kyle asked.

Tara nodded. "Trapped there by the Riprap man." She and Kyle had debated for a while about her going back to Miss Lucy to get another potion, so she could go and visit one of the other captured witches. She wasn't sure what they'd be able to tell her, though. They'd failed, and had been captured. Maybe they could tell her what they'd done wrong, which could be useful.

However, what Tara really needed to know was what she could do right to avoid both the Riprap man and the potential floods all together.

"I'm wondering if the Riprap man took their souls the night before they died," Kyle said softly. "Their bodies had no choice but to leap off those bridges, trying to get back to their souls, trying to make themselves whole again."

Tara nodded. The same thought had occurred to her. "So he tears the soul of a witch out from her still living body, then binds it. How does he do that?"

"You know that Miss Lucy would have a much better idea of how to go about that," Kyle pointed out.

"She was very clear about not wanting to see me again," Tara said. "I'm bad luck, remember?"

"Just had to ask," Kyle said, holding his hands up in surrender. "I'm not sure if knowing the exact process is as important as figuring out why he's doing it."

"It's to defend the bridges, right?" Tara said slowly. "The witch's soul acts as a guardian."

"Why?" Kyle asked. "Why would a witch go ahead and protect the place that she'd just been killed for?"

"Dorothy can't leave," Tara pointed out. "Cell sweet cell," she repeated.

"Imprisoning a witch's soul, and creating a guardian for a bridge, are two different things," Kyle stated plainly. "So which is it?"

"Hmmm," Tara said, pausing at the scenic view and looking out over the water for a moment. The breeze lifted her hair off the back of her sweaty neck, carrying the scents of the water marshes just beyond the brambles at her feet. "Though it's a cell, as long as the bridge stands and stays strong, the witch will continue to live. So maybe she'll guard against it failing that way."

"That's possible," Kyle said. "But the bridge has to be under repair, or being built for the first time, for the witch's soul to be used. So I keep thinking that the Riprap man takes more than just their soul for the bridge."

"Wait a second," Tara said. She tried to remember something else that she'd heard. "Oh! I know! It's the other version of London Bridges. It talks about taking a witch's heart."

She brought out her phone and brought up the children's song. She'd copied it down as closely as she could remember it after Davie had sung it to her. She showed it to Kyle.

Build it up with stone so strong,
Dance over the dead lady.
With a heart it will last so long
From a gray lady.

"So something about a witch's heart," Kyle murmured. "Heart. Feelings. Fire," he continued on.

"I think you're onto something," Tara said after a moment. She still felt the fire banked inside her, warming her core.

That fire was her heart. Somehow, the Riprap man wouldn't just take her soul, but her fire, her magic, her heart, and bind those to the bridge.

After another long moment, Tara finally turned to Kyle with a grin. "I think I have a plan."

SEVEN

As a man of science, I can't help but question. How did the river god come to be? Was he always a god or at one point had he been a man? Without a doubt he is great and terrible. Like the angels, the first utterance he must speak for any coming into his presence is, 'Fear not.' So I have banished my fears and hold myself ready for his great plan. My thirst for knowledge is as boundless as the mighty waters in the river. I carry a part of the river god with me as I return to the shining city of Portland, along with the potions and spells necessary to bind a witch's heart to the next bridge, marking it as sacred to the river god, so that He will Know it and not damage it. I will mark all the bridges this way, as well as the city Herself, so that the devastation I saw at the beginning of my journey can never happen again. This knowledge has changed me, but I'm willing to sacrifice myself to the greater good. I pray to all the gods that my success will inspire others to the same task; to denounce all witches, to be reborn in the fires of knowledge, and to purify themselves in the sweet waters of redemption.

Wilson Evermore, pact holder and witch hunter, 1899

TARA MANAGED to sleep for a few hours that evening, in part due to the potion Kyle made for her. While her body quickly succumbed to the soothing drink with peppermint, chamomile, lavender and red cedar, her mind continued to race with thoughts and plans. She dreamed of endlessly running away, the unseen monster behind her never quite catching her, but she never fully escaped either.

The dream faded after Tara awoke with her alarm, around ten PM. She showered again, then used the stimulating oil that Kyle had spent the afternoon making for her, rubbing it into every inch of her flesh. It smelled of pungent pine, ginger, new spring grass and wild roses.

Tara dressed in her ratty robe when she left her bedroom, walking into the living room. Sharon was already locked away in her bedroom, supposedly working on the next great American novel. Kyle had prepared as well. He looked like an oiled bodyguard, his black skin glistening. He wore a brightly colored gold-and-green striped vest, with no shirt, and loose brown cotton pants that were cropped around the knees.

"Are you ready?" Kyle asked solemnly.

Tara shook her head no, but still replied, "As ready as I'll ever be."

"We have a little over an hour until midnight," Kyle said. "What do you want to do until then?"

Tara took a deep breath then let it out in a loud sigh. She honestly didn't know. What did you do the last hour of your life? She had no one to contact or hold. She had already done her best to prepare. Studying or learning anything more would just confuse her.

"What does your heart desire?" Kyle asked when Tara still hadn't answered.

Tara closed her eyes and *listened.*

"I want to walk next to the river," she said, surprised at the answer. She'd been avoiding the river walk for a few days, since this had all started. But she missed it. The river, for all its threat and danger, still held her heart in many ways.

"Then let's go walk," Kyle said. He lifted a single eyebrow at Tara when she walked to the front door still wearing her ratty bathrobe and slippers.

"Look, we both know he's going after my magic as well as my soul," she said. "I may as well be comfortable defending myself."

"What, you think you're going to strip nude and distract him?"

"I have nothing to be ashamed of," Tara said. "And I don't think he's quite human. Besides, the strongest magic is generally performed without clothes on. You know that."

"I know that's what we've been taught," Kyle pointed out. "I've spent much of the afternoon questioning that learning."

"I understand," Tara said. "I've been doing the same. But this feels right."

Kyle gave her a sudden grin, the light of it warming her. "Then I'll make sure I have bail money ready if you get arrested for indecent exposure."

"What, you're not joining me nude to go dancing in the moonlight?" Tara teased.

Kyle gave an exaggerated shudder. "Gonna leave the dancing up to you tonight, darling."

"Then let's go," Tara said. She turned and looked over her apartment for one last moment. She didn't know if this was the last time she'd ever see it or not. The living room didn't contain that much that was hers—the beige couch and matching loveseat had been Sharon's, only one of the standing bookcases contained Tara's books, and the small round table and four chairs were both Tara's and Sharon's, found used at a garage sale.

The balcony had all her plants, which she would miss. The kitchen was the heart of the place for Tara. She had an entire cupboard filled with her dried herbs and potions, oils and medicines. It was where she concocted her teas, which were as much a part of her magic as the spells themselves.

She was walking away from all of this, however. The material possessions had come to mean so much less in the last few hours. She and Kyle had prepared a will for her that afternoon. She couldn't leave notes for her family—how was she going to explain to them that she'd died at the hand of a supernatural creature?

Kyle accepted her keys, phone, and wallet, sliding them into various pockets in his vest. He'd take care of everything if…if.

She had to survive.

The air outside had a brisk chill to it. Tara pulled her robe tighter, questioning her choice. But she stubbornly didn't turn back, and instead, led Kyle through the locked gate of the apartment complex directly onto the river walk.

Dark waters ran in the river tonight, swift and deep. It had been a really wet winter, and the waters were still running high, even though it was already June. Above the rush of the cars in the street beside them, the cicadas gave their cycling call. The night smelled clean, the wind pushing away the stench of the city.

Without thinking about it, Tara turned automatically toward the Burnside Bridge. She knew that the choice was probably being influenced by the events sure to happen later that night. However, she also wanted to see the bridge, feel its strength and its structure, touch the iron and the concrete, listen to the hum of the cars.

They walked slowly up the pedestrian stairs, supported by separate pillars, not really part of the bridge itself, something Tara hadn't known until she'd started researching the history of the bridge. Tall banks of construction lights illuminated the bridge deck, banishing the darkness that Tara felt gathering around her. The smell of tar overwhelmed all the other scents.

Construction crews had narrowed the traffic lanes so there was merely a single lane for traffic going either way. Despite the late hour, too many cars still wanted to cross. Their impatience was evident from how they would race forward whenever they got the chance. Tara counted at least three times when there was almost an accident if not for the miracle of modern brakes.

Kyle walked beside Tara, a pillar of strength. She didn't know how she could have survived even that day without him. "Thank you," she told him again as they neared one of the two fancy operator booths on the side of the bridge.

"No reason to be thanking me," Kyle said. "I was just doing what anyone with a heart should do."

A little anger seeped out with his words. That afternoon, Tara had just had a taste of how furious Kyle was at the rest of the coven for abandoning her, how betrayed he'd felt. They were his home, his safe place. That they'd abandoned one of their own had filled him with rage.

Tara's attention was drawn to the circle of silence that radiated out from the center of the bridge. It was as if the noise of the street traffic had suddenly been halted.

The Riprap man stood there.

He appeared mostly human, not made of riprap, as he'd appeared in her dream. He still wore an old fashioned suit, though this one was more formal, made of black wool and cut differently, with smaller lapels and a longer tail. Instead of a bowler he wore a top hat, also made of black, with a shimmering white rose tucked in along the brim.

She still couldn't see his face clearly. Instead, it appeared as though he had two dark ponds where his eyes should have been and a gaping hole for a mouth.

Tara stopped. Kyle looked over at her.

"Do you see him?" Tara asked, not pointing directly at the Riprap man but waving in his direction.

Kyle looked forward, searching. Then he shook his head. "I sense a dark spot up ahead. Something I would walk around and say a blessing as I passed. I don't see a man."

"Okay," Tara said. She was a bit disappointed. She'd hoped that someone else would have at least been able to see what she saw. At least Kyle knew to avoid the spot where the Riprap man stood.

Tara turned to Kyle and held out her hands. "You need to stay here," she told him gently. "I have everything I need."

Kyle's hands wrapped around hers. She hadn't thought she was cold, not until she felt the heat of his palms against her fingers. However, Kyle had a stubborn look around his jaw. "I still don't like this."

"I won't risk you," Tara said. "You've been such a good friend to me. I won't stupidly endanger you."

Kyle gave her a crooked smile. "Too late," he said.

Tara shivered as a searing cold wind suddenly washed over her.

The Riprap man stood beside them.

"Say goodbye to your lover," he instructed.

Tara stood her ground. "He's just a friend. And one of the best."

The Riprap man seemed puzzled. Tara could tell his attention had switched to Kyle for a moment. He appeared to be intently studying the man in front of him. Then the Riprap man shrugged. "No matter. I will take his life as well if you don't come with me."

Tara swallowed hard. This was it. Her fire and powers about to be tested, by a much crueler taskmaster than the head of her former coven.

The stakes were higher as well.

Tara let go of Kyle's hands, her fingers suddenly cold. But before she could turn completely away, Kyle suddenly wrapped his arms around her and engulfed her in an awkward, sideways hug.

"You can do this," he said gruffly, kissing the side of her hair. "I won't lose my best friend to this Goodwill hobo."

Tara nearly snorted out loud when she saw how the Riprap man stiffened at the insult, his anger apparent.

Was it because he was an ancient white man, still used to thinking of African Americans as barely human? It didn't matter. His opinion held no importance.

"I will survive this," Tara promised.

She had no idea if she could keep that promise, but she intended to fight with everything she had—lore, training, and talent—in order to survive the ordeal.

"You better," Kyle said as he let her go.

Tara stepped forward in front of the Riprap man. *Do your worst.*

The Riprap man nodded as if he'd heard her unspoken challenge. "Witch," he said out loud, as if it were a curse word. "You are chosen."

A great sucking whirlpool of freezing water opened up at Tara's feet and sucked her down into the depths.

TARA FOUND herself at the base of one of the Burnside Bridge piers again, standing on the riprap. This time, heavy ropes wrapped not just around her wrists, but tied her body to the pier itself.

Dark waters surrounded her, billowing like storm clouds. The water tasted metallic, like cold steel. Ice pressed in on Tara from all sides, making her shiver.

She looked down, and found that her ratty robe had disappeared. For a moment, she was distracted and hoped that the robe hadn't been ruined. That was her favorite robe.

The ropes wrapped around her belly, then were looped around her shoulders, leaving her upper chest clear. Her legs, too, were tied tightly to the pier. She twisted, testing the limits of the ropes, but they didn't allow much movement.

Tara knew better than to believe that the Riprap man had left her chest bare so he could look at her tits, as nice as they were. He'd left that area clear so that he could rip the heart out of her body.

Surprisingly, Tara found that she could breathe easily underwater. Was that because her actual body wasn't down here? She hoped that Kyle was taking care of it, up on the surface, and would let it die if she didn't survive. She'd signed a "do not resuscitate" (DNR) order that afternoon along with her will.

She couldn't imagine how horrible it would be for her parents and friends if they came to visit her soulless body, kept alive by machines in a hospital.

The Riprap man suddenly appeared in front of Tara. She finally saw his true face, not the mask he'd worn before.

He was ancient. Furrows lined his forehead, then ran along the edges of his face, past his eyes and circling his cheeks, the skin sagging as if it were about to fall off. Age spots were splashed across his face, giving it a mottled look, as though he had a skin condition. His teeth had yellowed, and a few gaping holes showed through his ghastly smile. Watery, faded brown eyes covetously gazed at her. His suit hung loosely on his skeletal body. Bony hands formed into claws reached up toward her, as if to rake across her skin with his ivory-colored nails.

Everything felt as real as it had the night before, when she'd been tested in the meditation circle.

However, Tara knew that this was all, at some level, an illusion. Her body was still up on the Burnside Bridge, safe with Kyle.

The Riprap man started motioning with his hands, beginning an ancient chant. Tara could hear the words clearly this time, unlike in the dream. He was calling on the ancient spirit of the river, the god Mulinohana, to leave this bridge alone in exchange for the life the Riprap man was about to sacrifice.

Tara shook her head. The Riprap man thought he was doing the right thing by sacrificing her, a witch. Didn't he realize that humans had already interfered with the course of the river? It was possible that the area could still flood, but only after a catastrophic failure had occurred all along the course of the river.

No, her death wasn't necessary to protect the bridges. Probably none of the modern deaths were.

The waters surrounding the Riprap man grew darker. Was that the spirit of the river taking shape?

Tara started her own prayer, not to the river god, but to the water, itself. She remembered its spirit from the night before, how strong it had run, how powerful it could be. It would not be beholden to anything as puny as a mere river god. No, water, the element itself, was who she called on.

The dark clouds billowing behind the Riprap man grew more solid. It looked as though a giant mass of seaweed was slowly forming, with a solid core body and hundreds of arms. It stank of rotting ropes and dead marsh lands.

Tara shuddered. This was a powerful creature, she could tell that.

Was this actually the god of the river? The spirit of the Willamette? Or some monster who'd usurped the title?

Tara used the prayer she'd used before to sharpen her thoughts, to bring the knife's blade of clarity to the bindings holding her. They felt as real as the rope that Sheila had used the night before, abrading her skin as she fought against them. They dragged her down as well, their weight preventing her from rising.

For a moment, Tara had a spark of hope, as her spell cut through a strand of the rope fiber.

She quickly realized that it would take too long. The ropes were as thick as her forearm. It would take forever to cut through it a strand at a time.

No, she needed something more powerful. She and Kyle had discussed the possibility, and had already prepared healing salves should she end up needing them.

Tara took a deep breath and prepared herself as best she could.

Then she called forth the fire banked deep inside of her.

Flames burst out all along the length of the rope holding her.

Tara screamed at the pain that engulfed her. The smell of burning flesh turned her stomach and made her wretch. But she wouldn't hold back, or recall the flames.

The dark mass in front of her drew back, as if afraid of the fire. The Riprap man continued his chant, speeding up when he realized his prize was getting away.

Tara hung in the pain as the ropes burned. Her thoughts grew hazy as she endured the agony. She struggled to breathe, even as the fire stole all the air from around her. Despite the cold waters, she realized she'd started to sweat, giving her own water to that surrounding her.

Suddenly, the ropes fell away from where they'd been wrapped around her shoulders and her arms. The release of the pain made Tara gasp. She lifted her arms, waving them in the cold water.

The pain around her legs slowed next. Tara kicked her legs to the side, the ropes dropping off like a dried mask.

The bonds of rope around Tara's belly burned on, but the pain had diminished to mere discomfort. When she looked down, she saw that a single piece of rope remained, wrapped firmly across her center.

Cautiously, Tara peeled the still burning rope from her skin. While the rest of her body showed no trace of her recent agony, her belly had blisters on it, in a circular pattern.

Tara stood under her own power, facing the two creatures before her.

She was free. She knew that she could escape now. She had planted a strong rope herself, tying her soul to her body. If she reached out and twitched it with her magical senses, she could find her body. Possibly even rise out of this dream and flow back into it.

Plus, the bridge didn't really need her protection, not from a natural flood.

An unnatural flood, or these unnatural creatures in front of her, however…

The long arms of the river spirit slowly began to reach for Tara. She appreciated its caution. It knew that she could hurt it.

She'd proven herself a worthy opponent, even if she was a witch.

Now, she just had to turn the bad luck of the Riprap man away.

Tara bent her knees, bringing her arms up above her head as if she was about to dive into the water.

But instead, she dove head first into the embrace of the thing in front of her.

Bring it.

THE WATER that still surrounded Tara did not surprise her. The amount of light did. She'd been expecting to be engulfed in darkness while still being underwater. Instead, the water felt muted, the area surrounding her as crisp as a late fall morning. Mud squished between her toes. Her belly still ached. Though her physical body was somewhere else, she felt her heartbeat thrumming in the scars she now bore.

No words greeted her in this space. Instead, the water changed nature and tone, filling her ears with an amused chuckle at her audacity to seek the heart of it.

The Riprap man appeared beside her, still wearing his true face. The age didn't sit well on him. He had a sour look and a more sour smell, like an old man who'd spent his days eating cabbage. Close up, she could see his suit was actually badly tattered, the edges of the cuffs and collar ragged, the threads wearing thin.

"You don't need my soul to protect the bridge," Tara told the man. "The days of the massive floods are long over."

"You're wrong," the Riprap man sneered, shaking his head. "The river god demands a sacrifice. Something to mark the bridge as sacred. As His. Otherwise it will be taken."

Tara sighed. "The true spirit of the river would never demand such a thing," she said gently. "The waters themselves have no need."

Doubt crossed the Riprap man's face. Then he grew stubborn. "The river god has need."

"You're a fool," Tara told him.

"I've saved more lives than you ever will, witch," the Riprap man replied.

"Don't be too sure," Tara retorted, though she knew she didn't have a leg to stand on.

"If you don't believe in the river god," the Riprap man said, "then why have you come to the sacred hearth?"

"To bargain," Tara said honestly.

"The river god has no need for anything other than your magic and your life," the Riprap man sneered.

Tara didn't want to point out yet again that a true god wouldn't need such things. "Why mine?" she asked.

The Riprap man peered at her, as if she was an alien creature just born in front of him.

Surely the other witches had asked the same question…

"What makes me so special?" Tara insisted.

"Nothing," the Riprap man said firmly.

Tara felt the lie echo around the room. "That isn't true," she snarled. "Your river god wants you to tell me."

She felt it in the pressure of the water surrounding her. The presence they stood before had a reason for choosing her. It wanted her to know.

The Riprap man shook his head, but still responded, "Because you like the water," he admitted. "You're a witch, but you have an affinity for the depths. Not that it will save you," he added quickly.

"Did the other witches all have an affinity for the water?" Tara asked. Then she answered her own question. "No, they didn't. And this river god of yours is lonely."

The Riprap man blinked, surprised. "He has no other needs."

"None that he's told you," Tara said, suddenly feeling more certain of where she stood. "He wants more followers. He wants more believers. You've been a poor priest, as far as this river god is concerned."

"I've followed the true path, learned the knowledge of the inner circles," the Riprap man contended.

"So you're actually a witch," Tara countered. "If you know the way."

"No!" the Riprap man denied. "I am no witch. I merely studied my prey so that I could capture them more easily."

Loneliness washed through the space, a great echoing sadness that hurt Tara's soul. She felt a knot form in her throat, a hard lump of grief that made it difficult to swallow.

"No one will pray to you," Tara warned the river spirit. "No one will treat you as a god. But I can guarantee that there will be those who will scatter rose petals across your waters at the equinoxes each year."

"What?" the Riprap man said, affronted. "Who are you to make bargains?"

Tara gave him a soft smile. "I am a witch, someone with powers and magic, who has an affinity with the water. And you have outlived your usefulness." The rest of the words tumbled from her lips, passing almost without her knowledge. "As your own mentor Robin did, before you."

The Riprap man gasped and took a step back as if Tara had actually struck him.

"The river god deserves a sacrifice," he said, recovering quickly. He lifted his hands in front of him, as if to actually grab her shoulders and start to shake her.

"How about you?" Tara asked, sidestepping. She reached for a rope of awareness that she'd planted deep in her soul. "Why doesn't your river god take your soul for a change?"

Darkness rushed into the space, filled with the sourness of the Riprap man. The fire died with a quiet *whoosh*.

"I will sing songs for you," Tara promised both creatures as she tugged harder on that lifeline out of this place. "To you."

The scaly hands of the Riprap man grabbed hold of Tara's bare arms. She twisted her entire body, trying to break the hold. She couldn't see anything in the inky blackness. All the air fled her surroundings. She was drowning in glacially cold waters. She kicked away, trying to free herself. But no matter how she moved, the hands found her, held her tightly, and started to draw her back in.

Despite Sheila having cheated Tara of her proper status, Tara knew that she was worthy of being called a true initiate of the second circle. She focused on the air in the water, breaking apart the molecules, bringing herself bubbles of air to breathe.

Tara tried to call up the fire again, but she was too deep in the water's territory for it to suffer its mortal enemy's presence.

While the fire warmed Tara's skin in the icy cold, it couldn't spring forth again.

So Tara reached for the old oak she'd talked with the night before. The one who'd found its way to move through death.

She couldn't die down here. Couldn't let go like that. Her death would be true, the Riprap man would take her heart and suck it into himself.

But the river spirit understood the passing of the seasons, better than humans. It would understand what it was she did.

If the river spirit still demanded a sacrifice, and she was no longer available, it would turn on its one practitioner instead. Tara had promised it more followers.

Tara called the oak to herself, called up the winter soul, the dormant self who could weather any storm, the ice and cold, sleet and snow.

Then Tara reached for the ground that she knew had to be someplace below her. She knew where her body was, had a vague sense of the direction where it lay. The opposite way must be down.

So Tara pushed her roots *hard* into the earth. Down she delved, far under the pilings for the bridges, far past the lining for the river, down into the mantle of the earth itself.

She planted herself, and then refused to move, to bend, to be pulled or pushed or prodded.

Her breathing slowed as winter overcame her. Her blood pulsed with the slow beat of the seasons. Her body grew stronger than the manmade structure above her.

It took her a while to realize that the Riprap man no longer held her. He had moved on.

That was the true nature of water. To flow away, seeking the lowest possible point.

Tara shook herself awake, rising slowly out of her dream of earth and roots, of rocks and river silt.

A battle still raged to the side of her, the Riprap man and his former god.

She watched for a moment. They both employed massive amounts of ancient magic, grappling together with unfamiliar power. The battle wasn't between light and darkness, but dark and darker. If they'd been above water, in the air, she expected she'd see fireworks and bolts of pure energy passing between them. As it was, the water muted and slowed everything, turning her view wavy and indistinct.

Tara wanted to stay and see who was victorious, but her body was calling her.

Sweetly, Tara rose through the waters, like a kingfisher returning to the air, rising above her hunting grounds and back up into the clear blue sky.

TARA BLINKED. "OOOOF," she said as she took a deep breath, filling her lungs with sweet air.

Light shone behind her, and Kyle sat beside her. It took her a few moments to place where she was: one of the river walk parks. The dew had fallen hard, but dawn was on its way. The sound of the early morning traffic soothed her.

Just in front of her feet, the river ran, dark and solid, like black silk flowing from a loom. Warblers hunted for bugs on the water, while the robins chased across the grass for worms.

Tara shivered, then gratefully wrapped her ratty robe more tightly across her chest. She turned to look at Kyle, who was studying her carefully.

"Hi," Tara said. She suddenly felt shy around him. She wasn't sure why. But she felt raw and reborn, and wasn't sure what to do.

"Hi," Kyle said. "You back?"

Tara nodded. She reached out her hand.

Kyle took it and squeezed it, as if understanding that she needed something more to ground her.

"I'm back," Tara said. She swallowed and felt her shoulders drop further, relaxing into her new self. "I'm back—to stay."

LATER THAT MORNING, Tara sat out on her balcony, recovering and reassessing, well, everything.

Had the river god won? Or the Riprap man? As she felt no threat that morning, she'd assumed that it must have been the river god.

She needed to find a new place to stay, or at the very least, a new flatmate. She needed to find a new coven, or form her own, as Kyle had suggested.

And she needed to come to grips with the changes that her ordeals had wrought in her.

Tara had always felt so old fashioned, as she was the only person her age she knew who didn't have any tattoos. She had a few rings curled around the top of her right ear, with only three small holes in her left lobe. She'd tried piercing her eyebrow, but it had never felt right. Same with a nose ring.

But now, she didn't have a tattoo as much as she'd been branded. The mark on her stomach from where the fire had burned her had appeared on her physical body. She had a circle of raised flesh on her belly now, about the size of her outstretched hand, with four characters enclosed in it. They looked like ancient Chinese to her, with squiggly long lines, but a casual search on the internet hadn't turned up anything.

She suspected they represented the four elements—air, fire, water, earth.

Why had she been marked with these? What did they mean? She wasn't imagining them. She didn't have that good of an imagination.

In time, she was certain she'd learn their true meaning.

Not everything could be explained to the beginning initiate.

A hummingbird thrummed across the balcony, circling once, before settling onto its perch to sip at the nectar in the feeder. Then it flew up to the iron post holding the feeder. It looked at Tara, its head cocked to one side, as if asking Tara what she was going to do next.

"I don't know," Tara said, taking a deep breath. "But I have time, now, to figure it out."

The hummingbird *tsked* at her as if it was about time Tara finally understood that, before flying away to its busy tasks, leaving Tara to her day.

EPILOGUE

I drag myself onto the shore just as the night falls. The battle had been epic. I have survived. The bridges and the city of Portland herself are safe once more. But the cost…Ah, the cost. I find myself shaken to my core at the powers I have gathered. I had no idea how I had grown. I am no witch. Yet, I have absorbed much of the magic I have taken for my god. Former god. My holy quest has been forsaken. However, I still live. I will find a new quest, new deeds that need doing, tasks that would offend the gentle sensibilities of these modern people. That, as well as have my revenge on the one who so upended my world. That thrice-damned witch. Tara.

Wilson Evermore, the Riprap Man, 2018

CIRCLE OF FIRE

ONE

While I was at the headwaters for the mighty Willamette, I sacrificed an entire coven of witches to the river god Mulinohana, to ensure His forbearance when sending his flood waters toward the newly born city of Portland. Now that I have returned to the city, I need to renew the vows of the river god, to mark each and every one of the mighty bridges as His so that He might spare them. However, that means finding more witches. I need at least one for each bridge now being built or rebuilt, to lash a witch's heart to the footing and bind her there. The Hawthorn bridge is currently being reconstructed, with the project to be finished by 1901. I need to go hunting.

Wilson Evermore, Civil Engineer and Chief Magician, 1900

"STOP! STAY STILL!"

Tara froze. What on earth?

Okay, so maybe she was harvesting rose hips in public. But it wasn't as though she was doing anything illegal. She was in a public park. This was public property.

The day was sunny and unusually warm for Portland, particularly given that it was the middle of September. Still, it seemed the perfect time to harvest. Bright orange, red, and even purple rose hips peeked out from the green leaves and thorns of the *Rosa Rugosa* plants that ran through the center of the park. Some of the flowers had been confused by the hot summer, and were still blooming. As Tara had walked along the gravel path, their heady scent had followed her.

Tara started to turn around to address the speaker, to protest her innocence.

"Are you daft? Didn't you hear me? Stay still!"

Tara froze again, puzzled. The voice addressing her was female, and now that she thought about it, had a very slight British accent to it.

"Why?" Tara finally asked.

"There's wasps right in front of you!"

Tara looked closer at the roses nearest her. Sure enough, yellow jackets buzzed not two inches from her bare fingers.

As that type of wasp tended to be attracted by movement, and was also aggressive, the other woman's advice finally made sense.

However, Tara was also a powerful witch. She'd assembled a sachet for herself that morning to protect her from the thorns of the roses, as well as any insects. She'd combined lemon balm and chamomile to soothe and calm, borage and angelica for protection, as well as caraway, cloves, and rosemary for general good luck. The pouch itself was made out of plain cotton that Tara had first "fixed" with salt and magic (so the color wouldn't just wash out the first time she got the cloth wet), then dyed a gentle pink using rose petals.

The wasps wouldn't bother her. They hadn't even noticed her standing there.

Still, it wouldn't do for her to ignore this woman's advice. Most people knew nothing about magic. Tara wasn't about to show off her talent.

Instead, she stayed frozen a few more moments, as if she was making certain that the wasps weren't bothered by her. Then she slowly began to back away, stepping out of the rose bushes and onto the gravel path behind her. Only then did Tara turn to the woman who'd "saved" her.

A short young woman stood on the path. She had a mop of bright red curls on the top of her head, though it was shaved along the sides, giving her a cool, edgy look. Geometric tattoos—connected triangles and octagons—ran from behind her ears down her neck, as if streams of art just flowed naturally from her. A gold loop pierced her left nostril, and an entire row of rings ran up the edges of both of her ears, like modern armor, as well as bars pierced through her inner lobes.

She looked to be about Tara's age, in her mid-thirties. Freckles covered her pert nose and across her rounded cheeks, making her appear younger, while her green eyes held a depth of living. Her broad smile promised mischief.

She wore a baggy, long-sleeved, green-and-white striped shirt, jeans, and had a flowered sunhat that she'd pushed back from her face, hanging by a cord around her neck.

Tara pushed her own sunhat off her head so she could see the other woman better. Tara was dressed in a T-shirt, shorts, and sandals—then again, her coloring was darker than the other woman's. She would tan in the sun, whereas she was certain the redhead in front of her would fry to a crisp if she wasn't completely covered. Tara wore her own brown hair tied back in a tight ponytail, as usual. At five foot ten, she felt as though she towered over the other woman, who was five feet tall, at the most.

"Thank you," Tara said, smiling at the woman.

Then she noticed that the other woman held equipment very similar to her own: a pair of clippers in one hand and a cloth bag in the other.

"Oh! Were you harvesting as well?" Tara asked, holding up her own bag of rose hips.

The other woman nodded. "Seems a waste not to." The accent she had was very slight. How long had she been in the States? "Me Gran couldn't abide a waste."

"I'm just cheap," Tara said with a shrug. "Much less expensive for me to just harvest what's here. My name's Tara, by the way."

"Ginny," the other woman replied. She peered at Tara for a moment. "How will you process them?"

A deep rift existed between people who gathered rose hips, depending on the method used to process them, like a religious schism. Tara had witnessed two witches almost coming to blows over it at the shop.

"For tea, I'll process them the modern way, first drying them in a food dehydrator, then using a food processor to break them apart, and a sieve to separate out the hairs," Tara admitted. "For everything else, I'll do it the old fashioned way, slicing the rose hips and scooping out the insides before I dry them. How about you?"

Ginny gave her a big grin, then leaned closer, as if sharing a secret. "Much the same," she said. "Though me Gran would have a fit if she ever found out I'd been using those newfangled modern tools."

"I hear you," Tara said. "The—the woman who first taught me about plants would also throw a fit if she found out I was using, gasp, *machines*."

Ginny snorted at her. "Aye," she said. "So I've been coming up the path this way," she said, pointing behind her.

"And I've been working the other direction," Tara said. Between the pair of them, they'd just about covered one side of the path, starting at the ends and working toward the middle. "Should we switch to the other side?"

Just across the gravel path ran another long bed of roses. It wasn't as long or as deep as the first side, but Tara had been planning on harvesting on that side as well.

"Sure," Ginny said agreeably. "I haven't been in the city for long. Wasn't sure if this kind of thing was proper."

"I've been here since I finished college, coming up on fifteen years, now," Tara said. "No one's ever bothered me, though I've had lots of people curious about what I was doing. Where were you before this?"

"Ach, here and there," Ginny said. "Was born in Wales. Was there until me Gran died, ten years gone this fall." She was silent a moment, taking a deep breath, obviously still in mourning for her gram.

"I'm sorry for your loss," Tara said sincerely.

Ginny shrugged as she turned toward the rose bushes. "It pushed me outta the nest. Got me across the pond."

"Do you like it here?" Tara asked.

Again, the non-committal shrug as Ginny clipped a cherry-tomato-red rose hip from the bush in front of her. She trimmed both ends off before she dropped the hip into her bag. "Well enough. Still trying to find my way, you know?"

"I hear you," Tara said. Her own life had been turned completely upside down that summer. Though it had been no more than three months ago, it seemed like several lifetimes at this point. She no longer had a coven of witches to call her own. She was staying with her best friend Kyle for the time being, in his spare bedroom, but she needed to find someplace else and soon.

Tara still occasionally picked up shifts at *Ye Olde Magick Shoppe* in downtown Portland. However, even that remnant of her old life would dry up soon. The owner, Patricia, had finally found a permanent replacement for her. Not that Tara had wanted to leave, but none of the regular witches wanted to deal with her, afraid that she'd cause them bad luck. She had to find a job. Her savings would run out in a month's time. However, she felt stuck, unable to move forward, and she wasn't certain why.

Tara and Ginny worked together for a few moments in silence, each absorbed in selecting the perfect rose hips. Due to the hot summer, the hips had frequently gone past ripe and straight to withered. Tara would find one that looked perfect on top, only to lift it up and find that it was soft and squishy underneath. She settled for hips that were less ripe and more firm in an effort to fill up her bag, though they wouldn't be as flavorful as the hips that were fully ripe.

"Will you be making oil from these?" Tara asked as she clipped a vibrant purple hip. The color didn't affect the taste, but Tara still liked the purple ones the best.

"Aye," Ginny replied. "And some balms. I have a friend who lets me share her booth sometimes, down in the Saturday Market. And you?"

"I'll make tea as well as oil," Tara said. "Mainly, though, I hope to sell the processed rose hips. You know *Ye Olde Magick Shoppe* downtown?"

Ginny nodded slowly. "I do," she said. She looked over at Tara quizzically. "You think they'll take some of these for their supplies? In that fancy back room of theirs?"

Tara perked up. While the front of the Magick Shoppe was a tourist destination, complete with wands, crystals, and pyramids of energy that held no magic at all, the back room carried real supplies for the local witches and other beings of power. The room was hidden in plain sight. Most of the tourists didn't even realize it was there. The only people who even noticed it were beings who had magic, whether they knew it or not.

Ginny asking about the back room meant that not only had she seen it, she had power.

"They might take some of your processed hips," Tara said. "I work there." Patricia had told Tara that she'd buy any hips that Tara was willing to sell, primarily because Patricia would be able to charge a premium for them, as they'd been collected and processed by a witch.

"Oh!" Ginny said. She took a hasty step back and away. "You're one of them! A schooled witch. Sorry to be a bother to ye."

With that, Ginny took off down the path in haste.

"Wait!" Tara called after her, but the girl had disappeared. Had she used some sort of illusion to hide her from seeking eyes? She'd called it up quickly if she had.

What had spooked her? Had she had a run in with some of the other witches in Portland? And what did she mean by a "schooled" witch?

Tara shook her head. Yes, she might be considered a "schooled witch" by some. As part of her training in the coven, she'd had to learn not only the Latin names of the herbs she used, where they grew and how to cultivate them, as well as the traditional medicinal, culinary, and utilitarian properties of each, she then had to layer on the actual magical potions that the plants were used in. Often the traditional magic assigned to a plant was similar to the real magical power, but sometimes it wasn't.

However, since Tara had left her coven (or been kicked out for bringing *bad luck*, depending on how you looked at it) she'd stopped learning the traditional way, or at least cramming as much as she could into her head when she had spare time. Instead, she was starting to figure out her own approach to magic, as well as the herbs and plants she used.

Kyle had called her a *hedgewitch*, one that worked with the natural elements of things instead of following the strict traditions.

Tara was still trying to find her path, just as she was still trying to get her feet back under her from the blows of the summer.

But what did that make Ginny? Was she also a hedgewitch? Or just an untrained woman with power?

Tara considered for a moment. She wasn't content with just letting Ginny be. There was something there, some sort of connection that she'd had with Tara.

It was only Thursday. That weekend, Tara was going to the Saturday market, and see if she could find Ginny again.

TARA WAS elbows deep in rose hips, as it were, when Kyle came home that evening from his office job. He clerked for the federal court downtown, having decided early in his career that he didn't want to work as a lawyer on his own, though he had a degree in law. He always said he worked better behind the scenes, influencing a judge's opinions, rather than having to do all the case work himself.

Kyle always dressed the part of a powerful lawyer for work. That day he wore an expensive light-gray suit that looked good against his black skin, a brilliant white shirt, and a red power tie. Expensive, black-leather Italian shoes completed the outfit. His bald head just added to his gravitas, as did his physique, all the muscles he worked hard to keep up at the gym. He was also taller than Tara, six foot three, as well as older, as they'd just celebrated his forty-fifth birthday.

Though Kyle looked impressive and kept a serious demeanor, Tara counted herself privileged to know what a goof Kyle could be. They still had Friday night movie nights together, laughing themselves silly at bad seventies movies.

They'd been living together for two and a half months now, long enough for Tara to know Kyle's routine. He merely nodded at her as he emptied his pockets of his wallet, phone, loose change, and so on. Then he went directly to his bedroom, already stripping.

Tara had seen more of Kyle's body than friends normally shared. Then again, he was gay, and she had the wrong equipment.

She kept her head down, refocusing on the rose hips in front of her. She'd already set one large batch to drying, the hips that she'd keep for herself to make tea and sachets from. The rest, as she'd told Ginny before the woman ran off, she was processing by hand.

It was a long, fiddly business, slicing the hips apart and scooping out the insides by hand. She was doing them in batches, slicing a large amount, then scraping the insides out, then slicing another large amount. The hips themselves were slimy, and despite how Tara had tried to pick only the brightest, ripest hips, the seeds on the inside would stick and she'd end up scraping away too much of the skin.

She hadn't taken all of the hips from the park that were ripe. She'd just gone down "her" side of the row of roses, from the middle to the end, leaving the other half for Ginny if she decided to go back.

Tara had found herself thinking about Ginny off and on all afternoon. It wasn't sexual, Tara wasn't attracted to the girl. (Tara tended to be heterosexual, but she was open minded. It was Portland, after all.) It was more like meeting a long-lost friend. If the Saturday market had been open that afternoon, Tara would have already gone to it, looking for Ginny.

Once Tara heard the shower get turned off, she started packing up her mess, making room for Kyle in the kitchen. Part of Kyle's routine after work included first showering off the day, then meditating for a while before he came out to the kitchen and cooked dinner.

Tara had tried to cook dinner for them a few times when she'd first moved in, as part of her payment for the free room and board. However, Kyle insisted that he keep up his routine. Cooking was meditative for him. Tara actually understood that, and so always tried to vacate the kitchen and have everything cleaned up by the time he came out.

She needed to find a job. And a place to live. And a coven who would take her.

Though Tara had survived her encounter with the Riprap man, none of the covens in Portland would have anything to do with her. They considered her *bad luck*. That was what had happened in the past for any witch who had at least temporarily escaped the Riprap man. He'd come after not only them, but everyone they knew.

That hadn't happened, at least not as far as Tara knew.

Had the river god killed his faithful servant? Tara had assumed so.

Except that the last few nights, she'd started having nightmares again. Nothing obvious, no. She'd be doing something normal when she'd feel a pressure at her back as if someone was staring at her from across the room, but when she turned around, no one was there. The smell of water had started to follow her everywhere as well, dank and cold.

By the time Kyle came out of his room, Tara had cleaned up her mess, pushing the processed and unprocessed hips into two containers to the side. He gave her a grave smile as he passed her, making a beeline for the kitchen.

"Feeling human again?" Tara asked. He looked good. He wore a green and white shirt that looked inspired by afrofuturism, along with jeans and bare feet.

"I am," Kyle said solemnly. He opened up the refrigerator and paused, thinking. "How about stir fry tonight? We have leftover chicken and plenty of veggies."

That had been one thing that Tara had been able to get Kyle to change. He'd been in the habit of having bread and pasta and just drinking a veggie protein shake instead of eating real vegetables. Now he'd become a master at stir fry, particularly as Tara had slowly added more veggies to their shared fridge/freezer.

"Stir fry sounds great," Tara said. "What can I help with?"

Kyle scowled at the open fridge for a moment, before he slowly pulled out a bok choy. "I'm not even sure what to do with that, that, mutant cabbage thing," he commented.

Tara grinned. "Both the green leaves and the white stems are edible. When it was just me, I'd buy one of these large bok choy, chop it up, then throw half in the freezer for smoothies and half in the fridge for salads."

"Kewl. You could teach a cooking class, you know. Down at the local co-op," Kyle said. He was forever coming up with possible work for her, knowing that she wanted to find a new job.

That actually wasn't a bad idea. "Vegetables you may not know?" Tara said.

The question remained, however, did she just want to string together several one-off gigs? Or did she want to try to get just a single job, and a single, reliable paycheck?

A single job meant a reasonably regular schedule; however, Tara was well aware that she'd probably end up working retail, which meant lots of hours.

Being a permanent freelancer meant she'd constantly be hustling for work on the one hand. It also meant setting her own hours, and larger chunks of time for her magical studies.

She could always go back to being an *au pair* which would include room and board. However, those jobs also meant being at someone's beck and call, much like working retail, for worse pay.

Tara brought herself back to the job at hand, dismantling the large bok choy. She and Kyle worked together in silence for a short while, applying themselves to their separate chopping blocks. Kyle had started on the carrots, chopping those up, and had turned to the cauliflower next.

Tara had learned not to ask Kyle about his day job. He kept a strict separation between it and his home life. It was one of the ways he was, to use his words, "able to stay a nice guy and not turn into an asshole lawyer type."

After a while, Kyle did ask, "How did your day go?"

Tara told Kyle about meeting Ginny, and the feeling that she had about needing to go find the girl, as if they had unfinished business.

Kyle had already started frying the carrots and celery by the time she was finished.

"Witches form covens," he said slowly. "While there are some who work alone, most work together in a group. A tight-knit community."

Tara nodded. She'd had her friend Richard—a research librarian who always needed more work—look up the history of covens. There was an ancient tradition of them, dating back to Egyptian times (though Richard had complained long and bitterly about how much more difficult it was to research anything Egyptian since those stupid teenaged vampire movies had come out).

"I don't think it's in your nature to work alone," Kyle continued.

Tara sighed. "You're right," she said. While she didn't consider herself an extrovert, one of the things she missed most about working in the shop was more interaction with people. Which was why working at retail might turn out to be her best choice.

"We've talked before about you forming your own coven," Kyle said. He splashed some vinegar into the pot, causing the cooking vegetables to sputter. "Do you think Ginny might be part of that?"

Tara blinked, surprised by his suggestion. However, she immediately felt the rightness of his statement. "Wow," she said. "I would never have thought of that. I think you may be right, though."

Kyle nodded. "Your coven won't be traditional," he said with a grin.

He'd said that before. Tara had always just agreed with him. Finally, though, it occurred to her that they might have different ideas about what that meant.

"Tell me more about what you see for a non-traditional coven," Tara said. She was still unwilling to commit to calling it *her* coven. She wasn't a practitioner of the inner circle, and those were generally the only witches to collect a coven to them. Officially, she was only at first level, in the circle of thought. She'd been trying to move into the circle of air when the lead witch of her coven had cheated and Tara had failed the test.

Unofficially, Tara considered herself a witch of the circle of air, because of how close she'd come, as well as how difficult the test had been—much more difficult than the standard tests. Plus, she would have passed the test if the head of her old coven hadn't cheated.

"You're going to have different people in your coven, different from the norm," Kyle said after a moment. "People like Richard."

"What?" Tara asked, outraged. "But he isn't a witch! He's completely mundane!" The librarian was an old boyfriend of hers that she'd had to leave because he'd gotten too inquisitive about her magical side. Turned out he'd made some pretty accurate guesses about her being a witch, though he didn't really understand that she could do magic.

Or did he know? She'd never asked him outright. He was now seeing a lovely girl, Jeannie, who Tara had not only met but approved of. It made things much easier between them.

After a moment, Kyle continued. "True, Richard isn't a witch. He has no magical powers. But he has other powers, powers that you need, like his ability to look up old lore for you, find texts and passages. In a traditional coven, the eldest would keep the sacred books and would have a network for locating relevant information. You will need to build your own."

"Huh," Tara said. She'd never considered that Richard might be part of the coven. He could never be a full member, doing magic properly, but maybe she could make him an honorary one…

"Okay," Tara finally said after thinking it over for a bit. "Who else?"

"Well, me, of course," Kyle said, giving her a sly grin. He'd quit the old coven in protest over how they'd treated Tara. Aaloka, the second in command of the coven, had met with Tara afterwards, but had waffled about leaving. She, at least, had stayed in touch with Tara. They had a weekly coffee date every Friday afternoon.

"Do you need a coven?" Tara asked. Kyle seemed, well, pretty self-contained.

"I do," Kyle said solemnly. "I like the flow of energy that only happens in the circle, the way our prayers slide out into the world."

"Then maybe Ginny, and me," Tara said. "Who else?"

Kyle shrugged. "That's for you to figure out," he said. "Once you put your mind to it, the witches will come."

Tara had no answer for that. It was, however, how things frequently worked, that serendipitous magic.

It was time for her to set her intention and form her own coven. Whatever it might look like.

TARA DREAMED that night of fighting the Riprap man again. Only this time, it wasn't just her tied to the footing of the Burnside Bridge, far beneath the water. Five other figures were tied there as well. Though traditional myths always said that covens were composed of thirteen witches, six or eleven was more accurate. There were six circles, and a coven generally had at least one practitioner of each circle, or possibly two, with only one witch who practiced at the inner most level, the circle of circles, also known as anima, or essence.

In the dream, dark hoods covered the heads of her fellow captives. They struggled as she did with the hard, heavy rope tying them to the bridge. They all stood on the riprap—the boulders piled up at the bottom of the footing for a bridge to protect it from both the water as well as boats.

Tara tried to call out to her fellow witches, to encourage them, but the water carried away her words. The rocks under her bare feet were slimy, and she kept slipping as she struggled.

Though the water's temperature was comfortable, a cold current was snaking its way toward Tara, like a dark serpent. It foretold the coming of the Riprap man, the creature who had tried to sacrifice Tara to the river god earlier that year, just after the summer solstice.

Tara had made a separate deal with the river god, to honor him by scattering rose petals on the equinoxes. In the dream, she realized to her horror that she'd forgotten. The rose petals still filled the pockets of the jacket she wore.

If only she could get her hands free! She might stop the fate slowly rolling toward her if she could just reach the river god again.

But she couldn't free herself.

One by one, her companions all burst their ropes, either through physical strength (was that Kyle?) or through making the rope burn. One had even transformed the rope into a living vine which had then gracefully rolled away from its captive.

None of them tried to save her, though. As soon as they were free, they floated up toward the surface and were gone.

The Riprap man was coming for Tara's soul.

Tara tried calling up her powers, using what she'd learned. Fire fizzled around her. Try as she might, she couldn't direct it. The pattern of scars the fire had left during her last battle, the ones that circled her belly, seemed shrunken and blistered over. Bubbles of air lifted her up, but they weren't strong enough to pull her away from the ropes. The water surrounding her gave her strength. It was growing weaker though, as the dark waters carried by the Riprap man overtook the natural waters of the river. Tara stood on solid rock which wouldn't listen to her: she was more in tune with earth than stone.

In the distance, Tara got a glimpse of the Riprap man. His face was hazy even in the clear water. His torso still appeared to be made out of rocks, like the riprap she stood on. However, he seemed diminished, smaller than she remembered him.

As he drew closer, she could tell that the rocks which composed his body were no longer as well assembled as they'd once been. Before, he'd looked more like a superhero drawing of a rock man. Now, he shambled, the rocks piled up haphazardly. One shoulder stood higher than the other, as if he'd become a hunchback. He also limped now, one leg shorter than the other.

Dark magic swirled around his head, pouring out filth into the river.

The sluggish, oily cloud reached out to Tara, encasing her. She shuddered at the clutching feel of it, how it circled her arms and her chest. Slime that covered her, seeking to pollute her soul.

She had to get her hands free! Had to grab her rose petals. Had to go find her friends, the rest of her coven, even though they'd abandoned her.

Before the dirt and grime swallowed her whole.

At least now her water power helped by trying to keep her skin clean. The battle seemed endless, though. As soon as Tara switched her concentration from her hands to her legs, the filth came pouring back. Itchy welts raised across her bare skin, infected sores filled with pus.

Cold black eyes stared out from the face of the Riprap man, sucking at her like dark whirlpools, willing her soul to rise up out of her body.

"No. Never," Tara said.

Only then did she realize her mistake. By opening her mouth, she gave the filth surrounding her the opportunity to dive straight into her.

The blackness slid down her throat, more bitter than one of Miss Lucy's potions, curling around her tongue and making her gag. She felt the long worms sliding through her stomach, then blooming outward, infecting her limbs, her heart, her lungs.

Tara cried out the one word that she knew might save her.

"DREAM!"

The realization that she was merely dreaming woke her right up.

She sat up, finding herself still in Kyle's spare bedroom. The cold from her nightmare followed her, making her shiver. With a shaking hand she reached over and turned on the light on the end table, banishing the dark shadows.

Books covered the walls, old law books and text books, stiff and formal, not comforting. A chest of drawers made from a dark wood stood at the foot of the bed, matching the bookcases, heavy and masculine. Tara's bright blue suitcases gathered in the corner next to the chest, the only color in the room, the rest of her clothes there. A single window facing west filled much of the adjacent wall, the shade letting too much light seep through.

Tara made herself take a deep breath, then another. She couldn't get warm, though.

What she really wanted to do was to get up and take a shower, both to warm herself up, as well as get herself clean again, really clean. However, that would wake Kyle up, and he had to go to work in the morning. It wouldn't be fair to him.

Instead, Tara pulled her ratty but soft and warm green bathrobe out of the tiny closet that mostly held Kyle's winter suits and wrapped it around her before going out to the kitchen to make herself some tea. Kyle would sleep through that if she was quiet.

She didn't turn on any lights in the two-bedroom condo, the windows of the patio shining with enough light from the city outside. With practiced movements, Tara found her large mug and her electric tea kettle, filling it with just enough water and plugging it in before she opened the cupboard dedicated to her herbs.

Without thinking about it, Tara pulled out lemon balm,

peppermint, and chamomile to help calm her down. To that mix, she added some stinging nettle, for cleansing, as well as a pinch of lavender, which would do double duty, both for calming as well as spiritual cleaning. She hesitated, but finally added a pinch of borage as well, for courage.

When her tea had finished steeping, Tara sat down on the cool leather couch facing the sliding glass doors, her hands wrapped around her mug, and thought about her dream.

It had been more than just a nightmare. That much she knew. The dream had the same foretelling quality of the first time she'd dreamed of the Riprap man.

Tara now knew that the Riprap man had survived his battle with the river god. Had he killed Mulinohana? Was that why Tara hadn't been able to call on the river god? Had the Riprap man bound the spirit of the river? Or had the pair of them come to a new agreement?

She had no answers, only more questions. Why was the Riprap man coming for her now? Why hadn't he started his attack the next day?

With a start, Tara realized that the fall equinox was six days away.

Last time, she'd started dreaming about the Riprap man a week before the solstice.

He was coming for her again, either on the night of the equinox, or more likely, the night after.

Why hadn't he come for her friends before now? It was why the other witches didn't want anything to do with her. The few witches who had escaped him before her had been ostracized because the Riprap man had cursed them. The bad luck of the witch who had survived eddied out around her, affecting every other witch they came in contact with.

The dream had let her know that the Riprap man didn't care about her friends, or the rest of her coven.

He was focused on her.

The Riprap man was yet again coming for her soul.

And she didn't have any idea how to escape this time.

TWO

Wilson Evermore, Witch Hunter and Chief Magician, 1901

TARA HAD MANAGED to get back to sleep after she'd finished her tea, much to her surprise. Though her dreams didn't contain any more hauntings, she still woke up tired.

She wasn't surprised to find a note from Kyle on the kitchen counter, asking what was wrong. He'd woken up while she was having her tea, and so knew that something was up.

What could she tell him, though? *The Riprap man comes for me next Wednesday, on the equinox?* While that might be accurate, it seemed a bit melodramatic. She finally settled on texting him, *Bad dream. Talk more later.*

And she would talk with him. He'd been there to take care of her, watch over her physical body while her soul had battled the Riprap man. She'd never wanted to have to do that again. It had taken her time to recover, as if she'd gone through a long illness. Sometimes she still felt as though her soul was no longer fully attached to her body.

Tara went through her usual morning routine, a slow roll into the morning as she liked to call it. It wasn't that she couldn't wake up first thing. She just preferred to take her time rising out of the unconscious to discover her conscious self.

She made herself a salad for breakfast, clipping basil, marjoram, and sorrel from the long row of pots that Kyle let her keep on his balcony. To that, she added pine nuts, bacon, and a poached egg, breaking the yolk so it warmed up the greens and made the dressing creamy. Only after she finished eating did she make herself tea. That morning, she chose a bright green tea, adding strawberries, ginger, and a touch of cinnamon to liven up her senses, along with a touch of buckwheat honey.

When her tea had finished steeping, Tara went out and sat on the uncomfortable metal chairs that Kyle had out on his balcony. His view showed the courtyard of the condo, a very small green area six stories below, but mostly just the buildings on the other side. She *missed* her river view, even if the river was perilous for her. Water was still her element.

Kyle's place had been wonderful. A great port for her to rest in while she had tried to get her life together.

But it was really past time for her to get moving. Just because that asshole—the Riprap man—was haunting her again didn't mean she couldn't start moving forward.

She realized as she sipped her tea that she'd been in a holding pattern, afraid of exactly what had happened, that the Riprap man would come back to haunt her.

Now that she knew he was there, coming for her again, it was time for her to get on with her life. She wasn't sure why it worked that way, but it appeared to.

How was she going to defeat him? This wasn't like the previous times that he'd taken a witch's soul. Did he still think that he needed to bind her to the Burnside Bridge? The bridge had already been reopened, without a witch's soul. Was this just for revenge? Or was there some other reason he was stalking her again?

Tara had too many questions. She could ask Aaloka, though she wasn't sure she could trust her former teacher's answers. She could also talk with Miss Lucy, who at least wouldn't lie to her.

And who else did she want to recruit for a coven? *Her* coven, though it was still uncomfortable for her to think along those lines.

Richard, though he couldn't stand in any of the circles. Or could he? Would having someone mundane spoil the magic of the circle? Did he have to have power? Was he even interested? Did she want to invite him when there was potential danger?

Kyle, who wouldn't abandon her. Tara had never had such a good friend before. She now had a much better idea of what she wanted in a partner—some of Kyle's better tendencies, as well as some of Richard's.

Ginny—if Tara could find her again.

That left two more for Tara to find. Possibly before the equinox. How did one find disenfranchised witches? Advertise on Meetup? Or should she look at a dating site?

Tara suddenly felt as overwhelmed as when she'd tried looking for work. There were too many options, too many things she didn't know. Too many pieces she had to piece together.

She knew what would settle her the best: a long swim, down at the Y. It was why the river spirit had spared her. He'd grown tired of the Riprap man and wanted someone like her to honor him. She had an affinity for the water, unlike the Riprap man.

How could Tara move forward? How could she beat him? What was she going to do with the rest of her life?

She needed a direction, something more to live for, more than ever.

But what?

TARA MET with Aaloka at their usual spot, Urban Tea, northwest of downtown in the neighborhood called *Uptown*, close to the vegan bakery that Aaloka liked to visit. The shop made their own flavored teas, and had one hundred and fifty different varieties. Tara had met Philip, the tea master, and the pair of them had geeked out over ingredients more than once.

That day, Tara had their Hi-Berry tea, a mixture of hibiscus, raspberry, and ginger. She might have added a touch of rose hips, to flatten it out some, but Philip wasn't there for her to make the suggestion to.

The tea shop was crowded for a Friday, students lounging at tables with headphones on and books scattered across their tables, taking up as much space as they could without being rude about it. The inside seating of the shop was always too dim for Tara, and she didn't really know how the students could read in such light. The pre-mixed teas were stacked in rows behind the counter, color-coded to indicate the type of tea.

Next to the teas stood three huge stainless steel containers that held the water the shop needed, each precisely kept at a different temperature, depending on the type of tea. Tara envied the shop's precision. Her electric tea pot had a thermostat in it so she could keep track of temperature; however, it wasn't that accurate.

Quiet indie pop played from the speakers, some band that Tara wouldn't recognize even if she tried. She just wasn't that hip. The smell of cranberry scones filled the space, the special of the day, served warm with clotted cream.

Tara had thought about applying to work at the tea shop, but she knew it would drive her crazy to have to serve someone else's teas. She would have always been wanting to add or subtract ingredients, to serve people the exact perfect tea that they were craving, even if they didn't know it.

In her ideal world, Tara would have enough money to open up her own tea shop. She wouldn't have prepared teas, or there might be a few standards. But for the most part, it would be bespoke tea, each cup hand crafted for that individual's needs.

However, she wasn't sure that would fly, even in hipster Portland.

Tara took her cup outside to sit at one of the sidewalk tables while she waited for Aaloka. A dingy white umbrella held off most of the bright sunlight beating down from the clear blue sky. Young people marched up and down on the sidewalk, coming back from school, heading off to their second or third job.

Damn it. Everyone was working but her. Why hadn't she found something yet?

Aaloka was late, as usual. As she'd once told Tara, she had been born with a loose relationship with time. But at least she wasn't too late this time, merely fifteen minutes. Tara had only just finished her first cup and had started contemplating her second.

"Tara! So good to see you!" Aaloka said as she came rushing forward, taking Tara's hands and squeezing them tightly.

Aaloka always greeted Tara that way. Was she at one point expecting that Tara wouldn't be there?

"Good to see you, too," Tara said.

Though Aaloka was petite, maybe standing only five feet tall, her personality always seemed so huge to Tara. Aaloka wore a beautiful matching lavender skirt and jacket, the color perfectly setting off her dark skin and black hair. While Aaloka had been raised in Sri Lanka, she only tended to wear saris for formal occasions.

Tara sat and waited while Aaloka went to go get her drink, though she returned with one of the scones for them to share.

Tara didn't really eat a lot of grain, which Aaloka knew. However, the other woman never seemed to remember.

"So tell me what has you so gloomy," Aaloka declared after portioning off the scone, handing Tara a tiny piece as requested.

Tara had debated what she would say to her former teacher all afternoon.

The moment was now.

"The Riprap man is back," Tara said.

Aaloka's dark eyes grew huge. "Really?" she asked, sounding breathless.

Tara nodded. "Yes. Seems his new date for taking my soul is the equinox, next week."

"Oh. Oh!" Aaloka said. "I'd thought—hoped—that he would let you be. That he'd let *us* be."

"Has he started bothering the other witches in the coven?" Tara asked. Surely someone would have said something. Or had he just started?

"Sheila claimed that he came to visit her in a dream last night, warning her against helping you," Aaloka admitted. "I…I hadn't believed her."

"What? Why?" Tara asked, confused. Aaloka would never stand up to Sheila, the head of her former coven. Though Aaloka had been angry at Sheila for cheating Tara of her proper place, she hadn't quit the coven. In the end, only Kyle had quit, along with Tara.

"Sheila says a lot of things," Aaloka said quietly. "Things that I know are not true." She shrugged. "I know you're a better person than who she claims you are. It is part of why we meet every week. So that I can see you, see the real you, not the boogieman that Sheila has made you into."

Tara opened her mouth then shut it closed again, her teeth landing together so hard they clicked. What was Sheila saying? And why would Aaloka just listen, and not actually say anything?

"Do I have a target on my back?" Tara asked, not bothering to hide the anger in her voice. "Are the other witches in the coven coming for me? As well as the damned Riprap man?"

"Shh, no, don't be silly," Aaloka said, glancing around.

Tara fumed. "Then what are the other witches going to do? Is Sheila going to suggest that I have an *accident* or something? That whatever bad luck falls my way is well deserved?"

Aaloka kept her lips pressed together tightly for a moment, all the blood leaving the pink flesh, before she finally spoke. "Sheila would never do something as foolish as that. You may not believe me, but I wouldn't allow such a thing. You left the coven, cut your ties. The Riprap man won't cause us harm as a way to pressure you."

"But he will try to hurt those around me," Tara said. "Or at least, that's always been his pattern."

"Since the first witches that he's claimed, yes. He has turned sister against sister," Aaloka admitted.

"When did he take his first witch?" Tara asked.

"We believe 1900 or so," Aaloka said. "It's never been that many witches. Just one here or there."

"Coinciding with the repair or rebuilding of any of the bridges," Tara supplied.

"Yes," Aaloka said. "I've been trying to learn about him, to look at the old texts, so that I could tell you. If he came back."

Tara thought for a moment. What the hell. "I'm forming my own coven," she said. "To fight him."

Aaloka blinked at her. "Really? Do you think that's wise?"

Tara shrugged. "He hasn't come after anyone else I knew. I don't believe he'll come after the others. He's changed. The battle with the river god left him weakened."

"And you promised to honor the river spirit with rose petals on the equinox, right?" Aaloka said.

Tara nodded, surprised that her old teacher had remembered. "That's correct."

"It's a trap," Aaloka announced suddenly.

"What?" Tara asked, confused.

"You can't go anywhere near the water," Aaloka said. "The further away from it, the better."

"You think I should run away? That I could run away this time?" Tara said. That hadn't even occurred to her, quite frankly.

"Yes," Aaloka said. "Run far and fast. It's no longer 1900. You have options, and can get away. He only has power here."

"But will he come after the others if I do leave?" Tara said. She could go and visit her parents back in Wisconsin for a while...

"I don't know," Aaloka said. She reached across the table and squeezed Tara's hand tightly. "I just know that in my heart, I wish you safely gone."

Tara nodded, understanding her former teacher's sentiment.

Even after Aaloka had left, Tara stayed sitting at the table, the afternoon throwing long, dark shadows along the street. People rushed along the sidewalk, scurrying to their homes and safe corners. The air had changed, and now smelled of a coming storm.

Or maybe that was just Tara being haunted again.

Should she go? Would everyone be safer if she did?

And if she did leave, could she ever come back?

<hr>

TARA HAD a long talk with Kyle that night over dinner, telling him everything: the dream, her conversation with Aaloka, thinking about a coven as well as considering leaving Portland.

Kyle had changed into his weekend clothes, a black Hawaiian style shirt with bright yellow sunflowers scattered across it, jeans, and bare feet. He wouldn't start wearing long sleeved shirts until it had grown much colder. The air still carried the promise of rain, and the temperature had dropped considerably.

They'd finished eating (leftover meatloaf from Tuesday with a huge salad) and now sat drinking their special brews of tea. Tara had mixed up a large batch of ingredients for Kyle so he could always make his own tea, with licorice, mint, chicory, and roasted dandelion roots—a hearty brew that was a good substitute for coffee in the evenings. She preferred something lighter and sweeter, as well as calming, and so had chamomile, peppermint, wintergreen, cacao nibs, and dried apple bits, with a splash of homemade vanilla.

They sat together on the leather couch, the material warming slowly. They'd lowered the lights in the living room so they could see outside, watch the clouds gathering.

It was cozy, but not. Tara was always careful to keep a formal distance between her and Kyle. He'd never been comfortable with physical touch—he'd been gang raped in his youth and still had both physical and psychological scars.

"I think," Kyle started after sitting in silence for some time, "that leaving doesn't make much sense. Since the Riprap man probably doesn't want your soul for a bridge, it doesn't matter where you are. He's a supernatural being. He can probably find you wherever you go."

Tara had come to the same conclusion earlier. "I am still going to talk to my mom about them getting me a ticket to go see them," she said. It had become so much more important, suddenly.

"That's a good idea," Kyle said. "Family's important," he added, throwing her a smile.

Tara gave him warm smile in return. She didn't know much about Kyle's parents, except that they lived somewhere on the east coast and didn't necessarily approve of their son's lifestyle. Kyle had talked about the importance of found family more than once.

She felt blessed that he considered her part of it.

"As for creating your own coven, you know I think that's a good idea," he said. "Talk with Ginny tomorrow. And with Richard. Let's see if we can gather together on the night of the equinox."

Tara snorted at him. "No pressure, right?"

Kyle shrugged. "I may, *may*, have another being that I'd like to suggest for a spot. I need to contact them first."

Tara was intrigued by his word choice. *Being*, not *person*.

Though Tara had been taught by her mentors that there were other beings of power, not necessarily human, she'd never been introduced to one. She'd always assumed it was because she wasn't powerful enough to handle such a being if they took a disliking to her.

Still, Tara knew better than to question Kyle. He wouldn't say anything until he was damned good and ready.

"I'm having dinner with Richard tomorrow night," Tara said eventually. Hopefully he wouldn't be too freaked out by her and her magic that he'd stop wanting to be her friend.

"He'll be fine," Kyle said, reading her worry.

"I hope so," Tara said. What would she do if she lost yet another friend? She still felt as though she'd lost too much already.

"Come," Kyle said, standing up. He actually held out a hand for her to take.

Tara did so, distrusting what her friend was up to.

"Let's do some magic," he said with a sly grin after he squeezed her hand and released it.

"Okay," Tara said slowly, though her heart leaped. Magic! She'd been practicing, but as Kyle had said to her earlier, she was a witch who preferred working with a coven, not being on her own.

Kyle led the way out to the balcony, stacking the chairs up and shoving the table to one side so they had more room.

"Won't the neighbors see us?" Tara asked, confused. She'd kept her practice indoors, though she preferred being outside.

In response, Kyle went inside, rooted around in one of the living room cupboards, then came out again, bearing three sachets that he carefully placed on the balcony railing. "For protection," he said, "distraction, and invisibility."

The small bags looked nothing like Tara's usual sachets. Instead of being made out of plain cotton, these were crafted out of black leather, blue silk, and a green-and-gold brocade. Each one was the size of a small dinner plate, though bulky, as if stuffed with herbs and other ingredients. She could smell the magic they contained, a dark sweet note that touched the roof of her mouth.

"Cool," Tara said, making a mental note to ask Kyle about the exact ingredients he'd used. Then she paused, thought for a moment. "Why didn't you tell me about these sooner?"

Kyle shrugged sheepishly. "I figured you could make your own. I know, I know, you don't think you're capable. But you're a lot stronger than you realize."

"I'm still only a witch of the first circle, of thought," Tara reminded him.

"And that's something we're going to have to fix," he said. "You and I both know that you're worthy of the second circle."

"But we don't have a meditation circle," Tara said, confused. Both Miss Lucy's coven as well as Sheila's coven had meditation circles that an initiate had to travel through in order to move within, tests to pass to go from one circle to the next.

"There are other ways to advance," Kyle said. "Do you trust me?"

Tara stood up straighter. "I do," she said. "With my life, my soul, and all my magic."

The smile that Kyle gave her brightened up the dark porch. "Then let's begin."

KYLE LED THE STARTING PRAYERS, as this was his place and his circle. Tara listened more closely than she usually did, knowing that someday, possibly sooner rather than later, she was going to be the one leading the circle.

They stood in the center of the darkened balcony, protected from curious or spying eyes by Kyle's magic and his sachets. They both stood barefoot: Even though they stood on concrete rather than dirt, Kyle insisted that they needed to feel the earth with their bare skin. Their hands were linked, but with only a single finger, as Kyle still didn't like being touched more than necessary.

"We thank the goddess Brigid, defender of the earth, for allowing us this space and time on Her plane," Kyle intoned.

Gone was the goofy guy who'd teased her about purposefully cutting up too many vegetables for dinner so that he'd be forced to eat the extras. The person who stood in front of her was a powerful orator with a presence that easily filled the small balcony. He would have made an impressive lawyer, appealing to the jury on behalf of his client.

Maybe that was part of why he worked behind the scenes—so that he wouldn't have to give persuasive arguments for clients he didn't believe in.

Even his bright Hawaiian shirt looked more formal, the yellow flowers like globes of armor across his chest.

Kyle continued. "We ask the god Samil, warrior for the people, to watch over us in the rightness of our deeds. May the old mother moon send her light and knowledge, for Hayvu and Eural to carry their justice to us on their winds. Finally, may Areebin, the protector of souls, guide us fairly to the summer lands, but only in the fairness of time."

Then Kyle started one of the older hymns that Tara had learned, about the fullness of time and the turning of the seasons. It was appropriate for the time of year, when summer still hadn't given up, though fall was bearing down on them hard.

Tara was pleased with how nicely her alto voice went with Kyle's lighter baritone. She'd expected him to be a bass, but was surprised to find that his voice, while mid-tone, was rich.

When they'd finished, Tara looked expectantly at Kyle, unsure what he had in mind.

From one of the back pockets of his jeans, Kyle fished out a tiny glass bottle. It was maybe two inches long, with an elaborate silver filigreed stopper that was almost as big as the bottle. Kyle bent over and placed it on the floor between them.

Even from where she was standing, Tara felt the power of the small bottle. It wasn't any bigger than her palm, but it bristled with energy. She nearly jumped when a single light blinked off and on, inside it, as though it had captured a tiny firefly.

More lights joined the first, yellowish and each as small as a pea. They seemed agitated.

"Where did you get this?" Tara asked, impressed. "And how did you hide it?"

Kyle grinned at her. "That cupboard is protected," he said simply. "You've never even been curious about what it contained."

Tara nodded, her eyes wide. "That's true. You enspelled it? Wow."

Kyle shrugged. "Mainly just made it a sacred space for my belongings. It kind of protects itself."

"I don't understand," Tara said. It was awfully difficult to permanently enchant anything. The spells had to be renewed often. Even if the item was handcrafted with magic, it still wouldn't "hold" the power channeled into it.

"Sacred spaces can be despoiled," Kyle said seriously. "But it takes effort. First you have to gain access. A space that's been dedicated to a specific person or group can gain an awareness, and provide some level of protection for itself."

"Okay," Tara said. She'd never even heard of such a thing. Though now that she thought about it, she had always wondered about the backyard that contained the meditation maze that the witches walked when moving from one circle to the next. The space had always felt isolated, cut off from the rest of the city. Maybe that was its way of protecting itself.

She looked back down at the glass bottle that still sparked between them. "What are we supposed to do with that?" she asked.

"That's a captured wind," Kyle said with a grin. "Oh, don't worry. It's tiny. But for your test to see if you can pass within, to the circle of air, let's see if you can tame this wind."

Tara gasped. "But how can you…how did you…what?"

"You're not the only one with powers," Kyle told her sternly. "And I've been preparing for this, for when you were ready to start fully practicing again."

Tara shivered. Kyle was right. Part of why she hadn't been moving forward was because her magic still felt raw, as if all the skin had been scraped off. She'd needed time to heal before she could start practicing again.

"Are you sure I'm ready?" Tara had to ask. Because she wasn't.

Kyle shrugged. "If you are ready, this will be a breeze, no pun intended. If you aren't ready, we can wait and try again in a few weeks."

Tara nodded. She understood why he was doing this. It would give her a great deal of confidence if she could do this. And it wouldn't completely break her if she couldn't.

"All right," Tara said after taking a few deep breaths. She readied her prayers and focused her powers, calling on the winds to protect her, as well as reaching deep inside herself for her own fire. "Let's do this."

"Blessed be," Kyle said, the words ringing out as if they formed a circle of protection around her.

"Blessed be," Tara acknowledged. She put the heels of her hands together, the fingers outstretched, as if she was an anime character, ready to catch a fireball.

Kyle crouched down and put one hand on the bottle, one hand on the stopper. Then he looked back up at her.

When Tara nodded, he slowly pulled the stopper up.

With a loud *pop*, the stopper came loose.

And the winds poured out.

Tara tensed as the winds flowed up, past her, seeking a way off the closed balcony. But Kyle had enfolded the space, so nothing could escape. She jerked her hands back when stinging lightning tickled her palms. Anger rose, as did the familiar exhaustion.

She wasn't ready for this. She would never be ready for this. Hadn't she already failed before? Must she fail so publicly again?

With an abrupt shake of her head, Tara pushed the negative thoughts away. Where had that come from? It had *not* been her fault that she'd failed the first circle walk.

Winds brushed the back of her neck, stirring her short ponytail. Tara forced her shoulders down as she followed the circling winds. They pushed, cackling, to the far corner, then back again, like a puppy racing to all the interesting parts of a room, then coming back to share *everything*.

They weren't trying to escape, weren't desperate or angry. Not like she'd expected them to be.

In fact, if Tara was any judge, she'd say that the winds wanted to *play*.

Tara paused. When was the last time she'd played?

With a jerk of her hand, Tara freed her hair from its usual ponytail. The winds picked up the strands immediately, tugging on them. She rolled her head, then stretched her arms out. Winds raced across her chest, to her fingers and back, again, like a puppy nosing her skin, learning all her different smells.

When Tara brought her arms down slowly, she brought the winds with her, until she was holding a ball of joyous frolicking energy, like a wiggling dog that was trying to lick her face while getting all its skin scratched at the same time.

The winds raced around and around the balcony when she let them go. Tara laughed at Kyle's grin.

So how to tame them?

Tara blew out a breath, then she blew again, aiming upward.

The wind rushed forward, trying to tangle with Tara's breath.

Tara sucked in abruptly as the wind brushed against her face in its haste, taking deep inside of her a bit of the wind. It tasted cold, like

April rains, with a hint of lavender thrown in. Or maybe that was purple heather.

Tara raised up her arms and started circling her hands in front of her, like she was spinning two large disks. The winds drew closer again, following her movements, twirling themselves around and around, like two mini cyclones.

After a few more moments of dancing with the winds, Tara spread her hands up and down, scooping up the bottom of the wind and pushing it together, compressing it like a spongy ball. It was the first time she'd felt some resistance—the wind didn't want to be tamed. But it settled down after a few moments, compressing down into a cackling sphere, about the size of a basketball, in between her hands.

Tara caressed the ball, calming it, before she looked up at Kyle. "Now what?" she asked.

Kyle snorted at her. "I have no idea. I've never seen someone work with the wind like that before. Certainly not someone who is merely first level. Winds aren't that friendly with me. Maybe you should tell me what's next."

Tara blinked at him. What was he talking about? Surely everyone managed balls of wind like this.

"Uhm," Tara said, glancing down at the ball she still held. The wind didn't like being compressed like this for long. She'd have to direct it or release it, soon.

"Let it hunt," Tara said after a moment. "I need to find Ginny, right? So why not see if the wind will hunt for me."

"Okay," Kyle said slowly, as if he'd never heard of such a thing. He picked up the middle charm from the balcony.

Tara could tell where the hole had opened, like an iris of gray across a darker black shade. She held the image of Ginny as firmly as she could in her head before she tossed the ball of wind through the hole. "Go find her," she commanded.

It leaped out of her hands, elongating into a sleek black greyhound as it flowed away, out into the night.

Tara glanced at Kyle, curious if he'd just seen the wind change into a dog or not. From the way his eyebrows rested at the top of his forehead, she figured he had.

"Will it find Ginny?" Kyle asked.

Tara shrugged. "It will try. I think."

Kyle shook his head, then held out his hands.

Curious, Tara took them, holding on with just pinkies, as usual.

"I hereby acknowledge that you have passed within, and proclaim you a full witch of the second circle, the circle of air," Kyle announced.

A shiver of magic passed between them, electricity tickling Tara's palms again. She gasped, unsure of what spell Kyle had just done.

But she felt it. Felt the difference. Something inside of her was now *free* to work with the wind and the air, as if she'd been blocked before and had never realized it, like looking through a dirty window that was suddenly clean.

"Wow," Tara said.

Kyle nodded. "I wasn't sure it would work," he admitted. "But I thought it was worth trying. You *should* have been allowed to pass the first time. You were more than ready."

"Can you teach me that?" Tara said, "How to acknowledge a new witch?"

"I can," Kyle said solemnly. "Realize, though, that you can only pass someone within who is at a lower level than yourself. Plus, normally, I'd warn you that not all witches have the ability. They need to supplement with potions and such. But I think you won't have a problem."

Tara shrugged, uncomfortable with the praise. "I might," she said.

Kyle snorted at her. "And now, I think it's time for a good bottle of wine and some bad 1970s sitcoms. You game?"

"Absolutely!" Tara said, happy to put aside the magic for a while, to recover in the snark and goofiness of a good friend.

And Kyle never said anything, even though Tara found her attention drawn again and again to the windows filled with night and the occasional breeze.

THREE

I may have miscalculated. There appear to be two classes of witches: those who are called 'schooled witches' who travel within, going from one circle of power to the next, and the 'hedgewitches' who have natural magic. The latter are generally not associated with a coven, but work on their own. While frequently an entire coven will attempt to fight me, they learn quickly to turn against the one I've chosen rather than battle the misfortune I bring to them. I had considered that it might be easier to go after one of the singular witches instead. However, their magic is too dissimilar to mine. We appear to be at a standstill. And the deadline for completion of the next bridge is approaching. I need to either finish her off, or choose another. And quickly.

Wilson Evermore, Chief Magician and Protector of Portland, 1905

CLOUDS and gray skies greeted Tara the next morning. She woke restless, needing to move from sleep to waking faster than usual, and finished with her morning tea just as Kyle came back from his run instead of just starting breakfast.

Tara nodded over her shoulder at him but didn't try to say anything. It was one of the reasons why she needed to find someplace else to live. While Kyle was lovely, and certainly supportive of her, there was a reason why he lived alone, and she always had flatmates, people she could talk with whenever they came into the room.

Tara made a second cup of tea—this time no caffeine, just rooibos, spearmint, lavender and lemon verbena, a bright, sweet mix—and was quietly sipping it when Kyle came out to join her. She had on jeans, thick socks, a plain red T-shirt, with an oversized soft, gray wool shirt over it. She'd stolen the baggy shirt from her dad. It felt good to dig into her suitcases and pull out a few of her warmer pieces. The summer had been weird, long, and hot.

Over his jeans, Kyle wore a University of Washington gray sweatshirt, something he'd picked up when he'd gone to law school there. He'd mentioned once that while he had the grades to go to one of the more prestigious law schools on the east coast, he didn't want to be that close to his family. He carried his own coffee mug.

Tara wished yet again that coffee tasted as good as it smelled, but it never did.

"You're up early," Kyle commented after he'd sat down and they'd enjoyed a moment of quiet between them.

"Restless," Tara admitted.

"Bad dreams?" Kyle asked. He didn't look over at her, but kept his gaze out on the horizon, as if he could see beyond the ugly block of condos directly across the courtyard from them.

"No," Tara said. "Just woke up and needed to move. Considered going on your run with you."

That got Tara a look. "Really?"

She grinned at him. "Just a brief moment of insanity," she assured him.

Tara didn't like to run. She much preferred to swim and do yoga. Though she had considered doing more physical activities, as she was getting older and it seemed it took more to keep herself in good shape.

"Good," Kyle said. "Or else I would have wondered if the Riprap man had already taken your soul and replaced it with someone else's."

"Yeah," Tara acknowledged. She still didn't have any idea how she was going to fight the Riprap man. At least last time she'd been working toward the next level of witchcraft, and so had a plan. Even if it had backfired.

This time, she really didn't have a clue, beyond trying to form her own coven.

"Feel different this morning?" Kyle asked after a few more moments of comfortable silence.

Tara paused, probing. "I don't feel stronger," she said. "My power didn't grow with the ceremony last night. I still feel clearer, though. As if all the cobwebs have been brushed away."

Kyle nodded. He appeared to be choosing his words carefully. "I wasn't sure what you'd feel, which is why I didn't warn you about anything. I can only tell you what I was told, and how I felt."

Tara smiled at him, encouraging him to speak. It was a different form of intimacy, to share this sort of knowledge, and Kyle still had difficulty with that.

"For me, I felt as though the line of power coming from my core had suddenly doubled, going from being a single wire to being two. I did feel much stronger, as do most. My guess is that you already had the power, you should have been passed within at the original ceremony. All I did was clear the path for you."

He paused, taking a sip of his coffee, before he continued. "My other assumption is that you're probably already capable of passing further inward. That you don't need to do a lot of work before you pass into the circle of fire."

"Really?" Tara asked, surprised. "But I don't know all the lore for that level yet!"

Kyle snorted. "Not sure you need it," he said. "I still think you're a hedgewitch, one who works with elements directly instead of herbs and knowledge. Just your power should be enough."

"I'll think about it," Tara said. It would give her a focus, to start studying again. "After the equinox," she added. She didn't want to have to split her attention again, like she had the last time, working so hard to pass a test that was snatched out from under her at the last moment.

"All right," Kyle said slowly. He paused again before he asked, "So what is the plan today?"

"I'm going to the Saturday market, to see if I can find Ginny," Tara said.

"Want some company?" Kyle said.

"That would be awesome," Tara said. She never assumed that he would want to go anywhere with her; he still had his own life and friends, apart from her.

"Then let's go," Kyle said.

Before Tara could spring up from her seat, he added, "After I finish my coffee."

With an exaggerated sigh, Tara sat back in her chair, pouting. She really did feel antsy, wanting to go.

"Have you heard from that tamed wind of yours?" Kyle asked after a moment.

"No," Tara said. "Honestly, it's felt as if the wind almost returned a few times. But then it would go chasing off after a new scent again. It's still a puppy, and not trained."

"I see," Kyle said. He looked at her and shrugged. "I have no experience with this whatsoever. You're kind of on your own when it comes to having a tame wind who's kind of like a dog."

"I don't know either," Tara said. She'd planned on asking Richard later that evening, when she went out to dinner with him. He'd respected her request to meet him alone, as Tara hadn't wanted to have to try to explain all the witchcraft to yet another outsider. At least, not yet.

Finally, Kyle finished his coffee. Tara felt like a puppy herself who'd been promised a walk when he announced that he was ready.

Was this going to be her natural state from now on? Gods, she hoped not.

———

THE SMELL of mini-donuts drew Tara and Kyle forward. Tara tried not to eat that much grain or junk food; however, the scent of fried dough and cinnamon sugar was still mouthwatering.

Though the Saturday market had only just opened, people were already in line at the front booths. Late tourists? Or locals already shopping for both Halloween as well as Christmas?

Then Tara realized both booths sold coffee. Of course, there were lines.

Could she open up a tea shop here? What would be involved with that? What sort of permits would she have to get? Could she survive just being open on the weekends? And would a town like Portland support another tea shop?

All questions for tomorrow.

If that silly wind of hers had returned by now, she might have asked it to go searching for Ginny. Instead, Tara and Kyle walked down the brick street, peering at the booths first on one side, then the other. What sort of booth would Ginny be at? Tara assumed it would be smaller, not the shop with hundreds of angel candle holders, or the one with row after row of necklaces and trinkets. But more like the shop with all the paintings done by a single artist, or even the shop that sold hand-blown glass ornaments and offered free lessons.

What sort of glass could Tara make, if she managed to pass within to the circle of fire? Was that even possible? She'd have to remember to ask Kyle later.

After wandering up and down the aisles both on the outdoor part of the market (with separate booths) and the indoor part (covered and too crowded for both of them) Tara felt something tugging on her attention.

She stopped and turned.

Out of the corner of her eye, Tara saw a black shape—no, a black greyhound, long and thin—glancing over his shoulder at her, then racing away, toward the outside booths.

"This way," Tara said, walking quickly in that direction.

Kyle followed without a word.

Tara wove herself through the crowds, which now all seemed to be coming from the direction she wanted to go in, like a salmon swimming upstream. It was odd. As soon as she saw a clear path, more people would block her way.

Frustrated after only taking a few steps, only to be forced to turn to the side again, Tara called up a spark of fire. It wasn't enough to set her skin glowing. People weren't suddenly going to brush against her and catch on fire, or even feel the heat.

The crowds now parted for her. The area was still overly full (and where had all those people come from?). However, Tara made forward progress.

Out in the open, past the covered area, Tara saw the dog again. He appeared to be looking for her.

There was no question that it was the same dog from last night, her personal wind, taken animal shape.

However, she would also swear that he'd doubled in size since the previous night. While he was still a puppy and had a young face, his body had grown considerably, and he now came up to her knee. Black fur had grown richer, making him seem more like a shadow. His dark eyes gazed at her with considerable intelligence. His ears were flopped down, but rose up to fine points when he saw her again. He gave her a nod, then turned and raced away again.

"Did you see that?" Tara asked Kyle as he came up behind her.

"See what?" Kyle said. "See that dog? That tamed wind of yours? Yeah, I saw him."

He didn't sound pleased. Tara wasn't sure why. "I bet he's found Ginny," Tara said defensively.

"I'm sure of it." Kyle pressed his lips together as if to prevent himself from saying more.

Why was the dog making Kyle nervous? Tara was going to have to ask about that later. "Come on," she said, walking forward.

Kyle stayed a few feet back, behind Tara, and to her right. Why wasn't he walking beside her?

It took Tara a few steps to realize that Kyle was in a defensive position. If they were facing a strong witch, he wouldn't be blasted first thing. No, just Tara would. While anyone trying to sneak up on her would be facing him.

Tara squared her shoulders and reached for the sachet in her pocket. She focused on herbs to help her see clearly, such as red raspberry, fennel, and ginko, as well as cloves and nettle for protection. She squeezed the sachet, willing the power of the herbs to aid her.

There. The crowds in front of her finally parted. Sitting at a small table, not even a proper booth, Tara caught a glimpse of bright red hair. Beside her sat another woman with dark brown hair.

This time, Tara would not be deterred. She called up more of her fire, making herself a force that people unconsciously turned away from, before she marched forward.

The table was small, barely big enough for the two chairs behind it. On the right side stood rows of homemade soaps, with beautiful swirling colors through the bars, each wrapped in a hand-labeled tag. The other side of the table had half a dozen mason jars filled with various dried herbs, like spearmint, oregano, sage, thyme, lemon balm, and rose hips.

Ginny looked up as if she faced her doom. The other girl leaned back, making it clear that this wasn't her fight.

"Look, I ain't bothering ye," Ginny said, exasperated. "Why can't you jist leave us alone?"

Tara stopped, bewildered. "I'm sorry?" she said. "I don't understand. I was looking for you so we could talk."

"Oh," Ginny said. "Ye aren't trying to order me out of yer territory?"

"What?" Tara said, shocked. "Territory? What are you talking about?"

"Some *people* who are 'schooled' don't like us who are home taught," Ginny said, sticking her chin up defiantly.

It took Tara a moment to translate what Ginny had said. Evidently some "schooled" witches didn't like hedgewitches.

She was going to have to ask Aaloka about that, as Kyle had never mentioned anything about some sort of feud between the various schools of witchcraft. Or possibly Miss Lucy, as her former mentor wouldn't lie to her, not ever.

"Though I'm 'schooled,' as it were, I've been told that I'm more like you," Tara said quietly.

Ginny nodded. "So that was your wee beastie following me this morning?"

Something cold suddenly struck Tara's left hand, as if a small fan had just turned on, then shut itself off again.

When Tara looked down, she saw the dog more clearly. It was as if he'd just stuck his nose into her palm, cold but not wet.

He looked up at her expectantly, as if waiting for a treat.

What sort of dog treats would a tamed wind find acceptable? Tara was going to have to figure that out. In the meanwhile, she met his eyes and smiled at him. "Good boy!" she said earnestly. "You did a really good job. Good boy."

Cautiously, Tara reached out to pet the dog. As her palm followed the contours of his head, the body solidified. She stroked the sleek, cool fur a few more times before turning back to Ginny.

"He's your first wind," Ginny said knowledgably. "Whatcha gonna name him?"

"Soot," Tara said immediately. She knew it wasn't the most imaginative name—that wasn't her forte. At least it was better than just calling him "dog," or "wind dog," which had been her first inclination.

"How did you know he was a wind? Or my first?" Tara asked.

"Ye schooled witches sure don't know a lot," Ginny said. She glanced at her silent companion, who shrugged. "I'm gonna take a break, and come back with more coffee," she announced.

That made her friend smile and nod.

"Come on," Ginny said, coming out from behind the table.

"Uhmmm," Tara said, turning toward Kyle.

He made a shooing motion with his hand. "You two talk. There will be time for introductions later."

"Thanks," Tara said.

Ginny looked between the pair of them before she turned and walked away. Tara quickly joined her. Soot followed her for a few steps, then melted into the crowd, following some scent or another.

"That your boyfriend?" Ginny asked.

"Who, Kyle? No," Tara said firmly. "He's my best friend. And also a schooled witch."

"Haven't seen a lot of guys in the circles," Ginny said.

"Only about a third in any coven are men," Tara said. "They aren't drawn to the craft like women are." She wasn't about to get into the long, involved arguments that she'd had with Kyle about the socialization of boys and why community building and working together with others had never appealed to men.

"Let me tell you a bit about myself," Tara said as they passed into the more formal areas of the market. "I quit my coven earlier this year because the leader cheated on one of my tests, so I couldn't pass. I had a supernatural creature hunting me, who's now come back. Kyle, my friend back there, thinks I'm a hedgewitch and that I need to form my own coven to fight the creature. With different witches in it, not just the schooled variety." Tara took a deep breath then blew it all out again. "I think that covers me. In a nutshell. How about you?"

Ginny snorted at her. "Quite a bit to just drop on someone, don't you think?" Then she held up her hand before Tara could apologize. "Sounds as though yer looking for help. And for members to join yer coven. Eh?"

"Yes. Exactly," Tara said. It wasn't the sort of conversation that she'd imagined having while walking through the crowds at the Saturday market.

Then again, no one appeared to be paying any attention to them. In fact, people kept turning away from the pair of them. It was as if Tara and Ginny walked together in their own separate bubble, apart.

Was she doing that? Or was Ginny?

"Tell me more about this supernatural critter of yers," Ginny said.

Tara told Ginny what she knew of the Riprap man, as well as the final battle, how he'd had to fight the river spirit and how it had changed him. "I don't know why he's coming after me now," Tara said. "Does he want to sacrifice me to a bridge? Is it revenge? Or is this part of a new deal with the river spirit?"

Ginny leaned over and sniffed Tara, then paused for a moment. "Yer a water creature, right?" Ginny said as she started walking forward again.

"I am," Tara said. "Can you smell the water?"

"The chlorine," Ginny admitted. "Ye go to the pool instead of to the beach."

"Ah," Tara said. "And you?" she asked, wondering if that was appropriate or not.

But Ginny didn't bristle at her. "Mostly winds and air," she said as she led them to the back of a long line of customers waiting for their caffeine fix. "Had to let the lot of 'em go when I came across the pond. They wouldn't aben happy 'ere."

"I see," Tara said, though she didn't. Evidently, Soot was a local wind. Good to know.

Would Tara be able to "tame" a water…source? A spring? A river? Or just an element? Like maybe a glass of water? Or a full water bottle? She had no idea.

"I was surprised to see yer wind come sniffing around this morning," Ginny told her confidently. "The schooled witches have lost all the old spells. Oh, it ain't that they're weak. Just got different strengths."

"Can you teach me?" Tara asked. They stepped forward. The line was moving much more swiftly than Tara had expected. Then she studied the people in line in front of them. Not all of them, but a few appeared to be suddenly called away, either by friends, or as if they'd just decided not to get coffee but maybe a donut instead, the winds carrying the sweet scent to them.

It took Tara a moment to realize this was Ginny's doing. Her winds were culling the people in line.

Clever. Tara was going to have to learn how to do that. Or would she be able to, given that her element was actually water and not air?

"Don't know what I could teach ye," Ginny said. "There's not a lot of formal teaching, ye know. Spells I do, you can't repeat. Different powers. Different people. It's why the schooled witches think they're so much better. Superior, like."

Tara could see that. It was the spirit of the modern age, to be able to repeat something reliably. To make it science, and not, well, witchcraft.

They got to the head of the line. Ginny ordered two large mochas with extra whipped cream, then looked expectantly at Tara.

Tara tried not to appear grudgingly as she pulled out her bank card. But she supposed it was fair, as she was trying to recruit the other woman.

"Don't you want any?" Ginny asked as they went to join the line for picking up their orders.

Tara couldn't help but shudder. "I've tried. But it never tastes as good as it smells, you know? I'd end up adding chocolate and sugar and everything else to it, just to cover the taste." She shrugged. "Would rather drink something that I actually liked. Like tea."

"Make your own?" Ginny said. At Tara's nod, Ginny added, "Whatcha have this morning?"

Tara recognized it as a sort of test. She detailed out the various ingredients of her first cup, starting with an Assam black tea base, then adding dried apple bits, dried ginger, and a few cocoa nibs to smooth it out.

"Huh," Ginny said as they started their walk back, cups in hand. "What about adding some marigold petals?"

Tara shook her head. "That would make it too bright," she said. "I like a darker tea for my first cup."

They discussed various teas and components all the way back to the booth. Tara recognized that they both were hungry to talk herbs with someone else who had the same level of knowledge, someone who they could each bounce ideas off of.

When they were in sight of the booth, Ginny stopped and looked over at Tara. "Now, I'd be daft to join ye and your coven. Ye know that, right? Ye got this creature after ye. The schooled witches don't care much for ye, and may be coming after ye at some point."

"I know," Tara said, swallowing down her disappointment. "But I didn't want to lie to you. Anyone who comes in has to understand the risk. Thank you for talking with me, anyway. And maybe we can go out for tea sometimes, and talk more about herbs and teas later?"

"Jist hold on," Ginny said. "I ain't done. What I was about to say was that me gran always told me to listen to me heart first. So I'll be joining ye and your fancy crew."

"Really?" Tara said, surprised. "Why? It is rather daft, you know."

Ginny grinned at her. "That's what me Gran would have said too.

But ye don't leave people in need. Not the ones you connected to." She paused, then continued. "Ye see how all the crowd ignores us?"

Tara nodded. "I figured that was something you were doing."

"Nope," Ginny said. "Tweren't me. Tweren't you, either. It's us."

"But how?" Tara asked, confused. Why didn't this sort of thing happen whenever she was talking with any other witch, like with Kyle?

"Don't know," Ginny said. "Just happens that way." She paused, then added, "Something that drives the schooled witches mad. Magic that just happens. No spell or fancy potion."

"I see," Tara said, nodding. Yes, that would make most of the witches she knew rather crazy.

No wonder the "schooled" witches didn't like the hedgewitches, if magic just happened that way. Or didn't, as it was uncontrollable.

They made plans to meet up again Monday evening, for Ginny to meet Kyle and maybe the other people that Tara had managed to recruit by that point.

"Thank you," Tara said just before she left. Kyle had texted her that he'd already walked back to the apartment.

Ginny gave her a sly grin. "Ye gave me a cause. Gran always said I needed one, or I'd just drift with me winds."

"You're welcome, then," Tara said.

Ginny nodded, then abruptly gave a sharp whistle.

About twenty feet away, a dark head popped out from between the crowds. Soot, looking at her expectantly.

"Ye'll have to learn how to do that yerself," Ginny said. "Git him to heel."

"I will," Tara said. "Thank you, again."

"Eh, off with ye. I got me work to do," Ginny said. With a final nod of her head, Ginny went back to the booth.

As Tara watched, more people were now blowing their way, Ginny attracting them.

Tara gave a sharp whistle and was pleased to see Soot walking directly toward her.

Good. Maybe training a wind wouldn't be that hard.

Tara's cheeks hurt from all the times she'd whistled for Soot. He only appeared to hear her and come about half the time. She stood out on Kyle's balcony, sending Soot to fetch things, like a stone she'd tossed from the balcony out into the courtyard below. She had the impression that he could fetch other things as well, but he hadn't managed to bring back the rose she'd asked for. She was more successful when she merely asked for leaves or petals. Still, he ignored her as often as he would come to her.

Was that how accurate a hedgewitch's magic was going to be? That anything she tried would only work about half of the time?

No wonder the schooled witches were so strict in their teachings. While it felt to Tara that their magic wasn't as powerful, it was at least reliable, if you used the right ingredients with the right spell.

Tara walked back into the condo, needing to get ready to go out to dinner with Richard that night. They were going to a hipster hamburger bar that she liked, a place with quiet corners where they could have a chat.

Kyle looked up from the book he was reading. He was sprawled out on the couch, comfortable, with bare feet, jeans, and just a T-shirt. He kept the temperature of the condo warmer than Tara liked, claiming that it was cold enough outside, he didn't need to wear sweaters inside as well.

"Getting ready for your meeting?" Kyle asked.

Tara nodded. "I was lucky with Ginny this morning," she said. "I just hope my luck continues."

"It will," Kyle said firmly. "It's the power of synchronicity. You have a need. The gods and goddesses will provide the people."

Tara smiled at that. Kyle didn't believe in the god he'd been raised with—particularly since that god wouldn't necessarily approve of him or his lifestyle. He did, however, have a small altar to the gods—Samil and Areebin, both protectors—in the corner that he sat in front of and meditated often.

Tara had always kept a very small altar in her bedroom, never out in the living room, as she'd always had roommates who weren't witches. She also didn't worship at her alter. Not exactly.

Unlike her former teacher Aaloka, Tara didn't have as strong a belief in the spirits that moved around them. Tara knew those spirits existed, felt as though she'd actually met wind and water spirits, as well as fire and earth.

Yet, it had never struck her as appropriate to worship them, but rather to honor the spirits. Most of the witches she knew only prayed to the spirits when in a circle.

Tara wasn't sure where she stood with all that. It was yet one more thing she needed to determine if she was going to choose her own path between the schooled witches and being a hedgewitch. Could she carve out a third road?

Tara changed into a clean green blouse and brushed her hair, pulling it back into her usual ponytail. Soot and the winds preferred it when her hair was loose so they could play with it, tug on it and tease her with it. But she wasn't going to need her winds tonight. She didn't bother with makeup, either. First off, it wasn't that sort of date. Second off, she rarely wore makeup anyway. She considered herself pretty enough with wide-spaced blue eyes and clear white skin that had a sprinkling of freckles from the summer sun

No, tonight was a perfectly mundane meeting with a perfectly mundane friend, just meeting for dinner.

A mundane who she was going to ask to join her coven.

Tara realized that she'd hide in her room for the rest of the night if she could rather than go and talk with Richard. She really didn't want to screw up his friendship. Like Kyle's friendship, it meant a lot to her.

The Riprap man was still hunting her, though. She knew that, even though he hadn't shown up again.

What did he want? How could she defeat him? And would asking Richard to be in her coven actually bring danger to him?

She still had too many questions. And only the faintest of ideas about where her path led.

Tara dug into her "wedgie" burger. The patty was part lamb, part beef, and all delicious, wrapped in a wedge of lettuce with bacon, guacamole, and a sharp cheddar cheese.

Heaven.

Richard was making good progress on his burger as well. He'd gotten a buffalo patty with an egg on it. They shared a basket of garlic-rosemary fries between them.

They'd arrived at the restaurant at the end of the dinner rush, so the tables around them were emptying out as they ate their dinner, the noise level decreasing to more comfortable levels. All the tables were orange plastic, with red plastic seats, but done in fall colors as opposed to bright and obnoxious. The music in the background was some sort of indie pop, a guy singing with a single guitar, so it was easy to ignore.

One of the nice things about the restaurant was that in addition to great burgers and fries, it also served beer, cider, and wine. Tara had a glass of the cucumber hibiscus cider that was as refreshing as tea but with a sweet kick to it, while Richard had a far too bitter triple-hopped beer.

After they'd finished devouring their burgers, they pushed their plates back simultaneously and leaned back.

"Oooof," Richard said as he reached for one of the last remaining fries. "That was good."

"It was," Tara said, nodding. She reached for her drink, trying to pick her words carefully. She had to admit that she just didn't want to say anything. More than a decade of silence was hard to overcome.

"So you said you wanted to see me about something important," Richard said gently, as if trying to break the ice.

Tara threw him a grateful smile. He really was a good guy. Goofy, with black hair that had a few more silver threads running through it than it used to, old-fashioned aviator thick-rimmed glasses hiding pretty hazel eyes, a broad forehead that sloped down to a pointed chin. He looked like the academic that he was, with a red-and-black checkered plaid flannel over the T-shirt that said, "Heisenberg may have slept here."

"I did want to talk with you," Tara said. She took a deep breath. "Look, there isn't any way to say this without just coming out and saying it." She paused again.

"You're pregnant?" Richard guessed. "And Kyle's the father?"

"No!" Tara said, glaring at him.

He grinned impishly.

"No and no," Tara said. She rolled her eyes at him. Richard knew that Kyle was gay, but he still teased her about living with another man. "Look. I'm just going to come out and say this." She sat up straighter, then turned in her seat to face him.

"I'm a witch," she announced.

Richard blinked. "Yeah, I know."

FOUR

Myths about witches frequently mention cats, especially black cats, as familiars. Yet the schooled witches never keep any animal companions. It turns out that the animal familiars appear to only be associated with the hedgewitches, and carry special powers, such as fire or wind. So while a hedgewitch may be alone, without a coven, she still has gathered her familiars to her, to protect and defend her. What she doesn't realize is that those beasts will be her downfall. I can draw those unnatural creatures to me, more easily than the witch can. She will not see the trap laid before her in her efforts to save her pets.

Wilson Evermore, Witch Hunter and Bridge Protector, 1904

"WHAT DO YOU MEAN, YOU KNOW?" Tara asked, surprised. She'd never told Richard. How had he guessed?

He looked at her, puzzled. "It was kind of obvious," he said. "You celebrate the seasons. You hang out with a group of other people late at night for no apparent reason other than to dance in the moonlight.

You know more about herbs and plants than anyone I've ever met, including several Ph.D. level botanists."

"Oh," Tara said slowly. "I guess that makes sense. But…I'm really a witch. I can do magic."

"Duh," Richard said, rolling his eyes at her.

"What?" Tara said, still shocked. "How did you…I don't get it."

With a grin, Richard said, "First off, Miss Lucy was your teacher at the time. If there's any woman I've ever met who I'd call a witch, it would be her."

Tara nodded. True, though Miss Lucy didn't look anything like a stereotypical witch with warts and a long nose, she still had a powerful aura that dispelled fools and weaklings.

"What else?" Tara asked. It couldn't have just been meeting Miss Lucy that made Richard think that Tara could perform magic.

"Next, you made tea for me. When we were dating. When I caught a cold."

Tara thought about it for a moment. She vaguely remembered him being sick once. She'd made tea for him other times as well, though. "What was magical about the tea I made?"

Richard sat and thought for a moment, his lips pressed together in a hard line. "I've never, *never*, had anything herbal or pharmaceutical that actually worked on one of my colds. But that tea basically cured me overnight."

"You might have had just a mild cold," Tara said. What had she put into it? She didn't remember.

"No," Richard said. "Every fall, since I was a kid, I'd catch a cold. I knew what its course was. I would turn into a snot factory for six days, then it would slowly taper off. But I wouldn't be well for ten days at a minimum. After drinking your tea, I was back on my feet after three. That had never happened to me before. Not ever."

"Okay," Tara said. "But why did you consider that magic? It might have been just the right herbs for you. No magic involved."

"Because I'd hoarded some of that batch, planning to use it the next year. However, it didn't work."

Before Tara could point out that maybe it was just the herbs had gone stale, Richard continued. "We weren't dating by that point, but you agreed to make me more tea. I watched you mix it up. The herbs jumped into your hand when you reached for them."

Tara frowned. She didn't think that actually happened. "You were sick," she said slowly. "Maybe you had a fever."

"That's what I thought at first. However, since we were no longer dating, you let me watch you more often. You were never in doubt about what to use because the herbs gave themselves to you. It was kinda freaky, but also, awesome."

"Huh," Tara said. She'd have to watch herself more carefully the next time she made a sachet or even tea. It wouldn't do for just anyone to look at her and know that she was a witch.

"So, was that it?" Richard asked with a cocky grin. "Was it national 'witch coming out day' or something?"

Tara sighed and shook her head. "I wish that was it. But I actually have a very serious question for you. You remember the research you did for me about London Bridges, last year?"

Richard instantly sobered. "I do. And the supposition that women died, or committed suicide, every time one of the bridges of Portland were either built or had major repair work done."

"There's a supernatural creature who binds the heart of a witch to the base of every bridge," Tara admitted.

"Really?" Richard said, his eyes taking on a certain intensity that Tara recognized from early in their relationship: She'd just awoken the research librarian, given him a mystery to unravel.

Woe to the ignorant.

"He's called the Riprap man," Tara said.

"Riprap—named after the boulders at the base of the footings of a bridge?" Richard guessed.

Tara nodded. "Yes. He sacrifices witches to the spirit of the river, supposedly so that the river won't destroy the bridge during the next flood."

"Ohhh," Richard said.

Tara could already see him forming his search parameters in order to investigate more.

A cold wet wind blew across the restaurant. Tara held up her hand before Richard could say anything more.

Cautiously, Tara looked around.

The Riprap man stared at her hungrily from across the now mostly empty room. He wore his human aspect, looking like an old-fashioned gentleman from the 1900s, with a brown wool vest, suit jacket, and pants. A black string tie was knotted around the collar of a brilliantly white shirt. He still had a bowler hat, though it was pushed back further onto the back of his head.

For the first time, the Riprap man's face appeared clear. He had pasty white skin and green eyes, a round face with high cheekbones, giving him more of a boyish look. His neck and chin were shaved clean of what probably would have been a sandy-blond beard.

He was disappointingly ordinary looking. Without the old-fashioned clothing, Tara wouldn't have given him a second look. And as it was one of the hipper parts of Portland, most of the other people in the neighborhood wouldn't notice him either.

The smell of wet ropes washed over Tara, overtaking the homey smells of frying meat and potatoes. She suddenly gulped at the air, feeling as though it had grown heavy with moisture, making it difficult to breathe.

Defiantly, Tara called up a light breeze around her, which allowed her to breathe more easily.

The Riprap man merely smiled at her, a cruel, predatory smile. The smile of a man certain that his target would never be able to escape.

Then he looked down.

Soot suddenly stood beside him, looking up at him warily.

The Riprap man reached out and petted the dog's head as if it were the most natural thing in the world.

Without giving Tara another look, the Riprap man turned and headed for the door.

Soot stayed right at his heels.

Tara whistled abruptly, hoping that Soot would hear her, that whatever spell the Riprap man had cast on the wind would break easily.

Both the dog and the man disappeared before they reached the door.

Tara shuddered. Did the Riprap man now have her tamed wind? Was he going to turn Soot against Tara? She had no idea.

"What just happened?" Richard asked quietly. "You were watching something I couldn't see."

Tara gulped again. "That was the Riprap man. I think…I think he has my wind."

"Huh?" Richard said, looking confused.

Tara couldn't help but smile. Finally, something Richard didn't know about.

Tara explained all that had happened, how she'd had to fight the Riprap man during the solstice, how she'd made a bargain with the spirit of the river, and then more recently, how there was more than one school of witchcraft and she was actually more of a hedgewitch. And she'd appeared to have tamed a wind that appeared mostly as a black greyhound.

"What herbs do you use to call a greyhound?" Richard asked.

"I didn't…Hmmm," Tara said, thinking. She hadn't approached the question that way. Kyle had initially gathered wind to him using "schooled" magic, as it were. Could she use a similar spell to bring Soot back?

"Thank you," Tara said after a moment. She paused and gulped again. "This is why I want to invite you to be an honorary member of my coven."

Richard sat up straighter but didn't say anything. She could tell he was thinking furiously about it.

"It may be dangerous for you, because of the Riprap man. And I don't know if you could ever be a full member, because you don't have any magic." Tara had checked more than once, but Richard had never appeared to notice the back room of Ye Olde Magick Shoppe.

"What would you want me to do?" Richard asked.

"What you do naturally," Tara said. "Since I'm starting my own coven, I don't have access to any of the ancient books of witch lore. And I have no idea what my powers might be as a hedgewitch. Any and all information you can bring would be greatly appreciated."

"I'd do that because we were friends," Richard pointed out. "Why bring me into the coven?"

"Because I want you to be part of it," Tara said. She tried to find the words. "When Kyle first mentioned it, I thought he was crazy. But the more I thought about it, the more you just fit."

Richard gave her a smile and nodded. "Like the herbs. You have knowledge about what should work. But you also follow your own instincts."

"Not as much as I could have, but yeah, like that," Tara said. She did make a special blend of tea every morning, depending on how she felt, not according to any lore.

"I accept your offer," Richard said.

"Are you sure?" Tara said, wanting to verify.

Richard gave her an adamant nod. "Yes. Besides, when else am I going to be able to watch other people perform magic?"

"You know you won't be able to tell anyone about this, right?" Tara added. Maybe she should have started with that.

"I know," Richard said. "It was the main thing that drove us apart, when we first broke up." He paused, then added, "At some point, I might ask for dispensation to tell Jeannie. I wouldn't right now, though. Not until I figure out if she's actually the woman I want to marry."

"Really?" Tara asked, surprised. Richard had always proclaimed that he wasn't the marrying type. He'd only been dating Jeannie a few months.

Richard shrugged. "We'll see. We're starting to talk about moving in together. But I don't know."

"Wow," Tara said, impressed. "I just want you to be happy," she added, despite feeling a slight tinge of envy. Not that she wanted to marry Richard, but it had been so long since she'd had someone in her life. Besides, Richard had been a dear friend to her for years. She honestly did want the best for him.

"I have a question," Richard said after a moment. "Are you looking to recruit other witches for your coven?"

"I am," Tara said. "What, do you know any?" Though she'd never thought about it, it really wouldn't surprise her if he did.

"Maybe. Maybe not. I can't tell, not for certain," Richard said, hesitating. "But if there's anyone who I've ever met who's possibly magical, it would be Kaede."

"Ka-ee-dee?" Tara asked, carefully pronouncing the name.

"Yes," Richard said. "Ze runs Hallowed Ground, a shelter up in the Lloyd district, off Weidler."

Tara blinked, surprised that Richard was that familiar with alternate pronouns. The name didn't give any hint of a gender either.

"You should go down tomorrow and volunteer," Richard told her firmly. "It's a good place, and ze could always use another hand."

"All right," Tara said slowly. What else did she have to do on a Sunday afternoon? Except to try to free Soot from the Riprap man.

Richard agreed to meet with Tara, Ginny, and Kyle on Monday night before the pair of them headed out the door.

To Tara's surprise, Soot sat just outside the door, waiting for Tara. He came bounding up, still part puppy, dancing around her, happy to see her.

She introduced him to Richard with the instruction, "Know his scent."

Richard held out his hand and let the dog sniff at it. Though greyhounds were more sight than nose dogs, Tara figured that Soot would be able to do both. After saying goodnight, Tara stood for a moment, staring at Soot.

Was the wind hers again? Had that whistle broken the hold the Riprap man had had? Or would the Riprap man be able to call Soot to him at any time?

Tara didn't know, and she didn't think Ginny would know either.

And Soot wasn't telling.

***

SUNDAY MORNING BROUGHT MORE RAIN. Tara was actually happy to hear it pattering against her window as she slowly came awake. It was a welcome respite from the long hot summer. She still took her tea outside to the balcony to drink it, even if she didn't sit on one of the wet metal chairs, but rather stared out over the small courtyard at the buildings just across the way.

Maybe the next place she moved to, she'd have a better balcony, one she could sit on most of the year.

First she'd have to find a job. It was time for her to move on from everything. She had a shift Tuesday morning at Ye Olde Magick Shoppe, as the shop owner Patricia had extra work to do before the equinox on Wednesday.

But that was Tara's last shift, as far as she knew. Patricia would probably never call her back, too afraid of the "bad luck" Tara supposedly carried with her as a victim of the Riprap man.

However, Tara was forming her own coven. It felt good, but odd.

After enjoying a second cup of tea, Tara finally felt ready to face the world. Soot wasn't around that morning. Maybe he'd been chased off by the rain. Tara didn't feel as antsy that morning either, not as she had Saturday morning.

Had that been part of her connection to Soot? Was it now broken?

Tara gave a sharp whistle, and was relieved when Soot popped up on the balcony almost immediately. "Good boy," Tara said, patting his sleek head. "Follow me today, okay?" she asked him.

Soot cocked his head to one side as if he didn't understand. Tara imagined herself walking along the sidewalk with Soot at her heels, on her way to the train.

Soot cocked his head to the other side, as if considering her request. Then he disappeared again.

Fine. She couldn't rely on him if she needed help. Message received.

Though she wasn't sure why she was feeling so hesitant. Kaede wouldn't attack her, would ze? Richard would only admit to having met Kaede at a volunteer event at the library. He still couldn't say why he thought ze was a witch. But he was adamant that ze might be.

As Tara walked down the street toward the MAX station, a cold wind nipped at her ankles. She turned around to see that Soot was there. He'd taken her command literally, and had done just exactly as she'd asked.

No more, no less.

Tara was going to have to read some dog training books.

Still, she praised Soot for following her, and imagined him there when she got off the MAX train.

Luckily, the Riprap man didn't appear on the train, as he had before. Still, she couldn't help but think about him and wonder when he'd make his next attack.

Downtown was still pretty quiet that early on a Sunday. Tara had checked the website for Hallowed Ground and found that while the general doors opened at noon, volunteers were expected to arrive by nine.

There was already a line at the front door by the time Tara arrived. Mainly chronic homeless people, with huge shopping carts piled high with all their personal belongings. A few street kids hung out as well, strumming a guitar.

Surprisingly, none of them bothered Tara as she walked by. Instead, one of the old women with only a few teeth left in her crinkly apple face pointed to the side of the building and said, "Volunteer entrance is that way."

"Thank you," Tara said.

Tara passed by the front of the building. It looked like converted office space, with a door in the center and large windows on either side. Cream-colored drapes hid the inside from the curious. Above the main floor, it looked as though there were three stories of apartments. All the windows were lined with aluminum foil to keep out the western sun.

Tara made her way along the side of the building and to the back. A large, hand-painted sign above the door said, "Volunteers only. Yes, that means you."

Cautiously, Tara stuck her head in the door. It opened onto a long hallway. She heard the banging of pots to her right, and either tables or chairs scraping against a floor straight ahead of her.

Taking a deep breath, Tara stepped across the threshold.

For a moment, she paused. She had a feeling of *something* present. It was similar to the feeling she'd gotten when she entered the garden that had held the meditation maze that the witches had used for passing within. It wasn't the same, however. This space wasn't as watchful.

It was still a *separate* space. Maybe not sacred, not as she understood it, but not completely mundane either.

Maybe Richard had been right.

Tara walked directly into the kitchen. It was a large open area, maybe thirty feet square, going up at least two stories. Industrial ovens, stoves, and grills lined the walls, most of them unmanned. A huge dishwasher stood in the corner, where large racks of dishes would be pushed through and sanitized.

In the center of the room, the volunteers had gathered around a series of tables, all chatting and chopping vegetables. Tara recognized the rhythm of people who had worked together for a long while— mostly women, but a few men as well.

A young woman came in from behind Tara, carrying a large basket of potatoes. "Can I help you?" she asked as she walked past Tara, delivering her goods to the table. She wore an artfully torn white T-shirt that showed off her black bra, along with jeans that were also torn deliberately instead of through use. Her blonde hair came straight out of a bottle, and she had the modern day armor of piercings scattered across her face, up both her ears, as well as in her collarbone.

Though the woman had a level of toughness to her, she was bird-thin and brittle. Tara felt as though she'd break this woman in two if she wasn't careful, even though they were roughly the same height.

"I'm here to volunteer," Tara said, keeping her smile friendly and non-threatening.

"Good! Good," the woman said. She returned Tara's bright smile, her pale blue eyes taking on an additional warmth. "Welcome to Hallowed Ground. This is your first time, yes?"

"It is," Tara said, nodding. She added, "I'm comfortable helping wherever you need hands."

The woman paused and looked at Tara more closely. "Ah," she said after a moment. "You need to talk to Kaede first."

"All right," Tara said. Had this woman just figured out Tara was a witch? Or was there something else about her?

"Ze is out front, setting the lines," the woman said. "I'm Alaska, by the way."

"Tara," she said, nodding.

Out front turned out to be about three times as large as the kitchen area. Tara had assumed that "setting the lines" had meant setting up some sort of rope line, in order to direct people. Instead, all the tables had been pushed to the edges of room, with the chairs piled up haphazardly on top, and would fall if someone wasn't careful getting them down.

The only person in the room—Kaede, Tara presumed—knelt on the ground in the center of the space and drew lines in chalk on the wooden floor.

A pentagram, Tara realized as she drew closer.

Kaede was chanting one of the hymns that Tara knew. As Tara didn't want to disturb the blessing taking place, bringing the warmth of the hearth into a new home, she joined along with the hymn instead, quietly adding her voice and her power.

Richard had been correct. Kaede was a witch, and a high-powered one at that. The strength of zir blessing flowed out to all the corners of the room, traveling up the walls and seeping into the building itself. Would Tara now feel the space as more sacred, if she'd entered after Kaede had finished zir hymn?

Tara stayed where she was, outside the pentagram, as Kaede finished. Ze looked Asian to Tara, Japanese, if she had to guess. Kaede wore zir hair shaved short, so it was just black fuzz across zir scalp. Ze had on a red T-shirt with white lettering, the name of some band Tara thought looked vaguely familiar, with capri jeans showing off muscled calves and bare feet. Ze didn't have any piercings or visible tattoos, which surprised Tara.

When Kaede finished the last line of the pentagram, timed with the last line of the hymn, ze stood up and frankly appraised Tara. "Alaska sent you out, didn't she?" Zir voice didn't give any indication of gender either.

Tara found herself curious, though she knew it was none of her business.

"She did," Tara said, nodding.

"Figured," Kaede said. "She assumed the little rich white girl would get freaked out by the pentagram."

Tara shrugged. "She was wrong." Though she probably did look like a "little rich white girl."

"That's Alaska's main problem. She always misjudges people. Both the good as well as the bad," Kaede said, shaking zir head. "So why are you here, Miss Witch?" Kaede leaned back and folded zir arms across zir chest.

"My name's Tara. And I did plan on volunteering for the day," Tara said. She didn't like how she was having to prove herself to these people.

Then again, it was their territory that she'd come into.

"And?" Kaede said, challenging.

Tara tilted her head to the side. She didn't want to invite Kaede into the coven if she didn't think they could work together. And she hadn't been in the other person's presence long enough to make that call yet, either.

"I don't know what 'and' is, or even if there is an 'and,'" Tara confessed. "There might be. But I don't know. Not yet."

Kaede nodded. "Got a story, don't you, Tara. That's okay. Most of the folks here have stories, and none of them are sweet. All right. We can talk after we get everyone fed and settled. Let's get this place ready."

Tara followed Kaede, as that seemed to be what the person wanted, carefully pulling down chairs and setting up tables. At least Tara was stronger than she looked, keeping herself in shape with swimming and yoga, so she was easily able to keep up with Kaede.

"Hallowed Ground came from the idea that the neighborhood has to take care of itself," Kaede told Tara. "There are no good corporations. Each and every one of them has blood on their hands. The only way you can achieve a working society is if everyone contributes according to their abilities, and only takes according to their need."

"Communist?" Tara couldn't help but ask, recognizing the quote as coming from Lenin.

Kaede rolled zir eyes. "The communist society, the worker's paradise, was doomed from the start. It was too large of an organization. You can't run a country that way. You have to start small. Dig deep roots and grow out from there."

"I see," Tara said, though she wasn't certain that she did. Covens tended to exist in their own sort of space as well, but it wasn't the same. The only members of their community were witches.

"We got more than a soup kitchen, here," Kaede said. "Will give you a tour later if you decide to stick around. Rooms upstairs to give people a way to transition off the street. After-school programs for kids. Mediation nights for people to solve their disputes. Regular education about government services."

Tara was curious about that. "Mediation? Education?"

"You know the best way to decrease the homeless population? Not to focus on housing everyone, but instead, to focus on prevention," Kaede said. "The number of people forced out into the street keeps rising along with housing prices. Every person you place gets replaced with someone else out on the street in less than three months. If you don't have as many people being forced out, you can actually decrease the number living out there."

"That's kind of brilliant," Tara said. She helped Kaede lift down another table, setting it into place. "Do you work with a coven?" She had to ask, though she suspected she already knew the answer.

"Don't talk to me about those stuck-up witches," Kaede said, anger deepening zir voice. "They only want to help their own. They wouldn't even contemplate bringing in a mundane."

"Ah," Tara said, nodding. That made sense. It was one of the reasons why she'd been so uncomfortable with Miss Lucy. The entire coven had just struck her as selfish, only wanting their own members to prosper. That, plus the fact that they cursed people, bringing them harm without a good reason, at least as far as Tara was concerned.

"What, you forming a coven?" Kaede asked, zir dark brown eyes peering intently at Tara.

"I am," Tara admitted. "And I have already invited a mundane to come and be an honorary member."

"What?" Kaede said. "Okay, Tara, you got my attention now. Why a mundane?"

"He's a research librarian. I don't have access to any books or ancient lore. He already had guessed that I was a witch, so he volunteered to help."

"Interesting," Kaede said.

"He was actually the one who recommended that I come to see you," Tara said.

Kaede picked up a few chairs and started hauling them to tables. Tara followed suit.

"I take it something happened with your old coven," Kaede said.

"Yes. And that's part of why I'm not sure there's an 'and' here," Tara said, referring to earlier in their conversation. "There's a creature haunting me. I don't want to bring danger to you or your community."

Kaede just nodded. "The people with the most need are the ones who show up at my door," ze said plainly. "The fact that you're here probably means you need to be here. We'll talk, more, after service."

"Thank you," Tara said. She wasn't sure what else to say. Hallowed Ground felt just like that to her, a sacred space, now that she'd been there for a short while. A place where possibly she could belong, if she was accepted.

After they finished setting up the long tables and chairs, as well as the tables around the edges for serving food, Kaede sent Tara back to the kitchen to help there. Tara chopped vegetables and helped prepare a simple meal for their service. While some of the herbs were fresh, most of the seasoning came in industrial-sized shakers. Tara took over one of the potato dishes, making sure that it was as tasty as possible, given the constraints.

At one point, an older Japanese woman came shuffling into the kitchen. She wore a beautiful peach-colored kimono with a pattern of lucky clouds floating across. Her black obi was tied tightly around her tiny waist, the folds perfectly pressed. White tabi socks stuck out under the kimono, along with old-fashioned bamboo and wooden sandals.

She regally nodded to Alaska and some of the other people in the room before starting the process of making a huge batch of barley tea.

When Kaede came into the room, ze just shook zir head at the old woman. "What are you doing here?"

The older woman replied in what Tara assumed was Japanese. Kaede said something in reply in that language. It quickly escalated into an argument, with the pair of them soon shouting at one another. Tara wondered if Kaede was telling the old woman to go home. But the woman flat refused, and instead serenely turned back to her tea as if nothing had happened.

Alaska came over to Tara and spoke quietly in her ear. "That's Kaede's grandmother. She comes by every day we serve to make tea. In proper robes."

"Okay," Tara said, confused. But then again, families were weird.

Just before service, Kaede called everyone together and had them join hands in a circle. Ze prayed for a moment, asking for Brigit's blessings, before releasing them to do the best they could that day.

Then the doors opened, and chaos ensued.

FIVE

Hedgewitches have turned out to be wily opponents. Of course they still lose, in the end. But I believe that, because a hedgewitch is on her own, she has developed more survival skills. I have switched back to hunting the schooled witches to do my mighty task, made more difficult by the rate of progress throughout the entire glorious city of Portland. The river god does not see the opportunities that I do; however, he does recognize the necessity to prolong the life of his most ardent follower. I shall have to travel back to the heartwaters of the river again. This time it won't be as arduous a task. Roads multiply like locusts. Rail lines choke the wilderness. The people grow soft in such decadence. Still, I have my sworn duty, and the river god's floods are just spats. Nothing mighty enough to wash away the city, though sometimes I'm tempted to direct His mighty wrath to do just that.

Wilson Evermore, Aging Magician and Weary Traveler, 1925

TARA WASN'T sure that she'd ever been so tired before, at least, not like this.

On the one hand, she liked people, and she'd honestly missed working at the shop, dealing with crowds.

However, this was something very different. She'd been a runner during the meal, as she was new and the community didn't really know her. So Tara had hauled pots of soup and potatoes, along with baskets of bread, from the kitchen to the serving tables.

Many, if not all, of the people who'd come to the soup kitchen line had brought something to donate, whether it be a pair of clean socks that they'd acquired and felt as though they could pass along, slightly worn shoes, clean-ish blankets, or food they'd received at a different food bank that they hadn't liked.

Tara had ended up carrying those into the kitchen as well, prepping the food so it could be shared, then bringing it back out and serving it. She'd also learned where the laundry room and supply room were, starting up a load so that the bounty that had been brought in could be redistributed among the community.

Though Tara had never worked in a soup kitchen before, she didn't think that this was the way one would normally be run. The homeless were just that—homeless. However, here the expectation appeared to be that they were to contribute what they could, when they could.

These people may have been sleeping out on the street, but they *belonged* to this place in a way that made Tara's heart ache.

It occurred to her that she wasn't the rich one here, not by a long shot. She did have a few good friends. However, even she had to admit that her covens had never been actual communities. Not like the people here.

They looked out for each other. Tara watched the more able fill trays and plates of food for those in wheelchairs, or who hobbled on canes.

Though Tara had never been so involved with any of the homeless before, there was only one person who frightened her. He was rambling about the government wiring his body together wrong, asking how much poison was in the bread, comparing the water to a river of piss.

He was so obviously insane that he struck Tara as an alien, barely human anymore.

One of the servers was familiar with him, and told Tara that he was a schizophrenic, off his meds, and unfortunately, high on something. Kaede took the young man out of the line and to the side, trying to get him to stop shaking. Ze made sure that he ate at least some of what was on his plate before issuing him back outside. He wasn't part of the community here, and he was too high—possibly a danger not only to himself but to others. One of the other regulars volunteered to go sit with him until he was able to take care of himself again.

After the food rush had passed, and everyone had eaten at the long communal tables, many stayed where they were, chatting with their neighbors. Tara thought she saw a bottle of wine being passed between one group, but no one else seemed to care.

The stately grandmother in her beautiful obi came out and served tea to everyone who wanted it. She moved with incredible grace in her wooden sandals, treating each person with a reserved dignity. It was like a moving ballet. Tara didn't understand why it was so important, but it seemed to her to be the final prayer in a circle, the blessing that all sought.

Tara wished that she could help, that she had something more to give to these people. They needed hands to help, of course. But she didn't have money she could give them. There had to be something she could do.

Kids soon broke out their school books. More than one of the older clients sat with them, helping them with their homework, listening as the kids talked. In one corner, one of the older men sat with a couple of very young children and told them stories.

Tara spent her time cleaning up, carrying away the very few remaining plates and used utensils—most of the people had bussed themselves. She also was pointed to a couple of pitchers of water, and delivered that to people still sitting around. She was debating where she was needed next. Only so many people could work running the sanitizer in the kitchen, too many bodies got in the way there.

It wasn't until she heard one of the kids complaining about being so stressed it was giving him headaches that she saw opportunity knocking.

"Tell me about your headaches," she said, drawing slowly toward the group. "Do they start in your neck? Or in your forehead."

"Back of my skull," the boy admitted quietly. He wore a white thermal-underwear shirt under a blue-and-white checked flannel shirt. His skin looked too pale, and his gray-green eyes stood out huge in his face. Dirty blond hair stuck up all over his head.

"I may have something for you," Tara said, getting an idea.

She rushed back to the kitchen. It was empty. The latest round of dishes were drying and the helpers had left. Tara reached for the cheap English Breakfast tea that she'd seen on one of the shelves. She tore off the string tying the folded teabag together, grabbed a bowl, then dumped the leaves (more like tea dust and twigs) out. Then she chopped up some of the mint she'd found, a pinch of dried ginger, and for luck, just a dash of cayenne, all the while humming a soothing melody.

After she retied the string around the ends of the folded teabag, she walked back out to the front room. "It isn't much," she said, handing the young man a single teabag. "But it should help calm your nerves, help you focus more. You need to get some hot water in a cup, put the tea bag in there for five minutes to steep, then gently squeeze it out. You may be able to get two cups from that."

"Wow, gee, thanks," the boy said, a little confused.

"Kaede sometimes makes sachets for people," one of the nearby girls said. "You make those too?"

Tara's fingers automatically found the sachet that she always carried with her, one for courage and protection. "You can have mine," she said.

The girl made a face at the faded pink bag.

Tara saw her mistake. "Though I should probably remix it for you. What do you need it for?"

The smile that lit up the girl's face warmed Tara through to her toes. "I got brothers," she said.

"Oh?" Tara asked, trying to be nonchalant but hoping that she wasn't about to hear a tale of abuse.

"They won't come here. They do stupid things, and are in a gang. You got something to help with that?" the girl said.

"They don't need courage," Tara said slowly. "Or protection. They need belonging."

"Yes! Exactly. I can't get 'em here," the girl said. "Where they might stand a chance."

What would promote being together? Sticky plants, like ivy and honeysuckle, Tara decided. And though Marshmallow wasn't like the actual food, maybe that too. "I can bring you something tomorrow," she said slowly.

"Great! I'll stop by after school, as usual, to do my homework," the girl said. "I'm Kaneshia, by the way. And that goof is Eric."

"Tara," she said, introducing herself.

It surprised her how the young people drew her into their conversation. It wasn't because she belonged there, she knew that.

It took her a while to realize that mainly, these young teens (thirteen and fourteen) really just wanted her to listen. None of the adults in their lives would. It was a huge draw for Hallowed Ground. The older people there considered it their job to listen, really listen, to these youth.

By the time Kaede came to find Tara, she knew that she would be returning regularly, whether Kaede became a member of Tara's fledgling coven or not.

Tara might have found a place where she could belong.

KAEDE TOOK Tara back toward the door she'd entered into the building, to a small side office off the main hallway. Now that Tara took a closer look, she saw that white chalk lines had been drawn on the white paint. They were barely visible unless she stared at them, and then they made the hairs on the back of Tara's neck stand up. They reminded her of designs Miss Lucy had used for protection, the kind of spell that promised pain to any who trespassed.

"I used to try to put sachets on the door, or above the door frame," Kaede said, indicating the lines of protection. "But too many people stole them, seeking something to help protect them out on the street." Ze shrugged and opened the door. "I don't blame them. So I had to come up with something to get them to respect this doorway and this office."

"Why?" Tara asked, stepping into the crowded space. The room was tiny, maybe six by six. A large gray filing cabinet loomed in one corner, papers piled up on top. A long desk jutted out from the wall. Papers piled up on it as well. To Tara it looked like organized chaos, as the stacks were all neat. The room smelled of the food they'd cooked in the kitchen, with an underlying dark scent of barley tea.

Kaede slid behind the desk and plopped zirself down in the old office chair there, while gesturing for Tara to take one of the two mismatched chairs on the other side of the desk.

"They need to respect someone else's space," Kaede said seriously. "They're out on the street and used to trespassing, considering everything theirs. As part of relearning to be in society, and being part of a community, they need this sort of boundary, though there's nothing here for anyone to see or steal."

Tara wondered about that. The room did appear to mostly contain paperwork. An ancient computer monitor sat on one corner of the desk, with an equally antiquated keyboard, both connected to an out-of-sight computer that was probably out of date as well. The desk lamp had seen better days. Dust covered the light-colored shade and the porcelain base appeared to be held together with duct tape.

"I like it here, at Hallowed Ground," Tara said. "I'd like to come back and volunteer, regardless of your decision about joining my coven."

That earned Tara a huge smile from Kaede. "I'd wondered. You seemed to fit, which, believe me, not all the volunteers who come through here do. So tell me about this coven of yours, and why you need another witch."

Tara told Kaede everything, from her own training starting with Miss Lucy, to Sheila, to being haunted by the Riprap man. Then she talked about Ginny, and how she was probably a hedgewitch herself, as well as about Richard and Kyle.

"What would you like to do here?" Kaede asked after a moment. "If you came back to volunteer?"

Tara explained about making the tea for the teen who was so stressed about everything, as well as making a sachet for the girl's brothers, to try to bring the family together.

Kaede sat nodding after Tara finished, a comfortable silence filling the small office. "I'm good with spaces," Kaede said after a few moments. "I'm a schooled witch, made it to the fifth circle, circle of water."

Tara sat up straighter, surprised. Kaede didn't appear to be that old. How powerful was ze?

"I started young," Kaede explained. "Grandmother made sure of that."

Given Kaede's sour expression, Tara had no doubt as to whom Kaede referred to, the older woman who'd served tea that afternoon.

"But I hated their structure, their strict rules," Kaede said. "They didn't fit me. Not the me I was discovering, the being that is neither male nor female, the inclusive one. I'd already started volunteering here, at Hallowed Ground. Discovered my true calling as an anarchist."

Tara saw much more research in her future. She'd thought that anarchists just tore things down. They didn't build communities, did they?

"Everyone should be expected to contribute to the community, not just sit at the top of the food chain and direct their human slaves," Kaede said hotly. Then ze grinned and shook zir head. "But you don't need a lecture. We'll just slowly indoctrinate you."

"Okay," Tara said, though she wasn't sure what that really meant.

"In your ideal world, what would you do?" Kaede asked.

"Open a tea shop," Tara said without pausing. She'd been thinking about that off and on for the past few days. "Not someplace that sold regular tea, or mixed blends. But a place where someone could come and get special mixes, specifically blended just for them."

Kaede smiled at her. "I was hoping you'd say that. How do you feel about working here during the week, afternoons and evenings?"

"What do you mean?" Tara asked, confused. "Like work here, like a job?"

Kaede rocked zir head back and forth. "Kind of. It wouldn't be fulltime. I can't afford that. But I have an opening for an another coordinator. Basically, it involves running the afterschool program."

"I don't have any experience doing that," Tara said. "I don't have any kids—never really wanted them." Wouldn't that type of coordinator need to have at least a degree in social work? Tara's degree was in English literature by default, not because she'd actually liked it.

"The program pretty much runs itself," Kaede assured her. "I need someone here to open the doors and let the kids in, count noses and keep track of things. There are a few adults in the community who come and monitor the teens. The kids are pretty well behaved for the most part, just need to be reminded now and again to not be such hooligans."

"But why me?" Tara asked, still confused.

"I can give you a monthly stipend for supplies for making your teas and sachets," Kaede said. "And I'm sure that you'll be able to sweet talk some of the covens into donating supplies as well. As for 'why you,' it's because I want you to set up that tea shop. Here, in Hallowed Ground."

"You want me to do what?" Tara said, trying to keep her voice modulated and not actually yell.

Kaede grinned at her. "Make your specialty teas. And your sachets. For the kids who need them."

Ze appeared to be thinking for a moment, before ze added, "Set up a barter system with the kids. Be creative with that. It might be passing a test, or spending an hour doing homework without interruption, or even wild gardening, harvesting things you need from the city parks."

"So my customers would be the kids who came in for the afternoon program?" Tara said, starting to understand. Starting to smile.

"The ones who need it the most," Kaede said. "Some of them need real magic in their lives. A bunch of them just require an adult who listens and who tries to help."

"Wow," Tara said. "I never...I never would have considered this."

She knew her answer immediately, however. "I would love to," Tara said, though she'd never thought that working with teenagers would have excited her. "I'll still have to get another job," she warned. A part-time salary from a shelter wouldn't cover her expenses.

Who would contribute supplies for her teas? Patricia would, certainly. Sheila, or more likely, Aaloka, might, if for nothing else, to assuage their guilt. Would Miss Lucy? Or the people Tara used to babysit for?

"That's pretty much everyone's life here," Kaede said. "Those who can, work a couple of other jobs so that I don't have to pay them."

Tara nodded, hearing the expectation laid out clearly in those words. Kaede would pay her at the start, but eventually, she should figure out how to make money from something else, while still volunteering.

"As for your coven," Kaede said slowly. "I'm interested. I'd really like to see a coven run on merit as opposed to a strict hierarchy. I'm not saying that I'll be able to stay, but I'd like to help, at least short term."

"Really? That would be wonderful!" Tara said. Kaede was a powerful witch, of higher level than Kyle. Still, she had to ask, "Are you sure?"

Kaede nodded. "Yes. I understand that this Riprap man may attempt to bring bad luck to the center, to my kids. But as I said, I'm good with spaces. Let him try."

Tara had the impression of Kaede growing larger, a suit of old-fashioned Japanese armor encasing zir, bearing a katana with a glowing blade.

The Riprap man had no idea what he was about to face.

Tara found herself pausing after she left Hallowed Ground, blinking her eyes against the dim afternoon light. She'd stepped out of one world and into the next. No wonder Kaede called zirself good with spaces. The community center was sacred, separate from the rest of the mundane world. Tara felt that now, deep in her bones.

She took a deep breath.

The smell of stagnant water overwhelmed her. She coughed, gagging.

The Riprap man stood at the corner of the building. His bare torso had the appearance of stones piled together, though he still wore pants and his bowler hat.

He placed one large, granite palm on the corner of the building and shoved, just once.

The entire building groaned, the timbers creaking. Cracks formed in the stucco walls.

Crap! Was he going to push it over? Tara readied herself to rush him, see if she could physically tackle the creature.

But the building appeared to fight back. A bolt of lightning raced across the wall closest to Tara, running from the door to where the Riprap man was touching the building. He jerked his hand back, surprised.

Yes, Kaede was very good with spaces, it appeared.

The Riprap man turned to glare at Tara.

She gulped, the air suddenly thick and hard to breathe.

"What do you want?" she demanded as she tried to clear the air around her.

The message came clear, carried on waves of rage and mortification. Tara was the Riprap man's rival for the river god's affection. He intended to show the river god just how badly He'd chosen.

The eventual battle between Tara and the Riprap man would be epic. But he would prevail in the end, and the river god would see the error of His ways.

Tara snorted. "Even if you defeat me, which you won't, your river god is still going to be on the lookout for someone more sympathetic. You're not a water person. Creature. Monster. Whatever."

"No," the Riprap man said. His features wavered, and suddenly the old-fashioned gentleman who Tara had first met stood in front of her. He had a clear tenor voice that cut through the still air surrounding them. "He will cleave unto me and no other."

"You do know that sounds like you're pursuing a homosexual

relationship, right?" Tara pointed out. If the Riprap man was a modern creature, she wouldn't have bothered saying anything. However, given how old the Riprap man actually was, she hoped that would bother him.

The Riprap man merely shrugged. "The meaning of the words have changed. Not the sentiment. You know nothing of devotion, of commitment. Of covenant."

Tara blinked, surprised that the Riprap man was speaking with her, that they were having an almost normal conversation.

"How do you intend to stop me?" Tara said. She figured she may as well ask.

The Riprap man gave her a sly smile. "That would be telling."

He turned and started walking away. He gave a sharp whistle just before he turned the corner.

A dark figure appeared beside him. Was that Soot? The Riprap man vanished out of sight around the corner before Tara could tell for certain.

She hurried forward, worried.

The Riprap man was nowhere to be seen.

And though she whistled and called, Soot never returned to her.

LATER THAT EVENING, Tara and Kyle sat in the darkened living room of Kyle's condo, sipping peppermint tea sweetened with a touch of warm apple cider and cinnamon. Tara told Kyle about Kaede, pleased to have another powerful witch join her coven. She was actually getting more comfortable calling it *her* coven, though she also liked Kaede's belief that the coven actually belonged to all of them.

The night felt warm outside the sliding glass door leading to the balcony, the clouds appearing orange due to their reflections of the city streetlights. Tara had stood out on the balcony for a while after she'd returned, whistling for Soot, but the wind hadn't returned to her.

Did the Riprap man now control her wind? Would Soot ever return? Tara was starting to feel the wind's absence, as if her lungs were somehow contracted and she could no longer take a deep breath.

Kyle looked worried. He wore his weekend clothes, a soft gray sweatshirt over brown jogging pants. He'd just shaved his head for the week, and the black skin glistened with the oil he'd rubbed in. "I had always thought that familiars were just a fanciful myth. Now, I'm wondering if there's some basis in it, that the hedgewitches have animals that are connected to them."

"I was thinking the same thing," Tara said. "I've sent an email to Richard, to investigate older accounts of witch familiars. I'm not hopeful that he'll find anything useful."

"Why?" Kyle asked, peering intently at her.

"Remember? According to Ginny, what works for one hedgewitch may not work for another. And whatever does work isn't necessarily consistent."

Kyle nodded and sipped his tea, his eyes still boring into her.

"What?" Tara finally asked. "You've been watching me all night." She tried to keep her tone light and not accusatory, but her worry about Soot nagged at her.

"I've never met a hedgewitch," Kyle said slowly. "But it seems to me that having so much power left unchecked is a disaster waiting to happen."

Tara blinked, surprised. "Go on," she said when he stopped talking.

"You left Miss Lucy because her magic was inwardly focused," Kyle explained. "You've said it yourself—Miss Lucy was selfish. But a hedgewitch is the same way. All that magic is just for yourself and your gain. Hedgewitches don't normally join or form covens."

"That doesn't mean that I've suddenly grown selfish," Tara pointed out. "I'm trying to create a coven, a community." His words stung more than she'd like to admit. Since leaving Hallowed Ground that afternoon, Tara had been thinking about where she fit, what it meant to have a community, to not rely on just herself so much.

"I know you believe that," Kyle said gently. "But think back to when we were at the Saturday market yesterday. You and Ginny turned people away, left and right, out of your path, without thinking about it. Your magic just did it for you."

"True," Tara said. It had surprised her how much her and Ginny's magic had cleared the path ahead of them, without either of them actually casting any spells or drinking any potions.

"Human nature is inherently selfish," Kyle continued, building his argument like the lawyer he was. "I don't believe that you would consciously use your magic for selfish gains. Unconsciously, though? When it's just a part of you?"

Tara had no answer for Kyle or his concerns. "I don't know," Tara replied after a bit. "I can try to be more conscious of it, when the magic just happens." She took a deep breath. "But as you said, this is new to both of us. I'm going to have to rely on you to be my conscience sometimes, bring things up if I don't notice."

Kyle gave her a grin. "You've been my evil conscience before, reminding me that there was more to life than just work. Now, to return the favor, I need to be your good conscience?"

Tara nodded and gave him a heartfelt smile. "Yeah. Thank you," she said.

"You're welcome," Kyle said, sipping his tea for a moment. He nodded, as if he'd come to a decision himself. "I may have another recruit for your coven. He is a being of power. He may have some human blood in him—I've never asked."

"Okay," Tara said, surprised. Though she'd known that there were beings of power, she'd never met one, or even really been taught about them. "Why would he be interested in joining my coven?"

"Honestly, he first expressed interest in you when you survived the Riprap man," Kyle said. "When I mentioned that the Riprap man had returned and you were forming your own coven as protection, he said, and I quote, 'Do keep me in mind for your little group.'" Kyle shrugged. "He's ancient. Came to the New World 'on a lark.' He's... uhm, alien."

Tara was surprised at the shudder Kyle gave. This being truly upset Kyle at a fundamental level, whether he realized it or not.

"How did you meet?" Tara asked after Kyle had taken a few deep breaths in order to recover his equilibrium.

Kyle smiled and rolled his eyes at her. "On a dating site, if you can believe it."

"What?" Tara said, completely surprised. "So you…dated? Are dating?"

"It's complicated," Kyle said. "He isn't human," he reiterated. "He has different needs. And he helped heal me and my psychic injuries more than anyone else. When he makes an effort, he's not that disturbing."

"Okay," Tara said, not sure what else to say. "What's his name?"

Kyle shook his head. "Lucius. That isn't his real name, though. He told me he took it after that wizard in the Harry Potter movies."

Tara blinked, surprised. "Why would he do that? Why would he take a name like that?"

"You'll see," Kyle said. "If you're game, you can meet him tomorrow at one P.M."

Tara paused, her mouth open. A part of her wanted to say, "Of course, I'll meet with him." Another part of her, however, was cautious, particularly in light of Kyle's misgivings about her power.

"I will meet with him," Tara said slowly. "But I will not guarantee that he has a place in the coven."

"Good," Kyle said. "That was exactly what your conscience was hoping you'd say. He represents a lot of power. But like your own hedgewitch magic, he's impossible to control. I would call him selfish. However, he would deny that. He has strict morals. They just aren't necessarily the same as yours or mine."

"I'll keep that in mind," Tara assured him. The other beings, the elders, those with power, were the basis of many human myths. However, as individuals, they were both more as well as less than the stories made them to be.

Who was it who had described elves as brilliant and perilous? Not that Lucius was necessarily an elf, though he might be considerably more dangerous than anyone Tara had ever met before.

Kyle smiled and relaxed. Tara suddenly realized it was the first time that he'd relaxed all evening, that he'd been tense, anticipating this conversation.

Was it because Kyle didn't trust Tara?

Or was it because he didn't trust Lucius?

SIX

The journey to the headwaters of the mighty Willamette took more than a year the first time I went. This time, it took merely three months. The end of my pilgrimage was the most difficult, going up mountain trails. My magic sustained me throughout. This wilderness sings to my heart. I am no painter or poet, however. Mere brushstrokes or words cannot capture the beauty of the mountains, the rocks and bones of the earth. I feel more youthful in this location. I assume that's because the waters are so fresh and new, though sometimes I wonder. It's as if the very earth itself supports me here. I have started to purify myself for the upcoming ceremony. The river god Mulinohana has only spoken to me once since I arrived, warning that the transformation may be painful. He assured me that I would become a better servant, as my life will be much extended. I welcome the trials that face me. Though the city of Portland will never know my name, or how I have protected Her, it is worth it, just to see her grow.

Wilson Evermore, Master Magician and Explorer, 1926

TARA COULDN'T HELP but feel nervous waiting for the mysterious Lucius. They were meeting at a coffee house in the Pearl District. The building was a converted warehouse, now divided up into a series of small stores. Huge wooden timbers held up the soaring ceiling. Old exposed brick made up the two outside walls, the mortar squished out like hard frosting. Only the floor was new: poured gray concrete that had been polished until it was shiny and slick.

After getting a bitter English Breakfast tea from the counter in the corner, Tara sat at one of the hard metal tables and equally cold metal chairs. As she looked around, she noticed that black and white photos hung between the windows, showing old Portland.

The photo closest to Tara's table fascinated her. It was of an old fire brigade boat pumping water at a flaming building. The fire was on the top floor of what looked like a fancy storefront. She couldn't make out the lettering that followed the curve of the façade, but the date underneath it appeared to be 1880. Smoke flew up from where the water and fire met, hazing the background.

It had taken her a few moments to realize that this photo had actually been taken during one of the huge floods. She'd originally assumed that the building that was on fire had been built next to the water. On closer examination, she realized that wasn't the case. The fire brigade boat floated in front of windows that were half submerged by the flood waters.

Was the fire on the second story of the building? The third? Tara couldn't tell. But it spoke of the desperate flooding that had occurred in Portland before humans had altered the course of the Willamette river, straightening it out as well as damming it.

"I was there. At that flood," came a deep, rich voice, a sort of "late night jazz" voice that sent cascades of goosebumps across Tara's shoulders. The voice had a slight British accent, something that Tara associated with "very posh," as it were.

"Really? You were?" Tara asked as she turned to greet Lucius.

A tall man stood next to her table, over six foot and wiry. He had thick silver hair that hung down past his shoulders. It was starting to recede from his forehead, making his face look long and thin. Brilliant blue eyes peered at her, pinning her in place. His thin lips curved in a sensuous smile, as if he liked what he saw. He had a slight cleft in his solid chin and an oversized nose, but all the parts fit together, giving him the appearance of a serious, intense older gentleman. His dark blue button-down shirt contributed to the effect.

"Yes, *really*," Lucius said, rolling his eyes at her. "Why you young people couldn't have come up with a better interrogator, I just don't know."

Tara bit her lips together so that she wouldn't end up grinning at the affronted man. "You must be Lucius," she said, rising from her table. "I'm Tara." She didn't reach out to shake his hand—Kyle had warned her that Lucius didn't enjoy casual touching any more than he did.

Lucius nodded his head to her. "Charmed, I'm sure." He glanced down at the table. "How's the tea here?"

Tara grimaced. "Not that great," she admitted.

"Coffee it is, then," Lucius said, turning abruptly and going to the counter to get his own beverage.

Tara understood why Lucius had chosen that name—he greatly resembled the character from the movie, especially given his long silver hair. He also held himself in a very stiff manner, as if he was uncomfortable in his skin.

Was that his natural appearance? Tara wasn't sure, and Kyle sure wasn't telling.

When Lucius came back, he sat without a word. He had a large mug of what looked like plain black coffee. Then he picked up a bare spoon and put it into the mug. As he stirred, a golden trail followed the path of the spoon.

"Honey," Lucius said when she looked back up at his face. "The real kind, not that fake sticky substance that they generally serve that's mostly made from corn syrup."

Tara wasn't about to point out that this place probably did have real honey. It was an indie coffee shop in Portland. She didn't know for certain, however.

"Thank you for agreeing to meet with me," Tara said after a moment. "I appreciate it."

Lucius nodded at her, as if she was only giving him the courtesy due him.

As he didn't say anything more, Tara continued, "I figure this is something of an interview, to see if you are a good fit for my coven or not. I have questions for you, but I'm also certain that you have questions for me. Would you like to go first?"

Lucius gave her a small smile. "Thank you. Tell me about your battle with the Riprap man. The first time."

Tara blinked, surprised. That wasn't what she'd been expecting him to ask about. She picked up her cup and took a sip, regretting it instantly as the brew was just too bitter.

Lucius pointed a finger at her cup. Instantly, she saw a swirl of golden honey dance across the surface of the black tea. It moved on its own, dissolving into the hot liquid.

"Now try it," Lucius prompted.

Tara hesitated. Wasn't there a saying about not accepting honey from a stranger? She glanced up at him, only to see him staring at her closely.

Was this some sort of test? To see if she'd trust him or not?

While Tara didn't know or trust Lucius, Kyle did trust him. And Tara trusted Kyle.

She took a small sip of her tea. The honey had added the perfect level of sweetness, as well as the taste of some sort of fruit. "Orange blossom?" Tara asked after a second sip.

"Indeed," Lucius said. He seemed impressed despite himself.

"Thank you," Tara was sure to say as she put down her tea. Then she started talking about the Riprap man, how her soul had battled him deep under the water, on one of the footings of the Burnside bridge. He'd polluted the water, sliming her skin, stealing the light and her air.

Tara found it difficult to breathe as she relived the horror of that battle, the unnatural creature she faced, the blindness of the river "god"—Tara still maintained that it was a spirit, not a god. A true god wouldn't be so petty. Or so she hoped.

She explained her bargain, how she had promised to honor the spirit of the river at the equinox with rose petals. She'd set aside a large allotment, and had already planned on spending most of the day on a boat on the water, sprinkling the petals and singing hymns.

"After I got free, the river spirit appeared to attack the Riprap man. I'd assumed he hadn't survived, not until he showed up in my dreams last week." Tara grimaced and shuddered, remembering the coldness of the water.

"Water is your element, yes?" Lucius asked.

"It is," Tara said. "And I'm not going to let the Riprap man or anyone else keep me away from it." She'd consistently gone swimming ever since that battle, even though the first few times it had been difficult for her to put her head under the water, even at the shallow end of the pool at her local YMCA.

"Describe the Riprap man, his appearance, the last time you saw him," Lucius commanded.

Tara tried not to let his tone bother her. "It's as if the rocks that made up his body have been dislodged. He's no longer symmetrical. His torso is still stolid, but at the same time, I keep wondering if he's been weakened."

"The Riprap man's element is not water, correct?" Lucius said.

"I think that's right," Tara said, particularly given the reaction of the river spirit.

"Would you say that perhaps, given his appearance, his element might be earth? Or stone?"

Tara's eyes widened. "That hadn't occurred to me. But you're probably right." Why had the river spirit chosen someone like the Riprap man to be its champion when water wasn't the Riprap man's element?

"Given your description, it sounds to me that it's the water that's changed his appearance. As though the rocks have been in the path of a mighty torrent for decades, and are being slowly worn away," Lucius mused.

"That's an accurate description," Tara said, thinking about it. It made so much sense to her now.

"You may well be able to use that in your coming battle," Lucius said. "Calling the water to you. Though that may just provoke him into calling the stones that he's named himself after. An interesting dilemma."

"Will we still be battling? If I keep my promise to honor the spirit of the river?" Tara asked.

Lucius gave a cold laugh. "He'll prevent you from keeping your promise. You need to be prepared for that."

Tara nodded. She'd assumed that he'd try to stop her somehow. "I will still fight," she said.

"You are human. It's what you do best," Lucius said. "Fighting against impossible odds. While any sane creature would accept that they've lost and move on."

"If you're so disdainful of humans, why would you want to join with us?" Tara said. "Why would you want to be considered for this coven?"

Lucius raised his eyebrows in surprise. "I'm not disdainful of your kind."

"Really?" Tara said, deliberately provoking him.

The sigh he gave her was worthy of any disgruntled teenager. "The majority of you aren't worth my time. Now, before you go off in a huff, let me explain."

He took a sip of his coffee while Tara tried to release her anger. Kyle had warned that Lucius could be difficult.

"My kind are long lived. Very long lived." He stared at her, his brilliant blue eyes taking on a pale light. She saw centuries in there. "How am I supposed to approach creatures who will only be around for a fraction of my lifetime? You're here, then gone. When I say you are not worthy of my time, I mean that literally. You rarely exist even long enough for me to notice you."

"I see," Tara said slowly.

"Do you? I doubt it," Lucius said dismissively.

"No, I do," Tara said. "When I was being tested, passing within the circles, the circle of earth, I had to become a tree. I had to experience the fall and winter, only to be reborn in the spring. An old oak led me through it."

"Interesting," Lucius said. "Kyle had said that I would find you fascinating. He may have been right. You're a strange mixture of natural and learned."

"Thanks, I think," Tara said. "Do you have more questions for me?"

Lucius cocked his head to the side as if the question itself puzzled him. "No, not at this time," he said slowly. "I assume you have questions for me?"

"I do," Tara said. She took a deep breath. She didn't want to piss Lucius off, but she had to make sure that he knew what he was getting into.

"The coven I'm forming is going to be different than a general witch's coven," she started with. "As you said, I'm a mixture of natural and learned, a hedgewitch who started off as a schooled witch. But one of the people I've invited is a pure hedgewitch."

Lucius raised a single imperial eyebrow at that but didn't say anything.

"I've also asked a mundane human to join us. He's a research librarian with mad skills. Since I have no ancient texts or lore, he's an incredibly useful resource for us, searching through old files and books. He has access to materials we don't."

"Fascinating," Lucius said. "Go on."

He actually did look interested. "Then there's Kaede. Ze is a fifth level witch who's left zir coven, who's an anarchist and runs a community center."

Lucius blinked. "I find it fascinating that humans have finally come to appreciate that gender is a continuum, not binary."

"Uhm, okay," Tara said, remembering that Kyle had emphasized more than once that Lucius wasn't really human. "What pronoun would you prefer? I apologize for not asking sooner."

That got her a real laugh, one that sounded warm and rich and full of honey. "He/his," Lucius said easily. "At least for today."

Tara wasn't sure if Lucius was being serious or not, if he really did change gender sometimes. "Thank you for telling me," she said. She took another sip of her tea. It was still perfect. "Then there's Kyle, who you know, and me."

"Are you the head of this coven?" Lucius asked.

"That's really the question of the hour, isn't it?" Tara said. "Generally, the head of a coven is the most powerful witch in the group. I'm not. I've only recently passed into the second level."

"I'm surprised by that," Lucius said. "I would have judged you as much stronger. You have the power." He paused, then asked, "Have you any familiars?"

"Kind of?" Tara said. She explained about Soot and how the Riprap man appeared to have captured the wind's attention.

"It makes sense that he'd have an affinity toward a familiar that was an element," Lucius said. "Given that he's already bound to a water spirit."

Tara sat up straighter. "Thank you," she said. "That explains a lot. But I don't know what to do. Do I try to call Soot back to me? Break the hold the Riprap man has on him? Or free the wind instead?"

"I can't advise you, I'm afraid," Lucius said. "I have had very few dealings with familiars and not a lot of insight. You might ask your other hedgewitch friend."

"I will ask her about it," Tara said, making a mental note.

"In the meanwhile, you might go about seeing if you can call a familiar for your current circle," Lucius said. "Some sort of fire element."

Tara opened her mouth and then shut it again. "What sort of creature takes the shape of a fire element?"

"That's something you'll have to discover, my dear," Lucius said. "I think that any sort of fire creature may help you in your coming battle."

Tara nodded, recalling the familiar spark deep in her core that still kept her warm. She'd developed an affinity for fire more recently, despite already having an affinity for water. What would it take to call a fire element? She was going to have to ask Kyle about it.

"So, for the sake of argument, say that I'm nominally in charge of this coven, though I'm going to listen to everyone and make this as much of a team effort as possible," Tara continued after a moment. "I think that strictly going by majority voting is a mistake." She knew that she'd end up fighting with Kaede on that point, but for now, Tara knew that she was right.

Tara turned a frank gaze on Lucius. "If I make a decision about something that you disagree with, will you follow my lead anyway? You probably have the strongest magic of the entire group."

"That depends," Lucius said. "If you've made an honest effort to listen to my council but still are convinced of your foolhardy ways, who am I to gainsay you? Though I will admit that if it happens frequently, I will be leaving your little group."

"Fair enough," Tara said. She swallowed. "Kyle has said that you're a being of power, not human, quite alien and occasionally alarming. You've been very accommodating today, which I thank you for. But I need to understand exactly why Kyle finds you so disturbing."

"Ah, you want the mask to slip?" Lucius said. He considered for a long moment. "Very well."

He nodded, then grew very still.

Tara found herself swallowing against a suddenly dry throat. Lucius's physical appearance hadn't changed, though his eyes had taken on a brighter glow.

However, the *presence* that Lucius projected had completely transformed.

Tara gripped the edges of the table and held herself in place despite how fast her panic rose, her fight-or-flight instinct growing stronger by the second. It was as if she was suddenly face to face with a monster. Though Lucius hadn't said or done anything, and still looked human, Tara felt at a gut level that he was *alien* in a fundamental way, terrifying and dangerous, as if through will alone he could cause her harm.

He reminded her of the schizophrenic she'd seen at Hallowed Ground. He, too, had been frightening because he'd been so insane and high at the time, a danger to himself and others.

Lucius conveyed the same feeling to Tara, of imminent violence from the least provocation, just because someone said, "Hi" instead of "Hello."

And he wasn't human. Tara had no doubt about that, deep down in her bones.

They stared at each other across the table for an endless time before

Lucius put back on his mask, as it were, then reached down and took a sip of coffee.

Tara blinked and shook her head. With shaking hands she reached for her own mug. The tea warmed as she touched it, her hedgewitch magic suddenly at work.

She took a sip, then another, before she brought her eyes up to look at Lucius again.

"All better now?" he asked, his smile sardonic.

Tara nodded, not yet trusting her voice. After a few moments, she finally said, "Thank you for showing me."

She'd thought that the Riprap man had been an alien creature. She'd not really known what alien was, though, before Lucius had shown her.

"Any more questions?" Lucius said.

"No," Tara said. She pondered the being in front of her, who didn't appear to take offense at her sitting there thinking for a moment.

Could she work with Lucius? Invite him into her inner circle? Knowing that he was so alien, so magical, so malevolent at heart? Or would she feel as though she was using him, just to gain his power for her use?

"I can see your hesitation," Lucius said. "And I honor that, much more than if you had immediately leapt to invite me. My people are solitary in nature. I'm considered quite gregarious among my kind. Would it make a difference to you to know that I believe I would enjoy the company of your coven, at least for a while?"

"Yes," Tara said, taking a sigh of relief. "I hesitate because I don't want to feel as though I'm using you."

Lucius gave her a bitter smile. "And that's where our fundamental philosophies differ. I have no problem whatsoever using you for my gain. My automatic assumption is that you'll do the same. There would be no hard feelings about it. It's just in my nature."

"How would you be using us?" Tara asked, perplexed. He certainly didn't need their power or their magic.

"For entertainment, of course!" Lucius said snidely. "Plus, you do seem as though you might occasionally listen to the wisdom of your elders, which, believe me, is more rare than you can imagine."

"Would the Riprap man come after you? If he knew that you were a part of my coven?" Tara said after a bit. The part about being Lucius's entertainment stung. However, she'd rather know the truth.

The smile Lucius gave her reminded her of a cat having found its prey sitting unaware. "Oh, I'm counting on it."

Though Tara had originally invited everyone to Kyle's complex for the gathering on Monday night, Kaede had volunteered Hallowed Ground that evening for their meeting instead. The afterschool program finished at seven, and the people sleeping upstairs had been told that the downstairs was in use that night, something that happened now and again.

Kaede had left explicit instructions for Tara and the others to knock on the front door when they arrived.

Standing outside the converted office space, Tara still felt hesitant. It was as if the very building repelled her. She peered closely at the door, but couldn't see any markings on it. The night behind her felt soft, despite the soft pattering of rain. The smell of wet concrete filled the air. She shivered when a slight breeze touched the back of her neck, but when Tara turned around, she didn't see anyone, or anything, there.

Telling herself not to be ridiculous, Tara raised her hand and knocked, though her brain screamed at her that she was just inviting the monsters in by doing so.

Kaede opened the door immediately. "Felt you out there," ze said with a grin. "Wondered how long it would take for you to overcome the repulsion." Kaede wore skinny jeans and a plain gray sweatshirt, which made zir look younger.

"How did you do that?" Tara asked, curious. When Kaede closed the door, Tara saw the pentagram drawn in chalk on the inside, as well as sachets hanging inside each point of the star. "Ah," she said, nodding. That was what she'd felt.

The tables and chairs had all been pushed to the walls of the room, looking like the first time Tara had seen it. The air still held the remains of the meal that had been served, the potatoes and industrial gravy. Tara hoped that once she started working here, she could teach the ones who cooked how to spice the food better, make it less bland, more appetizing.

Kaede directed Tara to put her jacket on one of the chairs next to the door. The air was cooler than Tara had expected. The cold found her skin immediately, casting goosebumps across her shoulders, though she was dressed in a loose black sweater over a white shirt, jeans, and warm boots. Her soul liked this place: the room itself felt comfortable —homey, even. However, Tara still expected it to be warmer. Maybe that was because she associated comfort with warmth.

"Don't want the regulars coming by and knocking when they see lights on in the windows," Kaede explained about the door. "The charms should keep out the rest. Plus, it will let you know if anyone in the coven can't overcome the spells."

"I do have a mundane coming, Richard," Tara said, worried.

"Tell him to text you when he arrives," Kaede suggested.

Tara did that, only to receive a text a moment later with Richard saying, "I'm here."

Tara opened the door to find Richard standing there looking worried. "I know I've been here before but I just couldn't figure out if this was the right place or not." He stood rigidly still, his eyes wide in his pale face. He wore a black coat over his standard T-shirt and jeans.

He jumped when Tara reached out and wrapped her hand around his arm.

"It's the magic," Tara explained as she tugged him across the threshold.

"Wow," Richard said as he turned and took in the back of the door. "I mean, I know you have magic and all. I've experienced it. I just…Yeah."

Tara grinned at Kaede, who gave her a nod in return. "I'm Kaede," ze said. "This is my space."

"I can tell," Richard said as he shucked his coat, putting it on one of the chairs next to the door, beside Tara's.

"Can you?" Tara asked. "Can you tell it's zir space? Or just that it's private?"

Richard thought for a moment. "Just private," he said after a moment.

Tara gave him an encouraging smile. She figured that would be his response. He was mundane, through and through.

Ginny arrived next. She had a big hug for Tara, which surprised her, though just a nod for the others. She wore a thick green wool jacket, with oversized sleeves and a long pointed hood—an elf jacket— over thick black leggings, solid boots, and a beige sweater that showed off her pale skin and copper hair.

After Tara introduced Ginny, she said, "I have a question for you, about my wind, Soot." Tara explained that what the Riprap man had done, how Tara hadn't been able to call Soot back since. The others listened intently.

"He's got ahold of it, that's fer sure," Ginny said, nodding. "Ye'll have to release him."

"How?" Tara asked, her heart sinking. She hadn't had Soot for long, but he still fit into her life, as if he'd filled a hole she hadn't known she had. She missed him more each day.

"Go to where ye called him. Open yer hands and spread yer arms and let 'im go," Ginny said. "Sorry, can't explain more than that. Just let 'im know your intent. That Riprap man will do the rest."

"Thanks," Tara said. One more thing to do before the equinox.

Lucius showed up next, wearing a timeless, scrumptious, long black wool coat over a black suit and white shirt. He had a cane with him that night, also black, with what appeared to be a silver dragon's head on the top of the cane.

"Interesting place," he said, looking sharply in all the corners, as if expecting large spiderwebs to be hanging there.

"Thank you," Kaede said through gritted teeth.

Tara had already warned all of them that Lucius sounded snide all the time. Each person in the coven needed to find their own relationship with him if this coven was going to work together.

Ginny, however, merely gazed at Lucius with wide eyes and had stammered hello when introduced.

Kyle came last. He'd insisted on going home after work, showering and changing before coming to the meeting. His mint-green long-sleeved shirt looked almost as formal as Lucius's suit, and set off Kyle's black skin nicely.

Had he felt the need to dress up for his sometimes lover? To show off? Tara wasn't certain.

Tara led them all to the center of the room. The floor had been washed clean, the pentagram no longer visible. The group stood in a circle. Though Tara knew she was supposed to be the main point, she felt as though Lucius drew all attention to himself, willfully or not. He stood directly opposite her, with Ginny and Kaede on either side of him. Richard and Kyle stood on either side of Tara.

Though Sheila and Miss Lucy had always stood in the center of the circle, drawing all the power to them, so they could focus it better, Tara deliberately stood with everyone else in the circle itself. That felt more right to her, and she suspected Kaede appreciated it as well.

"Thank you all for coming," Tara started off with. "I appreciate each and every one of you joining together in the circle tonight, to celebrate life and all its cycles. I call on the goddess Brigid to bless this endeavor, as she regularly blesses and guards the world with her grace and fortune. I call on the god Samil, warrior for all beings. I call on the fullness of the seasons, the turnings of the sun and the moon, the natural phases of the world everlasting, to witness our calling and our resolve," Tara said, her voice falling into a natural rhythm.

She hadn't planned out the prayer, though she knew she was supposed to. However, anytime she'd tried to do that, her words always came out stilted and monotone. She had some idea of what she wanted to say, then winged the rest of it, making sure to say "beings" instead of "people" where necessary.

Tara reached out to hold hands with Kyle, on her one side, and Richard, on her other. They in turn held hands with Kaede and Ginny, who reached out to Lucius last.

He made a face at her, but finally acquiesced, deigning to press his flesh against the mere humans.

A surge of warm power ran through the circle when it was finally made whole. Tara had never felt such a strong connection before.

Was this due to Lucius? Or was it because she'd chosen all these beings to be part of *her* coven? In the past, would she have felt something this strong if the leader of the coven had joined in the circle, instead of standing in the center of it?

Tara called on the moon to bless them, then directed the flow of power outward to heal the world. It was surely needed it at this point, though Tara realized that even their combined magical healing was just a drop in the bucket being rapidly emptied by man.

In a regular circle, the head witch would focus the magic thrumming through her and direct it toward some task. She hadn't really been able to think of anything that she wanted to get done, except to stop the Riprap man.

Would the magic being generated stop her enemy? Could they, as a group, utterly destroy him? She wasn't sure. She knew, though, that once she wielded that knife, destroyed another being with power, she'd never let it go.

Though Tara had left Miss Lucy, the allure of dark forces still haunted her.

Instead, Tara nodded to Kaede, who spoke, starting a new prayer. Effortlessly, ze picked up the threads of magic flowing between them and wove them together into a broad net. Tara couldn't see it with her physical eyes, but she had a sense of it, golden and glittering, expanding as it floated above the circle.

Then Kaede flung the net up, pushing the healing and goodwill through the ceiling, up toward those sleeping above them.

Tara admired zir skill, how ze shaped the power with words and prayers, bringing not just blessing but actual healing for those who were physically inside the structure Kaede commanded.

When Kaede finished, Tara said a closing prayer, thanking everyone again, before releasing the hands of those standing beside her.

"Wow," was all Ginny had to say, looking around the circle at everyone. "Is it always like that?" she asked. She sounded stoned. Tara felt the same way.

"No, not always," Tara said. "This is a particularly strong group."

"Pity," Lucius said. "I would consider joining more covens after you've passed if it was," he explained after a moment.

That made Tara smile. It seemed that even Lucius had been impressed by what they'd just done.

Kaede nodded. "It's because of the loose structure of the group," ze said, nodding zir head. "The tight hierarchy of the regular circle usually chokes off the flow of power."

Tara wasn't about to roll her eyes but honestly, she didn't think that was the case at all. She strongly believed that it was because of their combined power, due to a large part because of Lucius.

Richard looked lost. "Can someone explain to the blind guy what just happened?"

Lucius looked him up and down. "Despite being blind, as you so aptly described it, you actually contributed a small trickle of power to the rest of us. We, in turn, cast a healing for the poor souls who inhabit in this building. I believe that come morning, they may find that their reliance on drugs and other crutches has been greatly diminished. Well done," he added, nodding toward Kaede.

Though his words sounded like an insult, Kaede accepted them with grace.

"I've never been part o'something so strong," Ginny commented. "Not even dancing on the solstice with me gran during the full moon."

"Did we actually heal people?" Richard asked, still trying to figure out what he'd been a part of.

"Yes," Tara said. "We couldn't—we couldn't completely heal them. That would have taken too much energy—more than even this group could manage. But we did help all of those sleeping above us."

"Wow," Richard said. "I feel as though I've just run three marathons. But also as if I raised a million bucks by finishing. You know?"

Tara grinned at him. "I know." She turned to Lucius. "Were you able to feel each thread of power individually?"

"Yes," Lucius said. "Vaguely," he added with a dismissive gesture.

Tara found that interesting. She hadn't been able to figure out which strand of power came from which being—it had all flowed together like a grand river.

"If that's all the fun and games for tonight, then?" Lucius asked Tara.

"Yes, yes it is. Thank you for coming," she added. "We'll be back together Wednesday night." The night of the equinox. The night when the Riprap man would be coming for her soul.

For the first time in more than a week, Tara felt hope.

SEVEN

The river god had warned me about the transformation, telling me that it would induce a great deal of pain. I don't believe He understands the mortal agony of blood boiling away under the skin or bones crushing together into a new form. My shrieks and screams must have sounded as though I was being tortured by the devil himself. I cannot say how long the transformation took: a single night, or an entire eternity. Perhaps both. My new form is not displeasing to me, the rocks and boulders reminding me of the headwaters before me. However, Mulinohana appears dissatisfied with my new appearance. Perhaps He expected something different? I shall endure, though, as long as my new form shall last. Not forever, no, even mountains will be ground down to dust eventually. But I have promised to serve my new God until that day.

Wilson Evermore, Reborn and Everlasting, 1921

As SOON AS Kyle and Tara returned to Kyle's condo after the magical healing circle at Hallowed Ground, Tara stepped out onto the porch to release Soot. She felt both wired and exhausted. However, she also felt as if she had to let go of the wind as soon as she could. She'd never had asthma, but she imagined that it probably felt like this, unable to take a deep breath at least half the time.

Tara placed her own protection sachet on the porch railing, filled with angelica and Scottish thistle, hiding her from prying eyes. She called Soot, not expecting him to show up.

A wind swirled around her jacket and the dog appeared at her feet.

"Good boy," Tara said. Should she let him go? Now that he'd finally come to her call? Just seeing him filled her heart with a warm joy.

Soot pushed up against her hand, wanting to be petted. Her fingers followed the cool contours of his head, her fingers sliding across his soft fur. His tail thumped on the hard concrete of the balcony.

"Soot, you know I can't keep you," she said softly.

He merely looked up at her, as if awaiting her command. Did she want him to go chase something? Anything?

Tara took a step back. "I release you," she said. She opened her hands, palms out. Then she pushed her arms skyward, as if doing a yoga pose. "I release you," she said again. "You are no longer at my beck and call. Off with you. Be free."

Her arms raised above her head, Tara said again, "I release you."

She brought her hands down in front of her, palms together in prayer pose, closing her eyes. "I release you," she whispered again.

Winds whirled around and around, pressing against her legs, tugging at her ponytail, begging to be noticed.

"I release you," Tara said firmly, stubbornly.

Finally, the winds died down. Tara opened her eyes to find herself standing alone on the balcony.

Had it worked? She took a deep breath, her chest still slightly constricted, though not as much.

She regretted having to let Soot go. He remained special to her. She wished she could call him again. She pressed her lips together so that she wouldn't.

Damn it. She didn't like this part at all.

Maybe after she defeated the Riprap man she could call Soot back to her. She hoped so.

Blinking back tears that she didn't want to feel, Tara went back into the warm living room, ignoring the way the winds appeared to push at the windows for the rest of the night.

TARA BREATHED a sigh of relief when she let herself into Ye Olde Magicke Shoppe and saw that there was a large stuffed manila envelope with her name on it waiting for her at the counter. She quickly put her lunch into the refrigerator in the backroom of the shop, got the money for the register out of the safe in the supply room, counted it out, signed for it, as well as opened the shop for customers before she ripped open the end of her package.

The heady scent of roses flowed up and out of the container. Tara peered down at them.

Wait, was that something moving?

She shook the bag, then nearly dropped it when black beetle-like bugs came to the top of the pink and red petals.

They were eating her petals! Where had they come from? How had they gotten in there?

Tara was about to take the package into the backroom and blast the petals with a cleaning spell—maybe some lemon balm, rosemary, and angelica would do the trick—when the bell announcing customers merrily rang.

For the next three hours, Tara dealt with a steady stream of people coming into the shop. It was too early for Halloween; however, that appeared to be what everyone was shopping for. Wands and witch's hats and trinkets for decorating their houses.

By the time Tara got back to her packet of rose petals again, it was a heaving mass of beetles. The package wiggled in between her fingers.

Ugh! She couldn't clean the bugs out. The petals were ruined. She was just going to have to throw them all away.

Luckily, she had another stash of petals at home. They were under protective spells, or at least had been since she realized the Riprap man was still alive and coming after her.

The first thing she was going to have to do when she got home was to check that those petals were still okay.

Then the shop went crazy again, another stream of customers arriving.

When Tara had a few moments to breathe midafternoon, she went into the backroom of the shop to check on the jar of rose petals there.

While the front room catered to simple tourists with its pyramids of power, charged crystals and geodes, as well as focusing wands and protective rocks, the backroom held ingredients that real witches and beings of power used. The backroom was hidden in plain sight according Patricia, the owner of the shop—the only people who went back there, or who even noticed that it existed, were people who had magic in them.

Tara relaxed as soon as she stepped into the clean space. Brown wooden shelves lined the walls and held cannisters of ingredients. An old-fashioned balance stood on the counter in the corner, with the metal weights beneath it. Two large, silver refrigerators lurked in the corner, holding the fresh herbs.

With trepidation, Tara opened the fridge and picked up the cannister that contained the rose petals. She shook it, but didn't hear any scrabbling.

Cautiously, Tara opened the container. It still smelled like roses. She shook it gently.

No bugs spoiled the pink and red petals.

Tara measured out four cups of rose petals into a clean bag. Luckily they didn't cost that much, only a few dollars per cup; however, Tara didn't want to clean out all of Patricia's supply either. She carefully sealed the bag, labeled it with her name, then taped a sprig of rosemary to the outside, to help preserve the petals inside.

Of course, when Patricia arrived (late) Tara was in such a hurry to gather up her things that she forgot the package in the backroom. She didn't discover this until after she'd gotten back to Kyle's condo, after the store was closed and she was checking on her own supply.

"Can you believe that I forgot them?" Tara told Kyle, grousing about her day.

He raised both eyebrows at her. "It might not have just been coincidence. Would you call what happened to you bad luck?"

Tara nodded. Then understanding dawned on her. "It's the Riprap man, isn't it? A spell of bad luck has been cast on me."

"Exactly," Kyle said. "He's going to do everything he can to prevent you from honoring your promise to the river spirit."

Tara looked at her pitifully small collection of rose petals. She'd expected to have a dozen cups or more. Now, she had merely four. She was going to have to make every petal count.

Or else face the Riprap man in battle for her soul, once again.

Tara anxiously checked her rose petals in the morning, but no beetles appeared to have found them. Then again, she had put extra protection spells on and around the container. Kyle had contributed a couple of sachets as well.

Fortunately, Tara kept the container holding the petals—a solid white cannister originally designed to hold coffee—closed as she made her way from her room to the kitchen. An unseen line in the floor tripped her, sending her sprawling on her face, flinging the cannister in front of her.

Fearing the worst, Tara ignored her bruised elbows and knees and crawled over to check the container. Luckily, it hadn't shattered on impact. A large crack did now run across the base of it. She was able to transfer the petals, still bug free, from the porcelain container to a glass jar. Then she thought better of it, and put them into one of Kyle's plastic disposable containers instead.

When Tara tripped and fell again not two minutes later, she was glad of her choice. Normally, she wouldn't keep any herbs or ingredients in plastic. It was too porous, let in too much light and air, which would degrade the ingredients kept inside. But for a single day, Tara was glad to use it.

Now, she just had to get to the boat pier on time, without

dropping or losing her petals. Her protection sachet for the day mostly held goldenseal as a charm against bad luck, as well as hellebore, ginseng, and rue to guard her from evil. However, they didn't seem to be doing much to counter whatever it was the Riprap man was doing.

Tara dressed in a lightweight gray sweater, along with a bright blue rain jacket that would keep off any wind or water. She wore her rainbow patterned rainboots, along with her sunhat. The day outside was clear again, but Tara didn't trust the clouds on the horizon, promising plenty of rain later on. Crisp air reddened her cheeks and lifted her ponytail up from her back.

Tara had paid for a tourist type boat trip that day, traveling up and down the river so she could scatter her petals properly. Though the trip to the pier where she'd meet the boat should have only taken an hour, she left two hours early due to her bad luck.

Of course, the MAX train she boarded ground to a halt between stations. She ended up sitting for almost thirty minutes before it got moving again. Which made her miss her bus connection.

Tara clutched her bag to her like she was a crazed woman, never putting it beside her once. She knew that the moment she released it, she might forget it or someone would steal her petals.

The walk to pier was more empty than she'd expected. Not even the homeless were on the sides of the road. It felt eerie to walk along such an empty street, even half a block. Small one-story buildings were on either side, the front windows dark and sightless. Winds carrying the smell of rotting fish and reeds swirled around her. Clouds covered the sun, turning the day abruptly gray and chilled.

Tara kept looking over her shoulder, expecting to see the Riprap man or Soot or hell, even Lucius stalking behind her.

The street remained empty. Tara wondered it if was just her imagination or if it was part of the general spell the Riprap man had put on her that made her want to turn tail and run.

With great relief, Tara finally reached the small building from which she'd bought her ride. She'd called the night before to make sure that everything was still on track. The harried woman who'd answered had assured Tara that it was all still a go.

The gray siding on the walls had seen better days. Dirt-spattered raindrops covered the front windows. However, a faded red sign proclaiming the place as "Open" had been turned in the window for the door.

Tara opened the door with trepidation. "Hello?" she called into the empty office.

Two desks sat behind the tall counters. Piles of paper filled the desks and not in an orderly chaos. Ancient yellowing monitors sat on each desk. Cheap wood paneling covered the walls, and the air smelled like tacky pine air-fresheners.

"Hello?" Tara called again. She knew she was early for her appointment, but only by fifteen minutes.

She looked behind her, but there were no chairs for her to sit on. Just calendars at least five years out of date on the wall, showing washed-out pictures of boats gliding across the water on formerly sunny days.

From somewhere in the back of the building, Tara heard the sound of water gushing through plumbing. Finally, an older woman stuck her head out into the front office—April, if Tara was remembering correctly.

"Ah, Tara, you're finally here," April said. She had gray hair that stood at attention all around her face, with watery gray eyes set deeply into a tanned face. Her lipstick was an unfortunate pale pink, something that would have looked better on a teenager, not someone approaching sixty.

"Jacob has the boat all set and ready to go," April continued. She started sorting through the papers on the desk on the left side of the office, first looking at the papers at the top of one pile before shifting to the next. "Now, where did that final release form go?"

Tara kept a tight smile on her face. More bad luck? It appeared so. April had to reprint the forms for Tara to sign after fifteen minutes of fruitless search.

"Don't tell Jacob," April asked as Tara finally finished signing all the forms. "He'll scold me for them getting lost. I really did print them out once before," she assured her.

Tara didn't bother explaining that it was a supernatural creature affecting all of them. "I'm sure they'll show up as soon as I step out of the office," she said.

April gave a bright laugh. "Isn't that how it always goes! Now, here's your copy. Hurry down the pier. You'll see The Yellow Rose midway down, in berth 39, on the left."

"Thank you," Tara said. She didn't think that Jacob would leave without her. She'd expected to be one of the few paying customers that day. It was late in the season, and there wouldn't be that many tourists who wanted to go out on the river these days.

However, that turned out to be wrong. A group of twelve schoolchildren, around the age of ten, were already on the boat, along with half a dozen harried looking adults.

"Good, you got here," Jacob said, taking Tara's paper from her with one hand while helping her over the bow on the other. "I wouldn't have left without you, as it was our fault that the time was changed and you weren't notified."

"I see," Tara said. The kids all looked sulkily at her, predisposed to dislike her for having made them wait.

This was going to be even more awkward than she'd imagined. If she could have turned around and walked right back off the boat, she would have.

How was she going to sing praises to the river spirit while a bunch of kids watched? How could she keep them from disturbing her?

Tara cursed the Riprap man once again while making her way to a side bench. She was just going to have to figure out a way to make this work regardless.

Tara's first break came when the teachers and volunteers gathered all the kids to the front of the boat for their midmorning snack of cheese sticks and juice. Tara wasn't about to point out that hyping the kids up on the sugary drink probably wasn't the smartest move. However, at least it gave her a few minutes at the back of the boat alone.

Tara gave a sigh of relief when she opened the plastic container with the rose petals. They were still pure, no sign of bugs or beetles.

She grabbed a handful out of the container, then closed it up again immediately. For a moment, Tara closed her eyes and composed herself. Then she opened her eyes, looking out on the peaceful water flowing behind the boat and started quietly singing a hymn to the water spirits, thanking them for the mighty water for bringing all things life.

As she reached the end of short hymn, Tara reached out over the edge of the boat and opened her palm, intending to drop the first fistful of rose petals onto the surface of the water.

A sudden wind sprang up. The petals streamed to the nearest bank in a solid line instead of floating down to the water.

"Damn it!" Tara said. She guiltily looked behind her. Hopefully none of the kids, or their minders, had heard her.

She grabbed a few more petals, merely stating, "Thank you for your bounty," before she tried scattering them again.

This time, she actually saw Soot flowing through the air, snatching up every petal and sending it onward.

"Oh, Soot," Tara said. Her heart beat harder and a familiar ache set in. She abruptly realized that she hadn't let him go, not completely. However, he wasn't really hers to direct either.

The dog looked at her happily, as if they were playing the best game in the world. Anytime she let go of even a few petals, he chased them all away from the water. Then he would come back and sit at her feet, looking proud of his accomplishment and begging for more of this game.

Tara gave up after a while. She had barely a handful of petals left. Maybe she should just jump in the water with them in her hand?

When Tara peered down into the water, the face of the Riprap man grinned back up at her.

If she went into the water, he'd drag her down into the depths. Maybe she'd survive a physical battle with him. Chances were, she wouldn't.

What was she going to do? How was she going to scatter her rose petals across the water? It might have just been her imagination, but she felt as though the river spirit was growing tired of her failure.

Then the kids broke free from their imposed gathering, having finished their snack, and came racing back to the rear end of the boat again.

Tara leaned against the railing, her own dark cloud descending. There had to be a way for her to get at least a few petals into the water, without Soot chasing them all away, without the Riprap man dragging her into the depths like a waiting crocodile.

But how?

When the boat had finally finished its tour, Tara still had no idea what she was going to do. There were bridges, of course, that she could use for flinging her petals into the water, but Soot would be sure to stop her. What would happen if she went to the very edge of the riverbank and just stuck her hand into the water? She knew that she'd promised to scatter the rose petals across the surface of the river. Hopefully if she managed to scatter at least a few petals, that would satisfy Mulinohana.

Tara wasn't about to admit failure. Not yet. Though she knew that if she didn't appease the river spirit, it wouldn't help her when the Riprap man came to battle for her soul.

She suspected that it was just revenge driving the Riprap man. He wouldn't bind Tara to one of the bridges, but instead, would kill her just to prove a point, to prove that he was a better disciple of Mulinohana than she was, despite her affinity for water.

Most of the riverbank in the city itself had been built up, not just to prevent flooding but also to prevent accidental drowning. The city didn't want to be sued every time an irresponsible parent let their kid near the water. So the city officials had made access to the water difficult.

Tara ended up taking a cab to one of the boat launching areas south of the city. It looked like a driveway leading down to the water. Trees rustled on either side of Tara as she marched down the concrete. Cold winds blew off the river, making her shiver. The sound of constant traffic flowed behind her, people rushing home after a long day at the office.

Of course, Tara tripped before she got to the end of the launch point. The container of rose petals flew open as she flung it up into the air, the petals streaming out to either side, scattered among the tall weeds growing beside the driveway.

"Goddess take you!" Tara cursed as she carefully picked at her bleeding palms, trying to remove some of the small pieces of gravel imbedded there. Her jeans had torn on impact as well, and her knees were bloody.

Groaning, Tara forced herself back up, picking up the plastic container that sat at the water's edge. Almost all of the petals were gone. She was able to scratch half a dozen petals that had stuck to the inside of the container out with her fingernails.

Instead of being fresh and fragrant, the few petals that remained were creased and torn. Hardly an adequate offering.

Still, Tara did her best. She sat at the edge of the water and sang the praises of the water and the river spirit, thanking him yet again for his bounty as well as his restraint, for not flooding the city, for granting them passage along the waters. Finally, Tara grit her teeth and stuck her hand into the water, releasing the few petals she had managed to save.

She saw them float back up, onto the surface of the river, then swirl away against the current.

It wasn't enough.

The battle was coming.

And she'd just blown her best chance of weakening the Riprap man.

***

"I FAILED," Tara announced glumly when she met with the coven later that evening. They'd gathered at a coffee shop just up the road from Hallowed Ground. Tara wrapped her carefully salved and bandaged hands around her tea cup and explained what had happened to the group.

"Does he come for ye tonight? Or in the morning?" Ginny asked when Tara finished. The light sprinkling of rain they'd walked through still sparkled in her bright red hair.

"Last time, it was the evening after the solstice," Tara said. "So I think I'm safe tonight. I don't think he wants to use my soul, like he has the other witches. Instead, this is just revenge, because the water spirit chose me instead of him."

"Do you think it's possible that the Riprap man injured Mulinohana during their battle?" Lucius asked. He sat slightly apart from the rest of the group, his chair pushed back with a general air of disdain.

Tara blamed herself for his reaction. He might not have been so put out if she'd actually managed to honor the river spirit as she'd promised. Then again, he'd known that the Riprap man would try to stop her.

Ginny answered. "He might have. If this Mulinohana is just a spirit in search of a human to bond with."

"How did they bond in the first place? Why?" Richard asked. He was rapidly taking notes on his phone, research angles he wanted to explore.

"Perhaps he was the only one in the area at the time," Lucius said. "As I understand it, bonding is very place specific, correct?"

"Aye," Ginny said. "And if this Riprap man was at the headwaters when Mulinohana lost its other followers, it might have just chosen from the lot at hand."

"And the Riprap man is strong, right?" Kaede said. "Wouldn't the spirit have chosen the strongest available to it?" Ze presented zir question with the air of a student discussing an upcoming paper.

"Maybe. Maybe not," Kyle said. He shrugged when Tara threw a questioning glance his way. "I've been asking around, making inquiries about hedgewitches and their familiars."

Tara smiled at that. The Riprap man just happened to have a familiar that was stronger than most, the spirit of the Willamette River.

"I tried releasing Soot, the wind who I'd bound," Tara said to the group. "I really didn't release him, though. I'm not sure why, if it was because I didn't really want to let go, or because I was doing it wrong, or something else." She took a deep breath, then turned to Ginny. "Is it possible to break the bond between a witch and their familiar?"

Ginny looked at her with big eyes. "It's possible. Anything's possible. It just ain't easy."

Lucius raised his hand to draw the attention of the group, but then just sat there with his lips pressed together, not saying anything.

After a few moments of silence, he finally gave Tara a vicious smile. "How do you feel about being a distraction, my dear?" he asked.

Tara blinked. She hadn't expected that question at all. "As long as I don't end up being dead or forever soulless, I'm game."

"I can't guarantee your safety," Lucius said seriously. "We can only give you a fighting chance."

"I'll take it," Tara said.

Even a slight hope was better than none.

EIGHT

Though my new form delights me still, I have learned of a few drawbacks. I had never been intimate with a woman before, never having felt a grand desire, as well as wanting to save myself for matrimony. Now, I shall never know the delights of the flesh. I cannot hold onto the illusion of a man during intimacy. Even if I found a woman willing to bear my true foreboding nature, I no longer function as a regular man. It is yet another sacrifice I gladly make to the great river god Mulinohana. I wish only to please my chosen god, to protect the grand city of Portland, and to continue to marvel at the progress marching across the land daily. I do not let myself dwell on my faults, how difficult it is to commune with Mulinohana sometimes, how the witches fight me when they should be begging me to take their spoiling souls and dedicate their lives toward true goodness. But I shall prevail.

Wilson Evermore, Transformed Protector, 1936

TARA SPENT the morning preparing for her possible death. She already had a will, courtesy of the first time she'd fought the Riprap man. She called her mom, just to chat. Her parents had "retired" and now owned a hobby farm in Wisconsin. It was always fascinating to hear about their latest project. Tara had never considered her parents "handy" but they'd fully committed to the farm.

That morning, Tara had made herself a bright tea, starting with a base of organic green tea, then adding dried lemongrass, dried blueberries, and dried apple bits. She smoothed it out with a touch of vanilla and cinnamon. Though the morning was sunny, it wasn't warm. Tara had brought a thick blanket with her to wrap around herself as she sat out on the balcony sipping her tea and staring at the buildings in front of her.

She felt as though she'd had too many last days. She wasn't frantic this time. Instead, she felt resigned to her fate. She wasn't planning on dying, but she also wasn't fighting so hard for every minute, either.

Tara made the decision to start planning for her future. She made appointments to go see new apartments for both that day as well as later in the week. She wrote a long, impassioned email to Miss Lucy to ask for donations of ingredients to Hallowed Ground, so Tara could start helping the youth there.

Then, determinedly, Tara took herself to the Y for a good long swim. The smell of the chlorine as she walked into the building made her shoulders drop down as she relaxed. The waters of the pool itself looked blue and inviting. A water aerobics class for seniors was being taught along the front side of the pool, while the back was separated off into lanes for people to swim laps.

Tara felt her world suddenly right itself as she slipped into the water. *This* was right. *This* was home. When Tara had been much younger, she'd wondered if her spirit animal would be an otter or a porpoise, some type of water creature. However, she now realized that *she* was the water creature, herself. After she finished her laps, she spent some time on the other side of the lap lanes, treading water and just splashing around, playing, all the while ignoring the women glaring at her from the class.

When Tara finally left the water, she felt refreshed despite all the exercise she'd just had. She was still humming as she took a shower and washed her hair, cleaning off the chlorine. She'd take another shower later, as the evening approached, to clean and purify herself for the coming ordeal.

She knew she shouldn't feel as buoyant as she did. This was possibly her last day on earth. But she couldn't help herself.

Tara slowed as she passed the long information desk just inside the door. A "help wanted" sign hung on the front of the desk, something she hadn't noticed on her way in.

It seemed that her local Y was looking for a fulltime swim instructor.

Tara stopped and asked Casey—the tall African American woman who generally worked mornings. She was enthusiastic about Tara getting the position, insisting that she fill out an application right then.

"But my certifications for First Aid aren't current," Tara felt obliged to point out.

Casey pointed to the part of the job description that said that the Y would "facilitate the process of getting certified." Then she continued, saying, "You're the right person. You'd live in that pool if you could."

Tara grinned and nodded, acknowledging that Casey was right. "I'll apply," Tara said. She'd taught swimming lessons to kids before, as well as adults. She was certain that she could work around the hours that she needed to give to Hallowed Ground. And it would be the perfect match for her.

The job didn't pay well, but Tara had never needed a lot to live on. She'd be able to get by.

Excited by the prospect, Tara walked back out into the sunny day. She had too much going right at this point for her to lose the upcoming battle.

<hr>

Tara sat on the leather couch in the empty condo watching the black night through the sliding glass doors leading out to the balcony. She still smelled the lovely chicken curry she'd prepared for herself. It wasn't her ideal last meal—that would have been a ribeye, medium rare, with broccoli drenched in butter and garlic, along with a huge salad and a good glass of red wine.

The chicken curry was a good placeholder, however. It left her with yet one more thing to look forward to after the battle.

She found she missed Kyle more than she'd expected. He'd stood by her through the first battle, taking care of her physical body while her soul battled with the Riprap man.

However, he'd gathered with the others at Hallowed Ground, forming a powerful circle to aid her. She just had to keep the Riprap man distracted while they did their thing.

Tara pulled her ratty bathrobe more closely around her. She'd finished her peppermint tea and now sat quietly, humming snatches of hymns as they came to her.

Her phone sat beside her on the couch. She already had a text written out. She just needed to send it.

It felt to Tara as if a door or a window had just opened, letting a cold breeze blow through the warm condo. She glanced over her shoulder, wondering if Kyle had forgotten something, but the door leading to the hallway was still closed.

When she turned back around, the Riprap man stood on the balcony, outside the sliding glass doors. He wore his true shape, with boulders piled one on top of the other to form the rough form of his torso, arms, and legs. He still looked lopsided, as if the stones had been forced out of place. His ancient bowler sat jauntily on the back of his bare skull, as if he were some sort of gentleman caller.

Tara sent her text quickly.

The Riprap man was making a beckoning motion with his hand when she looked up.

Tara felt herself rise, cool air kissing her bare skin and raising goosebumps all across her shoulders and chest. She looked down, not surprised to discover that she was nude.

The circle around her belly where the fire had burned her during her last battle suddenly warmed and swelled up. She often forgot it was there, as it had faded back into her flesh.

When she glanced back, she saw her body slumped on the couch, her eyes closed, her mouth slightly open. It looked as though she was sleeping. Hopefully she wouldn't drool too much.

Tara floated through the glass of the closed door. The temperature didn't change, though she knew it was much colder outside than it had been inside.

"I have come to take your soul," the Riprap man told her in a clear voice.

"You'll have to fight me for it," Tara assured him. She sounded more confident than she felt, facing the creature before her. "And you'll lose. Like you did the last time."

"Ah, but the last time, you were aided by the great Mulinohana. This time, you must battle me alone," the Riprap man said with smug satisfaction. "I will prove to the river god that his choice of champion was ill suited to the task. As you have already proven."

Tara shrugged. "I'm sorry about that," she said softly. "I did try."

"You failed," the Riprap man said, glee tinging his voice. "And now you will pay for your interfering ways."

Though Tara wanted to point out that she wasn't the one who'd interfered the day before when she'd been trying to sprinkle her rose petals over the waters, she didn't.

Instead, she gave what she hoped was an evil smile to the Riprap man. She'd been practicing all afternoon, trying to channel some of Lucius's animosity. From the way the Riprap man suddenly blinked, she knew she'd succeeded.

"Bring it," she challenged.

Darkness came rushing at her and Tara felt herself falling into an endless black hole.

TARA FOUND herself standing beside a wildly rushing river, the sound of it deafening. Huge boulders stuck up out of the water, the tops covered in slimy moss. The sky had turned gray and overcast, iron cold and misting. Dark, ominous woods stretched out on either side of the river, with brambles cutting off any paths that might be found between the trees. Cold mud squished up between her toes.

Though Tara had never been here, she knew the place instantly: These were the very headwaters of the Willamette river.

The Riprap man came roaring up from behind her, intent on grabbing her and tossing her into the water. Though it was just her soul here, she knew that she'd never survive being battered in those rapids.

Tara dropped down into a crouch. The Riprap man missed his grip, slipping himself on the wet mud, sending them both crashing to the ground. He kept trying to grapple her, while she tried to squirm away.

Why was he using a physical attack? It didn't make any sense to Tara. Why wasn't he attacking her magically? Streaks of cold mud covered her skin, chilling her to her faraway bones.

Then she tried to pull up the fire she felt was always banked inside her. All she managed was a small spark, a flare that warmed her abruptly then faded away.

The Riprap man still let go of her, flinching back as if he'd been burned. "Your tricks will not work," he assured her. "Mulinohana reigns here."

"Why bring me to the headwaters?" Tara asked as she drew herself to her feet. She stayed crouched down in a squat, ready to drop to her knees if the Riprap man rushed her.

"So that Mulinohana can watch your defeat," the Riprap man said.

"No, it's so that you can rededicate yourself to your god," Tara said. "He's turned his back on you, making you wait until the equinox. But he still won't allow you to rebind yourself to him. Not unless you can actually kill me."

Beady black eyes narrowed at Tara. "You are too smart for a woman," he commented.

Tara snorted. "Get with the times. We have the right to vote and everything."

"Not for long," the Riprap man promised. "Or at least, you won't." He ran at her again.

Tara was prepared this time. Instead of staying crouched and grappling with him again, she leaped up, flying high, landing on the nearest boulder.

The moss beneath her bare feet was warmer than she would have expected. It also was less slimy. She balanced on the rock without effort.

The Riprap man paused on the bank instead of leaping up after her. He halted at the side of the riverbank, looking askance at the rapidly rushing water.

Tara was surprised that he didn't just jump up after her. What was he playing at? Were the rocks too far away from the earth for him to feel comfortable? She realized that she'd always seen him with his feet on the ground. He'd always marched around her and never swam.

"Afraid of the water?" Tara taunted from where she stood, out of reach. "But I thought the water god was your best buddy."

Growling, the Riprap man crouched down, gauging the distance from the river bank to where she stood.

Tara crouched herself. She knew she couldn't pass him in midair, switching places with him. That kind of thing only happened in chop-socky movies. She still timed her leap to match his, jumping to the side and landing squarely on the next boulder.

The Riprap man grabbed for her, but missed. He didn't even come close. He wavered back and forth, trying to get his feet under him.

"Balance," Tara taunted. "That's what water is all about. The balance between things." She remembered her fight with the water when she was walking the circles. She couldn't overwhelm such a mighty force. She'd passed within the fire, giving herself to it. The water would have washed her away. Instead, she'd needed to find the fine line between compliance and force.

"You don't have any balance in your life," Tara told the Riprap man. "You only know force. That is the way of rocks, stubbornly sitting in the way or plummeting down on top of you. The river is subtle. Water always finds a way through."

She knew that she wasn't speaking merely for him, but also for the benefit of the river spirit. They were at the headwaters. She still had a chance to prove that she was the more worthy companion.

"You are a fool," the Riprap man said. "You know nothing of power. The mighty Willamette destroyed the city of Portland many times before I came, before my sacrifices."

"What sacrifices?" Tara asked. "Because from here, all it looks like is that you killed a bunch of innocent witches. You forced your way through there, instead of making better bargains."

"I gave my life to the river." The Riprap man spoke vehemently. "I gave it everything. My body. My soul. To protect that great city."

"Your sacrifices were useless," Tara scorned. "Man straightened out the river. Built the dams. It was only through his works that the floods stopped. Not because of some bargain you made," Tara said. She'd done the research. The problem had been addressed far upriver of the city.

"No, you are wrong," the Riprap man said. He swayed where he stood, as if the water still buffeted him, though he was standing far above it. "My sacrifices were worth it."

While the Riprap man spoke, Tara turned her attention back toward the riverbank. Could she jump back from where she stood? Maybe. She asked Hayvu—the goddess of the western wind—to carry her away on strong winds as she leaped again.

The bank seemed to slide further away as Tara flew through the air. She felt herself clawing through the air, willing herself to solid earth.

The sound of the Riprap man behind her made her focus her will harder, sharpening the point of her awareness to a knife's point.

To her surprise, a smaller, more solid wind pushed her the last few inches so she landed on solid ground.

Tara didn't see Soot when she looked around. She still felt as though the wind had helped, and was able to take deeper breaths because he'd been there.

Now, standing on the cold mud, Tara faced the Riprap man. She would have thought that he'd be more comfortable standing on the rocks that resembled him. He looked worried, though.

"You will stop chasing me," Tara told him as she pushed her awareness under the cold waters rushing in front of her.

"Or else what?" the Riprap man sneered.

The voice of the water was so loud! It was difficult to hear him. When Tara tore her awareness away, she saw that he'd crouched down and was about to jump over to where she stood.

"I don't want to kill you," Tara said plainly.

"I'm sure you will be eulogized for your restraint at your wake," the Riprap man taunted.

"Destroying you, dislodging one rock from the other, breaking the bindings that hold you in a single form, isn't that difficult," Tara pointed out. While she didn't necessarily have the power herself, she knew that when she stood with the rest of her coven, she might.

She imagined the process, how a strong current would strike the Riprap man just under his chest, where his ribs would be, where the rock was already unbalanced. A wash of magic with a blow of pure power would start his torso crumbling. More jets of water would take apart his wrists and elbows. Bits of his body would fall, crushing his feet and ankles. His head would fall last, shattering as it struck the ground, the bowler hat rolling off to the side, undamaged.

Though the rock was too pale for Tara to see any change in color of the Riprap man's "skin," she still thought he blanched at the image she'd shown him.

"How could you…You haven't the power to do that!" the Riprap man sputtered. Then he narrowed his eyes at her. "Or the will."

Tara had to acknowledge that. "As I said, I don't want to utterly destroy you. That doesn't mean I won't. You need to forsake your vengeance on me. You've already outlived your original purpose. Portland is safe from the river spirit. Go and live in the mountains, where your true heart lies."

"No," the Riprap man said, shaking his head hard. "I will hunt you to the end of your days. Then I will kill your black lover and all your friends."

Tara cocked her head to the side. She was surprised that he wasn't threatening the coven specifically. Or had he not realized that she'd formed one? They had met at Hallowed Ground, a place protected by Kaede. And ze was good with spaces.

"You can try," Tara said. "But first you have to catch me."

Tara made as though to leap back onto another boulder, further down the bank.

She was surprised by how fast the Riprap man could move, flying back off the boulder he was standing on and landing on the bank beside her.

"No. The time for your arguments and pretty words has come to an end. Now, you must die," the Riprap man said.

This time, instead of trying to wrap his arms around her and throw her into the water, he wrapped his hands around her neck. Lifting her completely off the ground, he started to choke her.

Tara struggled. She bruised her hands beating at the solid rock arms holding her. She kicked out, contacting his torso with a thud, sending sharp pain through her foot but his grip didn't falter.

With a gasp, Tara pulled in as much air as she could. She knew she didn't have much time before this soul body blacked out. Her throat hurt and she couldn't breathe. Dark spots started to form in front of her eyes.

Tara reached deep inside of herself and grabbed the fire always banked there. She sacrificed a little of her precious air to bring it to a flame.

The Riprap man let Tara fall back to the ground. Through watering eyes, Tara watched the Riprap man beat out the tiny fires that had started on his bowler, scorching his head.

With a growl of disgust, the Riprap man finally knocked the hat to the side. The mud abruptly put out the flames.

"That was my best hat," he complained, turning his focus back to her. "Now, you must die."

He grabbed her neck again, holding it in a crushing embrace. She felt him prying at her as he stole her air. He was intent on sucking every bit of magic from her, as he'd stolen Soot. He would take the fire, the earth, and finally, her water abilities.

No, Tara said. She couldn't speak aloud, but she could deny his attack with every fiber.

She felt his hooks traveling inside her, along the quicksilver core of her being. She flayed them with fire whenever they landed, melting them to regain the power.

There were too many of them, all diving deep inside of her, trying to trawl out all of her magic.

Tara turned her focus outward again. *No*, she said again, denying him. *You are the one starting to come apart.*

She stared at his chest, that misshapen pile of rocks. With as much force as she could call up, she *pushed* at him, pushed at that weak spot, trying to get him to topple apart.

A massive shudder went through the Riprap man. His grip on her neck weakened and she took a gasping, shuddering breath.

"What are you doing?" he demanded, shaking her.

It was almost worse than being choked. All her limbs flew away as he shook, bruising her body further. She felt like a ragdoll in the mouth of a terrier shaking with all his might.

"I am *not* a killer," Tara croaked. "I will not merely slaughter you." She focused her power for one last push, sparking as she went, shoving against the creases of his chest.

The Riprap man dropped Tara on the ground. Her knees buckled under her and she landed on all fours. She gasped again, drawing more air in, though it felt like she was swallowing glass.

"I'm not destroying you," Tara said again. "I'm stripping you of your power."

The Riprap man turned huge, horrified eyes at her. "You—you can't!" he said. "You're just a witch!"

Slowly, Tara pushed herself up to standing. She swayed as though mighty winds whirled around her.

"You're right. I am just a sole witch. One with a powerful coven backing her," she said. She pointed her finger at him, directing all the power she felt swirling around the area. "Tell me. What will Mulinohana do when he realizes that you've forsaken him?"

Tara raised her other hand, then made a rending motion, tearing an imaginary veil apart. "Your bond is broken," she said, her words taking on a chanting quality. "I release Mulinohana. The river spirit is now free to choose its own companion."

"NO!!!" shouted the Riprap man. He made grabbing motions with his hands, as if trying to trap the pieces of himself that were flying away.

The river roared in response, an angry tide set on washing away everything in its path. Out of the corner of her eye, Tara could see the water leaping high, though it stayed within its banks.

"I free the water spirit Mulinohana from your bond," Tara shouted over the sound of the rushing water. "In this place where the bond was first formed. The water is free as it always should be, to find its own way. I release Mulinohana from the ties that bind you together. The water no longer has to accept your rock boundaries. Be free!"

The power of the coven swirled up around Tara. Instead of a golden net of healing, it was a dark cloud, sparking with fire, gibbering to itself as it descended on the Riprap man.

Groans of breaking rock overwhelmed the sound of the running water. The Riprap man shrieked again, as if his soul was being torn apart.

Tara made herself stay and listen. She was the one who wrought this. She needed to bear the consequences of her decisions.

The dark cloud rose up finally, streaks of blue now dancing through it. It flew out over the water, dissipating into mist, sparkling bits of magic falling down into the calming waters.

In front of Tara, a solid man of rock still stood. Except he'd shrunk in all his proportions, and now stood a head shorter than Tara instead of towering over her. His torso still showed signs of their battle, and creaked when the Riprap man took a small step forward.

It was his eyes, however, that showed what he'd lost. Tara would say that he had the look of a damned soul, with nothing but Hell before him.

"What have you done?" he croaked, his smooth voice gone.

"I've broken the bond between you and Mulinohana," she said. "Or rather, we have." She still felt a thread of magic tugging her back to where her physical body still sat. "The river spirit can now choose a more appropriate companion. I suspect it only chose you because you were there. Not because you were the best suited."

The Riprap man shook his head. "No. You are wrong. I sacrificed the others who might have taken my place. Mulinohana chose me because I was strongest."

"And came to regret that choice," Tara reminded him. "The river spirit longs for someone who is more aligned with him."

"No!" the Riprap man screamed. Though his voice had grown stronger, he still looked frail, as if the first strong wind might send the haphazardly balanced rocks of his body toppling. "You are wrong. And you are the one who will live to regret your choice."

"Do you really want to fight me again?" Tara threatened. She truly didn't want to destroy this creature, to wield that dark knife of power.

She would, though, if she had to.

"I won't be coming for you the next time," the Riprap man warned. "Mulinohana will. And I will give you no aid."

With that, the Riprap man disappeared.

Tara blinked, surprised. What did he mean that the river spirit was coming for her? The headwaters behind her still rushed, but they seemed much calmer, now. She couldn't sense any presence or malice.

After taking another painful breath, Tara sang a quiet hymn to the waters, fresh born and mighty, carrying their life-giving essence down from the purity of the mountains to the vastness of the oceans.

A cold wind blew across her hand. Tara looked down to find Soot sitting beside her. He looked happy to see her, eager to do her bidding.

Tara held the image of rose petals firmly in her mind, then of her scattering them across the water.

Soot disappeared in an instant, reappearing two breaths later. Only he wasn't in a solid dog form. Instead, he appeared to be made of petals himself, the red and pink forming the outline of a dog.

Tara directed him out over the water, blowing himself along, downstream, dropping petals as he went. Then she sang another short hymn of praise to the waters.

She had the sense that they were pleased with her action when she stepped back. The gray clouds peeled back from the sky, revealing the cool blue of autumn.

The threads linking Tara's soul to her body tugged on her again. She closed her eyes for a moment, giving thanks, promised to honor the waters again at the solstice as well as the equinox before she looked around one last time.

The waters appeared calm. She still didn't sense any malice in them.

Yet, there was an awareness in the river that hadn't been there before.

Would the river spirit really come after her? She doubted it. It should be grateful to no longer be bound to the Riprap man.

Bowing her head one last time, Tara followed the magical thread back to where her body awaited her.

***

TARA STUBBORNLY SAT out on the balcony of the porch, dressed in a sweater, jeans, leggings, and wrapped in a blanket. It wasn't really raining, just misting, hard. Tara welcomed the gray clouds, the turning of the season, from the overly hot summer to fall. She had what she thought of as an autumn tea, with chrysanthemum, rose, and borage petals, along with some lemon balm and apple mint.

Soot sat beside her. It had been easy to rebind him now that the influence of the Riprap man had faded, the words falling from her lips effortlessly. It would take a powerful coven to rend them apart.

She was aware that she belonged to him as much as he belonged to her. They needed one another. Some of the wind's carefree nature had been replaced with obedience to her. In return, Tara knew that she'd never breathe easy again without him near.

Kaede had suggested a *gotoku neko* for a fire familiar—a tri-colored Japanese hearth cat, with a short stubby tail. In folklore, it blew on a bamboo tube to coax flames from the coals.

Tara wasn't ready for another creature in her life. Not yet. Soot was going to be more than enough for the time being. Plus, once she bound a fire element, that would mean that she had officially passed further within, to the next circle, the circle of fire.

She needed time to just be.

Tara took another sip of her tea, looking out on the gray, soggy world. Tomorrow, she'd begin the process of moving to her new place. The room she was renting was only about the size of Kyle's guest room, so she wasn't upgrading there. And she was going to be sharing a house with three other people.

But it was house with a backyard and a garden, as well as a porch that she could just see the Willamette from. When she looked at a map, she realized that her life was now a triangle, with the three corners being Hallowed Ground, the Y, and her new home.

It felt right to her. Balanced.

She still wasn't sure what the Riprap man had meant that the river spirit would be coming after her. She'd gone to walk next to the river many times and it hadn't reached out to her or tried to coax her under the water. If anything, it felt more indifferent to her. She still sang to it on her morning walks, hymns of praise, and she scattered rose petals as well, brought to her by Soot.

Tara had thought that after her first battle with the Riprap man that she was ready to move forward. She'd been wrong. She'd needed to rest first, recover, accept her power and her position.

As well as build her team.

How long would it all last? Out of habit, Tara felt herself still holding her breath, metaphorically speaking, as if there would be another shoe dropping soon.

And there might be.

In the meanwhile, she was finally ready, and comfortable, with who she was and where she was going.

It was about time to stretch those wings of hers and fly.

EPILOGUE

Those interfering witches had no idea the trouble they have wrought. By releasing the river spirit, they have doomed the city. They can talk of man's mighty works all they want. They have no idea what true power looks like, have never stood in the middle of flood waters rushing unheedingly toward their homes. They will learn. My time has not been wasted. The witches I sacrificed not only protected the bridges, they satisfied the river god, so that he wouldn't punish man. No more. When they come to me, begging for help, I will laugh and turn my back on them. The city has never known the name of her protector. But she will learn the name of her destroyer. Tara.

Wilson Evermore, the Riprap Man, Unbound, 2019

CIRCLE OF WATER

ONE

Horrible flooding continues to plague Portland, the jewel of the Pacific Northwest. The mighty river god Mulinohana spares the bridges that I have marked as sacred. But He only spares those structures. The inhabitants of this city do not help their case, spewing filth and refuse into the clean waters. They are starting to be aware of their predicament, how they poison their own nests, and are planning to build what they're calling a seawall. Part of the work will divert the sewers from pouring into the river. While Mulinohana would be pleased with that, the wall itself displeases Him, as does anything that impedes His mighty flow. I will need to mark the wall as sacred, though I do not believe that a witch's heart placed at the base of the wall will be adequate. It is not a single base, unlike a bridge. I will need to find something else to sacrifice so that the seawall can be built and the city will have more protection from the ever capricious river.

Wilson Evermore, Civil Engineer and Protector of Portland, 1920

When Tara sat up in her bed, she saw yet another plain envelope had been slipped under the door to her room during the night. It wasn't addressed to her, but she knew it was meant for her, as all the others had been.

Though Tara loved her room in the house that she shared with four other people, the notes left her feeling uneasy. The smell of wet sisal rope washed through the air instead of the usual comforting scents of coffee and toast. She couldn't hear any of her roommates—they were either still asleep (like Tobias, who worked in a band) or already gone to work.

With a sigh, Tara pushed herself out of her bed, grabbing the ratty, dark green bathrobe that hung on the bedpost and wrapping herself in that. It enveloped her in a warm, soft hug. She sat down on the floor gracefully, thankful once again for the yoga classes that kept her limber even as she approached her thirties, tucking her straight brown hair behind her ears.

The envelope was manila colored and the size that would normally contain a happy greeting card. This one, like the others, contained a newspaper clipping from the day before, pasted to a white sheet of paper. The news reported two boats crashing into each other. One woman had been killed and three men hospitalized.

In block letters on the white paper was printed, "YOUR FAULT." The words looked as though they'd been drawn in red crayon. At least the words felt waxy, and she didn't think they were done in blood.

Tara shook her head. How could a stupid drunken boating accident be her fault? Yet, every time there was an accident on the river or a body was dredged out of the waters, someone—probably the Riprap man—sent her a clipping like this. It had been going on for the last six months.

It wasn't as if there hadn't been accidents when he'd still been bonded to the river spirit Mulinohana. Now that the water spirit was free, it wasn't suddenly causing a bunch of deaths, no matter what the Riprap man might think.

Though there had been more bodies found floating in the river during the last six months. Most of the cases were labeled as suicide or accidental drowning—there were very few homicides. For the previous two years, a body was found floating in the Willamette river about once every ten days, which was considerably more than any other city. Over the last two months, that number had increased to about one per week.

It wasn't her fault. Or at least she kept telling herself that.

Still, the envelope and the clipping were always distressing. Tara put the paper back down on the floor, her hands shaking.

Suddenly, a warm presence pressed against her right side. Tara knew without looking that Soot had just shown up, the tamed wind who took the appearance of a black greyhound. She put her arm over his shoulders and rested her head against him, letting his warmth comfort her.

Not to be left out, Tara heard a loud "Mrrr," and felt a head butting her left leg. She reached out to pet Teruko, the tamed fire spirit who looked like a calico cat, primarily white with brown and black patches, as well as a short, stubby tail. Teruko promptly stepped up onto Tara's thigh, then dropped down into her lap, purring hard. She, too, had come to comfort Tara.

One of the reasons why Tara had chosen this house was because her housemates let her have pets, though they frequently remarked on how quiet her animals were, as well as how they seemed to get in and out of the house on their own, without using a door.

Teruko turned her head up to Tara and issued another "Mrr"?

Tara looked down into the kitty's eyes, one pale blue, the other golden brown. She wasn't sure if Teruko wanted more pets or was asking what to do next.

Or maybe both, as she immediately head-butted Tara's hand when it got in reach.

"I don't know what we're going to do," Tara told her two familiars. Only hedgewitches had familiars and could tame elements. Schooled witches didn't keep them.

Then again, Tara would call Soot and Teruko merely half tamed. They would only do her bidding about half of the time. Otherwise, they ignored her, walked away, and went along on their own business. Ginny, the other hedgewitch in Tara's coven, told her this was normal.

It made someone like Tara, who tended to be logical and

organized, quite crazy sometimes. But she was trying to be more spontaneous. At least during her off hours.

Tara shook her head. "I have to get going, you two," she said after a few more skritches to both spirits. "Teaching this morning, volunteering this afternoon."

Teruko looked up at that. "Mrrr?" she asked.

Tara thought for a moment. "Yes, you can come," she said. While both spirits tended to follow her wherever she went, whether she wanted them around or not, they respected Hallowed Ground, the homeless shelter where Tara volunteered. It was Kaede's space. While Teruko and Soot could push their way through Kaede's protection spells, they both were happier when they didn't have to, when Tara granted them permission to come with her.

That afternoon, Tara was running the "teashop" in the homeless shelter. Having Teruko with her would be good. The cat would sit on one corner of the countertop, happy for people to pet her while Tara made up their order. It frequently allowed Tara to talk longer with the person, listening and asking questions, so that she could learn what the person really needed, not just what they'd asked for.

Soot helped too, playing with the younger children. He acted like a puppy around them, though the rest of the time he seemed like a mature dog.

"Okay, so let me get up and get going," Tara told her companions. With a sigh, Teruko got up on all fours, stretched her back, then languidly stepped first, onto Tara's thigh, then onto the floor. Soot snuffled her hair, rubbing his cold nose behind her ear, before he also stepped away.

Tara stood up easily, stretching her arms up above her head, then from side to side. It would be a long day today; however, she also knew that it would be satisfying. Nothing she did ever felt like work anymore. It was a strange place to be.

First, though, as she'd promised, she sent a mass email to everyone in her coven, letting them know that she'd received yet another missive from the Riprap man. She didn't have to face this on her own, though it was still difficult for her to ask for help. And it wasn't as if the Riprap man had challenged her.

The winter solstice had come and gone without incident. While Tara had had nightmares, they were of her own making, not dreams sent to her.

With a start, Tara realized that the spring equinox was only a week away. It was Thursday, and the equinox was the following Wednesday night.

Would the Riprap man try something then? Or was she still safe?

She included that tidbit in the email before she sent it off, then went to prepare for the long day ahead.

TARA WALKED UP THE STREET, heading for Hallowed Ground. Her hair was still wet from her shower earlier, rinsing off all the chlorine from the pool. She'd spent several hours teaching that day—seniors' water aerobics, beginning swimming for toddlers, as well as coaching a half dozen men who'd made an arrangement with the Y and were getting tips for their coming triathlon.

The building itself looked like an older office building, built in the 1920s. It originally would have had retail on the ground floor and goods displayed in the big picture windows on either side of the door in the center of the building, with three floors above it full of apartments. Now, the ground floor was a dedicated community space and soup kitchen, and the upstairs rooms were given to the homeless who were truly in need.

Tara walked past the front door, down the alley on the side, and around to the back where the volunteers came and left.

Kaede, the person who ran the shelter, was a fifth level witch, and was very good with spaces. It was extremely difficult to permanently enchant an artifact. Most of the time, a sachet filled with herbs only lasted a few days, then would have to be replaced.

However, Hallowed Ground belonged to Kaede, and ze protected the entire building. Every time Tara walked in, she had the sensation of stepping into another place, a location that was separate from the mundane world, sacred, in a good way.

Big signs next to the door proclaimed that this entrance was for

Volunteers Only—and that means YOU. The door was generally left unlocked, at least during the day. Because of the protections Kaede set in the building, very few people who weren't volunteers tried to come in that way.

Soot and Teruko appeared on either side of Tara as she opened the door. Though it was just an illusion that she was stepping into a dark, unwelcome hallway, it always gave her pause.

"Shall we?" Tara said as she stepped across the threshold. Her familiars walked in with her. Soot always gave himself a huge shake after he walked into the shelter, as if shedding the cold barrier from his fur. Teruko did the same, stopping to give the fur on her back a few licks.

The small hallway was still dark, but it no longer felt foreboding. Kaede's office stood behind the first door to Tara's left. Only when Tara stopped and studied the door could she see the white chalk drawn on the white paint, promising pain to any who tried to enter without permission.

Kaede had never been forthcoming about where ze'd learned such a spell, or even where most of zir training had come from.

However, the spells on the door always reminded Tara of her first mentor, Miss Lucy, who didn't necessarily practice black magic, but tainted magic, nonetheless.

Past the office door, on the other side, lay a huge kitchen, at least thirty feet on a side, with a vaulted ceiling that rose up two stories. Though the florescent overhead lights were off, enough light to see by came in through the second story windows. Industrial ovens, stoves, and grills lined the walls, while a huge dishwasher/sanitizer stood in the corner. The air still smelled of the soap used to clean the linoleum floor. The room wasn't heated—the stoves were enough to keep the place warm when it was being used.

That afternoon, it was empty, everything put away. Instead of a permanent center island, the kitchen had a series of tables that volunteers put together as needed. Even those had been folded up and stood stacked against the far wall.

From the laughter that came from the main room at the end of the hall, Tara could tell that the after school program had already started.

She wasn't late necessarily, but she would probably have a line waiting to talk with her as soon as she finished setting up.

A black curtain hung down over one of the long, industrial steel tables that had been pushed to the side, next to the dishwasher. That was Tara's space. When she reached for the curtain, the fabric scratched against her palms. Though this was *hers*, the spell on the curtain was so strong that it made even her feel uneasy.

A large collection of coffee containers full of herbs lay scattered across the lower shelf of the table. None of the containers were matched. They were the cheapest containers Tara could get at Goodwill. However, they all had good rubber seals on them, to prevent air from getting in.

Tara loaded all the containers onto a cart before flicking the curtain back down. She went looking for mugs next, but found the cupboard was empty.

Smiling, Tara wheeled her cart out into the main room. Long tables had been set up in three rows close to the hallway entrance, taking up just a small amount of space. A corner had been marked off for the younger kids to race around and play in. In another corner, an older member of the community—Stella, if Tara was remembering correctly—sat in a chair and read to a group of spellbound younger kids. Soot sat beside the storyteller, attentively listening with his tail thwapping.

One of the teens supposedly doing homework at the long table closest to the door came bounding up when he saw Tara—Eric. She'd made him a special tea the first time she'd volunteered at Hallowed Ground, and he'd become her determined helper ever since.

Eric looked better than when she'd first met him. He was still too skinny, with dirty blond hair that stuck up everywhere. But his gray-green eyes no longer looked so haunted, and his skin was no longer a washed-out white. He'd recently had a growing spurt, and was finally taller than Tara's five foot ten. He was just sixteen, and hadn't reached the end of his growth, she knew.

"I got out the mugs for you," Eric said as he helped her maneuver the cart next to the long table.

"Thank you," Tara said. The containers weren't marked, so Eric stood to the side, awkwardly shuffling from one foot to the other as Tara placed them in order. When she was finished putting the two dozen containers into three long rows, he cocked his head to one side and studied them.

"How did you order them this time?" he asked.

"What is your guess?" Tara replied.

He pressed his lips together and studied the arrangement. "The rose-colored short container has dried marigold flower petals. Adds brightness to a tea." He paused, then indicated the other end of the first line. "While hyssop flowers mellows out most teas, making them richer and darker."

"Very good!" Tara said. Eric had been fascinated by all the herbs she'd used, and had started learning the properties of each. He had no magic, at least as far as she could tell. He did, however, have a fantastic palate, and had been able to separate out the herbs of the "surprise" teas that she made for him.

She wanted to encourage him to get a job as a cook, and maybe train to be a chef. However, he was still too tightly wound to handle the stress of a kitchen. He would only meditate with her. Wouldn't do it on his own. Or at least not yet.

Eric helped Tara fill the giant jugs she used for water, then she filled her electric tea kettle and started the water boiling. She still envied the professional teashops and their massive hot water heaters that were able to keep the temperatures precise, based on the type of tea. Maybe some year, if she opened her own teashop, she could get some of those.

"Can I make you a tea?" Tara asked Eric, as a way of announcing that she was now open for business.

"Something to help me pass this next math test," Eric said with a grimace.

"You know the math," Tara told him. "You just have to stay calm."

"I know," Eric said, sighing. "It's just so hard with all those questions staring at me."

"All right," Tara said, thinking. "Payment is going to be five minutes of meditation every night this week. Just before you go to bed."

"I can't," Eric said, starting to sound panicked. "I can't—"

"Yes, you can," Tara said firmly. She caught the boy's hand and made him look at her. "You can learn how to breathe deeply at your father's house."

Eric wrinkled his nose.

Tara knew Eric's fear was irrational, that he'd take in too much of the air in his father's house and would somehow become more like him, an alcoholic who was at least functioning, unlike Eric's mom who was in prison.

"Remember, meditation isn't just about taking in the air, but also about releasing it. You can let go of everything you take in, every molecule of air," Tara said. "Maybe you should focus on that."

"Huh. I hadn't thought of that," Eric said. He considered the payment she was asking while Tara went ahead and put together the most calming elements she knew and started her tea.

"Fine," Eric said after a few more moments. "I'll meditate for five minutes every night before going to sleep, concentrating on releasing the air, not just bringing it in."

"Good," Tara said. The water had just started to boil. "Let this steep for five minutes," she said handing the cup to him. "And bring it back when you've finished. I've given you enough for two cups."

"Thanks," Eric said with a grateful smile. He took a deep sniff of herbs. "Chamomile, mint, and lavender?"

"Close," Tara said, impressed that he'd gotten all that just from the smell before tasting it. "Gingko, too," she said.

"Ah," Eric said, nodding. "I'll have to remember that."

He turned and went back to where he'd been studying, and the next customer came up, a pre-teen girl with beautiful black skin and her hair braided tightly in rows across her head. Tara gave her a tea with borage and other herbs to boost her self-confidence. For "payment," she wanted the girl to remember to use her twenty seconds of courage and do something she wouldn't normally do the next day.

All through the afternoon, the people in the community center would come up and ask Tara for different teas. Teruko stretched out in front of the containers of herbs, purring loudly sometimes to catch someone's attention, getting scritches as the person talked with Tara of their need.

Many of the teas Tara made were just tasty ingredients mixed together with a deft hand. While the ingredients did have medicinal properties, Tara was aware that for them to work the person would have to make tea from them on a regular basis, not just a couple times a week when she came to the shelter. That was the way of herbs—they didn't work immediately, and generally weren't as potent as modern medicine.

Sometimes, though, as she picked out the herbs she felt a spark pass through her, flowing out of her fingers and into the tea. She knew that her hedgewitch magic had just engaged and the tea would be extra effective.

By the time the community shelter closed up for the night, around eight PM, Tara felt exhausted, as she knew she would. But she didn't feel drained. It was always a weird energy, and she felt both wired and tired, as if she'd consumed too much caffeine after staying up all night.

Fortunately, she had both a long ride on the MAX, along with a long walk, before she'd arrive at the house she shared. That would help her relax before she tried sleeping. Plus, once she got home she'd make herself a nice tea.

The empty streets held an orange glow from the streetlights. It was misting out, not raining, the air full of moisture. Flowers had been in bloom for a while. Tara was looking forward to the lilacs that would start blooming soon, followed by the roses. Cars raced past her, hurrying to their important destinations.

Every once in a while, Tara thought about getting a car. But it would be such a huge expense. She'd arranged her life so that it was easy for her to get everywhere via public transportation. One big triangle, with Hallowed Ground to the north, the Y to the south and east, and her home to the south and west.

Soot suddenly appeared beside her. Tara didn't hear footsteps behind her, but normally, the tamed wind wouldn't walk her home unless there was some danger.

Tara stopped and looked back. It took her a moment to recognize the figure walking toward her. The cane gave him away, however. Lucius was following her.

On the one hand, Lucius was currently part of her coven and regularly performed magic with Tara and the others. On the other hand, Lucius wasn't human, but a being of power.

Tara still didn't know exactly what Lucius was. She knew that many of the myths of the elves were based off of encounters with his kind. He was completely alien. Fortunately, he wore a "mask" of humanity, so that unsettling difference was hidden most of the time.

"Hi, Lucius," Tara said as he stepped closer. He was about six feet tall, with thick silver hair that hung down past his shoulders. His face looked pale, long, and angular in the streetlights, giving him a more otherworldly appearance. The light was too dim for her to see his brilliant blue eyes, and tonight they seemed much darker and brooding. He wore an elegant double-breasted black coat that hung down past his knees. Water had beaded up across the shoulders, giving Lucius his own glow.

Lucius didn't address her, but looked down at Soot. "Why did you have to warn her?" he asked. He had a slight British accent and was unbelievably old. He'd come to the New World "as a lark" centuries before.

Soot gave the equivalent of a doggie laugh, sitting his butt down on the ground beside Tara and leaning against her leg.

Tara read the dog's response to be something along the lines of, "She's my mistress. What's it to you?"

"Never mind," Lucius told the dog before looking back up at Tara. "You received one of those nastygrams again this morning, right? Boating accident?"

Tara nodded. Again, she didn't see what the Riprap man's point was. She was not responsible.

"Have any of the missives you've received been about the harbor wall?"

"No," Tara said. "Just the deaths on the river."

Lucius heaved a great sigh. "Believe it or not, I'm starting to wonder if those notes from your nightmare man are just a decoy."

"What do you mean?" Tara asked, surprised.

"The Riprap man wants you focused on the deaths in the river, and feeling guilty, rather than paying attention to the rest of the river system and what's happening in the big picture."

"Okay," Tara said slowly. That seemed like a lot of work on the part of the Riprap man. Yet again, it had been effective. She hadn't been paying any attention to anything else regarding the river. "So… what are you saying? That there's a problem with the seawall?"

"There was a tremendous amount of snow this winter, up in the mountains," Lucius said. "Plus, that long freeze at the end of February."

Tara nodded. It had been colder and snowier all winter long, even in the city.

"We're possibly facing massive flooding as the snow melts," Lucius warned. "If we get another of those so quaintly called 'pineapple express' storms. We could see another flood, similar to what happened in 1996."

Tara couldn't contain her gasp. "But I thought the Riprap man wanted to protect Portland!"

"I think he did, before you broke his connection to the river," Lucius said.

Tara didn't bother pointing out that it wasn't necessarily her who'd broken the connection between the Riprap man and the river spirit Mulinohana. She'd been the decoy while the coven itself destroyed their bond.

"Now, who knows what he wants?" Lucius said. "He may have decided that the best way to get back at you is to destroy Portland, then blame you for it."

Tara gave an exasperated sigh. That sounded like so many of the spiteful men she'd run across over the years. "Swell," she finally said. She shivered. The night had grown colder while they'd talked, the mist heavier. It would soon ease over into rain. "So…what now? Should I have Richard look up problems with the seawall?"

"Yes, exactly," Lucius said. He sounded relieved. "And flood predictions for this spring."

Tara couldn't help but tease Lucius a little. "You know, you could ask him to do it yourself."

The look of horror mixed with disgust that crossed Lucius's face was priceless. While on the one hand, Lucius respected the results Richard brought the group, he also distanced himself from the research librarian as much as possible, so that Richard wouldn't be tempted to start researching *him*. Though Tara knew that Richard had already looked into Lucius as much as he possibly could without the other being knowing about it.

After a moment, Lucius composed himself again. "Oh, and one other thing."

He paused, seemingly lost in thought, until Tara prompted him. "And that is?"

"Like the bridges, I suspect that your friend the Riprap man did something to help protect the harbor wall," Lucius said slowly. "However, I doubt he used a witch's heart."

"Then what did he use?" Tara asked, puzzled.

Lucius hesitated. "I doubt that he was able to use one of my kind. But it wasn't a normal sacrifice."

"How do you know that?" Tara said, surprised.

Lucius merely shrugged.

She couldn't help but roll her eyes at his non-helpfulness. "How is Richard supposed to find out about something like that? Human deaths might at least be reported."

"I know," Lucius said. He shook his head. "We might need to go visit the spirit buried at the base of the seawall, however."

Tara felt all the blood leave her face. "Miss Lucy gave me a potion to go visit one of the witches at the base of the Morrison bridge," she said. The potion had been awful to take. Sludge mixed with rotten seaweed, and that was after oregano had been added to sweeten the taste. Her chest grew tight and she pushed down on the feeling of bile rising up.

"We'd do it differently, this time," Lucius assured her. "We might want to consider doing it on the coming equinox."

"Why?" Tara asked. "What could that spirit tell us? It isn't as if the Riprap man will make another sacrifice. He's no longer connected to the river."

"He may not be able to help himself," Lucius said. "Once a man gets a taste for the hunt, a taste for blood, it's difficult for him to let go. And the Riprap man has been killing for a long, long time."

"I didn't think of that," Tara said slowly. She was going to have to make sure that Richard expanded his search, to see if a woman had committed suicide on the winter solstice the year before. While the Riprap man hadn't been bothering her, that didn't mean he hadn't gone after someone else.

Was the Riprap man part of the reason why so many people jumped off the bridges in Portland? Was he blaming her for all the bodies pulled from the river, even though he'd been causing the deaths himself?

"Oh, I so didn't need to start worrying about this tonight," Tara said after a bit.

"I could make sure you had sweet dreams," Lucius said, his voice growing deeper, into that late-night-jazz announcer territory, sounding like smooth sex.

Tara held herself stiffly. This wasn't the first time that Lucius had propositioned her. She knew that he had, in the past, been intimate with Kyle, her best friend. They weren't exclusive, however, and Kyle had spent one awkward evening trying to explain to Tara that she was free to take Lucius up on his suggestions.

But that felt wrong to Tara. Particularly as she was the head of their coven. Being physically intimate with any of them would throw off their balance of power.

As Lucius appeared to still be waiting for an answer, Tara finally told him, "No, thank you. I will get myself home and make myself some tea."

"Your loss," Lucius said with a negligent wave of his hand. "I will see you on Monday," he said, turning and walking away, quickly disappearing in the mist.

Soot nudged Tara's leg, getting her to look down at him. He gave her a doggie eye roll, then got up and turned around, walking again toward the MAX stop.

Tara followed the tamed wind after a moment. She was never sure what Soot's relationship with Lucius was. The wind always seemed more *aware* around the other being.

At least Teruko hadn't suddenly appeared, draped across Tara's shoulders like a living stole, expecting to be carried home. Then again, the mist was getting a lot heavier. Probably the only reason the cat hadn't shown up was because she didn't want to get her fur wet.

Tara felt more tired now as she walked toward the train stop. She didn't know if she was in danger or not. Or if the danger was now to the entire city of Portland. She was going to have to get Richard to do some serious research.

In the meanwhile, time for home, tea, and bed.

TWO

I continue to meditate and consider my options for marking the seawall as sacred to the river god. While it would be possible to find a hedgewitch with a menagerie of familiars, it would be difficult to sacrifice all of them, as they're merely elements and don't have a "life" of their own. Possibly I could acquire an entire coven of witches, bind their hearts up and down the length of the wall, but that solution strikes me as too messy. I need a more elegant solution. I've asked the river god what He would prefer, but his answer wasn't satisfying, and presents me with another puzzle. "Find another Being."

Wilson Evermore, Civil Magician and Protector of Portland, 1925

"The harbor wall is collapsing," Richard announced when Tara called him the next day on her lunch break. She'd sent Richard an email the night before, telling him about Lucius's warnings.

"And good afternoon to you too," Tara said. She sighed. She'd been teaching at the Y all morning, filling in for one of the yoga instructors who'd called in sick. Tara would spend the afternoon teaching her swimming classes.

Currently, Tara sat alone in the staff breakroom. The smell of the tangerines from her lunch conflicted with the artificial scent of the lemon wax used on the gym floor next door. The room itself was maybe nine feet by six, with a round table in the center that had seen better days, the wooden top all scratched and scuffed. The countertops hadn't fared any better, and the gray material was stained in many places, including large yellow stains from what had probably been turmeric-loaded lunches. A silent TV hanging from the far corner showed the news, the rolling marquee at the bottom of the screen a constant commentary on what was happening in the world, most of it depressing and bad.

"The problems with the harbor wall aren't necessarily public knowledge," Richard said, sounding angry. "The city has commissioned some studies, then tried to hide the results. They're hoping that they can get by a few more years before they have to do any actual work on it."

"Okay," Tara said. "What does that mean, though? Is it going to collapse tomorrow? Later this spring if we get a heavy rain? Or in a couple years?"

"The wall wasn't supposed to last a hundred years," Richard said. "It's been eroding for a while. However, the city voted to put more tax dollars toward fixing the roads."

"Yeah, that makes sense," Tara said, nodding. That would actually be popular with more voters. Plus, if the harbor wall has been holding for a long while, why bother fixing it now?

"However, the confluence of events that caused the 1996 flood aren't unique to that year," Richard said. "All the events that happened that year, like the heavy snows up river and the surprising freeze that occurred at the end of February have both happened this year, in record amounts. All we'd need is a really warm, heavy rain for a flood to occur."

"Would the wall hold up if it got hit by a flood?" Tara asked, trying to follow along.

Richard sighed. "Possibly? No one knows." He paused, then added, "Unless there's something to Lucius's claim that someone, or something, other than a witch was used to bind the wall."

"Not sure I'm following you," Tara said.

"If the wall got hit with a wall of water, it would start to gradually give way. It wouldn't just explode. That only happens in Hollywood with good CGI," Richard explained. "You know that the seawall is haunted, right?"

"I didn't, actually, Tara said. "Truly haunted? Or just tourist trap haunted?" There were such things as ghosts and spirits, but they didn't normally interact with the living. They could be called by a strong witch or her coven.

"You're going to have to tell me that, actually," Richard said. "However, there have been legends of ghosts up and down that wall since it was first constructed. Or rather, a ghost. Tall and thin, willowy, with long silver hair."

"Lucius said it wasn't one of his kind who got taken," Tara said. "But I wonder if it's a relative of a sort."

"According to the legends, she's a siren, and has called men to their death. I haven't actually been able to find any deaths related to her, at least not in the neighborhoods that she supposedly haunts."

"She might just be placing the suggestion, so that the person goes to the nearest bridge and jumps off," Tara speculated.

"Great. Supernatural serial killers. Just what we need," Richard groused. "As if the Pacific Northwest doesn't already have enough."

That made Tara smile, at least. While Seattle seemed to be the home for more serial killers per capita than any other city, Portland still had its share.

"I also thought of something else." He cleared his throat. "What if the flood waters start rising and she finally has a chance to destroy the harbor wall? Instead of luring just a few to their deaths, she can kill thousands?"

Tara took a deep breath. "I don't know if that's possible. But

Lucius said that we're going to have to visit the spirit who lives at the base of the harbor wall. Possibly on the equinox."

"Oh," Richard said. "Can you at least promise to tell me all the details? Afterward?"

"Of course," Tara said. As Richard was fully mundane, he had no idea of what happened when the coven performed magic together.

"One more thing. A woman did jump to her death on the winter solstice last year. People thought she on something because she'd seemed so out of it. The police have closed the case, ruling it a suicide. They claim that she was depressed, not that she was drunk, so her tox screen had probably come back negative."

"That implies that the Riprap man might still be killing," Tara said. How was she going to stop him, if it was indeed him?

"Possibly," Richard said. "I've been trying to link the bodies in the river to possible suicides that he might have caused, but I haven't had any luck. He did *not* send you a newspaper clipping about Margo, the woman who committed suicide on the solstice last year."

"Huh," Tara said. Maybe he was taking responsibility for some of the people who'd died.

"But the number of deaths from suicide is disturbing," Richard said. "We're much higher than we should be for this time of the year."

"Could that be the river spirit?" Tara said.

"Hell if I know," Richard said. "The economy kind of sucks and the political climate isn't giving people hope. It could just be circumstantial."

"Right," Tara said, knowing that Richard was trying to make her feel better. However, she still had a niggling doubt that somehow, Mulinohana, the spirit of the river, was causing these deaths.

"I'll send you what I've found so far," Richard said. "You still coming over for dinner Saturday night?"

"That's tomorrow night, right?" Tara asked. She had a retail-like schedule, and Sundays were her actual Friday, with Mondays and Tuesdays off.

"Yup," Richard said. "Jeannie is looking forward to hanging out."

"Cool," Tara said. Though Richard and Jeannie were now living together, they'd made an effort to invite people over for dinner on a regular basis. "No surprises, though, right?"

"None," Richard said. "Wouldn't make that mistake again."

People who were couples tended to look at single people like Tara as a problem to fix. She'd endured their "surprise" guest who'd showed up for dinner once.

"What should I bring?"

"Just yourself," Richard insisted.

Tara smiled. He and Jeannie wouldn't ever allow her to bring anything for dinner, but they would gladly accept any tea that she made for them. She'd be sure to bring a few ounces of something for them to enjoy.

"So…are we going to tell her?" Richard asked after a few moments of awkward silence.

"Is it time?" Tara asked. Richard had been formally invited to be part of the coven, and knew about witches and magic, even though he was completely mundane. He kept the information to himself, even after he and Jeannie had moved in together.

"I don't know," Richard said after a few moments. "But…but it might be."

"I leave that decision up to you," Tara said. Both Tara and the rest of the coven had already approved of him telling Jeannie when the time came.

"I don't know," Richard said, whining.

Tara couldn't help but roll her eyes. Richard had always struck her as commitment-phobic. It had surprised her when he'd moved in with Jeannie after knowing her for such a short period of time.

"Do you want to marry her?" Tara asked quietly. "Spend the rest of your life with her?"

"Maybe?" Richard said. "I can't imagine living without her."

"You've said that before," Tara reminded him. "Are those just words? Just your comfort speaking? Or do you truly feel it?"

Richard gave a heavy sigh.

"I'm going back to work," Tara announced. "Give you more time to stew on things."

"Thanks. I think," Richard said.

"Talk to you later, see you on Friday," Tara said, swiping the phone off.

There really wasn't anything she could do for Richard. He'd have to make his own decision, sooner or later. She understood his hesitation though. What if he told Jeannie about the witches and the coven and she decided to leave? It was pretty weird.

But Jeannie was also a Portland native. Tara had faith that she'd take any additional weirdness in stride.

TARA DREAMED of floods that night. A wall of water was traveling down river, heading toward Portland. It towered above her, at least thirty feet tall. The water roared as it gained speed. Storm winds blew from the river, carrying icy sleet that stung her bare arms. The air smelled of the iron cold of winter storms. Dark clouds loomed ominously above her.

Tara raced to get in front of the wall. In the perfect logic of dreams, she believed that if she could get in front of the water, she could stop it.

She was somewhere north of the city. She could just see the city in the distance, the taller buildings and bridges shimmering and looking frail through the spray of water the wall generated.

Tara ran along a rutted dirt road on the river bank, with tufted green grass growing down the center of it. She managed to avoid the rocks and puddles that could have tripped her. However, people kept getting in her way. Slow walking couples who held hands and blocked the entire way. A giggling group of teenage girls who yelled insults at Tara when she pushed by them. Even a young man walking a group of a dozen dogs.

At the edge of a park, Tara grabbed a bicycle (a mode of transport that she never enjoyed). She finally was almost caught up with the edge of the water when a warning bleet caused her to pause.

Really? A herd of sheep?

Tara abandoned the river path and ran to the nearest street. Though she didn't know how to drive, she still stole an old truck. The streets were too far away from the river, though, so she cut across a wild variety of yards and meadows, finally able to roar down the dirt path.

Finally, Tara got in front of the water. She leaped out of the car and sprinted across the water, standing firmly in front of the wave.

"STOP!" Tara yelled, her hands out in front of her, all her magic focused forward. She built a large magical forcefield all around her, a bubble of safety.

The water didn't bother to even pause. It flowed around her safety bubble, parting like a curtain, leaving her standing behind it as it destroyed the city.

Tara woke up stiff and sore. Every muscle was tired as if she'd actually been running that much. Her jaw ached from how hard she'd clenched her teeth all night.

It was just a nightmare. There was no wall of water heading for Portland.

After a long hot shower, Tara finally read her email from Richard.

Which was all about the 1996 flood, how the weather had been similar that year, and how record rainfall was predicted for the following week.

TARA DRAGGED THROUGH HER MORNING, teaching at the Y. On the weekend, Hallowed Ground would get a lot more volunteers, people who worked regular hours during the week, so they didn't really need her. The Y, though, had classes all day.

She still managed to find all the energy the young ones needed, her first class. It was the most difficult class for Tara to teach sometimes, not because the kids were bad, but because it was so early.

Between classes, Tara made herself an extra strong cup of tea from an already prepared bag. She'd started with a base of a lovely Assam black tea, then she'd added Ginkgo Biloba, apple mint, hibiscus, and dried lemon peel. It was a really bright tasting tea, guaranteed to wake her up. Though she'd already had her caffeine before her first class, she knew that a second dose wouldn't hurt.

The rest of the day went by swimmingly, as it were. Despite her nightmare of chasing after a wall of water, Tara still loved the water. This was her home. This was where she felt most comfortable.

However, teaching all day left her tired, particularly after her poor sleep the night before. She decided to call it an early evening with Richard and Jeannie. They'd understand if she just ate and headed out soon afterward.

Though Richard had offered to come and pick Tara up at the Y, she didn't take him up on his offer. Instead, she took the MAX, then a bus up Foster. The traffic moved slowly, impeded by the construction.

It didn't make any sense to her why the city had decided to narrow the busy artery down to a single lane in each direction. Yes, it would be prettier. But the traffic was already atrocious. Making the streets harder to navigate wasn't about to cut down on the number of cars.

But she wasn't in charge. All she could do was sit and fume as the bus lumbered along from one stop to the next.

A change in the air of the bus made her look away from the construction outside.

Crap.

The Riprap man stood in the aisle of the bus, close to the rear exit. He looked far worse than the last time she'd seen him. He still wore his old bowler hat and trousers, but no jacket, and his shirt hung in tatters. His exposed torso appeared to be listing to one side, the rocks that made up his body bulging in first one direction, then the other.

What was he doing here? Why was he here? Was he coming for her again next week, during the spring equinox?

He glared at her from where he stood. His face was clear, and it no longer seemed as though he peered at her from under the water. His eyes appeared to be black holes, sunk deep above gaunt cheeks. He still had what she would call a weak chin, soft and undefined. She couldn't see his teeth, but the way his cheeks had sunk reminded her of the older homeless people who didn't have dentures.

She heard the words echo through the air, though she knew he hadn't spoken them out loud. "Your fault. You're to blame." He pointed an accusatory finger in her direction.

Tara felt the terror of the wall of water crashing toward the city from her nightmare the night before. The smell of the river and its marshes washed over her. Chills cascaded down her arms and her spine. She heard a dull boom as the harbor wall exploded, the waters cackling madly as they raced beyond their hated man-made borders.

"Your fault."

The bus drew to a stop and the Riprap man got off, disappearing as soon as he touched the sidewalk.

Tara shivered again, swallowing down the bile that had suddenly risen in her throat.

Richard thought there might be a flood soon.

The Riprap man was going to guarantee it.

***

TARA PUSHED BACK from the table with a replete sigh. "That was wonderful," she said yet again. Jeannie had gone all out that night, making a rolled pork roast that had blueberries, thyme, sage, and rosemary in the center of it, the perfect combination of sweet and savory. She'd served roasted root vegetables on the side—turnips, radishes, and rutabagas—cooked with pecans and hazelnuts to sweeten them. Desert would be a lemon tart that barely had any sugar in it, in an almond-meal crust.

Tara knew better than to believe it was all for her. Jeannie loved to cook. She'd actually considered going into culinary school when she'd graduated college ten years before. However, she'd quickly discovered that she didn't want to turn her hobby into a profession. Instead, she happily invited friends over as it gave her an excuse to try new recipes and show off.

"I'm glad you liked it," Jeannie said with a happy smile. She was a petite woman, barely five foot two, with sandy-brown hair that she wore just past her shoulders. Despite her love of eating, Jeannie was very slim. She regularly fasted, eating only one meal per day, making that meal a feast. Like Tara, Jeannie didn't eat a lot of grains, but focused instead on healthy proteins with lots of veggies.

One of the agreements that Jeannie and Richard had quickly reached was that while Jeannie did the cooking, Richard did the cleaning. He was actually proud of the fact that Jeannie had never cleaned a single pot or plate. Period. No matter if she did the cooking or not.

Tara smiled as Richard grabbed Jeannie's hand and kissed the back of it. "Thank you," he said sincerely. She'd seen him do this before, to always express gratitude and mean it. He didn't toss the words off casually.

He really was in love with Jeannie. Tara could see it in his eyes, the way he looked at her. It made her feel warm inside, to be around such love.

Maybe someday she'd find that as well…but she honestly wasn't looking for it at this point. She had too good of a life, too much to do, to want to be weighed down by a relationship.

And that attitude was exactly why she shouldn't get involved with anyone in the first place. Not until she stopped seeing it as a burden and more as part of her support network.

Tara rose from her seat and started carrying dishes away from the table. Richard seemed to come back to himself, tearing his eyes away from Jeannie and standing himself.

"Sit," Tara said firmly. "Entertain your girlfriend. I'll carry the dishes away and make tea."

Richard sat with a loud oouuufff. "If you insist," he said with a lazy smile.

Tara was glad that they'd been able to remain friends after they'd dated. She was also glad that he'd found Jeannie, who was obviously perfect for him. He had a few more silver hairs running through his black hair and he actually looked older now than when she'd first met him, more mature than he used to be. That didn't mean he still didn't have an extremely goofy side. That night he wore a T-shirt with the slogan, "Because…SCIENCE!"

They'd been sitting around a small card table that had been set up in the middle of the living room, with the TV on one side and the couch of doom on the other (once you slid into the soft cushions, it was deceptively difficult to get back out). A sliding glass door opening up onto a patio was at the far end of the room. On the other side, a tall island separated the huge kitchen from the rest of the space, an open floor plan that Tara actually approved of.

She carried their plates and the leftovers from the table, taking her time as they chatted about Jeannie's next planned meal—a feast for their board game night the following week. She took it as a challenge to make gourmet finger food, as they wouldn't be sitting down for a complete meal.

Tara let their words fade into the background as she started preparing their tea for the night. Both Richard and Jeannie drank coffee, so Tara had made up a few ounces of a heavier tea for them. It started with a rooibos base (as it was late at night and they all needed decaf), then added chicory root, dandelion roots, barley, cacao nibs, as well as some dried vanilla. To the cups she added a touch of powdered dark chocolate.

When she walked back into the living room, cups in hand, she realized that she should have paid a bit more attention while she'd been making the tea.

The conversation had obviously turned serious in her absence. It felt like walking into the middle of a sermon.

Tara silently served each of them a mug of tea, then went back and fetched the cream and sugar.

The air felt sticky with anticipation. Tara felt like taking off the sweater she was wearing, as she suddenly felt overly warm.

"What's up?" Tara asked after she sat down.

Jeannie stared at Richard while Richard focused on his cup of tea for a few moments. He cleared his throat. "I have something to tell Jeannie," he said slowly.

"Okay," Tara said, nodding. "You can do this."

Richard sighed, taking a quick sip of his tea before turning back to Jeannie. "You know I love you, right?" he said, reaching out for her hand.

"Yes, but you're scaring me. Those words are usually followed by some sort of 'but,'" she said sharply.

At least she did take Richard's hand. Tara took that as a good sign. Richard clung to it like a lifeline.

"I have something to tell you. Something for Tara to show you. I need you to know this, about this part of my life," Richard said. "It is private, though. You can't ever, ever, tell anyone about this."

Jeannie looked from Richard to Tara, who nodded. "He's right. It isn't your secret to tell or to share."

Surprise crossed Jeannie's face. "Okay," she said slowly. "Now you're both scaring me."

"It isn't scary. Or rather, not that scary," Richard said, trying to reassure her. He cleared his throat. "You know that I get together with Tara and the gang on Monday nights, right?"

"Right," Jeannie said, nodding. "It's an eclectic group. You meet at Hallowed Ground, that homeless shelter. Do your volunteer work."

"It's more than that," Richard admitted.

"So you're having orgies," Jeannie said.

"No," Richard said firmly.

Tara couldn't help grin. He'd done the same thing to her when she'd tried to tell him about being a witch.

"Really? That's too bad. Lucius is quite a looker. I'd imagine he'd be rather…intense in bed," Jeannie said with a teasing grin.

Tara snorted. It wouldn't have surprised her in the least if Lucius had propositioned not only Richard but Jeannie the few times he'd met her. That was exactly his speed.

"We're not having sex," Richard said. "We're doing magic."

Jeannie peered at him, puzzled. "Like…how?"

"We're a coven of witches," Richard said. "I don't have any magic," he quickly assured Jeannie. "I've just been invited to participate."

"A coven?" Jeannie asked. She turned to look at Tara. "I suppose you're part of this."

"It's my coven," Tara said firmly. "I put it together."

"And you believe that you do magic," Jeannie said, glancing from Tara to Richard and back again.

"Yes," Tara said.

"Show me," Jeannie said. She sat back in her chair and crossed her arms over her chest.

Tara tilted her head to one side, studying Jeannie. She seemed angry. Tara wasn't sure why.

"All right," Tara said. She pushed her chair back from the table and stood. "Just remember, you can't ever tell anyone about this."

Jeannie snorted. "No one would believe me."

Tara shook her head. This was not going to end well. She could tell.

Still, she'd promised Richard that she'd show Jeannie her magic if they ever got around to telling her.

"Do you remember my dog Soot?" Tara said.

Jeannie nodded. She didn't care much for dogs.

Hopefully, that wouldn't stop Soot from showing up.

Tara gave a long whistle, her usual call for the tamed wind to show up.

Jeannie gasped as Soot materialized out of thin air, sitting at Tara's feet, looking up.

"Fetch," Tara said. She held in her mind the clear image of a daffodil, one of the ones that grew in the gardens at the base of the condo. She hated having to pick one of the flowers there; however, she needed to be able to show Jeannie exactly where the flower had come from if she should ask.

Soot nodded and flowed out the closed glass door of the balcony.

Jeannie sat stiffly in her chair, her arms tighter across her chest, hugging herself in fear.

After a few moments, Soot flowed back through the glass, placing a long daffodil at Tara's feet. "Good boy," Tara said, praising the wind and patting his smooth head. She picked up the flower and put it on the table in front of Jeannie.

"Home," Tara told Soot.

He whined at her. He was bored. He wanted something more to do.

Tara had seen a homeless encampment set up along a street near here. She held the place firmly in her mind. "Comfort those you can," she said softly.

Soot nodded and vanished.

Tara turned to Jeannie who still stared at the daffodil on the table as if it were a poisonous snake about to bite her. "Do you want to see more?" she asked quietly.

"No," Jeannie said firmly. She finally looked up, fixing her glare on Tara. "I believe you."

"But?" Richard asked.

"If you can do this magic, why haven't you healed the world?" Jeannie asked. "There's so much that's wrong. So many places broken down. So much hurt and evil. Magic should be able to stop all of that. Why haven't you?"

Tara sighed and sat down at the table. "There's only so much we can do," she said softly. "We do try to heal the world. To bring peace to troubled souls. To clean up the messes others leave behind. There aren't enough of us, though. And I don't have endless energy."

"I see," Jeannie said, still angry.

"Plus, not all witches seek the betterment of others," Tara felt she had to add. "Some seek their own selfish goals."

Jeannie gave an expressive sigh at that. "Of course," she said. "Human nature, right?"

"Exactly," Tara said.

"What magic can you do?" Jeannie said, turning her burning gaze on Richard.

"I can't do magic," Richard assured her. "Nothing beyond my mad researching skills."

"You can't? Or you can't show me?" Jeannie asked. She still sounded hostile.

"I don't have magic," Richard said.

"He's completely mundane," Tara added. "Doesn't have any magic at all." She'd been hoping that possibly, after being involved in a few circles of power, that he might start to show a spark. He still had no magic at all, though Lucius claimed that Richard did have a primitive power that he was able to add to the circle, though it was completely undisciplined.

"I don't believe you," Jeannie said. "Why, if you're so powerful, do you need him? Why not invite other people instead?"

"He does have mad researching skills," Tara said. "And I need those. We're kind of a renegade coven. I don't have access to the books of lore that the other covens have."

Jeannie just shook her head. "You could use those skills without making him part of all…this."

Tara wasn't exactly sure what she meant by "all this." "True," Tara said. "And I gave him that option. I wanted him to be a part of the circles, though."

"I need to think about this," Jeannie said, pushing herself up to standing. "You get the couch tonight," she told Richard firmly as she marched off toward their shared bedroom, closing the door behind her firmly.

Richard looked as though he'd been kicked in the gut. "Sorry about that," he said after a few moments.

"Don't be," Tara said. She sighed. "Hopefully you'll be able to bring her around."

Somehow, she doubted it. Jeannie appeared to have some real prejudices against witches, or those with power. Richard associating with such people, despite having no power himself, seemed to just add insult to injury.

Richard gave Tara a watery smile. "Give you a ride home?"

Tara accepted gratefully. They didn't talk much on the ride home, and as expected, Tara had further nightmares that evening, only this time, after the flood waters took out most of the city, the ghosts of the dead came after her.

THREE

I have finally discovered what could be a solution to my dilemma about the wall. The witches, while powerful, are sedentary. They don't travel far, except to consort with each other. For the wall I need a creature who will roam up and down the entire entity. Though I did not originally believe it, there appear to be beings who are not human, beings of great power, who walk among the humans in disguise. I have been learning how to recognize such creatures. There is one race known to the others as the Travelers. They are rare, extremely solitary, and do not stay in a single location for very long. I will have to find one of those, trap its soul and bind it to the sea wall. And I must hurry. The start of construction draws near.

Wilson Evermore, Hunter and Protector, 1927.

THE HAPPY SHOUTS of children playing in the water echoed off the tall ceiling of the pool. Tara stood at the shallow end of the warm water, holding up one of the younger ones while he kicked hard,

learning how to better propel himself. He almost had the hang of it—
it was more a matter of coordination than anything else.

Finally, a loud buzzer sounded, announcing the end of the hour.
Tara blew on the whistle she wore clipped to the shoulder of her red
bathing suit. "Time!" she shouted.

Though she didn't consciously add magic to make herself sound
louder, her wild magic caused it to happen anyway, her voice booming
across the room. Tara knew if she really tried, she could shout loud
enough to cause the water to ripple.

As it was, all the kids stopped playing abruptly, the silence itself
shocking.

"Time," Tara called again, this time in a normal voice.

The kids started making regular kid-like noises again as they
splashed their way to the side of the pool, hauling themselves out and
heading toward either their parents who sat around the edges of the
pool, or the locker rooms.

"Thank you, Ms. Tara!" several of them called, waving after they'd
gotten out of the pool.

"See you next week!" she said in return.

Gradually, the pool room emptied. Tara checked the clock. Did
she have time to do a few laps on her own before she hit the locker
room herself? Probably.

She grinned and dove into the water, pulling herself forward with
hard strokes, aiming for the far end of the pool.

Though she always expected the Riprap man to bother her here,
when she was in the water, he never showed up. It finally occurred to
her that while the Riprap man had been bound to a water spirit, he
himself was an earth spirit. It made much more sense for him to
bother her on solid ground than in the water. Or on trains, that
were like bridges, not set in a single location but spanning more
than one.

Still, Tara felt as though the water started pushing against her as
she began her second lap. She stubbornly swam on as the water grew
heavier, denser. Finally, panting, Tara reached the end of the lane and
popped up above the water.

The lights flickered. The comforting smell of chlorine that always said *home* to Tara was replaced with the smell of the river, damp and fecund. Tara shivered as the water around her grew cold.

High up, near the ceiling, storm clouds gathered. What fresh hell was this? This wasn't the Riprap man, that much Tara knew. Lightning raced across the darkness in streaks. Winds howled furiously, itching to take apart anything that stood in their path. Tara shivered as the temperature dropped.

The air changed abruptly. A strange, warm wind blew around her, then raced up, challenging the colder winds above. Tara smelled rain. If the storm continued, Tara knew that it wouldn't be drops of rain falling. No, it would land in sheets of water, as if buckets were being dumped.

Just as quickly as it had come, the storm vanished, leaving Tara breathless.

She couldn't shake the feeling that she'd just had a vision of what was coming: a massive storm guaranteed to flood all of Portland.

Trembling, Tara pulled herself from the pool. Her muscles ached as if she'd done an hour's worth of laps. She quickly toweled off and headed toward the locker rooms.

How long had she been in the pool? Most of the kids and their parents were long gone. Just a couple of teenagers remained, blow drying their hair and gossiping. She snuck a quick peek at the clock.

Holy cow. Forty-five minutes had passed without her realizing it. Had she been actually at the edge of the pool that entire time? Or had she been swimming?

Tara headed for the showers. It took a long while for the hot water to soak through her chilled skin and into her bones.

A storm was brewing, heading for the city. She'd check the weather reports, but it honestly wouldn't matter what they said.

Richard had said that all the other pieces were already in place, replicating what had happened in 1996. All they needed was a really heavy, warm rain.

She was going to have to find a way to control the river, stop it from smashing against the harbor wall and probably destroying it, flooding the city.

But how?

"WHAT ABOUT MARIGOLD PETALS?" Tara asked as Ginny perused Tara's shelves, looking for the perfect element to balance out her Irish morning breakfast tea. They stood in the kitchen that Tara shared with the rest of her flatmates. It was late Sunday evening, and though Tara felt especially tired, she hadn't cancelled her meeting with the other hedgewitch. She had too many questions. Besides, Monday was actually the start of her weekend, and she'd be able to sleep in.

"Aye, that might do," Ginny said, reaching unerringly for the glass jelly jar.

It gave Tara an insight into how she must appear to others as she made up her own teas, never hesitating, the jars occasionally leaping into her hand when she raised it.

It was a good reminder to her that she had to be extra careful when her flatmates were around, so they wouldn't start questioning her like Richard had.

Ginny felt as though she belonged here. Then again, that seemed to be one of her knacks, to always fit in everywhere she went. She'd let her bright red curls grow out some, to keep her head warmer during the cold months, but she still shaved the edges of her head, giving herself a floppy mohawk. She'd recently gotten her left eyebrow pierced with a gold ring to match the one she wore in her right nostril, making her look more balanced, though her green eyes and wide smile still promised all kinds of mischief. She wore a comfortable bulky sweater in a color that Tara would call oatmeal, as well as black leggings that had geometric patterns in white. They matched the tattoos that Ginny had running from behind her ears and down her neck, connected triangles and octagons.

Tara sometimes felt like the uncoolest witch in Portland, especially compared to Ginny and the others. She wore her straight brown hair pulled back in a ponytail, and tonight wore a comfortable dark gray sweatshirt over light gray sweatpants. The only color she had were tall slipper socks in red, gold, black, and blue.

She leaned against a counter as she watched Ginny work her own magic putting together her own concoction. The kitchen was warm and empty, just the two of them. In the living room, the TV blared a soccer match that Erin had recorded earlier.

Ginny gave Tara a grin over her shoulder when Erin exploded in loud cheers. "'Tis a good house, here," she said, nodding.

Tara agreed. "Good mix of people, too." A musician, a writer with a day job, and two travelers who needed someplace cheap to live so they could save money and go on their next great adventure. They all took care of the house, the chores divided between them. They had monthly dinners, followed by their house meeting and airing of grievances.

As a result, the kitchen was generally clean, everyone taking care of their own dishes and cleanup, the floors washed once a week. The space was large and inviting, with a gourmet stove with six burners, a huge farm sink, and plenty of counterspace. There wasn't enough refrigerator space, so Tara had invested in a small fridge that she kept in her room.

Ginny hummed as she finished adding ingredients to her teabag, then poured the already boiled water over it.

Tara shook her head. "I don't see how you can drink caffeine this late at night."

Ginny shrugged. "Never seems to bother me one way or the other," she admitted. "Can go without for weeks, then drink it all day, never notice a difference." Ginny's slight British accent softened her words in an enchanting way, making Tara feel even less cool.

"But," Ginny added, "as lovely as the tea and company is, you have questions, I can tell."

"How can you tell?" Tara asked. She'd made a real effort to be polite and not just pounce on the other witch.

Ginny paused, considering. "There's an electric quality to the air. Charged, you know? No one else would notice it," she assured Tara. "It's just that our magics work well together, and so your impatience is spiking mine."

Tara nodded. That made sense. Their magics did work well together, combined without either of them willing it, making the little, day-to-day tasks easier.

Kyle still didn't trust it. He often questioned Tara when she unconsciously did magic, her wild magic taking care of her. And she still could see his point, that such power, unbridled, could lead her down the wrong path, making her arrogant.

As Ginny's tea steeped, Tara told Ginny about her vision that afternoon, of the coming storm. "I've never had a vision like that before," she said. "Not a waking dream. The Riprap man sent dreams to me when he was coming after me."

Ginny brought her finished tea over to the kitchen table where Tara was sitting. As she drew near, Tara felt their combined magic flare outwards.

None of Tara's flatmates would come into the kitchen now. Their magic had just seen to that, though neither Tara or Ginny had willed it. Tara wasn't even sure she knew how to make that happen, not without a sachet and a strong spell.

The natural magic was easier, and sometimes so much more powerful. Though it wasn't consistent. They had just as good of a chance that the magic would have flared and suddenly all of Tara's flatmates would be in the kitchen with them, drawn inexplicably there.

Ginny gave Tara a grin. "Seems we're here for a talk, then." She grew more serious. "Wind's my element," she said after a moment. "I can always follow it. It tugs me here or there."

Tara nodded. She'd come to realize that while getting to know the other witch better. Ginny had at least a dozen tamed winds who would go walking with her, though rarely all at the same time. They appeared as various breeds of dogs, from a huge mastiff to a tiny Pomeranian princess.

"The winds bring me news," Ginny said. "They've also told me of the huge amount of snow melting up river, and the coming storm."

"Really?" Tara asked, surprised.

"I did set them seeking, once I heard the news," she admitted. "But they confirmed what you and Richard have said. Now, your element is water, right?"

"Yes," Tara confirmed. She couldn't help but add, "I always feel at home there."

"But you haven't called a water spirit to you," Ginny said. "How else is the water to tell you what's coming if it doesn't have an easy way to talk with you? Other than to send you visions while you're surrounded by it?"

"Okay," Tara said slowly. "That kind of makes sense. Some water spirit brought me the vision. So that the water could protect me, right?"

"Eh, water's always tricksy," Ginny said. "Most of the stories of merfolk and water spirits is all about them pretending to be helpful so that they can drown folk."

"So was the vision of the storm to get me to do something foolish?" Tara said, trying to puzzle out what the intention actually had been.

"Who knows?" Ginny said, shrugging her shoulders. "Maybe a bit of both. A warning of a coming trial, that ye may or may not survive."

Tarra thought about that for a moment. It sounded like just the sort of thing a water element might do. She remembered when she'd been walking the circle of water, and that in order to finish she'd needed to find balance. "What form does a water spirit take?" Tara asked after a few more moments.

"I don't know. I've never met a witch with a water familiar," Ginny said. "Or at least not as I know." She paused, then added with a grin, "Could be a horse."

Tara nearly snorted her tea out her nose. "Right. Where would I keep a horse? It couldn't just live in my bedroom, not like the other two." She couldn't help but grin at the idea of a tiny pony curled up on one side of the bed, with her in the middle, and Soot and Teruko on the other side. She'd have to get a bigger bed.

"They also appear as people," Ginny said. "At least according to legends and myths."

"I'll ask Richard to get me a list of the different forms a water spirit takes," Tara said.

"Then you'll try to call one to ye?" Ginny asked. The air between them suddenly sparked with excitement. "Tomorrow night?"

Tara took a deep breath. She hadn't thought about moving between the circles of the schooled witches for a while, not since her coven had turned their back on her. Kyle had been the one who passed her inward the last two times, first to the circle of air, then to the circle of fire where she now practiced.

But maybe she needed to move further inward, traverse another circle. Call a water spirit to her and bind it, so that she could face the river and the flood.

"Okay, I'll do it," Tara said. She hadn't been studying, but since water was her element, surely she natively knew enough to be able to do it?

"Yay!" Ginny said. She raised her tea mug in a toast. "Here's to taming another spirit."

Tara clinked her mug with Ginny's. Monday night was going to be fun.

Ginny and Tara talked about what they needed to do in order to call a water spirit. Ginny reminded Tara that location was important. Tara had called Soot to her on the porch of Kyle's apartment. She'd called Teruko to her while standing beside a bonfire in the backyard of her new house. She needed to find someplace more neutral for calling the water spirit, so that she could get back to it easily. (Kyle might move from his condo someday, and she wasn't going to live in her current house forever.)

After they'd found a park that was close to Hallowed Ground, Tara sent an email to all the members of her coven, explaining what she wanted to try Monday night.

At least she had a long, restful sleep that night. She suspected that in part, it was due to being in Ginny's presence, her own magic calming as it meshed with Ginny's.

Tara spent Monday morning sitting on her bed, studying on her tablet with research books sprawled everywhere. Teruko complained that there wasn't enough space for him to lay down as well (even though he had the entire foot of the bed). So she had to shift the books around so the cat could curl up next to her thigh, sharing body heat.

At least Soot was probably outside playing somewhere and wasn't demanding her attention as well.

There wasn't enough time for Tara to memorize everything that she'd need to know for passing within, to the next circle. As a hedgewitch, she didn't need all this lore. As a schooled witch, she knew she'd fail the test because she didn't know all the uses all these herbs could be put to. She still intended on whizzing through the practicum.

Tara was just enough of a perfectionist that she really wanted to pass the lore part of any exam as well. Plus, she was learning useful things! She was going to have to start studying on a regular basis again.

When her phone rang, Tara took it as a welcome respite. "Hi, Kaede," Tara said happily, laying her book beside her.

Teruko opened one sleepy eye and glared at her for shifting her position.

"Hello, Tara," Kaede said. "How are you feeling this morning?"

"Rushed," Tara said honestly. "There's so much to study!"

"Cramming for the exam, eh?" Kaede said. "Good thing you don't really need to pass one in order to call a water spirit."

"That's the truth," Tara said, feeling relieved and yet guilty at the same time. "So what's up?"

"I would like for you to reconsider your plans for this evening," Kaede said.

"Okay," Tara said, concerned. "Why?"

"I want you to call your water spirit here, in Hallowed Ground," Kaede said.

"Oh," Tara said. She hadn't been expecting that at all.

"I know, part of the reason why you wanted to be in a park was because it would be more easily accessed. I will give you my solemn vow that you'll always have access to Hallowed Ground," Kaede said.

"I don't want to invade your privacy," Tara said, shocked.

Kaede smiled at her. "You wouldn't be. We would conduct a spell together that would ensure you had access without disrupting me."

Tara nodded, thinking. "But what if the developer who owns the building sells it?"

Kaede gave a merry laugh. "I own the building. No one's about to sell it out from under me."

"Really? I didn't know that," Tara said. Though she didn't ask the question about where Kaede had gotten so much money, Kaede answered her anyway.

"Oni loaned me some of the money," Kaede said with a sigh.

Tara had learned that was the name of Kaede's grandmother, the elegant Japanese woman who came in every Saturday and Sunday and poured tea for the people who came there. It was her way of showing the people in the community respect. Even though they may or may not care for the tea, they needed to feel included that way. It was her own special magic, though Kaede claimed that Oni had no actual magic of her own.

"It's why Oni feels she can show up every weekend, as she claims the building is partly hers. I'm paying her off as quickly as I can, though," Kaede said.

Tara wasn't sure she wanted to know more about how the money worked for the charity, or how Kaede was getting more of it.

"How could a spirit enter the building though?" Tara asked. It was another reason why she'd wanted to work in a park and not at Hallowed Ground. The building was too protected.

"I'll crack open the spells for the evening," Kaede replied. "I was going to redo them during the spring solstice anyway. Remember?"

Tara nodded, then said, "Yes." The coven had been planning on meeting twice that week, on Monday for their usual circle, as well as on Wednesday to celebrate the solstice and redo the spells for Hallowed Ground. And possibly now call on the spirit of the harbor wall, though they might agree to meet on Tuesday to do that.

"Will the building still be safe?" Tara asked, concerned. "Before you put the spells back in place?"

"I didn't say I'd take them down, just crack them open a little," Kaede said, zir tone chiding. "Nothing else will get through."

Tara had to believe the other person. Kaede wouldn't do something rash or endanger zir community.

"All right," Tara said after a moment. As it was supposed to rain that night, it would certainly be nicer to hold the ceremony indoors. Though she'd been counting on the rain, to use it as part of her spell…

"I'll let you tell everyone the change of plans," Kaede said breezily.

"Thank you," ze added.

"You're welcome," Tara said, swiping off the phone. She leaned against the headboard for her bed and thought for a moment, idly reaching out and petting Teruko's warm fur, getting rumbling purrs in return.

Would she have any problems calling the water spirit in the community center? Did she have to be outside in order to do it? She was already concerned about doing it in front of a large group of people, even though they were all part of her coven.

She'd have to bring a large bowl to contain the water she'd need, as the other times she called a spirit she'd already had some of that element nearby.

She sighed and told herself that it was all going to be okay. Water was her element. She could do this.

⁎ ⁎ ⁎

Normally, when Richard wanted to gain entrance to Hallowed Ground, he texted when he was just outside the door. He was such a mundane that Kaede's protection spells had him doubting that it was even the right building.

So Tara couldn't contain her surprise when Richard opened the front door and poked his head in. "Good," he said when he caught sight of Tara.

"How did you do that?" Tara asked, coming over to where he gingerly took off his soaking raincoat and shook off some of the excess rain outside the door.

"Took all my courage," Richard said. He gave a huge sigh. "Still got butterflies, you know? But I did it." He gave her a big smile.

"Richard the lion hearted," Tara teased him.

"Damn straight," he replied.

It took Tara another couple of moments to realize that Richard's supposed ease and happiness was just a mask. He was broken and crying inside.

"Oh, dear," Tara said.

He stopped her from hugging him. "Don't," he said, his word

clipped. "Or I'll just break down again."

Tara felt a lump form in her own throat. "Still fighting?" she guessed.

"I'm losing her," Richard said, carefully studying the floor. "I don't think she'll ever forgive me, or be able to fully trust me after this."

"I'm so sorry," Tara said. And she was. "Let me know if there's anything I can do to help, that the coven can do." She felt guilty about Jeannie walking away, though it wasn't necessarily her fault, not directly.

"Yeah," Richard said. He gave an audible gulp, then looked back up at her, his mask firmly back in place. "So we're calling a water spirit tonight, eh?" he said giving her a determined smile.

"We are," Tara said, taking the hint to not ask him any more about Jeannie or his relationship. "I'm just about finished drawing the pentagram."

"Is there anything I can do?" Richard asked as he did every time.

"Not with this, no," Tara said. "Tell me if you've found out anything new about water spirits," she asked instead.

"Lots of cultures had water spirits," Richard said, falling easily into research librarian mode. He certainly looked nerdy enough, in his huge black-rimmed glassed, his old blue jeans, and a red T-shirt that proclaimed that it was actually blue if you approached it fast enough.

"Most of the time, a water spirit either appears in the form of a person, or has another shape and can also take the form of a person. There are a few exceptions," Richard said, nodding to Kaede as ze came into the room. "There are water dragons, in Chinese myth. Though those usually either represent the sea, or thunderstorms. Mesoamerican myth is more concerned with rain than with sacred waters or streams. The Chaac usually have a human body with fish scales, and a snake-like head."

"That would be cool," Kaede offered. "If your water spirit manifested as a snake."

"At least that's a pet that I could easily keep," Tara said as she finished drawing the last line of the pentagram on the floor of the common room. "Instead of, say, a horse."

She'd drawn the pentagram in white chalk. Sitting in the center was a huge glass bowl with pretty flowers etched along the rim. It was full of pure water that Tara had blessed. She planned on using that as her water element.

Richard snorted, also seemingly amused by the idea of a horse manifesting.

"Did you loosen the protection spells for the building?" Tara asked, remembering that Richard had for the first time been able to get in without someone else opening the door first.

"I did," Kaede said. "Can you feel it?"

Tara extended her senses outward, seeking the perimeter of the building. It had always seemed so closed off to her, the space inside sacred, set apart from the mundane.

Now, instead of a hard border that protected the occupants, the wall had transmuted. It was still thick, but permeable.

"I think so," Tara said after a moment. "Still don't know how you do it."

Kaede smiled at her. "We all have our strengths," ze said.

Ginny was also able to enter the building without hesitation. Lucius had never noticed the barrier in the first place, as it had never been enough to hold back one of his kind. Kyle came in, his face quizzical, as if he had sensed the missing protections.

Normally, the group stood together in a circle, holding hands and sharing their magic.

Tonight, Tara had drawn out a protective pentagram in order to better focus the magic around her. Each of the other members of the coven would stand at their point of the star while she'd stand in the middle. It was the first time she'd done this, asked them to direct their magic to her instead of letting it flow around the circle. Kaede had agreed that this would probably be the best way for Tara to find her water spirit and bind it to her.

After everyone had taken their places, Tara stepped into the center of the pentagram. She heard Richard's gasp as the lines suddenly flared bright white.

Tara hadn't expected him to be able to see the magic, but she was glad that he could.

"Thank you for coming and being part of this calling tonight,"

Tara said solemnly. "I also thank the goddess Brigid for defending the earth. I thank the warrior Samil for defending its people," she said, continuing her prayer. She called on Hayvu to carry her words on the western winds to all the parts of the earth, and Eural to carry her words on the eastern winds. After also thanking Areebin, the protector of souls, Tara finally asked Bonana, the goddess of the water, to send one of her spirits forth.

Winds suddenly swirled through the large room, circling those standing at the points of the pentagram. Tara felt the wind tugging on her hair, which she'd worn down that night. She couldn't help but grin.

Now, Tara reached for the magic the others had generated. It wasn't as cohesive as when they were all connected in a circle. The edges were more diffuse, frayed by the growing wind. Instead of a magical mass, Tara had to reach for threads of magic, finding Lucius's strong cool line that tasted like wintergreen tea, then reached for Ginny's pepper-laced thread, then finally gathered together the others, pulling the power toward her.

She couldn't hold onto each thread individually, however. The easiest thing for her to do was to weave all that power together into a large golden net, as Kaede had done on more than one occasion when they threw their collected power upstairs, to heal the people sleeping above them.

While a net was easy, the back of her mind chittered at her. It wasn't the right shape, not for drawing in a water spirit. But she'd never thought of the form the magic would need to take for water, not specifically.

Tara continued on despite her misgivings. "I call on Juhali, spirit of the rain! I call on Onosh, spirit of the ocean! I call on the water spirits of the Columbia and Willamette! Come. Bring me a piece of you, that I might better know your will!"

The sound of falling rain filled the room, a quiet, comforting spattering. Tara's skin didn't get wet, however, and she couldn't actually see the drops. The winds died down, as if the rain was hushing them, dampening their power.

Suddenly, the bowl of water sitting at Tara's feet lit up, as if a spotlight had hit it. White mist began rising out of it.

Tara tried to see what form the water spirit was taking. However, the form was shapeless at first, looking like billowing fog as it grew.

The golden net that Tara had gathered grew stronger between her hands. She raised her arms up above her head, then threw the net over the top of the mist.

The net passed through the mist and landed with a splashing sound on the floor, spreading out across the rest of the pentagram until it touched the toes of the rest of the coven.

Tara frowned. She'd suspected something was wrong with the net, that it wasn't the right shape to draw a water spirit to her. She didn't have time, though, to refocus and reform the magic flowing around her.

The white mist rising from the bowl was as tall as Tara now, and began to coalesce into a human-like figure. She couldn't tell if it was male or female.

Before the form took its full shape, it drew one foot up out of the water.

Tara caught her breath. Was it about to step out, onto the ground and come to meet her? She started humming a hymn of praise and welcome.

The figure kept raising its leg up, drawing the knee up to its waist.

However, instead of stepping out of the bowl, it stomped down with its foot.

The glass bowl shattered with a loud crack. Slivers of glass flew everywhere. Tara felt the sting of the shards striking her face and her bare hands. She took a step back, accidently smudging the pentagram and breaking the circle of power.

Water sloshed everywhere, much more flowing out of the bowl than what it had contained. The tops of Tara's shoes were suddenly soaked. At first, the water raced along the lines of the net that Tara had dropped. Then it spread, seeking all the corners of the room. It moved quickly enough that small, four-inch waves formed on top of the water in all directions.

"Contain it!" Kaede shouted. "Before it attacks the building!"

Soot suddenly appeared, pushing back against the water, not

letting it touch the southern wall that he guarded. Teruko helped as well, the warm corner he protected suddenly water free. Ginny brought in her dozen winds as well, pushing back the water from where it wanted to creep.

Lucius clapped his hands. A loud crack of thunder followed. Water sizzled in the direction he glared, drying up instantly.

But it was too late. The wild water had soaked into the building, through cracks in the floor.

"I'm losing it," Kaede moaned. Zir face had grown pale. "The water is wrenching the building from my control."

"Join hands!" Tara commanded, racing over to stand beside Kaede. "Form a new circle!"

The coven gathered around quickly. Once they joined together, the magic surged in a strong pulse between them.

Before Tara could try to weave their magic into a coherent shape, Lucius had gathered all the threads together, pushing the newly joined power toward Kaede.

All of Tara's strength was suddenly drained from her. She tried not to fight it, though she could tell her magic wanted to resist. She wasn't an earth person, but a water person. Opposing the water was difficult.

Instead, Tara tried to focus on what Kaede was doing, how ze was shoring up the protection spells for the building. Zir spells went deep under the foundation, as if the building itself had roots that went through the earth, past the compacted dirt and down into the bedrock, resting on the stones there.

No wonder the building always felt so protected, the barriers so strong! Kaede didn't depend on the brick walls themselves for her spells.

Tara tried to ride along with the others and pass the wave of magic to Kaede, for her to bolster the roots. She still felt as though only half of her power was able to be tapped, the rest still fighting her, wanting to reach out to the water instead that rested just a little bit beyond the rock.

Finally, after a timeless time, Lucius narrowed the pull of power from each of them, like he was slowly closing off a spigot. The world blinked back to life.

Tara found herself swaying where she stood. Kyle collapsed to the floor as soon as she released his hand. Richard as well. Ginny stood with a dazed look on her face, probably identical to the one that Tara had on hers. Only Lucius and Kaede didn't seem diminished by the amount of magic they'd just passed.

"What…what happened?" Tara asked as she knelt beside Richard, checking to make sure he was okay. His eyes were open and glassy, but he nodded at her and mouthed the words, "I'm okay."

Kyle had pushed himself up to sitting, his head hanging down between his drawn up knees. "That was intense," he said softly.

Tara was worried about how he started to tremble.

"The water was trying to break down the building," Kaede said after a moment. "Tried to get into the walls and the floors. They're too structured. The water didn't want to be contained." Ze sighed. "I'm sorry, Tara. I shouldn't have suggested that you call a water spirit here. I hadn't realized how…formless water can be."

Tara gulped and nodded. "Neither had I." She herself was more of a structured person. And yet, water was her element.

Kyle looked up from where he was seated, glaring at both of them. "How much research did you do before you called us all here?" he said, the smooth-jazz tone of his voice buzzed off and jagged.

"There wasn't much she could research," Ginny said hotly. "What works for ye schooled witches isn't the same for us."

Tara nodded. "I did some," she admitted. "But there wasn't time to do a lot."

Kaede spoke up. "You're going to need to do a lot more. And soon." Ze grimaced. "That water is still mixed in the roots of this building. When the next rain comes, it will start eroding the foundation. If there's a big flood, the building will collapse."

Tara sighed, the weight of the problem landing hard on her shoulders. Though Soot and Teruko came up and offered comfort, she knew there was little they could do to help.

She had to figure out how to tame a water spirit so she could draw the water out from Hallowed Ground. And quickly. Before the promised rains came.

FOUR

Finding one of these traveler creatures has been more difficult than I initially believed. They are rare and skittish. However, I think I have developed the perfect trap. I had originally been haunting the rail stations, looking for travelers heading back east. A long journey isn't what these travelers are seeking, though. They go short distances, explore, then take another quick hop. I've moved my gaze from the railroad to the river. Short boat trips north of the city have appeared to capture the interest of more than one traveler. The next one will be epic, the boat overturning as it runs into an unexpected sandbar. And I will capture and use the souls of all those who perish in Mulinohana's waters.

Wilson Evermore, architect of the harbor wall and protector of Portland, 1928.

TARA BLINKED SLEEPILY at the text she received from Kyle the next morning when she finally got up around nine thirty.

Breakfast?

The text seemed innocent enough. But Tara had the impression that Kyle was still angry with her over her failed attempt to call a water spirit. He must have taken the day off, though, if he was asking about going out with her.

The coven was meeting again that evening, though not at Hallowed Ground. Instead, they were meeting at the harbor wall. They were going to try to engage with the spirit tied to the wall. Lucius insisted that while it wasn't a witch, it wasn't necessarily one of his kind either. But still a being of power, just someone…different.

Tara wasn't sure why he was so insistent that they try talking to the creature first. What sorts of insights could the being give them? He wanted to learn more about the construction of the harbor wall first hand, and the soul tied to the wall was their best bet. But Tara hadn't been able to come up with a different plan. The rains were coming. Chances were the harbor wall would fail. Soon.

They needed to do something.

Tara looked again at the text on her phone. She knew she couldn't come up with some lie about not receiving Kyle's text. She wouldn't feel good about doing that. Plus, she'd never be able to hide the fact from him, not when they'd be sharing magic again that night.

So Tara texted back that she'd only just gotten up (which was true) so could they do a late breakfast?

Pick you up at 11?

Tara knew there was no escaping, so she said sure before she tottered off for a hot shower and a long think. However, her brain wasn't cooperating that morning. She found herself staring off into space after she'd made a morning concoction of a bright green tea with chili flakes, rose hips, ginger, then added some lavender and vanilla to smooth it out.

Tara sat in the middle of her bed staring out at nothing. She had books to study. Herbs to review. Richard had sent her even more information about water spirits and myths. But her body was so tired. Listless. As if the water inside of her had grown muddy and dull.

She'd never felt this bad when she'd been fighting the Riprap man. Never this exhausted. What had happened? What had tapped her magic so hard? Had it been Lucius the night before?

No, that wasn't it. Or rather, that was only partially it.

Her magical self had been fighting the strengthening spells that Kaede had been trying to erect. It went against her watery nature to be so confined.

Yet, Tara was going to have to help on Wednesday night, when Kaede tried to rebuild all her protection spells again. She wasn't sure how, though, to balance the two sides of her nature.

Tara had moved her musings to the street corner by the time Kyle showed up. It was nice to have a friend who had a vehicle that morning. She wasn't sure she could face either a bus or the MAX.

Kyle still drove a chocolate brown Mini Cooper. It took an effort for Tara to fold herself into the seat as always. However, the cooper had more than enough headroom for both of them.

"Took the day off?" Tara asked Kyle, as he was dressed in light green sweater that looked amazing against his black skin instead of his one of his fancy suits.

"I have so many sick days piled up it isn't funny," Kyle told her with a grin. "I'm getting to the stage of 'use them or lose them' though. So I figured breakfast would be a good idea today."

"I'm glad you called me," Tara said, mostly truthfully. She did in fact miss her old friend. They still had regular movie nights where they'd sit and watch bad 1970s TV and giggle. But they weren't as close as they'd once been, not when they'd been living together. Plus, Tara was so busy all the time now.

Kyle drove them to a neighborhood dive, "J's Breakfast." It was an incredibly popular restaurant during the weekend, with a line out the door and up the block. However, on a Tuesday, mid-morning, it was relatively empty.

J's was one of the skinniest restaurants Tara had ever been in. Just inside the door to the right ran a long bar, all the way to the back of the restaurant, with a dozen padded stools that swiveled attached to the floor in front of it. And that was it. There was no room for extra tables. On the other side of the wall behind the bar ran the long kitchen. At the end of the bar was a single multiuse bathroom, as well as a door leading out to the alley out back that was frequently open, carrying the scent of eggs, waffles, bacon, and rich coffee out to the neighborhood.

The Formica of the countertop had been replaced sometime in the last few years, as it was still mostly smooth and gray, not stained and cracked like the older version had been. Some of the pads on the stools had been replaced as well so they were no longer split and cracked, the padding falling out, or held together with duct tape. But that was all that had changed in J's since the place had opened back in the 1930s.

Behind the stools, the cheap '70s paneling was covered with framed photographs of parties held at the restaurant through the years, including the suits of the '40s and the wildly colorful kaftans of the '80s.

Tara surprised Kyle by ordering coffee as well, though she asked for merely half a cup and a boatload of cream.

"What?" she asked in her defense when the two large mugs were plunked down in front of them. "I need the caffeine," she explained after dosing the coffee with cream and pouring a steady drizzle of sugar into the cup.

Kyle nodded. "I get that," he said.

They both ordered omelets. Now it was her turn to be surprised, as Kyle ordered the garden omelet.

"What?" he said, deliberately teasing her. "If I didn't get it, you'd start pointing out how I wasn't eating enough vegetables."

Tara had to acknowledge the truth in that. They talked of recent news, not of magic, covens, or floods. Tara felt herself relaxing despite the extra caffeine. She really had missed her old friend.

Finally, after Kyle had insisted on paying for breakfast, they both got extra coffee in to-go cups and decided to take a nice walk through the neighborhood. It would be another day or so before the clouds blew in, and the March sunshine was warm and inviting.

As soon as Tara stepped out of the restaurant, Soot appeared at her side.

"Everything okay?" Kyle asked as Tara paused to spend a moment petting Soot's head.

Tara wasn't about to admit that Soot had picked up Tara's worry about Kyle. "Yeah," she said after a moment. "Just checking in on me."

"Good," Kyle said. He grimaced. "I wouldn't have to want to try to defend myself from him."

Tara opened her mouth then shut it again. Kyle wasn't wrong that Soot would attack him if he tried to hurt her.

But Kyle wasn't about to attack her, was he?

They slowly made their way down the street, pausing to look at the many windows of the ma and pa shops that still occupied most of the storefronts. The bookstore didn't interest Tara, as it was mostly computer and technical books, but one of the shops had cute nautically themed T-shirts for sale, and she really liked the octopus one where the tentacles were dissolving into numbers and magical symbols.

"So I know that you didn't take me out to breakfast just for my scintillating conversation," Tara said as they reached the corner and turned up the quiet side street, away from the traffic and other pedestrians.

Kyle grimaced. "I'm worried about you. You did ask me to play your good conscience, you know."

"I know," Tara said, nodding. "So what would my conscience say to me this morning?"

"That you need to watch yourself so that you don't fall into the trap of being arrogant," Kyle said bluntly.

"I...what?" Tara said after a moment.

"You didn't know how to call a water spirit," Kyle said. "Not really. You just figured you could wing it as water is your element."

Tara bent her head, acknowledging her guilt. She really hadn't spent the time she needed meditating on the form, not like she had before she'd called Teruko.

"I know you're a hedgewitch as well as a schooled witch. But you should have been better prepared."

"You're right," Tara said quietly. She really should have taken more time and been better prepared.

"There are still things you can learn from the lore," Kyle insisted. "If you'd studied more, you would have learned about sachets that could have been placed in the corners of the building, to protect it from the water or floods."

Tara sighed. Kyle was speaking the truth. She shouldn't have just assumed that she knew enough to call a water spirit. She remembered the time when she'd tried to walk the circles, to pass inward to the circle of air. How Aaloka, her former mentor and teacher, had pushed her even when Tara hadn't felt ready.

Aaloka had told Tara that she was ready, and was standing in her own way.

This time, Tara really hadn't been ready.

"I admit that I fucked up," Tara said. "And you're right, I was starting to get arrogant. Instead of studying and preparing, I thought the spirit would just come to me, as water is my element." She took a sip of her overly sweet coffee, the sugar tasting bitter now.

Kyle nodded and looked relieved. "Good. I'm glad I don't have to be more of an asshole this morning."

Tara gave him a reassuring smile. "Sometimes, it's necessary for even my friends to be assholes and tell me where I've screwed up." Then Tara took a deep breath. "The question is, what do I do now? I don't have a lot of time to study, to prepare. But I have to be able to call a water spirit to me. And soon. So I can help repair the damage the first one did—is doing—to Hallowed Ground."

"Do you?" Kyle asked, raising one eyebrow in her direction. "Don't you think that Kaede can handle it zirself?"

Tara heard the underlying question that Kyle was really asking: was she just being arrogant again, assuming that she had to fix the problem?

"Water isn't Kaede's element," Tara said slowly. "Earth is. You know ze's a fifth level witch, right?"

Kyle nodded. "I did know. I still don't know where ze studied, however." He sounded frustrated. "I've asked around, but I can't find a coven that once admitted zir."

"Ze talks about zir grandmother ensuring that ze started studying magic at a young age," Tara commented. "Perhaps it wasn't a formal coven, but just friends and relatives."

"That would make sense. But again, back to the original question. Do you need to help Kaede fix the protection spells?" Kyle said.

Tara wanted to point out that the entire coven would be helping

Kaede fix the spells on the equinox. However, that wasn't really what he was asking about.

"I do need to have a better understanding of water and water spirits if I'm to help zir exorcize the one that's in the building's roots now," Tara said. She nodded, the words and images coming to her as she thought about it. "The water is trying to break the earth free. We don't need to capture it, though, or draw it out. Instead, water will always take the path of least resistance. We just need to provide it a hole it can flow down into."

"Huh," Kyle said, nodding. "That makes sense. But you're still going to have to nudge it along that path."

"And that's what I need to study," Tara said. "How to entice the water to follow me."

Soot had been a puppy, and had eagerly wanted to join with her, be a part of her life. He hadn't been lonely as a wind, not exactly. But he'd been willing to be tamed.

Teruko had taken a lot of coaxing to bring him out of the flames. Then again, Tara had studied fire more, and had been able to talk of the hidden gods, worshipped by the fire itself, the ones that had no human names. That she'd had the knowledge of those had at least gotten Teruko to listen to her. That, and the fact that Tara still always carried a spark of warmth within her.

The water though…it was just a part of her. She didn't know how to draw more of it to her.

"With both Soot and Teruko, you had a specific source of that element," Kyle said.

Tara shrugged. "I had that bowl of water. Look how well that turned out." She sighed. "Ginny did say that water was always tricksy. That it would both try to protect me at the exact same time it would try to drown me."

"Lovely," Kyle said. "Are you sure you even want a water spirit as a familiar?"

Tara gave a choked laugh. "Yeah, I do." She paused, considering. "It isn't arrogance," she assured Kyle. "It's honestly the next step. It's the next part of my journey. It's where I have to go from here, or die trying."

Kyle sighed, obviously not believing her. "But why?" he asked again.

"I just do," Tara said. She wasn't being obstinate. It was the right thing for her to do.

Kyle still made a face. "I still consider you my best friend," he said after a few moments of tense silence. "But we're just going to have to agree to disagree about this one."

"All right," Tara said. A small lump formed in her throat.

She'd known that this day was coming. Kyle was a schooled witch. He didn't understand Tara's hedgewitch powers. And she was never going to be able to explain them to him.

Hopefully, however, they had enough other things connecting them that he wouldn't leave the coven.

TARA SPENT the rest of the afternoon cramming, as it were, studying all the herbs she needed to learn for the next level if she was passing within, like a schooled witch. Her eyes hurt. She squeezed them tightly together, pressing her palms against them, trying to bring more moisture back to them as the shadows grew longer.

Finally, though, Tara put the books to the side of her bed. She reached forward, stretching to grab her ankles and stretch out her back.

Teruko hopped onto the bed at that moment. "Mrrr?" he trilled as he head-butted her leg.

"Fine, yes," Tara told him, skritching him under the chin. "I know. It's awful. I haven't been paying any attention to you at all all afternoon."

Teruko stopped rubbing his head all along her leg and looked up at her, his golden and blue eyes staring hard at her.

"What?" Tara asked. Obviously the spirit wanted to tell her something. "I had to study before I called you, too," she told him.

The cat tilted his head to one side, still observing her. If she was to guess, she would say that he had a contemplative look on his face and was thinking deep philosophical thoughts.

Or he was just considering the best way to get her to pay more attention.

Teruko very deliberately turned his head and licked the side of her hand. Instead of a raspy tongue, a trail of fire raced across Tara's skin.

"Ouch!" Tara said, jerking her hand away, drawing it up to her chest. "What did you do that for?"

Teruko jumped from the bed and stalked away, disappearing before he reached the door.

Obviously, the cat believed that Tara was doing something wrong. But what? Or was he just pissy because she was studying an element that wasn't his?

She wasn't sure what had upset him. But she knew better than to try to call the cat back. He would spitefully ignore her, probably for the next week or so.

With a sigh, Tara reached for her books again. But she didn't want to study anymore. Her head felt full of mush. Instead, she picked her books up, lightly put them on the floor beside the bed, set an alarm on her phone, and curled up for a quick nap.

TARA DREAMED of walking in what looked to her like an English garden. While there were wild roses growing along the edges of it, and ivy taking over the wall, the grass had been trimmed to within an inch of its life. All the flowers were in their beds, the daffodils separate from the crocuses, which were separate from the bluebells and the lilies of the valley. Nothing was out of place. Artistically laid out rocks formed a spiraling path through the area.

Tara found she couldn't step off the gravel walkway, that instead, she could merely walk the tamed roads. It frustrated her. The path never led close enough to the roses. Their scent tantalized her. She could hear them whispering on the slight breeze. She had to get to them, but she didn't know how.

Around and around the garden Tara walked. It was worse than the meditation maze she'd walked when passing within. She was so close to her target, only to be led away with the next few steps. She stopped and leaned over to get closer to the roses, maybe even bend over enough to touch a branch. As soon as she reached for one, though, the winds sprang up and pushed the roses back.

The winds also tried to force Tara from her path. But she knew, in that perfect logic of dreams, that as soon as she deviated from the rock walkway, the greenery would eat her alive.

Long afternoon shadows stalked across the green lawn. The air grew chilly. The delightful scent of the roses was now mingled with decay. Tara wasn't going to be able to capture her rose before it had stopped blooming.

Finally, unable to take it any longer, Tara forced herself to step off the path.

The grass tickled her now bare feet, soft and springing on top with good, solid dirt underneath, cool and carrying its own earthy scent.

But the grass grew more spongy. The roses against the wall seemed to retreat. Though Tara had stepped off the path at where she'd been closest to the rose trees, there was now an entire field between her and her prize.

She made the mistake of starting to run.

The grass no longer grew on solid earth, but floating on a pond.

Tara quickly sunk knee deep in the waters. Her feet slipped against the slimy mud. Then the ground tried to catch hold of her, sucking at her toes, making it more difficult with each step.

She couldn't go backwards. An endless ocean splayed out behind her.

She could only go forward, toward that distant shore, even though the water was rising and she was sure to drown.

For the first time, Tara felt afraid of the water. She tried to bluster through it. Water was her element. She shouldn't be afraid. She could swim out.

But she knew she couldn't. The roots of the grass would form a net and hold her, while the water would slip through.

Night was coming quickly. She had to get out.

Water was all about a balance, finding the point between raging and trickling.

Tara woke up still floundering. She sat up in her bed, panting.

Though she coughed, no water came up out of her lungs. She still felt waterlogged.

The fiery path across her hand that Teruko had licked suddenly came back to her.

Obviously the cat had been trying to tell her something, something about her own very nature.

But what?

THE BUS LET Tara out a few blocks away from where the coven was meeting. They'd found a park midway along the harbor wall. Though there were no clouds, the air had stayed warm. Tara knew it was the start of the pineapple express winds blowing their way, sure to dump several inches of warm rain on them starting tomorrow.

Even with the dim light, Tara could tell this wasn't the best neighborhood. Tags covered the garbage cans on the corner. Graffiti murals were painted across the fronts of the garages. At one point this neighborhood had probably been cute, but it had gone to seed. The sidewalks were cracked.

An encampment of homeless stretched along the driveway of an abandoned house. Tara would have to remember to come back and talk with them, to let them know that the area might be flooding tomorrow and that they were directly in the path of the water.

They wouldn't necessarily believe her, of course.

And their deaths really would be her fault, as the Riprap man was sure to claim.

Tara hurried along, drawn toward the light she saw just down the street. Lucius had prepared the area for them. The light that Tara saw came from the top of his cane that he held aloft like a torch. Anyone outside of their coven would be repelled by the light.

Lucius wore his usual impeccable black coat, though he'd added knee-high black leather boots that evening. They had a square toe and looked much more solid than Tara's own short waterproof boots.

"I'm glad you're here first," Lucius said, nodding to Tara. His silver hair gleamed in the light he held, though his normally blue eyes appeared black. "I wouldn't presume to give you advice—"

"Yes, you would," Tara snapped at him.

His eyebrows raised up at her.

"I'm sorry," Tara said. "I'm just tired. And I don't know what to do. How to stop this flood from coming."

Lucius nodded. "I see," he said.

"You wouldn't presume to give me advice…" Tara prompted him after he'd been quiet for a while.

"True," Lucius said. He sighed, and seemed to come to a decision. "You need to decide what is right for you," he said after a moment. "Just think about it."

"What do you mean?" Tara asked, confused.

"Part of the issue with you humans is that you're always racing off to do something or another," Lucius said, "instead of thinking about it. Forming a plan. Perhaps considering the consequences or even what the correct path is."

Tara forced her hands to unclench, though she really felt as though she wanted to slap Lucius and his smug attitude from his handsome face. "I've been doing trying to do that," she said, her jaw clenched so she wouldn't scream. "I've been studying. Thinking."

"Ah, there's your problem," Lucius said. "You need to be meditating and feeling deeply. You're a witch. That means seeking the answers within, not without."

Tara nearly growled. Hadn't that been how she'd gotten into trouble in the first place?

"Meditate on it," Lucius said, though the words sounded more like a command. "Don't just grasp at the first solution that comes to hand."

"I don't have time," Tara pointed out.

"Make the time," Lucius said. His human mask slipped a little.

Tara felt a shiver of fear run through her. She refused to take a step backwards, away from this being, though the power flowing off him buffeted against her skin like harsh waves.

"How? How do I make the time?" Tara asked. She found her hands balled up in tight fists and didn't bother releasing them.

"Go deep," Lucius said. He seemed amused by her aggression. "Think deeply." He looked past her. "Ah, Kaede. Welcome."

Tara couldn't help the anger that still radiated off her. She was trying, damn it! Trying to learn enough. To be enough. To do enough so that she wouldn't lose thousands of lives.

How could going deep help her? She'd drown if she went deep. She couldn't pass through the water as she had passed through the fire. She couldn't live and die as she had with the old tree. She had to do something else with the water, find that balance.

And soon.

<hr>

THEY STOOD IN A CIRCLE, holding hands beside the river. Though Lucius had killed the light from this cane, he still generated a soft glow so they weren't standing in complete darkness.

The sound of the rushing water soothed Tara's nerves, as did the smell of the wet grass. It was too early to hear crickets or frogs, but they'd start their singing soon. She held hands with Ginny on one side, and just held pinky fingers with Kyle on the other.

They stood in a different order tonight, the one that Lucius had put them in instead of the order they normally stood in. There was no doubt, though, that Lucius was the center of the circle, despite how he stood beside them, joined physically with the rest of them.

Tara still led the group in their initial prayers, starting this time with Bonana, the goddess of the waters before thanking the fires by their unknowable names, the earth underneath their feet and the winds. Only at the very end did she make a mention of the defenders of the people and the guardian of souls.

It just seemed to her that the elements were more important that night, rather than the other spirits.

Lucius took up the prayer next. He thanked gods and goddess who Tara didn't know, the names rolling off his tongue. His voice would have graced any chapel, the deep tones ringing solemnly through the air. He actually sounded sincere, and not sarcastic for once.

She should have realized that of course, Lucius and his kind had their own gods and goddesses, though she didn't really see Lucius as someone who would spend a lot of time being grateful or in prayers.

Tara added her magic to the threads being gathered. It felt easier this time, as though her magic wasn't fighting against her. Then again, it also felt as if she pushed her magic along, instead of having it pulled from her.

Lucius formed a bubble of magic around them. It felt vaguely familiar to Tara. It took a moment for her to remember her dream, where she'd been trying to hold back the wave on the river. She'd formed a similar sort of bubble shield around her.

Huh. So it was actually a thing? Not just something her imagination had come up with?

Then again, Tara knew she wasn't the most imaginative person in the world. She tended to be very practical and not fanciful.

She was going to have to remember to ask Lucius about this spell later, to see if it was possible for her waking self to make something similar.

Then Tara's stomach lurched. Sour bile rose up and she swallowed hard to get rid of it.

The group had started to sink beneath the ground. The last time she'd done this had been using Miss Lucy's potion, and her stomach still associated the two.

Tara looked across the circle to Richard, whose eyes were so wide they appeared to be popping out of his head. She tried to send reassurance to him as the ground rose up, the cool earth now the level of her knees. At least he didn't look as though he'd bolt and break the circle. Probably his fear, as well as his curiosity, held him in place.

Down they went, starting off slowly then rocketing, like a high-speed elevator. The cold quickly sank into Tara's bones. She tried to call up the spark of fire that lived deep within her but it was sluggish in response.

It, too, was still tired.

When Tara had visited the witch at the base of the Morrison bridge, she'd landed in what looked like living room carved out of the rock, with a cold fireplace despite the bright blue flames and solid rock walls.

Or as the witch had called it, "Cell sweet cell."

The group landed in a vaguely round chamber. This wasn't someone's home. The walls were plain rock and soft dirt lay under their feet. It looked like a cave, with several tunnels branching off of it. The rock gave off a strange white glow, as though living mist covered it. A slight breeze blew around them, tugging at Tara's hair and carrying the scent of dust and ancient dirt.

Before anyone could ask if this was the right place, a figure came out of one of the tunnels.

She was taller than Tara, over six feet. Long silver-white hair flowed straight down from her center part, ending close to her waist. Her skin had the same pale glow as the rock, as did her clothing—a loose pair of trousers with a long-sleeved shirt hanging over it, belted at the middle. Her bare feet seemed out of place. Tara would have expected solid boots.

Though Lucius still physically stood with the rest of them in the circle, what appeared to be an avatar of the being pulled away, turning to face the woman. His avatar took on that same whitish glow as the other spirit.

Neither of them were ghosts. Though they had the same glowy white coloration as a ghost, she couldn't see through them. Ghosts were always transparent. This was a spirit form that she'd not heard of before. Could witches do it? Or was this just an ability of beings of power?

Or was her spirit form more colorful, as she had traveled without her body before.

The wind whistled more loudly through the chamber. Tara also thought she heard the sound of rain pattering around her. The smell of the river suddenly loomed, full of wet moss and decay.

"You have come," the woman whispered. The wind suddenly died down. "As promised."

Lucius pulled himself more stiffly upright at that. "I didn't promise anything."

"Ah, no, not you. The other. Who first took my soul," the woman said, swaying. "The Riprap man."

A spike of fear ran through Tara. That didn't forebode anything good.

A sigh filled the chamber. The sound of rain increased.

"I just have to wait until the rains come, now," the woman said. "And I will be free."

Tara didn't understand what was happening. Mist sprang from the walls, blocking her view of the two spirits.

Ginny called up a quick wind to clear the way.

The woman now had her hands on Lucius's shoulders. His spirit form stood frozen in place.

Tara gasped when she realized that his boots were dissolving. She knew that once his bare feet touched ground, he'd be stuck here forever.

The spirit would change places with him. He would stay here and she would be free.

"Up!" Tara commanded. "Back above the earth!"

Tara thrust Lucius to the side, drawing the focus of power to herself. Kaede wove the rest of them together into a single unit. Tara could tell that ze had some difficulty with Lucius, who now stood there like a dead weight.

Fortunately, Tara had experience with this sort of travel and had a good feel of where her physical body still stood in the circle above the ground. She grabbed onto the threads of her soul, still planted in her body, and *pulled,* trying to lift the entire group back up above ground.

It was slow going at first. Tara's metaphorical arms ached and shook as she tugged at the threads above her. The bubble enclosing the group felt too heavy. She couldn't drag such a large structure with all these souls up. She wasn't strong enough.

Then Kyle's strength flowed into her, giving her the power to start to lift them.

Once the group was no longer touching the ground of the chamber, Tara was able to lift them much more quickly through the earth. It wasn't a high-speed elevator this time, though. More like an old fashioned clunky one, that tended to get stuck between floors.

Tara couldn't split her attention, couldn't look over at Lucius. She stayed focused on that thread up above, pulling her up. She had to get them all safe.

The sound of water buoyed her spirits and renewed her determination. She could follow the sound of the river. The others were hearing it too, whether they realized it or not. That made lifting the bubble of magic so much easier as it wasn't merely her senses drawing them up.

Finally, they popped up above the earth. Tara settled easily into her body, stepping into her skin and breathing a sigh of relief.

She blinked and looked around at the others. They all stood with her, various expressions of shock and relief on their faces. They still all held hands and were joined together in a circle.

Then the circle broke, their hands no longer joined.

Lucius fell to his knees, then over onto his side.

Kaede reached him first, though Kyle was right beside zir.

Even in the dim light, Tara could tell that Lucius had grown incredibly pale. Almost as white as his spirit form.

Finally his eyes blinked open. "It was a trap," he said, his normally smooth voice grating and harsh. "Eunida—she stole…she stole as much of my power as she could," he added.

Tara looked around at the others. She had no idea what that meant. No one else seemed to have a clue either.

Lucius closed his eyes and took a deep breath before continuing. "It means that now, when the rains come, Eunida can destroy the harbor wall when she escapes. Blow it to pieces." He coughed, his voice starting to return to normal. "Unless I take her place."

Tara couldn't help but gasp. "No," she said plainly. She wasn't about to let that happen.

Lucius chuckled. "Of course, that's a very noble reaction," he said, his tone returning to its normal sarcastic gait. "But are you sure that you wouldn't rather sacrifice one being for all the souls in Portland that you might save?"

"There has to be another way," Tara said. The others in the coven all nodded.

"But you forget, I'm not human," Lucius said. The mask slipped, whether on purpose or by accident, reminding Tara and the rest of just how alien this creature laying on the ground actually was.

Richard took a step back, visibly shaken. So did Ginny. Tara stood her ground, grinding her teeth together, as did Kyle and Kaede.

"I always said I'd be using you and expected the same in return," Lucius reminded her. "No hard feelings if I become the sacrificial goat."

"Do you want to be bound to the wall?" Kyle asked. He seemed choked up. Then again, Lucius had been his off and on lover.

"Of course not," Lucius said. "Don't be silly."

"Then we'll figure out something else," Tara said firmly. "We're not sacrificing you or anyone else."

Lucius merely chuckled at her pronouncement. "For now."

FIVE

TARA WOKE FEELING RESTLESS. When she'd gotten home, she'd tried going deep as Lucius had insisted, but she'd just ended up falling asleep. She sat up in her bed, trying to remember her dreams in case they had any hints or clues about what to do, but nothing brilliant came to her.

She couldn't help but groan when she saw an envelope had been pushed under her doorway. Who else had died? Whose death would the Riprap man blame her for this time?

She delayed getting up for a few more moments, checking her phone for messages. Kyle had taken Lucius home from the park and had promised to look after him for the day. Richard was going to do more research to see if he could find either Eunida or a myth that covered her type of being. According to Lucius, she wasn't one of his kind, but something called a traveler.

No important messages or emails. With a sigh, Tara got up, wrapped herself in her robe, and shuffled over to the door.

While the envelope was the same, instead of being a clipping about a death, it was about the failing of a dam just north of the city. Again, the words, "YOUR FAULT" were printed in red crayon.

Tara wasn't sure what the Riprap man was getting at. How could the fault at the dam be her fault? What did it matter?

Then she realized that the clipping was from that morning.

The dam had failed because too much water was pouring down from the mountains.

The chance of flooding in Portland had just gone up significantly.

And more rains were coming.

***

Despite the rain already pouring from the sky, Tara kept her promise to Mulinohana and spent the morning standing on one of the piers, throwing rose petals into the water.

Tara sang hymns to the water and the river, praising the coming rains as well as thanking the river for its bounty. Water dripped off the wide brim of her black rain hat and onto her bare hands. Her pretty purple waterproof boots were up to the task of the onslaught, as was her bright orange rain jacket. Her jeans, however, were soaking wet where they were exposed to the elements, from the top of her thighs to just below her knees.

However, Tara didn't call up the spark of fire that lived inside her to keep herself warm. Fire and water were fierce enemies. It felt disrespectful for her to call the fire while fulfilling her promise to the river spirit.

Tara sang and scattered pink and red rose petals across the water. The last time she'd done this, at the winter solstice, the water had sucked at the petals eagerly, pulling them under. Tara had taken it as a sign that her offering had been accepted.

This time, the petals stayed on the surface of the water, floating quickly downstream, as if Mulinohana really didn't like this offering.

Tara wasn't sure what to do, despite her misgivings. She finished her ritual, shaking the petals off her wet fingers then jamming her freezing cold hands into her pockets. Though the air felt warm, the rain was still cold. She stayed where she was, rocking back and forth on her feet, thinking.

The river flowed swiftly under the wooden pier, a dark, brown-gray color. Tara stared into the depths, trying to understand what the river was saying.

It didn't seem to care that she was there, fulfilling her promise. It had its own intent, to flow mighty and free. It resented everywhere man had interfered with its flow.

With a shock, Tara realized that the river itself was looking forward to flooding Portland.

But what about those places marked Sacred to You?

The Riprap man had sacrificed the witches in order for the bridges to be safe.

Would you break your Word?

Tara felt as though only part of the river acknowledged her claim. But the waters had divided, somewhere upstream. They'd swollen with so much snowmelt that the composition was no longer the same.

Mulinohana still existed, but his will had been diluted.

And the rest of the waters were angry.

Do not break your vow, Tara warned.

The waters didn't bother sneering at her. She wasn't important enough for that.

They were planning on running their course, no matter what the consequences.

———

Tara called Richard as she walked toward Hallowed Ground. She was working there for the rest of the afternoon, would take a quick dinner break, then meet the rest of them. Normally she'd be teaching at the Y that afternoon, but she'd arranged to take the days off around the equinox months before.

"Tell me you have some good news," Tara begged as she slogged through the rain.

"According to the weather forecasters, the pineapple express won't start really dumping water on us until later tonight," Richard said. His voice sounded grim. "All the pieces are in place for a huge flood. The city has already put all of its emergency crews on high alert."

"Not sure that's good news," Tara said sourly.

"It means the city is taking the threat seriously," Richard said. "I do think that's good news. There's a chance fewer people will die because we're expecting the worst."

"No, they're not," Tara said. "They're expecting some sort of flooding. Not that the harbor wall will explode as a mythical creature blows up her prison, fed by the energy we gave her last night." She was still pissed that they'd fallen for such a trap.

Why had Lucius insisted that they go talk to Eunida? Or was it a fate that he hadn't been able to escape? Had Eunida been calling to him? Or was this something that the Riprap man had done?

"Was Lucius serious when he thought that you'd actually sacrifice him? To save the city?" Richard asked.

Tara sighed. "He was." She took a minute to shake her head, sending drops cascading down from her wide-brimmed rain hat. "He isn't human," she added after a few moments. "He'd do the same thing to one of us in a heartbeat."

Richard gave a low whistle. "That's what I thought. I'm starting to understand just what that means, though." He sighed and paused.

"What?" Tara asked. Obviously he wanted to say something else.

"Well, Jeannie has kind of been following along with the flooding and everything," Richard said slowly.

Tara rolled her eyes. She hadn't forbidden Richard from talking about what they'd been doing recently. Maybe he thought telling Jeannie about the coming flood would help. Or maybe he was just trying to warn her away, trying to save her.

"She said that if we can prevent the flooding, maybe she'll accept that witches can do something good," Richard said all in a rush. "I mean, no pressure or anything. Save a couple thousand people, millions of dollars in property damage, and my relationship all at the same time."

Tara had to chuckle, as Richard had intended her to. "I'll do my best," she promised.

"I know you will," Richard said. "You'll come up with something. You have magic, right?"

Tara shook her head. Magic couldn't solve everything. Otherwise, as Jeannie had pointed out, the world would be in much better shape, wouldn't it?

"I'll see you later tonight," Tara said. They were still going to try to shore up the defenses of Hallowed Ground.

Tara swiped off her phone and took a moment to zip it carefully into one of her jacket pockets, getting it out of the rain. Then she took a deep breath and turned the corner, seeing the building for the first time in a couple of days.

Curses bubbled up out of Tara. The building suddenly looked old. The bricks no longer seemed perfectly aligned. The second story sagged in the middle, as if the supports had suddenly weakened. Peeling white paint covered the window frames. The smell of rotting drywall seeped over Tara, as if mold now grew between the walls.

And that was what the building felt like from the outside.

Tara steeled herself as she approached the volunteer door in the back.

Wait, was that graffiti? It disappeared as soon as she approached it.

The building was vulnerable to all attacks now. Human and non-human.

As were the souls inside.

Tara kept looking around the front hall. As the room felt so different she kept expecting for it to look different as well. Nothing had changed physically, though. The floor was still plain, scarred wood. The walls were decorated with drawings from the youngsters, as well as with government posters advising where people could get help, numbers for the homeless to call.

The same three rows of long tables were set up near where Tara had her "teashop." But no adult sat in the corner reading to the kids. Instead, the kids wandered with books in their hands, looking for someone to read to them. The activity corner was loud and crazy, and one child stood in the corner in time out, crying.

Soot and Teruko hadn't accompanied Tara that day, probably not wanting to face the chaos. Plus, only a few of the teens had asked for teas that afternoon.

If Tara had to put a name to the sour tang on the air, she'd call it hopelessness. This room used to be full of hope, of determination to be better, do better. Now, it was barely a refuge for those it sheltered.

It broke Tara's heart to see how the energy had flowed out of the room. She was determined to patch the building back up. Hopefully, just drawing the water out of the ground, purifying the spells there, would fix most of what had broken.

She wasn't sure it would be enough.

Was this why the Riprap man sacrificed a spirit at the base of new construction? So that his protection spells would last? Though he'd hunted and killed witches, probably needlessly, his intentions had always been good: he was there to protect the city of Portland.

Eric came up just as Tara was starting to load her canisters on the cart and take them back into the kitchen. "Hi," Tara said, trying to give him a big smile.

It mostly worked.

"Hi," he said, seemingly shy. He stood in front of her table, shifting from one foot to the other. His skin had that waxy look to it again, his eyes too big for his face. His black hair hung stringy down over his shoulders. He hunched over in his jacket, as if he couldn't get warm that afternoon. (Tara had had the same feeling, though she knew consciously that the room was the same temperature it had always been.)

"Is there something I can make for you?" Tara asked when Eric still didn't say anything after a few moments.

He looked up at her, his lips pressed so tightly together the skin around his mouth had gone stark white.

Tara waited. It was something she'd learned, having the patience to wait until one of the teens finally figured out what they wanted to say, not rushing them, but giving them the space and time they needed to find their words.

After a few long moments, Eric said all in a rush, "Look. It probably isn't my business. But I know something's wrong. We all do. The magic isn't working."

Tara nodded slowly. Kaede had never hid that ze was a witch from zir clients. Almost all of them believed it was a pagan thing and that it was just words, not power or actual magic.

"If you need help tonight, call us," Eric said. "Not just me. All of us. We can help."

Tara wasn't completely surprised at Eric's offer. They did work as a community, and the members of the community frequently helped each other. "Thank you," Tara said, though she had no idea how she might use any of their help with what the coven needed to do that night.

"Tonight's the spring equinox," Eric continued.

That surprised Tara a little more, that the boy knew the significance of the date.

"You'll be doing magic tonight. More healing," he said. He sounded both scared as well as determined. "There's a lot here that needs fixing," he added, gesturing vaguely around the room. "I'm serious. Let us know if we can help."

Tara gave him a smile. "Thank you," she said again. "Your offer means a lot."

"No," Eric said, shaking his head. "Don't blow me off. Use us. Use our power or energy or whatever you need. Fix this."

Tara opened her mouth then closed it again. "That isn't how it normally works," she said slowly.

"This place doesn't work like normal places," Eric said with a shrug. "Believe me. I've been to other food banks and soup kitchens. The people who run those places are trying to make the world better, but they're still doing it from a higher place than the rest of us. They care, but not like Kaede and the others here. They also don't expect anything from us." He fixed her with a hard stare. "You do. You expect us to contribute. Even the poorest of the community always brings in something to share. Don't suddenly cut off that source, thinking you can fix this yourself."

Tara paused, considering. The circle had always been able to use Richard's power, as weak as that might be. He contributed something to the circle.

"Let me check with Kaede," Tara said after a moment. Maybe there was something they could do, some amount of power they could draw from the community.

Tara wasn't certain if the coven's problem lay in a lack of power or a lack of knowledge. She also didn't know if it would take more power to coordinate a large group of mundanes than they would bring in.

"Good," Eric said. He handed her a scrap of paper with a phone number on it. "Call me. I can reach the other teens in the afterschool program. We're all prepared to drop everything and come here later tonight if you need us."

Tara reached across the table and took his hand. The skin was rough but warm, the grip firm. "Thank you," she said again.

Eric nodded, then turned and went back to his books.

Tara suddenly found tears in her eyes. She'd gotten so much better about relying on the rest of the coven instead of trying to solve every problem herself.

Seemed as though she still wasn't reaching wide enough for her solutions.

JUST AS THE last people were leaving the community center, a bright redhead slipped through the door. Tara looked up, surprised. "Ginny? What are you doing here?" she asked as the young hedgewitch made her way across the floor.

Ginny's coat was dark green, setting off her pale skin. It was two sizes too big for her, and she had to roll back the sleeves in order to free her hands so she could unzip it. "Here to take ye out to dinner," she said firmly. "We need to talk."

Fear spiked through Tara. "Okay," she said slowly. "I just need to finish up here." She'd already sent a text message to Kaede about Eric's offer, which the other witch appeared to be seriously considering.

Ginny rolled her eyes at Tara. "No, I'm not about to break up with ye," she said. "I love this coven. This group. It's the first time I've felt really welcomed, as a witch, ye know?"

Tara nodded, relieved. "I just have a few more things to put away," she said, indicating her little teashop. The others had already folded up the tables and put away the chairs before they'd gone for the evening.

"Can I help?" Ginny asked.

Tara silently handed Ginny the still full tea kettle, which Ginny carried back to the kitchen to empty out. Tara quickly packed up the rest of her gear onto the cart and went back into the kitchen herself.

Ginny came over and curiously fingered the black curtain Tara lifted that hid her ingredients. "Interesting," she said. "Not sure I could do that," she said after a moment.

"Sure you could," Tara said. "It's the same as making a sachet. Just...longer, I guess."

Ginny shook her head. "It's more permanent than what I make," she said after a moment. "My magic gets blown away by me winds too quickly."

Tara wasn't sure what to say about that. Then again, she was both a schooled witch as well as a hedgewitch, so she had a better handle on how to keep her magical elements separated.

"Where do you want to go?" Tara asked as she pulled on her own rain jacket.

"There's a pub I know," Ginny said with a grin. "Serves a brilliant fish and chips."

Tara kept a smile on her face. She tried to not eat a lot of fried food or grain.

"They serve big, juicy burgers as well," Ginny added after a moment. "With bacon and avocado."

"Now you're talking my language," Tara said with a grin.

They stepped outside into the rain. Tonight, their magic wasn't combining well. Maybe it was because Tara still was nervous about what the other witch had to say. Then again, the wild magic only worked about half the time. This may have been just one of those times when it wasn't working.

"Storm's coming," Ginny said as they waited for the bus.

Tara merely nodded. She felt it in her bones, the way the winds pushed at her and made her restless.

"It'll be a bad one," Ginny promised.

"Is there anything we can do to deflect it?" Tara asked. The thought had occurred to her that afternoon, that perhaps her wind, combined with Ginny's, might be able to alter the course of the storm.

Ginny shook her head. "Nope. And that's the problem, I think."

"What is?" Tara said.

"Let's get some food in us first," the other witch insisted. "Then we'll talk."

Tara nodded. She could wait. Just as she'd had the patience for Eric earlier that day, she could give Ginny the time and space she needed.

Tara just hoped that Ginny would talk with her soon. They didn't have much time.

THE PUB TURNED out to be on the river. Tara hadn't realized how nervous she was of the water until they'd started walking beside it.

It pissed Tara off. She wasn't afraid of the water. It was her element. And yet, the dark rushing river filled her with a strange anxiety. Rain came down harder now. If it continued, they'd get several inches over the next few hours.

More rain than the harbor wall could handle, particularly given the broken dam upstream.

The pub was dimly lit, with neon beer signs on the walls providing most of the light. There were two long counters, one at the bar and a second that ran under the front window. The rest of the floor was filled with sturdy high top tables, more than a dozen. Flat screen TVs hung from every corner, each showing a different sport. The smell of grease lay heavy in the air.

Only a few of the tables were filled. One group in the corner suddenly cheered on the soccer players shown on the TV they'd sat beneath, making Tara grin. Despite how dim this place seemed, it felt more welcome now.

Ginny insisted on sitting at the counter that ran under the front window, so they could stare out across the gloom to the river. The front of the pub held a wide deck. When the weather was nice, Tara imagined that it would be quite lovely to spend an afternoon, drinking and watching the river.

A harried waitress came and took their order, then left them in peace. The pub did serve big juicy burgers, with sweet potato fries and apple-onion kraut. Tara licked her fingers as she finished. She was going to have to remember this place.

As soon as the waitress collected their plates, Tara felt their magic swell together. She knew that they wouldn't be bothered for the rest of the evening, though they didn't have that long before they needed to meet up with the rest of the coven at Hallowed Ground. Ginny nursed along a dark pint of porter while Tara had stuck to water.

"Ye asked me about us blowing away the storm," Ginny said after a moment. "But ye didn't understand why it wouldn't work."

Tara nodded. "True," she said.

Ginny took another sip of her porter before she replied. "Me winds are local," she said after a bit. "It's why I had to release all of me old winds back in England before I left. Couldn't have brought them with."

Tara nodded. She remembered. And she remembered that Ginny had told her that Soot was also a local wind. "So what does it mean that a wind is local?" Tara asked after a few moments of silence.

She felt a pressure to get going, to start moving, to do something. Anything.

"Yer wind won't blow other places," Ginny said. "Ye try to call Soot to ye when you're in Seattle, and yer likely to be disappointed. Don't know his range. But he's a young wind. It won't be very far. Might not even reach Clackamas."

"Winds travel farther as they age?" Tara asked, surprised. She would have thought that as a wind grew older, it wouldn't be as strong.

"Aye," Ginny said. "Some of 'em. Some of 'em just peter out." She paused, then added, "Me winds are all local and young as well. Now, if a storm was blowing up in a couple dozen years or so, we might be able to do something about it. Might not."

Tara nodded. That sounded about right—maybe the wild magic would work. Maybe it wouldn't.

"So our winds are local, just blowing around Portland," Tara said, wanting to make sure that she understood what Ginny was saying.

"Aye," Ginny said. "And yer cat is local too."

Tara blinked, surprised. She hadn't thought about it. A wind being local made sense. Not necessarily a fire.

"Ye called him with a local bonfire, one ye lit yerself," Ginny pointed out.

"I did," Tara said. "In the backyard of my house."

"It's why location is important, when yer calling a spirit," Ginny said.

"Oh!" Tara said, putting it all together. "So I wouldn't necessarily have to be in that exact backyard if I needed to release Teruko, just nearby."

"I think that's right," Ginny said.

"Why didn't you tell me this earlier?" Tara asked, feeling a little aggrieved. She might have been able to use this information before.

Ginny shrugged. "I hadn't ever thought of these things myself, ye know. I've just been doing them. First time I've been digging in, trying to figure it all out."

Tara nodded. Ginny wasn't a schooled witch. She never thought about the magic she performed. She just did it. She didn't learn lore or spells, just relied on her instincts to pull ingredients together for her sachets or soaps.

"So my wind and my fire familiars are both local," Tara said.

"And yer water spirit needs to be local too," Ginny said firmly.

"Okay," Tara said slowly. She thought she'd been trying to call a local water spirit to her before. Hadn't she?

"I've been thinking on it," Ginny said. "Trying to figure out what went wrong that night. With ye calling the water spirit."

Tara nodded, encouraging Ginny to continue. She still hadn't figured out why the spell had gone so horribly awry, except that she knew she'd been using the wrong type of magic to draw it to her. The net had merely passed through the water spirit, who'd then turned around and used it to sink into the floor of Hallowed Ground.

"When ye were calling on that water spirit, trying to form it in that bowl of water, it wasn't local enough," Ginny said after a moment. "It was just…a water spirit."

"But wasn't that what I did with Soot and Teruko?" Tara asked. "Just called up a wind? A piece of fire?"

Ginny shook her head. "All the myths about water spirits have them in specific places. A stream. A lake. A place on a river. Ye cast yer net too wide."

"Oh," Tara said, nodding. "So even being in a park wouldn't have worked," she said after a moment.

"Probably not," Ginny said. "Not unless ye formed a mud puddle and called a spirit out of that. But it wouldn't be a strong one."

"Got it," Tara said. "So what do you suggest?"

She knew what the other witch was going to say before she even spoke the words. She still wanted to hear them out loud.

"We're gonna march right out on that pier over there," Ginny said, gesturing with her glass, "and call up the spirit of the river. Bind it to ye."

"Without the rest of the coven?" Tara asked.

"They can't help ye," Ginny insisted. "Hell, I can't either. Yer gonna have to do the calling yerself."

It felt so different than the offer Eric had made that afternoon, to help with the community center. Then again, the coven couldn't share in the power of the water spirit. It really would be a singular creature, only bound to Tara herself.

"Are you sure?" Tara asked, watching Ginny down the last of her pint and stand up.

Ginny at least had the decency to shrug. "I know ye have to do the calling. Can't tell ye if you'll succeed or fail."

The other witch's eyes suddenly bore into Tara's. "But ye better pray to Brigid and beyond that ye find yer water spirit. Nothing else is gonna save the city."

Tara grimly nodded. Ginny was right. She needed to tame the river if they were going to have a fighting chance.

SIX

The harbor wall stands finally, and the latest spring floods have bypassed the city. I keep finding myself drawn back to it, though. I wonder if another might have served better as the wall's guardian. Eunida does her best, wandering the endless tunnels she's built there. Mulinohana pushes harder against that structure than against the bridges. I wonder what else I need to do to strength the wall. I have heard rumors that Eunida is able to haunt the ground above as well, that she calls humans to their death. I will try to set a net to trap those souls she damns, so that it isn't just a single soul who protects the wall.

Wilson Evermore, Master Magician and Hunter of Souls, 1932

THE WINDS HAD GROWN fierce while Tara and Ginny had eaten. They howled out of the south, warm and wild. Tara's jeans were quickly soaked. The darkness of the night settled heavily around them, the shadows hiding them even without their magic.

Just past the restaurant a private pier jutted out into the river. The water wasn't high enough to slosh over the top of it yet, but the rain had soaked it thoroughly, making it slippery. An orange streetlight bravely tried to light the path despite the heavy rains.

A locked gate stood at the foot of the pier. Wire fencing wrapped around the edges of the gate and up the pier so that someone would have to swim deep into the water in order to gain access. Neither Ginny or Tara thought anything of it. A simple touch of the hand brought the winds who slipped the tumblers into place, the door sliding open silently.

Tara took a deep breath before she set foot on the pier itself. The earth had always seemed to support her. Now, she would be floating, standing above the water, connected to the ground but not on it.

Somehow, that seemed significant to her. She thought back to being at the headwaters of the Willamette, where she'd delayed the Riprap man so they could break his bond with Mulinohana. She bet that the original ceremony had been done while standing on the boulders there.

She would have to tell Ginny about this, if the other witch ever wanted to call a water spirit to her. Then again, Ginny's element was the wind. She might never progress to other spirits.

Would Tara ever try to call an earth spirit to her? Or would this be the last spirit she had? She didn't know, but thought that at some point, an earth spirit might be kind of cool as well. She still thought fondly of the old oak who had helped her traverse the circle of earth.

Tara shook her head, the rain dripping off her hat, reminding herself to focus.

"Ye can do this!" Ginny shouted over the wind, encouraging her.

Tara took a deep breath, nodded, and walked out onto the pier.

The winds tried to push Tara into the water. She didn't bother calling Soot—he was no match for these. She did bring up that spark of fire that always lived deep within her, just a little something to chase the cold away.

She recognized her mistake as soon as she did. The wind was working with the water, who recognized its ancient enemy. Tara's next step wasn't straight but to the side as a gust nearly knocked her over.

Fine. She'd be cold. She let go of the fire, trying to appease the storm.

The winds backed off slightly, so that she was able to mostly walk a straight line to the edge of the pier. Dark water rushed before, off the edge. She couldn't see the far bank through the storm, so it felt as though she stood at the very end of the world. The rain struck her face, blowing sideways, stinging with cold. The lovely burger she'd just eaten now sat like a bloated sack in her belly, throwing her off balance without grounding her.

Why was she doing this again?

Tara suddenly felt warmth at her back, as if a ray of sunshine had miraculously broken through the clouds. When she looked over her shoulder, she saw that Ginny had followed her there to the end of the pier. Though the other witch couldn't help Tara calling her water spirit, it still made her heart glad to know that she wasn't alone.

Someone would be there to either witness her success, or to help her bear the weight of her failure.

Tara spoke her prayer out loud, though she doubted that even Ginny could hear her. She thanked not only the eastern and western winds, but those that blew north and south as well. She thanked the retreating winter spirit for its duty, teaching them the stillness of the season, the need for reflection. She welcomed the coming spring as well as the growing light, without forgetting to thank the darkness of night, keeping balance in all things.

The winds whipped her words away, casting them far and wide. She didn't know if any of them reached the river itself. It reminded her of the first time she'd tried to scatter rose petals on the water and Soot had chased each one away.

Tara had always felt comfortable in the water, had always lived near it so she could regularly see it and visit it. However, unlike the fire, she didn't feel as though she had a "spark" of the water inside of herself that she could draw from.

She blinked out across the dark river rushing under her feet. Wind drove the rain almost horizontal at this point, slamming into her. The winds howled as they whipped past her, drowning out the sound of the water at times. She shivered in the cold, fighting to stay on her feet.

She couldn't tame the storm. It was too big, too wild. Maybe if she had the full power of the coven behind her, but even then she didn't think it would work.

However, she still had to do *something*. The winds made it impossible for her to think, let alone perform magic. She still felt that itch inside to move, though she knew if she raised her arms or danced that the wind would catch at her jacket and throw her into the waters.

She felt more than heard Ginny's word, coming from behind her. *Local.*

Tara drew herself up and closed her eyes for a moment. She needed to focus on what was right in front of her, the local surroundings. Not the entire storm or the full river.

Stinging rain lashed against her face. The cold had seeped into her very bones, freezing her in place. The smell of the river was very faint, but she still tried to draw it closer.

Then she called Soot to her. She thought about his slick, warm fur and clear eyes, his boundless, puppy-like enthusiasm. She couldn't free her hair from her hat, but she thought about how he liked to tug on it.

Suddenly, the winds around her lessened. She could hear again. The rain hitting the pier made a hollow sound. Ginny hummed behind her, the sound making her heart lighter.

The pressure of a warm body leaned against Tara's soaking jeans. She could barely make out the dark shape of Soot at her feet, but he was there, protecting her. His local winds rebuffed the storm, at least in the area directly around her, and hopefully Ginny as well.

Tara took a deep breath, feeling as though she'd just stepped into the eye of the storm. It still howled all around her, but she had a few moments of peace. "Thank you," she told her familiar, her wet fingers scratching the top of Soot's rain-slicked fur.

The dog looked up at her, expectant. What else did she need?

Tara shrugged. She had no idea. She wasn't about to call Teruko out into this mess. Not that she'd come. She *hated* the water. Wouldn't stand for her fur to get all wet. Plus, Tara had no idea how the river would react to a fire spirit out on the pier. The river might decide to tear down the structure just to get at the creature.

Maybe it was time for Tara to try calling a water spirit. She'd prepared the space around her as well as she could.

It was time to try.

TARA SAID HER PRAYERS AGAIN. This time, she felt as if they went into the river waters. Not by casting the words out in front of her, off the edge of the pier, but by making them sink down, beneath her. The cone of calm around her went deep into the river.

Finally, she was getting somewhere. The river wasn't necessarily paying much attention to her. She still knew that she'd at least gotten some of the racing water to heed her.

Now, it was time for her to try to call up part of that water, to draw the local water spirit to her.

Tara didn't know the name of the local waters. The only water spirit she was familiar with was Mulinohana. Though his base was up at the headwaters of the Willamette, he traveled this way. His waters mingled with the rest here.

However, Tara didn't speak his name. Instead, she tried calling on the local waters. Some of the river eddied at this point, around the pier. Was it a deep enough pool for it to have its own water spirit?

At first, Tara wasn't sure if the local waters heard her or not. They were overwhelmed by the rest of the river running headlong down its course.

After another call, Tara finally found a thread of awareness at her feet. Beneath the pier sang a small, shy voice. It was a joyous song about the rain, the rushing waters, the depth of the river before it. Yet, this spirit held itself separate, bringing life to the banks here, celebrating the frogs and the birds who lived nearby.

Tara called to this local spirit of the water, tried to draw it closer to her. She praised its wisdom of staying nearby, of taking care of the creatures in its environment, of not spreading out across the entire width of the river.

Slowly, Tara coaxed the spirit up. It was such a tiny thing!

Was it not a water spirit, but maybe a water sprite?

Tara had read of such things in the lore that Richard had set her. She hadn't thought to ask about the differences with Ginny or the others.

Soot could take the shape of a large dog, until he was the size of a small horse if he felt very threatened. Teruko was the same. Though she normally was the size of a large, twenty pound cat, she, too, could stretch and lengthen out. Tara had never pushed Teruko to see her full abilities, but she imagined that the cat could, in fact, grow as large as a small car.

This water spirit—or sprite—would fit comfortably in the palm of Tara's hand, and would never grow much larger. Tara had an image of it standing like a tiny fairy in front of her, not even six inches tall. It didn't have much magic, or really much power, either.

Still, Tara was desperate. She slowly drew the water sprite up. For a few moments she actually saw it, dancing like a delicate, glowing butterfly in front of her. It cruised on the winds that Soot provided, then fluttered closer.

Tara reached out her hand. She knew they had to touch in order to become connected.

However, like all spirits, the little sprite was a contrary thing. It wouldn't come to her hand easily. It flew around her, teasing.

Then, it made the mistake of trying to fly further away. Tara had the feeling it wasn't necessarily rejecting her plea, or trying to escape. It was just playing.

Dark winds caught the tiny water sprite as soon as it left the quieter area around Tara.

"No!" Tara called. "Come back!"

The water sprite, even if it had wanted to, couldn't heed her call. The storm winds shredded its delicate winds, howling in glee. Tara heard the poor shriek of the little creature as it was tossed around.

Damn it! Tara tried to reach for the sprite, tried to snag it with her magic and draw it closer to her.

Too late. The being was ripped from her grasp. Tara watched the tiny light tumbling down stream, buffeted by the winds.

Tara stood, horrified. She had never meant to cause harm. Now, she'd deprived an area of its magical protection, what little the sprite had been able to provide.

Bowing her head, Tara grieved. She hoped the little sprite could find its way back home after the storm had finished playing with it, that she hadn't killed it by calling it up.

A hand reached out and touched her shoulder, lending her warmth and strength. Ginny had seen what Tara had done, how she'd accidentally called forth the wrong creature.

"Ye must try again," Ginny said.

Tara heard cold steel in the other woman's voice. Or maybe she couldn't actually hear it over the rushing wind, and just felt it, the knife's blade prodding her forward.

"Did I kill it?" Tara said softly.

"Eh. Maybe. Maybe not," Ginny assured her. "'Tweren't the right creature anyway. Ye can come back here and give a blessing on the place, see if ye can call it back later."

Tara nodded, sighing. She would do that.

"Ye gonna have to call the big one," Ginny said.

Tara couldn't help but gulp at the thought of that. She knew that Ginny meant Mulinohana, the water spirit that the Riprap man had been bound to.

At least that gave Tara a new thought. She'd felt as if she'd bound both Soot and Teruko to her. They had form in part because she'd given it to them.

Was that enough for the water spirit? Or was Tara going to have to give it something more? Give it part of herself?

Be as bound to the spirit as it was bound to her?

"I'll try," Tara said, nodding. She had no choice. The storm was dumping too much water into the river. When the harbor wall broke, the flooding would be epic. The angry river would see to that.

She immediately missed the warmth of Ginny's hand on her shoulder when the other witch stepped back again. The rain continued to assault her, the winds beyond her calm spot howling not only for her blood, but the blood of everyone it came in contact with. River water surged up, splashing across the top of the pier, intent on washing away everything in its path.

Tara had to tame at least one part of this storm or she'd lose a lot more than a single water sprite to the rain and winds.

She took a determined breath, and started again.

———

TARA RECALLED her prayers and recited them a third time, though this time she started off thanking Bonana the water goddess for her wisdom first before calling on the other gods and goddess to aid her in her quest. When she finished, she began a hymn to the waters, thanking them for their bounty, for bringing life and light.

Though Tara felt as though all of her prayers were reaching the rushing river that still overflowed the pier, she still felt ignored. The waters were too varied between the local waters, the snow flow, as well as the pieces she felt were part of Mulinohana.

What could she do to call attention to herself? To get the waters to heed her?

Before, while preparing to walk between the circles, Tara had performed a lot of spells that used the elements, such as wind or fire. She hadn't done as many spells that required water. She understood her ignorance as well as her arrogance, now.

Still, water was her element. There had to be something she could do.

She tried calling up the water, but it was moving too fast beneath her. She couldn't control it.

Tara felt her rage increase. She would *not* be ignored. Water was her element. She drew a small pool of water up around her feet, causing it to swirl slightly, circling where she stood.

The amount of water that she could control wasn't big enough. Not in the face of the raging river.

Fine. She'd get its attention another way.

Tara deliberately called up the spark of fire that always dwelled inside of her. She reveled in the warmth for a moment, ignoring how the storm picked up around her.

It took some time for Tara to call up fire into her hands. She'd only done it before with the proper components sitting beside her, as well as three powerful sachets. She didn't have time for any of that, however. She called on the secret names of the fire gods, begging for their help as she gathered her strength together.

Eventually, Tara had a small glowing fireball crackling between her palms, perhaps six inches in diameter. She fed it her anger, causing the hissing sparks to fly up high, defying the water around them. Tara found herself sweating for the first time in forever. She raised the ball up above her head, calling again on the water to heed her, to pay attention to her call and her need.

With all her strength, Tara threw the fireball down, directly at her feet. It passed through the pier and went into the waters there. Gleefully, the fire continued to burn, fighting the dark waters surrounding it.

Tara knew the battle was hopeless. The water would eventually overwhelm her little fire.

Still, she'd finally gotten the attention of the river. The river deigned to communicate with her at last. Not in words, so much as with images and feelings. It showed her its leaping progress, how it was climbing the manmade banks. How it would spew over everything, an orgy of cleansing. How it would at first tear away everything in its path, then slow to a trickle that would seep in everywhere and be impossible to clean away.

Tara tried to calm the waters, reminding it of its other nature, how it could be life giving as well. How playfully the river could be, how much joy it brought.

For a moment, Tara thought she had a chance. The waters around her slowed and the winds lessened. The rain fell down steadily, not as angry as before.

"Mulinohana!" Tara called. "Remember your promises! The structures that have been marked as sacred to you! The lives already sacrificed!"

Tara couldn't see far beyond the edge of the pier, yet she felt a presence growing there. A dark form rose out of the water, like an inky cloud. "I remember," it boomed at Tara, sounding like boulders smashing together. "You no longer have power over me, human."

"You will heed me," Tara commanded, though she felt like an ant trying to stop a wave.

"Or what?" The river actually appeared to chuckle, to laugh at her.

Tara couldn't call up another fire. The water would also laugh at that effort too.

"Or you will be forever alone," Tara told it. "Seeking comfort and never finding. Seeking companionship but always racing away. Seeking honor but remaining nameless, with no one to sing praises to you."

"I don't need you," Mulinohana sneered.

"Need? No," Tara said. She knew she wouldn't get anywhere trying to force the water into one path or another. "Want, however? You want people to remember you. To not take you for granted. To praise your coming and the life you bring."

"They will fear me," Mulinohana boasted.

"And then they will box you in more," Tara reminded the waters. "As they already have."

A dark being suddenly loomed up above Tara. It took on the form of a huge wave, curling above her head. Or maybe a mouth, ready to swallow her whole.

"I do not fear you," Tara said calmly. "You are of me. With me. You will be a part of me."

The water paused, black drops of freezing rain dripping on her face.

"No. You will be a part of me," the river declared.

The water crashed down, sweeping Tara from her feet and into the river.

<hr>

TARA DIDN'T SCREAM, though she wanted to. That would just give the waters the chance to drown her. Instead, she called up her air power, giving her a pocket to breathe in, at least for the moment. It wouldn't last long. Soot stayed by her side, not in dog form but as a flowing wind, circling her head.

It took some effort, but Tara crunched herself down into a ball. Flailing arms or legs were sure to get broken by rocks or trees carried in the water. As a smaller target, Tara could at least float in the water. She willed herself up, to get her head out of the water and take a deep breath.

Except…being that high in the water wasn't where she belonged. She couldn't swim, not against this current. She would freeze in a short while as well, her magical fire giving her a chance to survive, but eventually it, too, would die out.

Instead, Tara willed herself down toward the floor of the riverbank. She had to find a spot to take a stand.

The current wasn't as strong there, deep under the water. Darkness enclosed her. There was nothing to see except black waters. Though her body wanted to float up, Tara dug herself into the ground, her toes seeking the muddy soil.

Finally, Tara was able to stand. The waters rushed around her, seeking to make her bow or to carry her away. It took all her strength to stay where she was.

Despite how little Tara could see, she knew when Mulinohana had arrived, his dark shape surrounding her. The temperature of the waters dropped. Tara shivered, but kept her breathing shallow. She wouldn't give the waters the chance to drown her. Not yet.

Tara remembered the first time she'd deliberately sought the water's embrace, the warm fire fed by river rushes, the brown flames cackling contentedly, the only fire that the waters would allow. The humor of the river as she had faced it, its admiration for her audacity to come closer when she could have swam free.

Mulinohana no longer had a space for her, though. It had grown wild without any humanizing influences, because while the Riprap man wasn't exactly human, he had been at one point.

Instead, they stood in the raging waters, facing off against each other.

"You have nothing to bind me with," the waters said gleefully. "Any net you throw will pass through me. And nothing, really, to offer me."

"How did the Riprap man bind you?" Tara asked. She'd always been curious about that.

Despite being in the cold waters, Tara felt her skin blanch as a dozen souls dropped into the headwaters, fed there by the Riprap man. He'd sacrificed an entire coven, as well as his mentor, in order to take his place beside the river spirit.

"What do you have to offer?" the river asked slyly, knowing that Tara wouldn't give it any such sacrifices.

Tara pictured the rituals she'd preform at the riverside, the songs and praises. She thought about bringing the entire coven with her, so that they could help, but decided against that. The river needed her attention, and hers alone.

It wasn't enough.

River grasses sprang up all around Tara, binding her legs. She might be able to burn them away, but it would take time. She'd probably drown first. Even if she did get away, she still had to find the strength to make her way out of the water, fighting through a stream that wanted to drown her.

She was going die here, her soul enough of a sacrifice for the river.

Tara felt the dark presence of Mulinohana turn away from her. It had other business. Other humans to hurt and kill.

"No!" Tara screamed.

The river ignored her.

There had to be some way to get its attention. To bind it to her, as it were. A net wouldn't work. Nor would another fireball.

She needed something else.

Something floated past her line of vision. She blinked, peering hard.

A single rose petal undulated softly in the waters.

Tara suddenly had an idea.

Would it work?

She could only die trying.

SEVEN

It turned out to be a brilliant stroke of luck, but every soul that Eunida takes now strengthens the harbor wall as well. If I could find another such creature, I'm sure I could bind it to one of the bridges. However, since I've taken Eunida, all the other beings of power have started avoiding this place, not just the travelers. It's just as well. There are too many witches still, who don't deserve such honor as protecting this fair city. Still, I take their pitiful lives and turn them into something useful. Mulinohana sings my praises for each and every soul, though He teases me by buffeting the bridges I have marked as Sacred to Him.

Wilson Evermore, Taker of Souls and Defender of Portland, 1935

TARA RECALLED the hymns she'd sung to the river when she'd dropped rose petals into the water, both on the winter solstice as well as earlier that morning. Those petals were hers, freely sacrificed for the river.

She couldn't sing out loud, not without risking drowning. The grasses wrapped around her legs at least gave her more stability so she wasn't fighting to hard against the river and was able to stand up straighter. The cold also pressed against her and she couldn't help but shiver. Blackness like an inky abyss formed all around her.

Still, Tara strove to find those petals, remembering throwing handfuls of them out onto the river, singing praises to Mulinohana and thanking the river for its life-giving waters.

First one, then another of the petals suddenly floated in front of her. They glowed with soft red and pink light. They grew in mass, like a hunk of crimson seaweed waving slightly in the current.

Tara sent them streaming out to Mulinohana. They were his in the first place.

The rose petals found where the river spirit lurked, maybe twenty feet away from where Tara was trapped. They swirled around the dark form, outlining it.

"Come here," Tara ordered.

"No!" the river spirit raged.

The petals increased their speed, whirling now like a tornado. They made their own sharp humming noise, cutting through the sound of the rushing waters with a deep bass.

As soft as the petals might be, roses still had thorns.

They dragged Mulinohana across the space, bringing him to stand before Tara.

"I have kept my bargain with you," Tara told the reluctant water spirit. "Now, you will heed me and remember your promises as well."

The water spirit gave a heartfelt sigh. Tara had the impression that it both wanted to be bound as well as fought it at the same time.

"I claim you," Tara said, risking speaking the words out loud while still held so far under the water. "And I give myself to you as well."

A tendril of rose petals reached across the gulf between them.

Tara gulped. Was it a trick? Would the water spirit drown her anyway if she took it?

She had no choice, though. She had bound it, now she had to let it bind her.

Tara reached out her hand, her fingertips brushing against the soft petals.

The petals swirled around her arm, gaining speed.

Tara felt herself yanked forward into darkness.

WHEN TARA BLINKED her eyes open, she found herself standing near the headwaters of the Willamette, that same place where she'd distracted the Riprap man and destroyed his bond with the water spirit. She wore a mere slip instead of her jeans, raincoat, and boots, so she knew that she wasn't there physically, but just her spirit.

In front of Tara, water rushed over the boulders in the river. Clear blue sky arched overhead. Green moss edged the bank, and pines, dark and ominous, stood across the way. Cold mud squished between Tara's toes, but she didn't feel as though she was about to slip and fall. No, the mud held her as firmly as if she stood on solid dry ground.

A contented sigh spread across the wind. Standing next to Tara, she finally saw the form of the river.

He appeared Native American to her, with long black hair braided down on either side of his face and dark eyes. Despite the age of the waters, he appeared to be in his mid-twenties. He gave her a smile that warmed her heart.

Despite his appearance, he wore western style clothing, a long-sleeved shirt hanging over dark black trousers, with a brown suede vest. His bare feet and long toes dug into the mud beside her.

"You see me," Mulinohana said, surprised, his words hissing like the river.

"I do," Tara said.

"Wilson Evermore—the being you call the Riprap man—could never see this form," Mulinohana said.

Tara nodded. She didn't know if that was because water wasn't the primary element of the Riprap man, or due to his prejudices, as he was a white man born in the 1880s and would never have seen a Native American as anything worthwhile.

Mulinohana sighed. "I cannot stop the flood," he said. "The waters are too fierce. Outside of my control."

"Thank you for letting me know," Tara said, though her heart sank. She'd hoped that just calling the water spirit would have been enough.

"I will calm the waters once they've broken through the harbor wall," Mulinohana promised. "That much I can do."

Tara knew that would help tremendously, if the waters didn't rage after the harbor wall had fallen. She didn't ask Mulinohana if he could help strengthen the harbor wall, that went against his very being.

Cool strength flowed into Tara the longer she stood there, calmness seeping into her heart. After a few more long moments, Tara finally said, "I need to get back to the pier."

"I will help you with that," Mulinohana said. He gave her a wicked smile. "But you need to visit me often."

"I will," Tara promised. She knew the words bound her soul to his, in some way.

"Then I release you," Mulinohana said. "Call on me later, when you need some unruly water brought to heed."

Tara wasn't sure what the river spirit meant by that. But she found herself in a whoosh of water, darkness descending once again.

Suddenly, Tara was standing on her own two feet again, on solid land. No, not earth. The pier. The winds pushed at her, angry that their prey had been taken from them. Tara found herself suddenly blown to the side. It took some fancy footwork to stop herself from going over the edge again.

Had she actually, physically gone into the water the first time? Or had that just been a spirit form?

She turned to ask Ginny.

The other woman was nowhere to be seen.

Had the waters taken her? Had the storm? Tara called out, using her magic to carry her voice. It wouldn't do her any good to search the immediate vicinity—if Ginny had been dragged into the river, she would have been carried far from here by the rough waters by now.

Rain continued to pour from the heavens, no longer bothering to form drops but instead, coming down in huge sheets. Tara felt waterlogged. She called up her fire spirit to warm her, but even that extra warmth wouldn't be enough to dry out her clothes anytime soon.

Tara stomped down the pier, angry at herself for having risked her friend. She nearly stumbled once, then twice, as Soot tried to get in her way.

However, before Tara spoke sharply to the dog, she looked at him.

He raised his eyes beseechingly to her.

"What is it?" Tara asked. "Do you know where Ginny is?"

She shook her head, calling herself a fool. She didn't need to find Ginny on her own. Soot could find the other witch much faster than Tara could.

"Go find Ginny. Fetch Ginny here," Tara said.

Soot continued to look up at her, his tail thumping on the wooden pier loud enough for Tara to hear it over the pounding rain.

"Good boy," Tara said belatedly. She reached out and scratched the top of his head, between his eyebrows. Soot closed his eyes in bliss.

"You were so good!" Tara said after another moment. "Thank you so much for giving me air while I was underwater, for supporting me through all of this. Good boy. Good boy."

That appeared to be what the wind needed. Soot finally gave her a doggie grin.

Tara had just taken on another familiar, an incredibly powerful water spirit. It left Soot feeling unsettled. She would have to remember to reassure Teruko as soon as she saw her.

"Thank you," Tara told Soot again. "Now, can you find Ginny for me?"

Soot turned and flowed away. His wind form maintained the head and body of a large black greyhound, but his legs were replaced by dense fog that carried the dog along quickly.

By the time Tara had unlocked the gate at the end of the pier, she heard a soft bark.

Peering through the darkness, Tara recognized Ginny's bright turquoise rain jacket rushing toward her.

"Oy! Thank all the spirits! Yer alive!" Ginny said. She raced over and hugged Tara, nearly knocking her down.

"The water took me for a ride," Tara said, hugging the other witch back. Suddenly, the rain appeared to lessen, at least where the pair of them stood.

"I was so worried for ye!" Ginny said, her tone turning scolding.

"I'd been waking the river, calling to ye. Trying to give ye a place to come back up."

"Thank you," Tara said, hugging Ginny again, soaking up the warmth and bright spirit her friend gave away eagerly.

After a few moments, Ginny pulled back and looked hard at Tara. "Ye found yer water spirit, didn't ye?"

"I did," Tara said. She couldn't help but grin. "Mulinohana."

"I knew ye could," Ginny said. "So's he stopping the storm?"

Tara sighed and shook her head. "No. He has no control over the rain, or even over all the waters. All he's promised to do is to not rage over the ground if the harbor wall breaks, but he can't prevent it from breaking."

"Gotcha," Ginny said, catching Tara's hand and putting it in the crook of her arm. "Let's get to the main street over there, eh? See if we can hire us a car."

The rain beat down on them, trying to hammer them into the ground. The winds had done their job, and so had died down some. Water ran in the streets, the sewers unable to handle the onslaught. All Tara could smell was wet and cold, though her internal fire was keeping her warm. Even out on the main street, only a few cars crept along, windshield wipers knocking the water off furiously but inadequate to the task.

How many inches of water were they getting an hour? In the 1996 flood, they'd had several inches of rain in the first hours of the storm. Would they be able to save the harbor wall?

Tara had felt so good about working with Mulinohana. Though she would deny that she'd had any holes in her soul, it was almost as if he filled pieces of her that she hadn't known were missing.

Looking at the disaster waiting to happen all around her, Tara pushed away at her sense of hopelessness.

They could do this.

She just wasn't sure how.

It took longer than either Ginny or Tara anticipated to get back to

Hallowed Ground. Buses weren't running, and most of those who drove others around had stayed home. Tara had already called ahead and let Kaede and the others know what they'd done, where they were.

Tara couldn't help but gasp when they finally reached the building. It looked as though a dark cloud loomed over the roof, pummeling the area with rain. The brick held on staunchly, but Tara knew it wouldn't last for too long. The water was determined to undermine the foundation.

For a moment, Tara caught the scent of wet rope and marsh grasses. She gulped, fear driving through her, though she didn't understand why.

They just had to fix this place. Soon.

Tara and Ginny hurried inside. Everyone else had already gathered, and they were ninety minutes late. Kaede's anger flared out at them as they entered. So did Kyle's. Richard at least seemed relieved.

And Lucius…Lucius wasn't noticing much at all. He lay flat on his back in the center of the room, as still as a statue. His mask was firmly in place, and he at least seemed human, but Tara could tell that it was a struggle for him. His skin looked as pale as his white hair, and his closed eyes seemed sunken into his face.

"So you finally decided to join us," Kaede said, zir words biting.

"We got here as soon as we could," Tara said, her own anger rising in return. "There's a huge storm out there, in case you haven't noticed."

"You said you managed to tame a water spirit," Richard said. It surprised Tara that he would try to play peacemaker. Then again, he had no magic, so he was unaware of the other energies flowing through the room.

"I did," Tara said. "Mulinohana, the water spirit of the Willamette."

"How did you manage that?" Kyle said, sounding impressed despite himself.

"It wasn't easy," Tara said.

"So you exhausted yourself adding to your collection of familiars before coming here to help us," Kaede said bitterly.

"No, not at all," Tara said, stung. "I wouldn't do that."

Except that she hadn't realized that Mulinohana would renew her strength, not when she'd started.

Kaede looked as though ze didn't believe Tara.

"Mulinohana has promised that the river won't rage if the harbor wall breaks," Tara said. "But there's too much rain. He can't stop the storm or the water from rising."

"So we still need to sacrifice a soul to the harbor wall, so it doesn't explode," Lucius said from his place on the floor. He didn't sound like himself at all, his words as cold and emotionless as the statue he was imitating.

"No," Tara said immediately. "I'm not about to sacrifice you or anyone else."

"Then how are we going to stop the harbor wall from crumbling?" Richard asked, still trying to sound reasonable to everyone.

"I have an idea," Tara said, turning to Kaede. "Did you bring everyone here?"

Kaede nodded. "I did. They're all in the kitchen."

"What are you talking about?" Lucius said. "You mean that mob of unruly teens in the other room? What can they possibly do?" At least he was starting to sound a little more like himself, being dismissive of everyone else.

"We don't have to sacrifice your soul," Tara said. "We just need to siphon off enough energy and power to protect the harbor wall. Eunida will leave. We can't, and shouldn't, prevent that. Let her soul be free. We'll have to protect the wall in another way."

"Will it work?" Kyle asked quietly.

"It has to," Tara said. "Or we'll all be lost."

KAEDE WORKED with Eric and the other teens from the community center who sat in a circle on the floor in the kitchen. Ze got them arranged, holding hands. A few adults had joined them as well, wanting to help.

Tara didn't try for a fancy pentagram again, though she knew that she'd be directing the energy. Maybe there would be times when she needed to stand apart from the rest of the coven, but not that night.

It was close to ten o'clock by the time they were ready. Tara, Ginny, and Kyle had created a few powerful sachets to protect the room they stood in, placing them in the corners. The scent of lavender and rosemary flitted through the air, as well as the smell of pine and sage. Outside, the sound of rain continued to beat down.

As they took each other's hands, the lights flickered. It didn't surprise Tara that the power was being finicky. Trees had probably already started falling, their root balls compromised by the water, then pushed over by the winds. More than one transformer had probably already been destroyed by falling tree limbs, though she hadn't heard any explosions.

Lucius had risen to his feet, but barely seemed able to stay there, swaying from one side to the other, as if he'd topple over at the slightest provocation. At least that brought a familiar grimace to his face.

A huge surge of power flowed through the circle as Tara started leading the prayers. She continued with her thanks to Brigid, though her eyes flickered over to Kaede, who nodded.

Huh. Seemed that ze was able to harness a lot of power from the mundanes sitting in the other room. Tara suspected that wasn't normally the case, but these people were part of their community. And demanded the right to help tonight.

When Tara finished thanking the gods and goddesses who looked after them, she gathered the group together in the same shape that Lucius had taken them before, that strong bubble of magic around them, as she went seeking the harbor wall.

At first, she couldn't find it. It was dark outside, all around her. She had no guiding points. At least when they'd been at the harbor wall, all Lucius had had to do was to direct them down.

She had no idea what direction to go in. Their soul form had no point to direct them. Everything felt shapeless, cold and dark.

Finally, Tara found a landmark: the river. It flowed like a lifeline across her own soul. It occurred to her that she could now be anywhere in Portland or possibly anywhere in the world and she'd always know where the river ran.

As Tara drew them closer to the river, it was easy for her to find the wall. Its hard, straight line irritated her. It felt unnatural to her water sense. She had to bring back in her human senses, to remind herself of the good the wall would do, before she butted against it in disgust.

Diving deep under the river, she was able to find a chink in the wall, and slide the group through, into the empty space where Eunida lived.

You've come.

The words echoed around them. Cold rock walls encased them, and even colder winds blew through the tunnels. The dirt under their feet felt as powdery as ash. A ghostly light—like that from beyond the grave—emanated from all around.

And here, you'll die.

Sharp points of energy tried to pierce the protective shell that Tara maintained around the coven, like a bevy of arrows.

Most of the points bounced off the magic shield that Tara maintained. The only one that got through reached Lucius. It was like a harpoon, meant to drain out his soul into the wall around them, the point connected to a solid line, as thick as Tara's arm.

"No," Tara said. She burned the rope connecting Lucius to the harbor wall in a flash.

Tara felt more than heard the sigh as the other being turned away.

It's all on your head, then.

It surprised her that Eunida appeared to give up so easily, only sending a single volley their way. But the being was leaving.

Would she go peacefully?

A rush of energy filled the chamber they stood in, as if a spigot had just been turned on.

Damn it! Eunida was intent on destroying the prison that had held her for so long. Not that Tara blamed her for being vindictive. She might have done the same after being held against her will, imprisoned when all she wanted to do was to roam free.

Still, she had to stop the other being from destroying the harbor wall, particularly as they were reaching the critical point in the flood.

Tara tried a familiar net to sling around Eunida, to try to contain the energy surging around them. However, it was as effective as it had been for catching water.

Kyle surprised her by stepping forward. *Let me.*

It was the first time that he'd tried directing the energies of the coven. It wasn't that he wasn't comfortable with the group. He'd just never believed it to be his place.

Yet, Kyle was a fourth level witch. He'd walked to the circle of water right after Tara had met him.

Tara saw her mistake immediately. The circle of water wasn't just about the element. It was also about process. It was the ability to put plans into place, to work with the entire coven instead of focused on an individual's power.

Plus, Kyle's greatest strength lay in his ability to stay calm under fire. Though he didn't practice as a lawyer, he still got into debates regularly, and had to stay cool when regularly faced with challenges.

Kyle's power washed over Tara like a soothing balm. She hadn't realized how angry and fearful she'd been feeling. If she'd been a cat, her hackles would have been raised all along her spine, her tail bushed out.

Though she'd teased Kyle about having a great, late-night jazz, smooth voice, she hadn't ever thought about the fact that he did in fact, listen to jazz on a regular basis. The sound of a saxophone, low and sweet, floated through the air.

Eunida didn't manifest. Tara never caught a glimpse of the being's ghostly form. However, she did feel as though the creature settled down, the music calming her explosive energy, dampening down her frantic flight.

Tara and the others shored up Kyle's power, sending more his way so he could slow down Eunida's haste.

Finally, with a loud sigh, Eunida left the area, her soul freed from her prison. Tara didn't know where she would go. Had the being died? Or would she roam and haunt someplace else?

The circle all gave thanks to Kyle for diffusing the situation.

However, all this meant was that the harbor wall wouldn't explode as the waters climbed.

They still had to stop it from breaking to pieces.

Somehow.

As the group paused before starting the next phase of their battle, Lucius's power suddenly rose up. The being tried to grab at all the power of the coven, direct it toward himself.

Was Lucius about to sacrifice himself? That seemed so selfless and out of character for him.

Still, his grab had the feeling of finality to it.

"No," Tara said. She knew she'd said the word out loud, her body, left far behind, speaking it.

That appeared to startle Lucius enough that Kaede was able to take the reins of power instead.

Your loss, he appeared to say.

Tara sent a surge of reassuring thought his way. They weren't about to lose him. Not tonight.

He didn't appear to appreciate it, however, shrugging it away like a duck shedding water.

Even though this was not Hallowed Ground, Kaede was still their expert on buildings and structures. Ze understood how things were built.

And ze had the power of the community behind zir.

Kaede took all their consciousness down further, past the chambers where Eunida had spent her exile, into the very foundation of the harbor wall itself.

The concrete forms bulged here, no longer straight. Decades of pressure from the structure above, as well as being pushed at by the river, had deformed them. In addition, the concrete itself was beginning to crumble.

They couldn't save the wall, make it into a formidable structure again. That would take even more power than what they had, which was a considerable amount. Tara felt as though she rode at the top of a powerful wave, carefully surfing, always just on the edge of being engulfed and drowned.

Kaede did what she could to strengthen the foundation. She siphoned off the power of the community, using those individuals to hold up the wall instead of the coven's magic.

It surprised Tara how easily the slight energy from the teens slid into the concrete down here. It wasn't until she started paying closer attention that she realized what had happened.

Richard had reported that Eunida had sung more than one soul to its death. He couldn't prove her influence, but he believed that she'd killed people regularly through the years.

Somehow, the souls that Eunida had taken had slipped into the wall itself, helping to hold it up. They weren't enough, not on their own. But they'd reinforced the structure.

Had that been the doing of the Riprap man? Had he formed a trap, so that the people Eunida killed wouldn't go to waste?

As Kaede shored up one section at a time, weaving in the strength of the community without leaving their spirits trapped there, Tara finally saw those other souls escaping. Wisps of fog slipped out from between the cracks and crevices. The soft sound of sighs floated around her. She smelled the river strongly now, the scent of decaying reeds all around her.

Finally, Kaede drew back. The harbor wall wouldn't hold for long. The damage was too extensive. However, instead of exploding or completely disintegrating, it would slowly erode, failing over the next year instead of minutes.

Lucius appeared to recover his immense strength as they finished. He put a hard shell on the wall, giving it a little extra life, before he gently took them all back, up to their bodies waiting patiently for them in the community center.

Tara opened her eyes to darkness as she let go of the other's hands. The power had gone out. She shivered, suddenly cold.

No, it wasn't that. Something else had gone wrong. A muffled booming sound came from deep beneath her, setting the soles of her feet to tingle.

Something was attacking Hallowed Ground.

Was it Eunida? Had she given up her revenge on the harbor wall in order to attack them here?

No. It wasn't her.

It was the Riprap man, finally come for all their souls.

EIGHT

Though I am bound to Mulinohana, I was originally an engineer, familiar with stone and brick. I marvel at how Portland continues to build and thrive. While I cannot protect all her buildings, I can make it easier for new ones to grow, by helping to clear out the old structures that are in the way. I still know rock and stone, and helping to tear down a rotting structure has become its own joy.

Wilson Evermore, Protector as well as Destroyer of Portland, 1935

HALLOWED GROUND CREAKED, the old timbers complaining, as if a great wind pushed at them. The windows rattled, shaking in their casements, shuddering at the mighty pressures being exerted. Cold bit at Tara's nose and fingers, seeking to encase her bones and make her creak as well. The smell of rotting beams rose up, as if the wood had been long submerged in dank waters.

Like the others, Tara felt exhausted. Repairing the harbor wall had taken everything she'd had. She'd been hoping that Hallowed Ground could hang on for one more day before they got around to strengthening the protection spells.

They'd run out of time.

It made sense that the Riprap man would attack now, while the building was at its most vulnerable and its defenders were drained.

Rock was his element, after all, not water.

"Form the circle again! Quickly!" Kaede commanded, reaching out to gather the others to zir.

Tara gulped down her disappointment. She just wanted to rest. Even her soul felt bruised at this point.

Reluctantly, Tara reached out lead-weighted hands to Kyle on one side of her and Richard on the other. They were both as exhausted as she was. Their sighs filled the room.

Shake it off.

Tara felt as much as heard the words. She wasn't sure where they were coming from, who'd spoken them. She tried to squelch the resentment she felt. There was a *reason* why she was so tired. It wasn't whining or complaining.

Kaede started her prayers, calling on Brigid and Sammil to defend the earth and its people.

A breeze tickled Tara's neck, distracting her and sending shivers across her shoulders. It took her a moment to realize that it was one of Ginny's winds, not Soot.

She felt the encouragement from the other hedgewitch to call up her own familiars. Tara didn't see how they could help. Hopefully, calling them wouldn't drain her further.

The image of the black greyhound formed in Tara's mind, his fur warm and sleek under her fingers. A sudden gust raced around her, like a puppy chasing its tail, before she felt the warm pressure of a dog's body pressed against her leg. He'd grown slightly in size, and his head reached her hips.

All that happy energy from Soot welled up inside Tara. She couldn't help but smile at its bubbly nature. She did what she could to spread it out to the other witches. There wasn't a tremendous amount, and it wouldn't last, but it was a nice boost. Ginny's winds also helped, giving them one last push.

Tara knew she should be paying more attention to Kaede and the welcoming prayers. She had a job to do.

Still, she reached out to Teruko. The cat was not interested in leaving her warm bed. She didn't want to come to the cold community center. After a little coaxing, Teruko finally deigned to drape herself around Tara's neck like a living fur muff.

Tara shared Teruko's warmth with the rest of the coven. Teruko gave a rumbling purr of approval that finally, she was being appreciated.

Kaede nodded in approval as ze continued zir prayers, leading the others in a hymn of gratitude.

Tara found herself wishing Kaede would hurry up and finish so that they could get to the task at hand. Then she chided herself for her impatience: they needed to weave themselves tightly together in order to do the important work ahead of them. It wouldn't do to just rush in.

Was Mulinohana the source of some of Tara's impatience? She thought he might be. Though Tara considered herself disciplined, happy to be like water and just drip, slowly seeking her way in, another part of water was its rushing nature, how it overflowed and overwhelmed barriers.

Tara reached out to the water spirit, then was surprised to find that he already stood beside her. She would never have to call him like she did the others. He was as much a part of her as her own breath. She hadn't added him so much as become more aware of her own water nature.

Could the rest of the coven see him? Feel him? She doubted it. All they probably saw or felt was herself, extended.

Kaede finally finished her prayers and started weaving the group together. This time, though, it wasn't a net. Instead, it felt airy to Tara, as though Kaede spun them into cotton candy. However, there were sharp bits woven into the fluffy cotton. It took Tara a while to realize that what Kaede was crafting them into was more like heavy duty insulation.

What good would that do against the Riprap man?

Tara knew that he was still there, deep under the earth, gleefully ripping out the roots of Kaede's spells, infecting the space beneath them with soft sand that would cause the building to sink further, disrupting its solid foundation. Given enough time, the building would crack and fall over.

Kaede directed the consciousness of the coven downward. Tara felt the solid footprint of the building all around her. Kaede pushed out their awareness, shoring up the walls, stuffing every crack and crevice with their insulated magic.

Only after a piece was in place did Kaede harden the substance, making the walls solid again. Tara finally saw the wisdom in starting soft, as a harder substance wouldn't mold to the broken surfaces.

However, it wasn't going to be enough. They didn't have enough magic or strength.

The Riprap man was just going to come behind them and tear out everything, undo all the work they'd just done.

Kaede was fantastic at building community, bringing together a force that was greater than just the individuals combined.

They were going to have to have an actual confrontation with the Riprap man this time. Not merely act as a distraction.

Tara pulled back from the rest of the group, leaving as much of her energy with them as she could. As Lucius had done with Eunida, his spirit turned away to confront the other being, Tara turned as well, coming face to face with the Riprap man.

He looked better than the last time she'd seen him. No longer under the influence of a water spirit, he'd been able to solidify his body. He still wore pants and a bowler hat. Strangely enough, his string tie had also reappeared around his neck, black against the brown stone. His chest was bare, showing his rock torso. He no longer hunched to the side. The rocks weren't solid, one against another; they still looked like individual stones piled up. However, they were more balanced.

She could also see his face clearly, his pale blue eyes, broad forehead, and weak chin. He gave her a cruel smile, telling her just how much damage he intended to cause.

"You will leave this space," Tara commanded firmly.

The Riprap man just laughed at her as he reached down and grabbed something at his feet. As he stood, he tore out another one of Kaede's protection spells. It took the form of a great root, dangling in his hand, twitching. He didn't even deign to speak to Tara as he went searching for another spell to destroy, his eyes trained on the ground beneath him.

Tara tried to call up a spark of fire, but her spirit form didn't have that much substance to it. Instead, it just caused her to glow brighter down here in the darkness.

Besides, how could fire damage rock? Wind wouldn't do her much good down here either.

The Riprap man glared at her. Suddenly, Tara felt the press of solid earth all around her. She was trapped in the dirt.

He couldn't drown her in water, so now he tried to do so in earth.

The soil clamped down all around Tara, caging her in, stealing what little heat she had. It held her arms at her sides, intent on entombing her.

The Riprap man found another of Kaede's spells and yanked it from the earth.

Tara found her words were silenced. The earth had no need for sound. It wouldn't carry her threats or her promises.

How do you stop rock?

The comforting sound of rushing water reached Tara's ears. Mulinohana had been bound to the Riprap man for more than a century. And the water had also almost destroyed the creature, knocking the stones out of place.

Tara called forth Mulinohana. The spirit joyfully rushed forward, knocking the Riprap man from his feet.

"You!" the Riprap man thundered. "You will not turn against me. I know you."

The water ignored the Riprap man as it streamed around him, intent on pushing the rocks that formed his body apart.

The Riprap man grew dark, his stone turning from a light brown to an inky black. He roared through the earth, his hands grappling with the water pouring all around him.

Mulinohana ignored the Riprap man and continued his slow but steady work.

"You will obey me!" the Riprap man howled. "You made me!"

Mulinohana didn't pause. "And I can unmake you," the water hissed.

"You failed before," the Riprap man boasted. "You will fail again."

"He will succeed, this time," Tara said. The earth released her and she took a step closer.

The Riprap man sneered at her. "Why? Because you'll help him?"

"Yes," Tara said. She threw all her power at bolstering Mulinohana, strengthening the flow of the water.

"No!" the Riprap man called out in surprise. "Stop!"

"Why?" Tara asked. She had no doubt that she could do this. She would tear the Riprap man to pieces, shatter his stones and cast the dust to the winds.

He gulped, appearing shaken by the images he saw.

The darkness in Tara's soul held no surprise for her. She'd always known those abysmal places lurked, deep inside of her. Her destructive urges were cool and calculating, not hot and rash. She always speculated about choosing the worst path, of doing evil instead of good.

"You'll never be free of the stain," the Riprap man proclaimed. "You'll always be a dark witch if you do this."

Tara blinked at the vision the Riprap man gave her, of how much she'd seek death, how the dying of others would begin to delight her. How bored she would grow of the light, looking for the dark side in everything.

Was that how Miss Lucy saw the world? Tara wouldn't doubt it. Her former mentor had a darkness to her that no amount of sunlight would cast away.

As much as Tara might regret it, she knew she shouldn't kill the Riprap man. She'd known it before, when she and the rest of the coven had broken his bond with his water spirit, Mulinohana. If she chose to use that dark power to kill the Riprap man now, she'd never be free of that influence.

"Then leave," Tara said after a few moments. "Never threaten this place again."

The Riprap man glared at her, his fists clenched.

Was he determined to sacrifice himself? So that she would have to live with the shame of killing him?

"I will go," the Riprap man announced, as if the idea had just come to him, and not been suggested by not merely a woman, but a witch. "I will not return here. I will leave your special space alone."

The water surrounding the Riprap man lessened from a stream to a mere trickle. When it had finally diminished to merely a small puddle at his feet, with one last glare, the Riprap man disappeared.

Tara knew that wasn't the last of him. She'd have to battle him again. But finally, true healing could begin.

Without Tara asking him to do it, Mulinohana rounded up the wild water that had seeped into the building's foundations, drawing it up and out, so that Kaede's spells could take hold once again. Tara felt the rushing of the water as it left, trailing across her fingertips as though she'd just stuck them into a cool stream.

It wasn't an apology from the wild waters. Not exactly. Just acknowledging the one who'd called them forth in the first place, as well as her right to send them away.

Tara turned back to the rest of the coven. Kaede was busily shoring up the foundation with their help.

A new surge of power went through the group, bolstering their power. Tara felt as though she could suddenly take a deep breath. What was that? Was it just the ominous presence of the Riprap man, finally gone?

No. Tara had been working on drawing apart the various flavors of power of the coven, trying to identify each strand. Ginny's ran red hot, of course, as brightly lit as her hair. Richard's was the most similar to hers, though he didn't have the strength of any of the witches. At the same time, his always felt like a bass line to the music they played. Not exciting, but solid and reliable.

Lucius was all things string, frenzied and powerful, lifting them up. Kyle's, for all his smooth jazz, was still a drumbeat like a heart, solid and steady, giving them strength. Kaede's matched Kyle's the closest, though zirs was more tinkling, almost like a piano.

Tara didn't know what her own power sounded like when joined to the others. Perhaps she was the wild flute that stirred them and led them on.

But this new surge of power didn't have the feeling or sound of any of the rest of the coven.

It took Tara a moment to place the chorus that had joined them.

This was the singing of the choir, the community. Eric and the others. How had they managed to send down more power? What was helping them? It wasn't the Riprap man, Tara knew that.

The mystery wasn't solved until Kaede had finished her work among the roots of Hallowed Ground, reweaving all her protection spells, making them firmer than ever.

The coven would still have to spend time during the summer solstice to bolster them. However, the building was no longer vulnerable.

Tara opened her eyes to soft light. Candles and oil lamps surrounded them.

As did a wide variety of the homeless, as well as the adults from the community.

As Tara released Richard's and Kyle's hands, she heard the hymn the group was singing. Out of tune and dragging, but the effort made their words shine brightly. *Amazing Grace*, leading them all home.

Tara found herself in tears as she turned around. Eric stood close to her, grabbing her before her legs failed her and she collapsed onto the ground.

"Did you call them?" Tara asked, not sure if she should laugh or cry or both.

"Yes," Eric said. "You needed more than we could give."

Tara knew that Eric had no magic. He was as mundane as most of the rest of the community. Still, he'd felt the coven's need and done what he could to sustain them.

"You were right," Tara said. "Thank you."

He beamed at her. Suddenly, the lights flickered back on. Everyone gave a ragged cheer.

All the witches sat on the floor, surrounded by helpers. Even Lucius, though it was an older man who sat with him, a vet who'd been out on the street for years but had finally found his way back. He and Lucius sat silently together, brothers in arms, sharing strength.

The room felt *right* again, in ways that Tara couldn't describe. Warmth flowed through the air, not necessarily brought by the ancient radiators along the wall. The light seemed clear and bright and cast no shadows.

Suddenly, the smell of tomatoey goodness filled the room. Alaska, one of Kaede's primary volunteers, came into the room bearing mugs of soup, followed by a few others. Tara wasn't sure how they'd managed to heat it so fast, given that the power had been out. She gratefully accepted a mug, warming her fingers around it. It smelled heavenly, as though they'd added not only butter but sweet carrots to the industrial base that came out of the huge cans in back.

"Cheers," Tara said, clinking mugs with Eric.

Warmth spread all the way to Tara's fingers and toes as she sipped the soup. Quiet conversations had petered out as everyone shared their meal.

"Are we safe?" someone asked into the silence that held the group.

Tara understood the question at a base level. Was Hallowed Ground going to be all right? Was the community still at risk of attack?

Kaede replied. "We are safe. For now."

Tara had to agree. Another battle with the Riprap man loomed. She didn't know what shape it would take. How he could come at her, her community, her city.

She did know that she couldn't take him alone.

Fortunately, she didn't have to.

TARA WOKE up and stretched in her bed. Though it had been a week since her most recent battle, she was still feeling the effects. She'd run a marathon, and was only now starting to regain her strength. As she stretched, she felt her muscles pull tiredly. It no longer felt as though she'd fall over when she stood up, but instead as if she'd just worked out too hard the day before. Fortunately, she'd taken the entire week off from the Y, so she'd only had to miss a couple of days.

Today, she was going back to work. It was finally time. She'd spent the day before being restless instead of listless. She took it as a good sign that she was ready.

The rest of the coven had been in touch via text and email. They'd all been feeling the same effects. Only Lucius had gone about his normal business the next day. However, he'd been able to take care of Kyle, who'd needed it.

Ginny, like Tara, had roommates to help. Kaede had zir family as well as the community to look after her. Jeannie had been there for Richard; she hadn't left immediately, but instead had decided to stay when the news reported about how close a call it had been to the harbor wall collapsing during the flood. Some flooding had occurred —that much rain in that short of a time period was unprecedented. However, it was minor, a few homes and farms instead of half the city.

Emergency funding had been allocated to rebuilding the harbor wall over the next year. It heartened Tara to see government finally moving in the right direction, though Kaede had had a few choice words to say about the matter.

However, even zir resources weren't enough to do that work.

Tara looked out the window to her right. Bright sunlight shone in the backyard garden. She'd spent much of her time there, wrapped in a blanket and sipping hot tea, not thinking about anything, not able to do much. She'd truly enjoyed her hiatus.

But now, it was back to work.

Tara groaned when she pushed herself up to sitting. Not because her muscles ached. Or rather, not just because her body still hurt.

An envelope sat on the floor directly in front of the closed door.

Damn it! Was the Riprap man going to accuse her of yet another death?

Though Tara would never get a straight answer from Mulinohana, she knew that the river spirit had been responsible for some of the deaths over the past six months. He'd sung to the hopeless, encouraging their sacrifice.

Tara didn't quite understand, but Mulinohana had been lonely without the Riprap man. He'd tried to capture the souls that died, but hadn't been able to keep them or talk with them. Yet, he'd kept trying.

Hopefully the number of bodies fished out of the river would go down, now that both Mulinohana as well as Eunida were no longer acting as sirens.

Tara called up both Soot and Teruko as she wrapped her ratty green bathrobe around her. Mulinohana wouldn't manifest physically most of the time, but she still felt his cool presence supporting her.

After a brief moment of quiet prayers, asking for strength, Tara folded herself up and sat neatly on the floor, her legs not protesting too badly. Teruko immediately claimed her spot in Tara's lap, sitting and purring up a storm, while Soot leaned against Tara's side.

The envelope felt like all the others, plain manila, unsealed. It smelled like paper, not the river or even like sunbaked stone.

Tara slid out the paper from the envelope and unfolded it.

It wasn't a newspaper clipping. Instead, it appeared to be a grainy black and white photocopy of a topo map. Tara hadn't spent a lot of time reading topo maps, but she believed the wavy lines indicated hills or mountains. She didn't see any rivers.

What drew her eye, though, was the red circle around the what appeared to be a valley. It was in the middle of absolutely nowhere. There were no roads running in or out of the area.

The words, "I AM COMING FOR YOU" were drawn underneath the circle.

Tara peered more closely at the map. She finally made out the name of the valley that the Riprap man had circled.

Forest Green.

That name sounded familiar. Teruko protested as Tara picked her up and moved her to the side so that she could stand up and grab her phone.

Shock and horror filled Tara when she pulled up the news about the valley.

It had suffered a minor earthquake over the weekend. Not enough to damage anything, not really. Just shockwaves through the earth.

A practice earthquake.

The Riprap man was coming for them. For all of them. Everyone up and down the west coast.

He was going to make sure that The Big One finally hit.

And Tara was going to have to stop him.

EPILOGUE

I almost feel grateful that witch removed the bond I had with the water spirit Mulinohana. I had considered him a god. I can see how foolish that belief had been. There is no god, at least not down here on Earth. There are only mortals and spirits. But they shall all meet their true creator, one day. And some will meet it sooner, such as Tara and the rest. She removed the restrictive influence of the water, and has shown me where my true strength lies, in the earth. I have protected Portland for over a century. No more. Nothing binds me now.

Wilson Evermore, Destroyer of Portland and the West Coast, 2019

CIRCLE OF EARTH

ONE

The city of Portland has continued to shine as the only jewel along the western coast that has seen neither fire or earthquake devastate it. Not that there hasn't been threats. The pact with the mighty river god Mulinohana has kept the city mostly safe from flood. I have done my best. But now, we have the threat of all those immigrants, a flood of dirty, unclean scavengers, escaping from the dustbowl and all places east. I would guard the city better if I could. I take their souls, seeking to protect those who were raised here. There is only so much I can do. I know that a small earthquake would terrify them, send them scurrying away like rats off a sinking ship. However, Mulinohana will not allow it. So I bide my time and watch and wait. Sooner or later, my time will come.

Wilson Evermore, Civil Engineer and Protector of Portland, 1932

TARA SAT in the backyard of her house, on the porch swing, going over the Portland resiliency report again, the paper commissioned by the local government that studied how well Portland would survive an earthquake. Dew still sparkled on the grass where the sunlight peeked in through the trees. Buds tipped the tops of the roses on the perimeter of the yard, threatening to bloom early this spring. The sole lilac stand in the corner filled the air with their heady scent.

Though it was still early May, the day was already warm. Tara was comfortable in just a peach colored T-shirt and jeans, her brown hair still down around her shoulders. She'd probably pull her hair back and up, as well as change into shorts later..

For now, with her hands wrapped around her hot mug of tea, she was warm enough. That morning, she'd gone for a light Celon black, then flavored it with dried fruit—orange peel and currents—as well as ginger. It felt like the perfect combination of light citrus with spicy heat.

The one good thing Tara had to say about the government was that at least they'd put in effort studying the potential situation. She'd found plenty of papers and websites dedicated to "the next big one"— the earthquake that might end all civilization on the west coast.

Experts agreed that they were long since due for another major quake.

The problem was that while the government had done some things —like moving schools out of old fashioned buildings and into more modern ones—they were merely stopgap measures at best. It appeared to her that less than a quarter of the work had actually been done.

If (when?) a big earthquake hit Portland, the death toll would be astronomical. Plus, only one of the ports had been retrofitted. Neither food nor water would be easily shipped in, as the roads would all be unpassable.

So even after the quake, people would starve to death, or else die of things like dysentery, as there wouldn't be any clean water.

Or, as Tara had read on one of the forums—they were really only a few weeks away from an MCE—a Mass Cannibalism Event.

How was Tara and her coven going to prevent an earthquake from destroying not just Portland but the entire coast? Particularly since the Riprap man appeared set on causing it?

In the six weeks since the Riprap man had sent Tara that map, highlighting the location of a small quake some distance away from the city, more tremors had been reported in those hills. Tara had read at least one official report of increased seismic activity in the area. Were they all caused by the Riprap man? Or had his initial quake created some sort of instability?

Tara had no answers. She'd asked Mulinohana how to contact the Riprap man, or call him forth. As the river spirit was no longer tied to him, the spirit had no idea. However, the spirit did promise to avert what water it could from the city, direct it into smaller channels if the earth suddenly shifted and huge waves threatened to engulf Portland.

However, there was only so much the river spirit could do as well.

A sudden warm spot appeared next to Tara. She put down her tablet and reached down to skritch the ears of Teruko, the fire spirit who took the form of a calico cat. Teruko needed little encouragement, and had already placed his paws up on her thigh, looking for a lap to crawl into.

"Fine," Tara said, pushing herself back on the seat and making more of a lap for the currently tiny kitty. Teruko frequently changed size, going from what Tara considered normal cat size—about ten pounds—down to kitten or up to Maine Coon, depending on the situation.

Right now, there wasn't that much room in Tara's lap, so Teruko had shrunk himself down a little.

"There, is that better?" Tara asked as the cat settled down, purring hard.

Teruko pushed his head up against her arm.

"Fine," Tara said. "Both hands." She gave into the pleasure of petting and skritching a purring kitty in her lap, letting him calm her.

She still didn't know what she was going to do. And it was difficult to imagine that a catastrophe awaited on such a pleasant morning.

But it did. And Tara had to do something about it.

What, though, she had no idea.

As it was Monday, Tara met with her coven that evening, at Hallowed Ground, the homeless shelter that Kaede ran. The evening meal had already been served, and the residents of the building banished to the upstairs rooms.

Tara had no problems entering the building anymore, not since she and the others had helped Kaede rebuild the protection spells that sank deep below the foundation. No one loitered outside the door, as those same spells worked on everyone outside the coven, sending them to other locations for the night.

The tables of the main room had all been pushed to the side and the chairs piled up in the corners, opening the large space up. The building itself had been built back in the 1930s, with the ground floor originally set up as a store, and the upper floors as flats. Shades covered the two bay windows at the front of the room on either side of the door, as well as over the door. The lights came from high overhead, adding a golden touch to the walls and floor. The air still smelled of the spicy spaghetti and garlic bread that had been served for dinner that night, a homey smell that suddenly made Tara hungry despite the dinner she'd eaten earlier.

Kaede was kneeling on the floor when Tara entered, drawing a large chalk six-pointed star on the scarred wooden floor. Ze looked up and smiled at Tara before going back to zir work, still humming and chanting. Ze wore three shirts, all sleeveless, showing off surprisingly large muscles for such a petite, Asian-looking person. Zir skull was still shaved, making zir face seem larger and more fierce.

When Kaede finished zir work, Tara felt the spells take hold, sanctifying the entire building. While she had seen Kaede do this every Sunday, before food service for the homeless, Kaede hadn't necessarily done it every time the coven had met.

However, tonight was a big night. Richard had been keeping track of the tremors as well, and had located one that had occurred late that afternoon.

The coven hoped that by tracking the instability of the earth that they might be able to find the Riprap man.

Tara waited until Kaede stood up and came to join her.

"I wanted to make sure we were safe, here," Kaede explained. "The building will withstand an earthquake, now. I've made sure of it. But there isn't anything we can do about water or food."

Tara nodded. They were going to be seeking the Riprap man again that night, seeing if the coven could at least find or track him.

The others arrived shortly. Richard, who still had a hangdog appearance, as Jeannie, his girlfriend, had left him shortly after the floods, unable to reconcile her mundane world with the magical one that Richard was pursuing. His heart was healing, but it would take time. Though is large, black, nerdy glasses weren't colored or shaded, they still managed to hide his eyes effectively. More silver threads ran through his black hair than she'd remembered from before, probably from all the energy he'd been expending. He wore one of his many geeky T-shirts, this one saying, *Come to the Math Side. We have ∏.*

Lucius and Kyle arrived together. Lucius still looked ridiculously formal even in his tan button down shirt and beige chinos. He'd cut his long silver hair, though, so he looked a little less like his namesake from the movies. Kyle wore one of his dashikis, the green one with white embroidery that looked so good against his dark skin. He kept his head shaved bald and gleaming. He looked more like a hipster and not at all like a high powered law clerk.

Lucius raised one perfectly sculpted eyebrow at the increased protection spells, but didn't say anything. Kyle just nodded and said, "Good. Was expecting trouble tonight."

Ginny arrived last, looking as flustered as always. The new tattoos of dripping water that she'd added to the geometric sequence of triangles down her neck were healing nicely. She'd figured that since she'd survived the floods with the rest of them, that she deserved her own badge of honor. Despite how protected the room and the building were, Ginny still appeared to be surrounded by winds swirling around her, tugging at her torn purple sweatshirt and nipping at the tight black pants with the holes torn out of the knees.

Tara called them all together, placing them each in a point of the star. She started with Richard, putting him with Ginny on one side and Kaede on the other. Richard was the only one without power in the group. She'd found that when she put him beside Lucius, he'd end up falling over tired, as Lucius managed to pull so much more power out of him than anyone else.

She placed Lucius next to Ginny, then Kyle, then herself standing beside Kaede. Kyle had been working hard to overcome his aversion to touch. He'd even talked of someday passing further in, along the circles, and moving from the circle of water to the circle of earth.

However, the circles weren't just about the elements. While the circle of water was associated with process and the stomach, the circle of earth was associated with roots as well as sex. Kyle had trauma from being gangraped when he was in his twenties. Now, twenty years later, he was finally starting to truly leave his experience behind.

Lucius was helping, for which Tara was grateful.

Once everyone was in place, Tara reached out and took Kyle's hand first, just holding on with pinky fingers. Lucius did the same.

Power rocketed around the group when the circle was closed. It always made Tara grin. She'd never felt such a strong circle before, even in Miss Lucy's coven, the first one she'd joined.

Surely they were going to succeed tonight.

"I call upon Areebin, the protector of souls, to set a watch over us tonight," Tara said at the start of their prayers. The names of the gods were many. It had always surprised her that all the covens appeared to call on the same gods, no matter if their focus was on the light and life of others or not. "As well as Samil, the warrior for the people, and his bright shield and spear. Brigid, the protector of the earth, hear our call and help us keep the very firmament stable. I also call on the Hayvu the goddess of the western wind to carry words on her winds, as well as Bonana, goddess of the water, to feed our intent far into the ground. I call on all the protectors, big and small, to help us in our quest. We seek to protect the life of the city and the souls found here. Aid us in our seeking."

Tara took a deep breath, then pulled the focus of the group's magic to her. "We seek the Riprap man. Now."

Richard had sent Tara that map of the area around the latest tremors. It was to the west of the city, in the Tillamook state forest, up in the foothills there. Tara felt herself flying, seeking the trail the sun had blazed across the sky. While her physical body remained behind, sustained in part by the rest of the coven, her mind projected far.

A sharp yip drew her attention. Soot, the first wind spirit she'd called to her, flew beside her. His sleek, black, greyhound body appeared to swim through the air. Soot's eyes had turned golden and he gave her a great doggy grin as they flew.

We seek the Riprap man Tara told the dog, holding her last image of the man in her head for the dog to seek.

She doubted it would do any good. While Soot was great at finding and retrieving things, he seemed to have a blind spot when it came to the Riprap man.

Probably because the Riprap man was able to call the wind spirit to himself, wrestling Tara's control away. Or at least the Riprap man had been able to do that. Tara wasn't certain if he'd still be able to do that or if Tara herself had grown strong enough to be able to hang onto Soot.

Every other time Tara had sent Soot out after the Riprap man, the wind had returned empty handed. Tara wondered if Soot wasn't able to find the man, or if the Riprap man had just been able to turn the dog away.

However, this time, Soot nodded and nosed to the right a little.

Huh. Where was Soot taking her? She was going to have to drop down soon, find her way through the water and creeks that ran through the area. She hadn't moved within to the circle of Earth—none of them had. So she couldn't necessarily trace trails on the ground.

Dark forest spread out beneath Tara. She heard the hooting of owls. Soot dove down under the dark canopy, leaving behind the open air.

Tara took a deep breath and followed him.

Was this a trap?

Soot swam easily between the trees, skimming over the wide spread of bramble and bushes. Tara had a quick wish that her physical body could do the same. It was a beautiful, wooded area. While it was lovely at night, she wished she could travel through it for real during the daytime, as herself.

The scent of wet pine filled the air. There wasn't enough sunlight due to the canopy of trees for blackberry bramble to take over the area. Tara sensed a river to her right, then had to pull her sensing back, or else she'd be overwhelmed by the number of small creeks and trickles of water running through the ground.

Soot slowed as he left the trees and entered a small, natural meadow.

The Riprap man stood in the center of the open space.

Tara instinctively pulled all the power of the coven to her, floating up in a bubble of power.

The Riprap man looked better than the last time she'd seen him. The rocks that made up his torso were no longer out of alignment. Instead of looking as though he'd been built out of individual stones that had been piled up on top of one another, the rocks had been fused together, giving him a much more cohesive appearance. He still wore pants, perhaps out of a sense of decorum, as he'd been born over a century before. His hat and string tie were nowhere to be seen.

It was his face that amazed her. It, took, had grown much more rocklike. He still had a weak chin and piercing blue eyes, but the ridge of his brow now looked as though it was chiseled out of pale white stone. His cheekbones, also, had grown hard, and the planes of his face had flattened out.

Whatever mischief he'd been up to, it had strengthened him. Not weakened him.

Tara prepared herself for the blast of power sure to rip loosed from him.

She wasn't prepared for his laughter, bitter and mocking.

"I allowed you to find me tonight to thank me again for releasing me from that water spirit," he said. "While Mulinohana gave me great life and a purpose, you have freed me to become who I truly was meant to be."

Tara wondered at the Riprap man's voice. It still held the cultured edges that he'd been born with. However, the hoarseness of it made her wonder. His voice was now rough and gravelly, as though the sound was being made by grinding boulders together.

"And what is that?" Tara asked. "A killer?"

The Riprap man laughed again. "Do you understand the damage that man has done to the wilderness? Can't you see? I remember what this place was once like, before humanity arrived. No, they are the greater plague."

"You protected them for a century or more," Tara pointed out.

"That was my mistake," the Riprap man assured her. "I should have let the first big flood just wipe them out."

"Are you certain?" Tara said. "What about all those beautiful bridges?"

Tara saw a shadow of doubt cross the Riprap man's face. He still had a soft spot in his hardened heart for Portland. "Those people there don't deserve to all die. They need the chance to make the world a better place. They can help. Tearing the coast apart will not solve the problem. It will just make it worse."

"You are wrong," the Riprap man said. "It will take time for the locus to return to strip the corpse of the earth bare. I will be ready for their re-infestation."

"So many innocents will die!" Tara protested.

"None of them are innocent," the Riprap man declared.

"We will stop you," Tara said. She drew more power to herself.

The Riprap man laughed again. He shot down under the earth.

Tara willed herself after him.

Surprisingly, the ground appeared to welcome her. It was as warm as the pool at the Y where she taught classes. The loam flowed around her like thick fog. Boulders appeared like dark clouds, easily passed around. The taste of the rich soil actually delighted her, like fresh morel mushrooms.

Up ahead, tauntingly close, she saw the shape of the Riprap man. He was pale against the dark ground. He looked over his shoulder and appeared surprised at how close she'd gotten.

He dove forward, then shifted to the right, as if that would be an easier route.

Tara followed, though the nature of the soil changed. It grew distinctly colder and she stopped moving as quickly.

She realized that the smooth dirt had turned to clay. Instead of sliding through the soil, she found herself slowing as the clay thickened.

Then slower still.

It dawned on her that this was a trap. The Riprap man planned on holding her here. She didn't understand the magic, as it was merely her projection, not her physical body. Yet she was slowly getting stuck. It was more and more difficult to move herself through the massive pile or clay.

The Riprap man was nowhere to be seen. He'd trapped her, and had taken off.

What was it about the nature of this dirt? Was it the stones mixed in? Tara tried to taste the area, see what it was that was so very different about the clay.

It was wetter, here. Colder. The clay was denser than the rest of the dirt.

The coven far behind her pushed more energy her way. She reached out again, tapping into the water of the clay. Could that aid her?

No, but it was in part why she was entrapped here. Like called to like, and the water called to her.

It was a clever trap, she had to admit. The water calmed her even as the heavy dirt sucked away all her power and magic, keeping her in stasis.

Tara tapped the energy from her friends and violently pushed her way out of the center of the clay pit, heading up, straight toward the surface.

It was only after she'd reached the regular soil again that she realized her mistake.

By destabilizing the ground in this area, she'd just set another tremor into motion.

Tara swam up above the forest and watched in horror as it swayed in a breeze she didn't feel, the ground shifting and waving beneath her. A deep moaning groan washed over her as the very earth undulated. Trees knocked each other over, their root balls suddenly exposed in the air. Birds exploded into the air, screeching their dismay. All the small creatures hidden among the trunks raced out of the area, breaking through the bramble.

The area directly beneath Tara—maybe a twenty-foot radius circle —settled down quickly. She could see the ripples moving out. At least as the area spread the effect grew less. Trees stopped being toppled and merely waved. The stillness of the night returned gradually.

Crap.

She had really been trapped by the Riprap man. He had grown much more dangerous now that he was on his own. Not only could she have died under the earth, she could have done much, much more damage escaping.

Tara tugged on the thread that connected her soul with her body, flying back to Portland and Hallowed Ground. Soot joined her after a short while. He seemed so happy to see her. He didn't understand that she'd just messed up, but good.

The bright lights of Portland just made Tara feel worse. What would happen if there was a huge quake? Would those lights ever come on again in her lifetime? She flew north, over the bridges and up to Hallowed Ground.

The building also appeared to have its own light, safe and warm. She knew that mere tremors wouldn't rock its foundations. Kaede and the others had sent the root too deep.

They couldn't do that for the rest of the city, though. And even if the houses and buildings didn't collapse, that still left the roads disintegrated, as well as the ports.

No, Tara and her friends needed to stop the Riprap man from bringing his tremors into the city itself.

But how?

Tara dropped her friends' hands and took a step back, breaking the circle. The air in her lungs still tasted of mushrooms and dirt. Though her skin was dry, she'd swear that the clay still coated her back.

"I don't see how we're agonna stop him," Ginny grumbled. She looked more pale than usual, which worried Tara.

How much of her group's strength had she siphoned off that evening? Richard seemed to be holding up well, but Kaede and Kyle were both listing as well.

"You're not dreaming big enough," Lucius said. He lightly tapped his cane on the floor, drawing all their attention to him.

"What do you mean?" Kaede said. Ze sounded more angry than tired. "We know who it is we're fighting against."

"You're focused on this group, on this coven, being able to contain that madman," Lucius said. He sounded as though he was sneering at him. Then again, he always sounded that way. "Why should it be us?"

"Because we're the ones who broke him from what little was containing him?" Richard asked, sounding just as condescending.

"You misunderstand," Lucius said. "While I might argue responsibility, I would still suggest you're still thinking too small."

Tara made a gesture, urging him to continue.

"While you are all delightfully powerful, I would suggest that it might be time to call on some other groups as well," Lucius said.

"What do you mean?" Kyle asked, his own expression growing hard.

"You've been associated with at least two other covens," Lucius said with a nod in Tara's direction. "Three, if we might include your former one as well," he added, looking at Kaede.

Ze just crossed zir arms over zir chest and shook zir head.

Lucius shrugged. "So we have connections with two other covens. Why not bring them in? Bind all their power together into one massive, giant spear, and use that to attack? Before the actual earth under the city of Portland shrugs us off?"

Tara swallowed against a suddenly dry throat. She didn't want to have to approach Sheila, who would have gladly thrown her to the wolves, or Miss Lucy as well.

However, Lucius had a point. This threat was bigger than all of them.

In the past, Tara had had to be reminded not to try to fix everything on her own, but to rely on her community.

Maybe it was time for her community to expand to the other two covens as well.

TWO

I do not care for how the bright lights of Portland have been dimmed by the influx of so many strangers. She is doing her best to feed and clothe all those who are dumped on her shores. There are so many mouths to feed! I relieve her burden, taking souls when I can. However, even the river can absorb only so many. The conservative local government isn't helping, too proud to take the money freely offered by the federal government, content to have the shanty towns sprung up beside the river, Hoovervilles. I have come up with a plan to take care of quite a few of them, all at the same time. To send them into the tunnels and then collapse them all. It would work, if the river god will allow it. He isn't certain, as those souls wouldn't technically belong to him. I am still imploring him, though, to let me do the deed.

Wilson Evermore, Defender of the Wealth of the Land, 1933

TARA CONTACTED AALOKA, the second in command of her former coven. Though it had taken much persuasion on her part, she'd finally gotten Aaloka to agree to talk with the head of the coven, Sheila, and try to get her to meet with them on Wednesday afternoon.

While Aaloka wouldn't make any promises about Sheila actually attending their customary tea and treats, Tara was betting the older woman would show up. She would be too curious not to. Plus, merely sacrificing Tara wouldn't satisfy the Riprap man, not anymore. He was determined to destroy the city he'd spent so long protecting.

They agreed to meet at a coffee shop closer to where Sheila lived, so in northern Portland. It wasn't too far from the beautiful tree-lined neighborhood that Miss Lucy called home.

Like most of the coffee shops in Portland, they had a wide variety of teas as well, though all of them were commercial. Tara settled for a blackberry-hibiscus tea, iced, then made her way outside, claiming one of the tables there. Aaloka approached first, hurrying along the sidewalk. Tara was surprised—Aaloka was actually three minutes early. That never happened.

However, Aaloka didn't seem too distraught. She merely waved at Tara before going inside to get her own beverage, and probably a slice of the olive oil cake, sweetened with honey and lavender. She was wearing a typical suit, this time in a beautiful navy linen, with white piping around the collar and cuffs, with a pretty lime-green shirt.

Before Aaloka could come back out of the shop, Tara saw Sheila coming up the street.

She was glad she had sat outside, even if the day was overly warm, just so she could study the older woman as she walked. Tara hadn't seen her former coven leader in over a year.

Though Sheila wasn't a tall woman, her presence pushed out at least three feet all around her, making on-comers swerve around her without knowing why. Normally, Tara would say that Sheila appeared to be in her thirties, half of her sixty plus years. Today, she appeared much older, perhaps in her late forties. While her gray hair was still completely concealed, the red in her hair had appeared to fade.

It took Tara a while to realize that the difference had nothing to do with how Sheila looked—she wore dark brown contacts to hide the faded color of her own eyes, and her skin still appeared smooth and freckle free. However, her walk was no longer as confident as it once had been. She was almost limping, actually. Had she been in an accident?

There was no question the older witch was still massively powerful. But something had drained her, recently.

Tara stood up as Sheila drew closer. They didn't shake hands, but did stare at each other for a bit. Tara wasn't sure what Sheila saw. Tara had her brown hair worn up in a ponytail, off her neck. Her sleeveless shirt showed off the muscles she'd developed swimming so much recently.

Sheila wore a bright shirt, as always, this one orange with white, red, and pink flowers embroidered around the neckline. The skirt she wore flowed down just past her knees, made out of a bold black and white print.

"You seem well," Sheila said after a few moments.

"You, too," Tara lied.

The old woman cackled at that. "Winter brought a bad fall," she said. She lifted her right leg to the side. Tara couldn't see any bruises or damage to the skin, but she had the impression that the energy that Sheila so effortlessly rode wasn't flowing correctly. "But it will heal soon enough."

"I'm glad," Tara said. And she was. She had never wished Sheila harm, despite how the older woman had kind of hung her out to dry.

Sheila had been working for the good of the coven. If she hadn't, perhaps the entire coven would have been punished with "bad luck" from the Riprap man.

"Are you?" Sheila said, tilting her head to the side to peer at Tara. "Well, you might be," she concluded before Tara could reply. "You were always like that."

Before Tara could ask what the older woman meant, Aaloka came out, carrying two cups, a small pot of tea, and a plate that held two pieces of the olive-oil cake.

"I'm so glad you could make it!" Aaloka gushed. She busied herself setting up the table with all their goodies, handing a fork to Tara, before sitting down.

Sheila sat down slowly, as if merely standing for a while had already led her joints to stiffen up.

Just how much pain was the woman actually in?

They sat in silence for a moment as Aaloka poured the tea for the pair of them and they all tried the cake, which was divine. Tara wondered if it would be possible to redo the recipe using almond or coconut flour instead of wheat.

"So you've survived," Sheila said after a moment.

"I have," Tara said. "And I have my own coven now."

"I heard," Sheila said dryly.

Tara had the impression that the older woman would have liked to roll her eyes at her. It wasn't really a proper coven, not done in the old tradition, where the main practitioner was of the highest circle, anima, essence, and everyone underneath her.

Tara's coven was much more egalitarian. And it had Lucius, who wasn't human as well as Richard, who was all too human.

"I'm not sure what you actually know about the Riprap man," Tara said after a moment. They weren't actually there to be friendly or to chitchat.

Sheila gave her a thin smile. "I know that you've defeated him, at least twice, now. He hasn't taken your soul yet, or been back to bother those of your coven. So I'm assuming he's been contained, at least for a while."

Tara nodded. She quickly explained how she'd stripped him of his connection to Mulinohana, the river spirit, while casually mentioning how she'd bound the river spirit to herself.

That at least got her a look, one that Sheila quickly threw at Aaloka.

"So you've bound a water spirit to you," she eventually replied.

"And a wind spirit. As well as a fire spirit," Tara said proudly.

Aaloka seemed surprised by that. "You're not a hedgewitch," she said. "You've been taught better than that."

"I am both a learned witch, able to pass within, as well as a hedgewitch," Tara explained. She thought that Aaloka had realized that.

"How?" Sheila demanded. "Normally, a witch cannot progress along both paths."

"Why not?" Tara asked.

"The powers aren't complementary," Aaloka said, as if explaining something to someone much younger than she was.

Tara merely shrugged. "They seem to be working together fine," she said. Though she wasn't about to admit that she occasionally had difficulty now when it came to creating potions and sachets.

"But despite that, despite the power of our group, the Riprap man is still a threat," Tara said.

"You took away his spirit companion," Sheila said.

"No, not exactly," Tara said. "You see, the Riprap man is associated with the earth. With rocks and stones. The riprap at the footing of a pier." She paused, considering her words. "He'd been bound to a river spirit. Something that actually deformed him over all those years."

She made herself say the conclusion she'd come to after a while. "The river spirit actually contained him. Confined him. And now, he has nothing that's holding him back."

"What does that have to do with us?" Sheila said. She had sat back and was starting to look defensive.

Tara wondered if the older witch already had a sachet in her purse for extra protection that she was itching to bring out.

"He protected the city of Portland for over a century," Tara said. "Killing witches to renew his pact with the river spirit. Now, he wants nothing more than to destroy the entire place. Wipe it out of existence."

"How?" Aaloka asked. "He can't flood the city any more, can he?"

"Mulinohana won't allow that," Tara said. "The river spirit. No, he's now calling on his natural abilities, to use rock and stone, the very land against us." She took a deep breath. "Earthquakes." The more she'd studied the potential, the more nervous Tara had grown, and she now started when a truck rumbled by.

Aaloka gasped.

"Brigid protect us," Sheila breathed out.

"Is he behind the increased tremors in the area?" Aaloka asked. "I saw something on the news last night about it, an unexpected fault letting loose in the Tillamook forest."

Tara nodded, aware that it had actually been her that had caused that latest accident. "Yes. He's been experimenting, causing a bunch of little earthquakes all around the city. We can't figure out why—possibly shaking out the cracks so that the big one will hit us all the harder."

Sheila had actually grown pale at the news. At least they were taking her seriously.

"We have to stop him," Tara said. "My group—as strong as it is—isn't strong enough to handle him on his own."

Tara didn't like the sly look that came over Sheila's face. "So you want to work together," she said. She gave Tara a smile that looked like the cat who'd just eaten all the cream.

"Yes," Tara said. "I'd like to bring your coven, and Miss Lucy's coven, and ours together to see if we can destroy the Riprap man once and for all."

Aaloka exchanged another look with Sheila. "So why not bind him instead?" she said. "You've brought over other powerful spirits."

Tara shrugged. "No binding lasts forever." She'd discovered that when the being bound to the sea wall finally escaped. "I don't want to create a problem that must be solved by a future generation."

"That makes sense," Sheila said slowly. "Do you know how to track him?"

"Maybe," Tara said. "We've been tracking the tremors, and following him back to them."

Sheila nodded. "That would make it difficult, then. Having to wait until a tremor was reported before being able to find him."

"Could you lay a trap for him instead?" Aaloka asked.

Tara kept her sigh to herself. She knew that her former mentor didn't understand what she was asking. However, Tara had considered that aspect herself already.

"We might be able to entice him into an area," Tara said slowly. At the nods she received from the other witches. "It's just that he would be coming after me, myself."

"We could work with that," Sheila said.

Tara didn't like how much that made her feel like bait. Dead bait.

"We'll see what we can do," Tara said after a bit. "But you'd be amenable to working together? Bringing the covens together?"

Sheila and Aaloka looked at each other. Tara wasn't certain what their look was saying, what silent words they exchanged. However, eventually Aaloka nodded.

"Yes, I think we could figure something out," Sheila purred.

Tara knew in her heart of hearts that agreeing to this was likely to put her, and possibly all of Portland into more danger, not less.

Still, she didn't see what else she could do.

She agreed, and the two witches shook hands on it.

<hr>

TARA HAD CALLED Miss Lucy to set up an appointment with her. It surprised her when the older woman suggested that they have lunch together, instead of meeting at her house. Tara had rarely seen Miss Lucy in a social setting, and not at her house instead.

But Tara agreed to meet her at a club that was south of the city. She looked the place up online, whistling softly at how upscale it appeared to be.

Jeans and a T-shirt were not going to do.

Instead, Tara wore one of her nicer dresses made out of a purple cotton with a pattern of large white irises on it. She actually got one of her housemates to braid her hair for her. She didn't bother with makeup—that was one step too far. She did put on a pair of nice black low heels, and carried a soft white knitted shawl.

Normally, Tara took the bus or MAX everywhere. Of course, there were no stops anywhere near the club. Those kinds of people wouldn't be welcome. Though she couldn't really afford it, Tara took a shared-ride taxi up, spending the entire time chatting with the driver about his brother back in Pakistan and how you had to work so hard here in America.

Expensive cars lined the street close to the club. Trees, too. Older houses sat back from the road, the yards covered in immaculate yards. However, Tara could smell the river as soon as she stepped out from the car. She knew she didn't have a lot of time, but she still walked north of the building, trying to catch a glimpse of the water.

Water had always been her element. She found that now that she'd bound a water spirit, she spent even more time near it. It called to her anytime she caught a scent of it and she frequently dreamed of floating on the waves, carried this way and that by the currents.

The sun shone bright down on the gray waters. Green banks rose up on both sides. Red-winged blackbirds called cheerily to each other, and she heard the industrial buzzing of bees traversing the blackberry bushes. The water itself smelled of the sea today, salty and moist.

After paying her respects, Tara made her way back to the dark club. She had to pause once she stepped inside out of the bright sunlight.

The hostess standing behind the reception area waited patiently for Tara to blink her way to clarity, not bothering to speak until Tara took a few more steps inside the room.

The front hallway was closed in, like a closet made out of fancy wood paneling. The reception desk was also made out of a heavy wood, with a discrete light shining down on the desk. Muted conversations rose up from either side, the restaurant apparently spread out to both sides.

"May I help you?" the hostess said. She wore a beautiful golden-silk blouse that probably would have cost Tara half a month's rent. Her teeth were perfect, as was her hair and makeup. Probably took her three hours every morning just to make herself look presentable.

"I'm here for lunch," Tara said baldly.

"Do you have a reservation?" the hostess asked, already looking down her nose. Well, as much as she could, as Tara stood at least half a head taller than her.

"Yes," Tara said. "Miss Lucy," she added after a moment. "Lucy Talbot."

"Oh!" the hostess said.

Tara grinned at the girl's reaction. Obviously, she hadn't expected someone as down and out as Tara to be meeting with such a high-powered client.

"Right this way," the girl said, hurrying off.

Tara continued to grin as the girl led her to a booth off to the left. Past the small bar, the room opened up. Large windows lined the wall, all overlooking the river. Miss Lucy sat in a small booth near the middle of the room, backlit by the bright sunlight.

She stood as Tara drew closer, leaning over the table to air-kiss both of Tara's cheeks. "So good of you to come to lunch with me, my dear," Miss Lucy said.

Tara didn't reply despite her confusion. She'd been the one to set up the meeting.

However, based on the gaping expression on the face of the hostess, evidently Miss Lucy had been setting her up.

After Tara was seated, a waiter came up to take their drinks order, with Tara getting plain water with lemon while Miss Lucy got sparkling water with a twist of lime.

"It's so good to see you," Miss Lucy told Tara. "You're looking well. Strong," she added. "You seem to be coming into your own."

"Thank you," Tara said. "You look good too." And Miss Lucy did. Her skin was a light colored brown, and she always wore hats to protect her face from developing freckles across her nose. She wore her black hair straightened, with a slight curl above the shoulders of her exquisite lemon-yellow silk top, with pearl buttons down the front. Her broad lips curved in a generous smile.

Miss Lucy was also in her sixties. However, unlike Sheila, she'd never tried to hide her age. Her brown eyes were faded, and obvious wrinkles crinkled around her mouth and the edges of her eyes. Power still emanated from her.

Tara hadn't seen Miss Lucy in a year, not since her former teacher had helped her reach the room of one of the witches who'd been buried at the foot of the pier of a bridge. They'd talked on the phone a couple of times, though not in depth.

"Tell me everything," Miss Lucy demanded after they'd ordered food.

Tara nodded and began, starting with the first battle she'd had with the Riprap man.

"I have a question for you darling," Miss Lucy said, interrupting Tara a minute or so after she'd started. "Where's that quiet coming from?"

Tara looked around, unsure what Miss Lucy was referring to. "Quiet?" she asked. She peered out, over the rest of the restaurant. "Oh! That's from me," Tara said. "The hedgewitch magic."

Miss Lucy frowned at her. "Hedgewitch?"

Tara shrugged. "I seem to have both," she said. "The ability to do learned magic, as well as natural."

"And the quiet wasn't something you spelled, was it?" Miss Lucy said as the noise in the restaurant started to trickle into the bubble that Tara had originally, accidently formed.

"It isn't," Tara admitted. "It just happens sometimes."

"That's always the problem with that sort of magic," Miss Lucy said, obviously disapproving. "It just happens. No control, whatsoever. I thought you were better trained than that."

Tara grimaced. "I've kept up my training," she said. "I've been passed within, a witch of the circle of water."

Miss Lucy nodded. "Good. Good! I always thought you should be at that level," she said. "You take nicely to water."

"Yes," Tara said. "I've bound a water spirit to me," she added.

Miss Lucy blinked, surprised. "Darling, you really do have to tell me all about it. Now, continue."

Tara smiled and continued talking. The sounds of the rest of the restaurant faded away again as Tara told her old mentor everything, all the battles she'd had with the Riprap man, all the successes she'd had as well.

By the time she'd finished, they were finished with their meal and contemplating dessert. Miss Lucy insisted that they split the flourless chocolate torte with raspberry ice cream.

"I assume that you're here for something other than telling me your tales," Miss Lucy said.

"Yes," Tara said. "We need your help. The help of your coven. We need more power than what we have to defeat the Riprap man. We'd like to have a group of covens, coming together, our power converging."

Miss Lucy nodded. "And you've already asked Sheila, haven't you?"

"I did," Tara said, surprised that Miss Lucy would know that.

"She will try to take over your coven," Miss Lucy warned.

Tara snorted. "She can try."

Miss Lucy tilted her head to the side to peer at Tara. "Interesting," she said. "You've grown into your powers. Much more than I would have expected."

"Did you ever suspect that I had hedgewitch powers?" Tara asked. She'd wondered that for a long while, actually.

Miss Lucy laughed. "All witches have the potential for using hedgewitch powers," she said. "They all have the ability. They just never tap into them."

"Really?" Tara said, surprised. She'd thought that there were actually two different breeds of witches.

"Tell me, which do you find easier?" Miss Lucy said.

Tara thought for a moment before she replied. She never would have admitted this to anyone else. Possibly not even her coven.

"I'm starting to have more difficulty with the schooled witch parts," Tara finally confessed. It was actually the first time she'd spoken the words out loud.

"I'm not surprised," Miss Lucy said. "You have too many familiars for the schooling to feel as natural as it once did. Plus, you were never one for learning through high school or college."

Tara shrugged. "I got good enough grades, but it really wasn't my thing." Unlike people like Kyle, who not only excelled at school but had actually enjoyed it.

"Exactly," Miss Lucy said. "You have power, my dear. You always did. It's always just been a matter of harnessing it. Directing it."

Tara didn't agree, but nodded anyway. Her problem with Miss Lucy had been much more fundamental: Miss Lucy and her coven weren't concerned with the betterment of others, but with more personal gain. And it showed—everyone in her coven was rich. Really, really rich.

While Tara and her coven were mostly poor. They worked actively to help those around them.

If there was some sort of catastrophe, Tara would want her crew around her, not any of Miss Lucy's.

"So will you join us?" Tara asked. "It won't do anyone any good if all of Portland gets destroyed. Along with most of the west coast."

"It won't work," Miss Lucy warned. "Whatever you have in mind.

In the end, you won't be able to pull the trigger and eliminate the Riprap man."

Tara shook her head. "If it's his life versus millions of others, I think I'll be able to choose him."

Miss Lucy gave her a sly smile. "It doesn't matter. I choose to work with you anyway. I am interested in meeting the others I your coven. Particularly this Lucius."

Tara nodded, her heart saddened but she should have expected it.

Miss Lucy would never lie to her. She didn't always state her intent out loud, but Tara had gotten very good over the years at reading between the lines.

While Sheila might try to take over Tara's entire coven, Miss Lucy had merely set her sights on the strongest member of Tara's group. Lucius.

And while Tara knew that Lucius enjoyed working with her and the others, he had no loyalty. He wasn't human. He'd always assumed that he would use Tara while at the same time she would use him.

She'd lose him to Miss Lucy, once they met.

She was certain of it.

THREE

The years have passed, and Portland herself is no longer the jewel she once was. I cannot stand the way that opportunities have been wasted by this local government of ours! At least the shanty towns have mostly been moved on as people leave the region. Portland is no longer growing, however. I miss the days when multiple bridges and projects were all going at the same time. I'm hopeful, however, that this conflict in Europe might bring more jobs to the region, as the last major war did. That perhaps our fine ports will be busy again. The great river god doesn't see the value of progress, doesn't understand how this stagnation will sour men's souls. I can only do so much to prod them on, however.

Wilson Evermore, Protector of Portland and Scourge of the Wasteful,
1939.

TARA GOT Lucius to agree to meet with her before the covens all descended on one another. They met in one of the parks just west of the city, where the trees met the water and great swaths of green grass filled the area. Though it was late, close to eight PM, it was still light out. Couples roamed the paths, as did parents pushing their SUV-sized strollers. The homeless were kept out of the park proper, and only took up one long edge, close to the street.

Tara still wouldn't want to go through this park at night. She could take care of herself, but she didn't want to have to.

Lucius strode up to the fountain she stood beside. He was carrying his cane that evening, an elegant black resin piece tipped on the bottom with silver. The top was in the form of a snake's head, a great cobra with the hood extended, also done in silver. Today he wore an impeccably tailored blue shirt that matched the intensity of his eyes, with cool gray pants.

"Good evening, my dear," Lucius said, giving her a frankly appraising look. "Don't tell me that you've finally decided to grant me my fondest wish of an intimate evening."

Tara snorted and rolled her eyes at him. She knew that Lucius was actually serious, and wanted to spend intimate time with her. She also couldn't even imagine what that would entail.

Lucius wasn't human. Anytime he let his mask slip, the alien nature of him made Tara's skin crawl. No matter how pretty the mask, she couldn't imagine getting closer.

"Then what task brings us together this evening?" Lucius said. His eyes practically twinkled at her as he grinned. "Perhaps some lovely magic, just the two of us?"

"No," Tara said, "I'd never even considered that, actually."

"Never thought about a *pas de duex*? Never?" Lucius said, teasing her. "You and Ginny do it all the time."

"We don't plan on performing magic together," Tara said. "It just happens."

"Your natural magic, yes, it ebbs and flows," Lucius said.

"Can you sense it?" Tara asked.

Lucius appeared to consider his reply. "In a way, yes. But only when I'm paying attention. Otherwise it will just flow past me like a soft, spring breeze. You don't pay attention to every spring breeze, do you?"

"No," Tara said. "But maybe I should." Ginny, after all, was really a wind witch, even though she'd developed something of an affinity toward water, now. Was part of their ability with each other because their winds interacted?

"So, no dancing, no magic, whatever are we to do?" Lucius asked. "Oh, wait. You don't want to do that either."

Tara sighed. "What I do want to do is to walk and talk with you for a bit," she said, starting down one of the paths.

Lucius caught up with her immediately. "Of course, my dear. What do you wish to discuss with me so far away from any of the others?"

"I've taken your advice," Tara said seriously. "I've asked both Miss Lucy and Sheila's coven to join with ours, to fight the Riprap man."

"Have you, now?" Lucius said. He sounded surprised. "I hadn't thought that you'd be able to share the power like that."

"I'm not sure how active I'll be in the group," Tara said.

"Do tell," Lucius said.

"We need to draw the attention of the Riprap man," Tara said seriously. "We can't just wait for another tremor, or bring the group together and hope that we get lucky enough to be able to find him."

"That's true," Lucius said. "So how do you plan on drawing him to you?"

"I will go out and challenge him," Tara said. "Someplace in the wilderness, where I would be more easily ambushed."

"You mean your physical presence? Not just a projected one?" Lucius said, his eyes wide. "I'm not sure I would recommend that."

"But it's the surest way to draw the Riprap man to us," Tara pointed out. "Mulinohana can't help us call him. Soot hasn't been able to find him, unless he wants to be found."

"It would be dangerous, you alone, out in the wild," Lucius said, turning serious for the first time that evening.

"I had hoped I wouldn't be completely alone," Tara said. Lucius was the most powerful being in her coven. She'd hoped that he would volunteer to help her confront the Riprap man.

"I see," Lucas said. He stopped walking, making Tara pause as well.

She felt her breath catch. Was this one bridge too far? Would Lucas not only say no, but leave the coven because she'd asked?

Lucas shook his head, sending Tara's heart plummeting. "No, I will not go with you."

Before Tara could say, maybe even apologize for asking, Lucas said, "Do you want me to call one of my brethren to help?"

Tara blinked, surprised by the offer. She'd never even considered that Lucius might be able to bring in more help. "Would that be possible?" she said.

"Let me make some inquiries," Lucius said. "There are never many of my kind in any single location. We tend to be solitary. However, with a threat like this, they may be drawn in. If only for the novelty, if nothing else."

"What, of possibly saving the world?" Tara asked.

Lucius's laughter ran coldly down her spine. "Oh, no. That would never appeal to anyone I know. No, it's the chance to work with one of your kind."

"What do you mean?" Tara said, confused. Surely Lucius and the others had worked with humans before. Witches, even.

"Just leave it all up to me," Lucius said with a negligent wave of his hand as he strode away, leaving Tara far behind.

Tara wasn't certain if she should feel relieved that Lucius had a plan and wanted to help, or if she should be terrified that she actually had no idea what he was up to.

Or possibly a little of both.

While Kaede and the rest wanted to meet at Hallowed Ground, Miss Lucy as well as Sheila didn't want to. It would put them distinctly ill at ease, being in another coven's sacred spot.

It took some negotiations, but they finally all agreed to meet at the waterfront park, close to the river. They would meet twice. Once as a dress rehearsal, to make sure that the three groups could mesh their power together, then again the following night, when Tara would be far, far away in one of the state forests nearby Portland, trying to draw the Riprap man to her.

Lucius assured her that everything was all set, she just had to let him know when she was leaving the next day. It didn't make her feel any better that someone, or possibly just something, would be invisibly following her.

Still, it was better to have some sort of backup rather than none at all.

The group met at seven PM. Tara and her friends actually got to the park early for a cookout. They grilled hotdogs and ate baked beans, as well as a lovely green salad that Ginny provided. They found themselves laughing and giggling over nothing, as if the stress had just gotten too much and they found everything funny.

Kaede turned out to be able to do a killer imitation of Lucius, including not just his snide tone but all his mannerisms. Kyle showed them the new skill he'd picked up: juggling. And Richard regaled them with old stories of Portland, how the area had been settled, the stupid things that some of the original settlers had done.

Tara hadn't realized how much she missed this sort of comradery. She performed magic with these people, hung out with them afterwards, but rarely shared meals with them. Except for Kaede, as they tended to eat together every Sunday after they'd served the homeless.

"Thank you," Tara said, beaming at all of them as they started cleaning up.

"We all needed this," Kyle said. He nodded over her shoulder. "Incoming."

Tara turned to see Sheila walking at the head of her coven. She carried herself like a warrior going into battle.

In many ways, Tara could see her point.

Miss Lucy and her folks appeared at the same time on Tara's left. They carried themselves differently, more like landed gentry walking toward the croquet fields. They were obviously here to do Tara a favor, and possibly to enrich themseslves. Nothing more.

Nothing important, like possibly saving the city.

Tara sighed and shook her head. There wasn't anything she could say to either group. As part of the negotiations between the three groups, she'd agreed to only speak to Sheila and Miss Lucy, and not try to recruit anyone beyond them. The other two had promised the same, though the time for recruiting had been very precisely limited.

It was an unusual enough gathering, to bring three covens together this way. Having some rules in place would help smooth out some of the inevitable conflicts.

Miss Lucy had brought twenty-one with her, while Sheila had brought fifteen. Tara felt dwarfed by the mere six she had supporting her.

Yet, when she strode forward to meet with the other two witches, she felt the strength of her people flowing toward her.

They believed in her. They would trust her to do the right thing.

"Miss Lucy. Sheila," Tara said, greeting them. "Thank you for coming tonight."

"It was our pleasure, darling," Miss Lucy assured her.

"The city has need of us," Sheila said. "We came."

Tara realized that if they were successful, no matter who had actually done the work, Sheila and her coven would claim all the credit.

Fortunately, Tara didn't care about that. Nor did Miss Lucy.

"Tonight is the dry run," Tara told the two women. "We're here to fine tune how we work together. Tomorrow night we'll go and see if we can track down the Riprap man."

"I'm assuming you have a plan for that," Sheila said.

"Yes," Tara said. "It's why I'll help bring the groups together initially, but then I will step to the side and let Kaede take over the focus."

"We agreed to work with you," Miss Lucy said. Her voice took on a dark tone. "Not some other leader."

"And you are," Tara said. "But I need to leave, physically, and trap the Riprap man."

"You're using yourself as bait?" Sheila said, her eyes narrowing as if she hadn't considered how it would be done.

"I am," Tara told them.

Sheila appeared to consider this new twist for a moment. "Yes, that will do," she said, nodding.

Tara wasn't certain what Sheila meant, exactly, if she considered this an easy solution to the continuing problem that Tara presented.

"You can be sure that we'll maintain our efforts even without you here," Miss Lucy said, obviously challenging Sheila.

"Yes, we will," Sheila said.

Tara wasn't sure who was going to be the adult in this group when she stepped away. It probably wouldn't be either of these two.

"All right," Tara said. "The first step is to get everyone arranged in concentric circles around us."

"Have you ever worked with another coven before?" Miss Lucy asked. She seemed intrigued.

"No," Tara said. "But I've studied the theory."

"Theory?" Sheila said obviously surprised. "What theory?"

Tara smiled at them. "Old lore that I've discovered." She didn't bother to explain that Richard, her research librarian, had dug deep into old archives, doing many inter-library loans, and had found the most interesting books as a result.

There actually had been a small pamphlet published back in the 1960s that explained exactly how to mesh the powers of more than one coven together. It had obviously been some handout for another group. She had no idea if it actually worked. But she intended to find out tonight.

Both Miss Lucy and Sheila were taken aback by Tara's assurance that she already had a plan, and that it came from old lore. Tara wondered if both of them had just assumed that they'd be the leader of the meshed coven, and not her and her group.

They ended up with three circles of witches loosely circled around the inner group of Tara, Sheila, and Miss Lucy. Tara faced the river, while the other two faced the city. Tara arranged the groups so that the strongest witches were closer in, and the less powerful one further out. Richard was in the outermost circle, while Kaede and Lucius were in the inner most. Both Ginny and Kyle were in the middle ring.

"It's important to stay in your place," Tara warned, speaking loudly enough so that everyone could hear her. "The circles have to be maintained."

The pamphlet had only had a single sentence warning about it, how the magic would explode outward it if wasn't properly contained by the circles, then drained away.

Finally, they were ready to begin. Kaede stood directly behind Tara, ready to trade places with her once the groups had all been joined.

Tara started off the prayers, asking for Brigid and Sammil to guide them. Sheila took up the next part, asking the winds to carry their prayers to all who needed to hear them. Then Miss Lucy spoke, asking the guardians of their souls and the protectors of the dead to watch over them.

Power suddenly started flowing between the three of them. It wasn't the warm strong power that she was used to with her coven. Instead, it was a much colder power, sleek even. It slid around them, instead of buoying her up. She thought of it as a blue ribbon that tied them together, as opposed to the warm, golden light that seemed to infuse her coven normally.

That ribbon was useful, though. Tara took the image in her mind and passed it back to the second circle, standing around them. She felt the power of the two groups as they got tied together. It was heady, standing on a wave of strength.

Why didn't witches come together more often to do this sort of thing? There must be a cost that Tara wasn't aware of. They could do so much good work this way!

Tara saw her mistake as she brought in the next group, tying them into the first two circles. Despite how powerful Miss Lucy, Sheila, and Tara were, controlling this much power was going to take tremendous effort.

Tara let the groups hum along for a few moments, trying to modulate the strength of the groups. There had to be a way of narrowing the firehose coming at her. She realized that all the hair on the back of her neck was now standing, as was the hair along her arms. The smell of burnt grass lay heavy on the air. Her stomach churned, her entire body unhappy with all the foreign magic flowing through her.

Tara looked at the other two women to see how they were holding up. Miss Lucy had her eyes closed and a grimace on her face. She was obviously straining as well to keep up with everything pouring into the three of them.

Sheila had her eyes open, but was staring off into space, not seeing anything that was in front of her. She panted slightly, as if she was walking quickly down the sidewalk. Tara could still feel where the flow of energy was off in the woman, how only one of her feet connected firmly to the ground.

Should Tara bring up the third circle of power? While they would be the weakest of the three, it would still mean adding more to an already creaking structure.

Was there a way of just adding a part of it? No. Each circle was a complete entity. She would have to add all of it, or none of it.

Tara tried to move slowly, very slowly, seeking to just allow the last circle's power to seep into what they already had. She found herself shaking with the effort. It was like trying to hold back a stampeding horse. Her arms trembled. Her legs grew shaky as well.

No. Wait.

She wasn't shaking.

The ground was.

Tara clung to the hands of the other witches. Had the Riprap man come to attack them?

A new presence lurked underground, directly beneath their feet. It would overwhelm them shortly.

Tara forced her attention *down*, into the earth, to try to stop whatever was there.

It surprised her when instead of staying in the cold, dank earth, she found herself in an open space, a room carved out of the rock. She was surrounded by a group of women, all holding hands. They chanted, channeling their power at her. They weren't chanting in English but used what sounded to Tara like nonsense syllables.

Tara tried to push back at the waves of magic washing over her, but it was like trying to stop the heat of a fire by merely waving your hands. The women were intent on…something. Helping her? Destroying her?

It took Tara a few moments to realize that this new coven was composed of the souls of all the witches who the Riprap man had killed and then bound to the bridges across the Willamette river. Dorothy Parkerson stood in front of her, still dressed stylishly in a maroon sweater and skirt, with dark curls drawn back into a poodle cut and a heart-shaped face.

However, like all the women, only the whites of her eyes showed. She looked like a woman possessed.

What were they doing? Why had they gathered? Why were they trying to overwhelm Tara and the connected covens?

"Stop!" Tara said. Or at least tried to say. The strength of their call was drowning her.

The ground trembled again, a tremor passing through the room like a cold wave.

Tara pushed her soul back up above the ground, rejoining her body. Both Sheila and Miss Lucy now looked at her, as if demanding answers that she couldn't give them.

Were the tremors real? Or was she just feeling them on the cosmic plane?

A scream filled the air. The power of the group suddenly spiraled out of control. Tara felt her focus release. The magic snapped loose, sparking like a powerline. That cool ribbon of power now jerked around the circles, shocking individuals when it touched them.

Tara turned to see the Riprap man advancing on them. He'd forced his way into the third circle, forcing two of the witches apart, breaking the circle, making them drop their hands.

He had his hands on the wrists of two of the individuals in the middle circle. Though his bare torso was made of stone, he still appeared to be struggling to make the witches let go of each other's hands.

What held them together wasn't their physical strength but the magical power flowing around the circle.

Tara had planned on an orderly releasing of the circles and the individuals. However, they'd all be damaged further if the Riprap man just broke them apart. She tried to untie the circles from where they'd been joined. The third circle had been torn loose.

She almost got the blue ribbons of power disconnected when the Riprap man forced the two witches apart.

Again, the backlash of power nearly knocked Tara from her feet. She stubbornly held on, gritting her teeth. She shook her head, trying to focus. She must untie the next circle before the Riprap man tore it apart.

The witches from the bridges kept pouring out their strength, distracting her from being able to do the work in front of her. Was that why they'd gathered? To act as a distraction? It had worked. She could barely see what was in front of her. The sound of their chanting suddenly filled her ears, along with the roaring of the ocean.

The blue ribbon of power had grown blazing hot. She still grabbed hold of it with both hands and tugged at the knot, drawing it apart.

A new power slid in beside her. Tara's first instinct was to push it away, snarling. It took her a moment to realize that Lucius was trying to help. She gratefully relinquished some of her control. He smoothly stepped in and untied the two groups before the Riprap man could finish his attack.

As the individuals in the group stepped away, back from each other, dazed, the Riprap man caught Tara's eye.

I'm coming for you next he told her clearly before he disappeared.

Tara shook her head and let go of Miss Lucy and Sheila's hands. They looked at each other, clearly shocked and stunned.

What had just happened?

The chanting from the coven working underneath them faded away as everyone came slowly to their senses.

Someone touched Tara on the shoulder. She turned to see Kaede pointing at someone who'd fallen to the ground.

Tara raced over to where Richard had fallen. He was still out cold, his skin waxy and pale. One of the other coven members held onto his wrist in a professional manner, obviously measuring his pulse.

"Heartbeat is rapid but slowing," the woman said. "He had a big shock."

"What in the hell were you doing bringing a mundane into the circle?" someone else demanded, a person Tara didn't know.

"He knew the risk," Tara said wearily. She pushed Richard's hair back from his forehead. "Come on. Come on back to me."

"Obviously, he didn't," Sheila said, coming up to stand behind Tara. "None of us did."

Tara hung her head. Sheila was right. None of them had ever tried anything like this before. And no one had had any idea of how it actually worked.

"Maybe with a smaller group—" Tara started to say.

"No," Miss Lucy said firmly. "I am not risking any more of my people."

Tara sat back on her heels and wearily watched Sheila and Miss Lucy gather their covens back together. She could never ask either of them for help, not ever again.

The amount of power that had poured through Tara and the others had been spectacular to behold.

It had also been far too much for any of them. Perhaps if they'd brought together two groups that had several level six witches as the leads, then backed the with much weaker witches, it would have worked. But the power levels were always going to be tricky.

"Ye didn't have a bad idea," Ginny said, coming up quietly. She sank down next to Tara, then reached out and held her hand. "We just needed more time."

Tara nodded. Time they didn't have, would never have. If she ever tried to bring together such a group again, the Riprap man would be there, sure to tear it apart.

Richard finally blinked open his eyes. Color hadn't returned to his face, but at least he was awake. "What…what happened?"

Surprisingly, Lucius was the one who responded. "A very interesting amalgamation of events," he said. "I suggest that tonight, we all rest. Then we should gather tomorrow night, as we had planned."

"Why?" Kyle asked. "We aren't still going after the Riprap man, are we?"

Lucius gave him an enigmatic smile. "I'll see you at Hallowed Ground," he said before he turned and walked away.

"Do you think he has a plan?" Ginny asked Tara.

"I sure hope so," Tara said. "Because I'm all out of ideas."

FOUR

TARA WOKE THE NEXT MORNING, feeling as though not just her body but her soul was bruised as well. She groaned as she stretched, resenting her alarm clock, the fact that she had to make a living and couldn't just call in sick to work, the realization that she was going to have to push herself all day just to make it through.

Teruko still lay beside her. He'd taken on a much larger form that night, so he could heat up her entire back. She was grateful to him, and his shared warmth, particularly how he'd purred and tried to comfort her.

Soot had even yielded his place on the bed to give Tara and Teruko more room, though he now poked his head up and looked hopefully at her. Though he was really an imbodied wind, and he didn't really need walks, he still needed to spend time with her on a regular basis, generally playing and chasing after things for her.

Tara did not want to move. Did not want to try to force herself up. She still made herself sit up on the bed, groaning again as she moved.

Outside, light shone against the blinds. At least it was going to be another sunny day, though rain was predicted for later that week. Tara stretched out to touch her toes, fighting off the wave of dizziness that overtook her.

She just needed some food. Then she'd be fine.

Her little room in the house that she shared with four other people still felt cozy to her. She didn't need a lot—just space for a small fridge where she could keep herbs and her own plants, the big bed in the center that she shared with her familiars, a dresser for her clothes and a desk where she could study. She had the rest of the house where she could go and hang out with the others if she wanted to, as well as a shared kitchen and the large backyard. She was only a few blocks away from the river. She could smell the water every time she stepped outside.

Tara gave Teruko a few more skirtches under the chin, ignoring his meow of protest when she finally pushed herself off the bed. She listed to one side. Wow. She hadn't expected to feel so dizzy. It was as if her inner ear was off balance.

That made sense, actually, given the way that the evening had gone. The great lashes of power that the group had undergone had roughed up all of her insides. It was as though her body, the container for herself, had been forcibly held still, while all of her insides had been vigorously shaken.

She just couldn't take the day off from the Y, though. She didn't have any more vacation days available, not unless she didn't take off time when the summer solstice came in a few weeks. And that wouldn't be right.

Tara pushed herself through her morning, walking with Soot to the MAX stop, throwing a ball that he could chase and bring back to her as they made their way along the few blocks. The day was already warm, and Tara was cursing her decision to wear jeans and not shorts that morning. She passed by a new encampment of homeless close to the stop. They were transient, wouldn't stay, she felt certain. Since she'd been working at Hallowed Ground, she'd become a much better judge of the various stages of homelessness.

It had made sense to her that Hallowed Ground focused on prevention, rather than just on taking care of people in the street. It was so much harder to get out of the cycle once you'd started down that path.

There wasn't anything she could do for this group of kids, however. They were pretty used to the street, had probably been there a few years. They would hold each other back if one of them tried to break out and leave. Groups like that needed to be rescued all at once, if at all.

Tara sank gratefully into a seat on the train when it arrived. It was still before seven, and many of the commuters had already gotten off downtown, before the train arrived in her neighborhood.

Though Tara found her body as well as her thoughts still moving slowly, she found herself circling back to what had happened the night before, thinking about the coven of witches who lived under the bridges, and finding herself comparing them to the posse of homeless kids she'd just passed.

What was the connection? Were they similar, in that if one of the witches tried to leave, the others would all hold her back? How did they depend on each other?

Tara had never forgotten going down to visit Dorothy. She and the others in the coven had discussed whether or not it would be possible to free those souls. However, the question had always come back to whether or not the witches would want to be freed. Yes, they were tied to their location, or as Dorothy had called, *cell sweet cell.*

But if they were freed, would they die? Probably. And that was the biggest problem. Did they want to die? To pass on? Or did they prefer their current existence, even if they were tied to a single place and unable to move around much?

Tara just didn't know. She wasn't sure if she wanted to try to visit them to ask, particularly after last night. Would they just attack her again?

Why had they attacked? Had it been them attacking? Or had the Riprap man somehow forced them into it? They hadn't seemed normal or right, with their eyes all rolled back in their heads. Had they been trying to help? It had been too much power coming at Tara all at once.

Somehow, Tara was going to have to communicate with that coven. Because she was *persona non gratis* with the living covens she had a connection to in Portland at this point.

TARA WASN'T sure how she made it through the day. She rested when she could between classes, even going so far as to catch a quick catnap in the breakroom when she was supposedly eating her lunch. There wasn't enough caffeine in the world to wake her up, though she drank black tea all throughout the day.

She didn't have time to go home after she finished teaching swimming at the Y—instead she caught a bus directly to Hallowed Ground. The solid building still appeared to be a sanctuary to her as she walked up. The walls were a white stucco, and looked freshly painted, though Tara knew that was just a spell that Kaede had put up.

Tara entered through the back, heading directly to the industrial kitchen. Alaska was there, preparing herself a snack. She'd been doing peacock colored hair recently, with dark green and blue highlights. She still had what appeared to be the requisite number of piercings on her face, through her ears, as well as a few exotic ones, like the bars across her collar bone. Today she wore what Tara would call modern grunge —a yellow and black flannel shirt covered over in patches, as well as black jeans with holes in them.

"You look as bad as Kaede," the younger woman said as soon as she saw Tara. Despite how tough and world weary Alaska tried to sound, she always gave Tara the impression of being bird-brittle.

"Thanks," Tara said, not bothering to hide her sarcasm. She yawned. "Sorry. Can't help it."

"How bad is it this time?" Alaska asked quietly as Tara pulled out tea supplies and put them on one of the carts, getting ready for her "teashop."

"Bad," Tara admitted. They still had no idea how they were going to stop the Riprap man.

"Do we need to call in the troops?" Alaska said. "Like we did last time?"

"No," Tara said with a shudder. "We tried that last night. Didn't work."

"Wasn't really your people," Alaska replied, her chin raising in defiance. "You should trust us instead."

"It isn't that," Tara said. "I just—we don't want you hurt."

Richard had checked in with Tara midmorning. Ginny had stayed with him overnight. He was finally recovering, though he said his insides were still spinning. He insisted that he was going to come see them that night, though he was planning on sleeping all day long.

How badly could it all have gone if there had been a large group of mundanes involved instead?

"We can take care of our own," Alaska said hotly.

"I know you can," Tara said. "And believe me, I'm grateful for all the help you can give. We all are. This is just…different."

"And bad," Alaska said.

Tara nodded. "And bad." She paused, then added, "If we can figure out a way of using you without killing you all, we will call on you."

Alaska blinked at her, looking surprised. "You're serious."

Tara nodded and shook her head, trying to prevent another yawn. "I am. Death awaits us. Hopefully only if we fail, and not necessarily if we succeed also."

That appeared to mollify Alaska some and she merely nodded as Tara left the kitchen with her full cart.

Someone else had already set up the table in the corner for Tara to work at, for which she was incredibly grateful. Three lines of tables had been set up across the back of the room, where a few different groups of teens diligently worked at their homework. Storytime was taking place in the far corner, with a group of younger kids enthralled by Sonja and her current yarn.

Tara slowly moved her tea carriers to the table, along with her tea kettle. The two large jugs for water were already filled and waiting for her.

After Tara slid the cart to the side, and let herself sit heavily on the stool thoughtfully provided, her first customers came up. They were fraternal twins, not identical. Tara guessed that they were both between seven and eight. The boy, DeAndre, wore his hair shaved close to his head with a cute half-moon pattern carved into at the front. The girl, DeLilah, wore her hair in a looser braid, though Tara had heard her threaten to just shave her head once she was older. They both had the usual T-shirts and jeans on, and at least looked as though they were eating enough finally.

"What can I do for you?" Tara said smiling at them. Though they weren't identical twins, they still shared some of that "twinness" that she'd only heard about. They frequently appeared to talk with each other without saying a word out loud.

They shared a look, then DeAndre took a half step forward, obviously intending on speaking for the pair of them today. "We need something to help us with math," he said seriously.

"Tell me more," Tara said.

DeAndre looked again at his sister before he continued. "I'm not as good at math as DeLilah," he said after a moment.

"Is there a problem with the numbers?" Tara knew to ask. "Do they dance around on the page?"

DeAndre looked horrified at her. "No! Why would they do that?"

"That's what some people see," Tara clarified. "The numbers reverse themselves." She needed to make sure that this wasn't some sort of dyslexia that the boy had.

"No. It's just they don't make come as easily to me as they do to her," DeAndre said, jerking his thumb in the direction of his sister. "And they should." He paused, then added, "I'm the boy. I'm supposed to be good at math."

Tara suddenly understood the problem. It wasn't that DeAndre was bad at math, she'd bet. It was that his sister was better.

And girls weren't supposed to be good at math. Everyone knew that.

"What if I tell you that some of the most famous mathematicians in the world were women?" Tara said.

DeAndre scowled at her. Tara snuck a quick peek at DeLilah. She was beaming. Tara could practically hear her singsong voice saying, "I told you so."

"It's okay if your sister is better at math than you are," Tara added.

DeAndre just shook his head no. That wasn't the way the world worked, at least according to him, as well as whoever he'd been listening to.

"What can DeAndre do better than you?" Tara said, asking DeLilah.

"Lots of things!" the little girl enthused. "He's a really good runner. And he can hit a ball harder than I can."

"How about in school?" Tara said, knowing that she might be getting into sticky territory here.

"He's really good at drawing," DeLilah said.

DeAndre just scowled harder.

"Everyone says so," DeLilah added. "You can draw just about anything you see."

"But what good is that?" DeAndre said.

Tara knew better than to try to convince him that he could do art someday. He wouldn't see the value in that. "You know the games you see some of the older kids playing on their phones?"

DeAndre nodded warily.

"Someone has to draw those characters, you know," she said. "You could become a famous video game designer someday."

"I don't need math for that?" DeAndre said, still suspicious.

"Maybe a little," Tara said, as she really didn't know. "However, just because your sister is better at math doesn't mean you're not any good. Right?"

"She's still better," DeAndre said, crossing his arms over his chest.

"What if I make you some tea to help you be a little bit better?"

Tara said, not speaking the full truth. She didn't have anything that would actually make DeAndre better at a specific subject in school. What she did have was a tea that would help him be more accepting of who he was, who his sister was destined to be.

DeAndre nodded, finally feeling better that Tara might be able to provide some help. "And I'll give you a tea as well," Tara said, turning to DeLiliah, "that will help you run a little faster."

"I'd like that," the little girl said with a big grin.

Tara made her first tea for DeAndre, adding hyssop, licorice root, ginger, then some hibiscus to brighten up the flavor, as well as some honey. Though she'd felt depleted all day, she felt her magic finally stir itself, and send a tendril of something into the cup. It would calm the boy, and help him in their current situation.

For DeLiliah, Tara mixed together borage for courage, as well as lemon balm and bee balm for quickness, not just of her body but of her mind as well, sweetened with some mint and honey.

The pair of them thanked her for their tea, promising to finish their homework early every night that week for payment so that they could help out more around the shelter.

Tara quickly fell into the rhythm of making tea, stirring in kindness and whatever else her clients needed. It was a very pleasant way to spend the afternoon. Mainly she listened, as that was what most of the kids needed—an adult who would listen to them and not immediately try to fix everything, not unless they specifically asked her to.

They didn't serve a full meal that night, opening up the doors and letting all the clients in. Instead, it was more of a family affair, the food all served family style—hamburgers, hotdogs, green salad and a red jello dessert. Kaede joined them, sharing a tired smile with Tara.

After they cleaned up, all the clients left and the rest of the coven began to show up. Ginny actually came early that night—possibly only the second or third time ever. She looked as pale and wan as Tara felt, the freckles standing out sharply across her nose and cheeks. At least her eyes didn't appear to be haunted, and she gave Tara a fierce hug when she came in.

The other arrived shortly. Richard looked like a dead man walking.

Even Lucius had a bit of dark circles under his eyes, though to a lesser extent than everyone else.

Tara didn't call everyone into a circle that evening. She didn't think they'd have the power between them to stay standing. Instead, she served them all a warming tea, made from lavender, peppermint, and lemon balm, with more honey than she usually served.

They did all end up sitting in a circle anyway, pulling chairs out to the center of the room.

"Well, we sure did get our asses handed to us last night," Kyle started out with. He sounded sour, and his dark skin seemed pale that evening.

"I didn't expect the Riprap man to come and attack us that way," Tara said, feeling as though she needed to explain herself. Most of his attacks previously had been on more of an astral plane, rather than a physical one.

"No one did," Kaede said. "But we should never make that assumption again. He has a physical form. And he's coming for us. All of us, this time, no matter how his attention appears to be focused on Tara."

Tara nodded. She had to agree. The Riprap man no longer held anyone, or anything, sacred.

"What called him there, do ye think?" Ginny asked. "Was it all that power?"

"Maybe," Tara said. "Maybe not. I wonder if he was preparing for us already." She explained seeing the other coven when she'd gone underground, how they appeared to have been under his control. Though she was just guessing.

Lucius nodded. "I think they were under his power," he said after a moment. His melodic voice sounded much rougher than usual, hoarse and strained. "I think he was in the process of coming after us, or using that coven's power for some ill deed, when we interrupted him and his plans."

"But what was he trying to do?" Richard asked. "And has he used their power in the past?"

"Someone is going to have to go and talk with them again," Kyle said grimly.

Tara shuddered. She did *not* want to have to do that again. The first time she'd managed it using a potion that Miss Lucy had concocted for her. It had been awful. She felt bile rising just thinking about it.

"Maybe not," Lucius said. "I think I have a plan that might work instead."

"Really?" Tara said, gratefulness overwhelming her.

"I had not anticipated that the Riprap man had such a physical presence anymore," Lucius stated. "I had believed that his presence is merely astral or mental at this time. But he still has a body. He just rarely uses it. And that can be used against him."

"Really? How? Tell us!"

Tara just sat still, thinking hard. She had never really considered that the Riprap man had both a physical as well as mental presence, and what that might mean.

"So you think that we can get at his body?" Tara asked finally, staring hard at Lucius. "Where do you think it is?"

She doubted that he was walking around in his physical body very often. In fact, she wasn't sure she'd ever actually seen him in the flesh, as it were. She might have only seen projections of him.

"Where was the first earthquake, that he blamed you for?" Lucius asked.

"Basically, out in the middle of nowhere," Tara said. "East of Portland."

"That's where we'll find him," Lucius said. "He struck as close to home as he could that first time. Now, he's branching out. I would bet he can't travel too far from it."

"I'd wondered, when he'd first started coming after me, if I could leave. Go to Wisconsin or someplace. If that would be out of his range," Tara said.

"I believe it would be, yes," Lucius said. "I consulted with a friend last night. He's game to go after the creature, in particular, his physical body, to help us."

"Do I still have to physically travel to there as well?" Tara asked.

"All will be made clear soon," Lucius said.

A knock suddenly sounded on the door.

"Kaede, can you let our guest in?" Lucius asked.

Kaede shook zir head, but stood up slowly. "Are you sure about this?" ze asked.

"It would be rude of him to do aught but what we ask," Lucius assured zir.

"And you can get him to leave?" Kaede persisted, not heading toward the door yet.

"Trust me, he isn't interested in you or your kind," Lucius said.

Kaede shook zir head, but slowly moved toward the door. "I will hunt you down and make your bones sing for their supper if any harm comes to me or mine," ze warned before ze opened the door.

"You may enter, but only for this evening," Kaede told the individual who stood patiently outside.

"But of course," came the smooth reply.

The voice reminded Tara of Lucius. The being who stepped into the room bore a superficial resemblance to him as well. They were both tall, arrogant looking men with piercing blue eyes. While Lucius's hair was silver, this person's hair was jet black. They shared the same hawk nose and dimpled chin, and perhaps the same tailor, as they both wore beautiful handmade shirts and trousers that were impeccably fitted.

However, the similarities were just skin deep. No matter how alien Lucius might seem when he allowed his mask to slip, he had a life and vitality to him.

This person, this creature, did not. Instead of exuding life, he drained it.

If Lucius and his kind had inspired myths of elves and other horrible but bright creatures, the one who had just entered would have inspired myths of vampires and their deadly, life-sucking kin.

Tara found herself rising to her feet automatically. Soot appeared at her side, growling. Teruko showed up on her other side, spitting and hissing.

"Now, is that anyway to greet an invited guest?" Lucius scolding, standing and walking over to his guest. "Hello, Martin," he said, sticking out his hand.

"Hello, Lucius," Martin said. He had the same smooth, sardonic quality to his voice that Lucius had. "So it this your little group?"

Tara was surprised at the beam of pride that Lucius gave. "It is," he said simply. "And we are asking your help."

"Read me in," Martin said. He effortlessly snagged a chair and floated over to where the rest of the group still sat.

Tara glanced at Kaede, who nodded and warily sat down herself. Tara couldn't get either Soot or Teruko to leave, however, she did manage to get Soot to lay down next to her, while Teruko leaped onto her lap and settled down there, still giving Martin the occasional baleful stare.

"Martin, as you may have guessed, is possibly better equipped for dealing with the physical Riprap man than the rest of us," Lucius stated.

Tara nodded. She could see that. This…soul stealer, could possibly do the trick, and be able to handle the Riprap man better than any of them.

Miss Lucy had told Tara that in the end, she wasn't hard enough to deal with the Riprap man on her own. Her former mentor may have been right.

So Tara waited with the rest as Lucius and Kaede explained their problem, waiting to hear Martin's solution, hoping that it would solve all their ills.

FIVE

The war draws to a close, and so does the latest chapter in Portland's historic growth. Vanport is draining. Too many are coming down to Portland again. The shanty towns will soon be rebuilt along the river. I cannot allow it. It is tempting to allow the River God his head, to drown all the rats who are now living along his banks. But I promised that I would protect those in the city. I just need to somehow stop those in Vanport from returning here, send them along to other places. It wouldn't take too much.

Wilson Evermore, Defender of Portland and the Hearty Souls Who Remain, 1947

AFTER THE GROUP had developed their plan and Martin had left, Kaede turned on Lucius. "Don't you ever, *ever*, invite someone like that here again," ze warned.

Lucius merely cocked one eyebrow at zir. "What, someone who could save our souls and help us destroy the thing that is intent on destroying the city?"

"You know what I mean," Kaede said. Ze closed zir eyes and bent zir head in prayer for a moment.

Tara felt power rock through the room, as if all the protection sigils deep under the foundation of the building just lit up.

Even Lucius appeared impressed by the display.

"Never again," Kaede warned before ze stalked off.

"I didn't know ze would feel that strongly about it," Lucius offered into the awkward silence.

"What is Martin?" Richard asked. Of course he would. He was a research librarian. Though they'd all been alternately scared as well as repulsed by Martin's presence, only Richard would be the one who would like to learn more.

"He doesn't suck blood or some such nonsense," Lucius assured them. "He doesn't really take souls or energy, either. He's much more attracted to lay lines, the natural power girds of the land."

"Interesting," Richard said. "How does he—"

"While Martin is a dear old friend, I don't know much more than that," Lucius stated, holding off Richard's questions. "It isn't any of my business. I suggest you ask him yourself the next time you see him."

"Which would be never, right?" Kyle asked. "There's no reason for him to come visiting any of us at night."

"True," Lucius said, sounding reluctant. "But if you really want to meet with him again, let me know," he added, nodding to Richard.

After the rest had left, it was only Ginny and Tara still standing on the sidewalk outside Hallowed Ground, chatting.

"Will it work?" Ginny asked, sounding much more timid than Tara had ever heard the other witch before.

Tara had to shrug. "Lucius and Martin seem to think it will." The plan did have a certain elegance to it, she had to admit. Instead of trying to ambush the Riprap man with the combined strength of three covens, they'd go the physical route instead, and have Martin ready to grab him. Just their coven would be involved, ready to distract any non-physical projections of the Riprap man.

The plan still involved using Tara as bait. That part hadn't changed. And Lucius had hinted that there would be yet another being involved who would be following Tara.

"I don't know about any of this," Ginny said. "I don't like the idea of going out and hunting someone. Even the Riprap man."

They started walking along the sidewalk, heading back toward the MAX station. The night was calm and soft. Tara still felt exhausted and unsettled from the night before, and the talk and planning that evening made her feel older still. Her bones creaked as she walked, her knees protesting every step.

"I also don't feel great about the plan either," Tara said. "But I don't see how else we can get the Riprap man to stop. We can't negotiate with him. There's nothing he holds dear that we could use to threaten him. He used to care greatly for Portland. Now, he's turned his back on his city."

"Wouldn't it be better to bind him?" Ginny asked.

Tara had thought about that as well, more than once. "It would be," Tara agreed. "But I don't want to bind him to myself, personally, to turn him into some other sort of familiar. I'm not sure I can, that I'm strong enough, and I think that's just putting the problem off to another day. Once I passed, he's become a problem again."

"Ah," Ginny said. She still seemed thoughtful. "I just don't feel good about gunning for his soul."

"I don't either," Tara admitted. "But I haven't come up with any other solution."

Ginny reached out and touched Tara's arm. "I know ye don't have the time," she said. "But ye got to keep trying other paths. Other ways. Not ending another soul like this."

"I will try," Tara promised. Besides, if this didn't work, they'd be forced to find another way regardless.

"Thank you," Ginny said. She strode off then, calling her winds to her with a sharp whistle. A mass of dogs appeared around her, like a dogwalker with a dozen clients.

Tara made her way to the MAX station with her own wind trotting beside her. She had the same misgivings at Ginny. However, they had run out of options.

The Riprap man was coming for them all. And she had to stop him. Even if it meant destroying his soul.

Tara slept heavy and deep that night. Her body seemed happier for the rest. She didn't have to work at the Y that day, having already changed shifts with someone else. Instead, today she was going up into the hills.

Far up into the hills.

She packed herself a hearty lunch, as well as made a large thermos of tea to share. Martin appeared in a Jeep promptly at nine AM, as promised. It was painted brown and covered in mud, as if he'd just driven it off from some dirt road. The vehicle didn't really have doors, just a front windshield and a rag top. It rode high on its knobby wheels and looked as though it could roll over just about anything.

Martin himself was dressed more like a quaint Englishman on safari, with a beige safari jacket with many pockets and wide brimmed hat. He also wore shorts, tall white socks, and black leather hiking boots.

However, the grin he gave her was that of a shark's. He seemed ready for a good hunt.

Fortunately, so was she.

They headed out of town, Martin unerringly finding the quickest route. It impressed Tara, as she'd assumed they'd be stuck in morning rush-hour traffic for a good hour. He quickly made his way east, up into the hills there.

Tara found that Martin was staring at her as he drove. It wasn't easy to talk in the Jeep. The sound of wind kept conversation to a minimum. But once they left the freeway and were heading more slowly along a winding, two-lane road, Martin asked her, "How did you meet Lucius?"

"He was introduced to me," Tara said. "A friend of a friend." Which was true enough. She didn't want to bring Kyle into the picture. She still was unsure what their current relationship was.

But Martin just nodded. "That was how I met him as well. Years and years ago. A friend of a friend. It surprised me when I found out he was working with you lot."

Tara shrugged. Lucius had only offered to stay with them for a while. She assumed that sooner or later he'd get bored and move on. She was almost surprised that he hadn't so far. It had almost been a year, now.

"He assures me that your group is something quite special," Martin continued.

Tara just smiled at him. Obviously, Martin was looking for information. Tara wasn't sure what he wanted. Eventually she replied. "I think our group is special as well," she said. "We have a range of abilities, not just a hierarchy, like a regular coven."

"I noticed that," Martin said. "I approve. I think that blended families work best."

"Blended families?" Tara asked.

"Yes. Your coven is like a family unit, as I understand them, correct?" Martin said.

"Yes, a family of choice," Tara said.

"I like that term," Martin said. "There's no such thing as a blended family for us," he said, sounding sad.

"Why is that?" Tara said, mainly because she felt he was expecting some sort of response.

"Well…my kind doesn't eat people. Not really. Not like your myths of vampires," Martin said. "But we do wear them down, eventually." He shrugged. "Just our nature, I suppose."

Tara nodded. She could see how that might be. Even just spending an hour or so with Martin had brought her exhaustion back to the forefront. She couldn't imagine what it would be like to actually have to live with such a creature.

They traveled a bit more up the two lane road until Martin told Tara, "Hang on."

She reached for the strap hanging off the roll bar as he made a sharp turn up a forest service road. He didn't bother to slow down at all once they did, instead, bouncing hard along the rutted gravel. Trees surrounded them. The smell of sunbaked wood and fresh pine rolled over her. Thick bushes grew under the canopy of trees. She saw tiny animals race off the road as they approached. All she heard was the racing of the engine, now.

Tara kept hold of the strap as they sped under the trees. She wasn't sure what the hurry was. They had most of the day ahead of them, until the coven met later that evening.

Martin had changed as soon as they'd gotten off the road. His eyes grew intent as he drove, and the look he gave when he glanced her way chilled her very soul.

This was the hunter that Lucius had described.

Martin branched off the service road onto something not much more than an improved animal track. It still had ruts from a car, but it was greatly overgrown with tall grass that whipped past them. They crossed into brilliant sunlight, then back under the trees again.

Tara had the impression that they were climbing again, albeit slowly. It wasn't until Martin pulled into a clearing and slammed the brakes on that she realized just how high they'd gotten.

Ahead of her spread a vast panorama. Trees filled the valley below. Birds flew above the greenery. Steep yellow and gray cliffs led down, boulders peeking out from under the grass. Far below, Tara sensed water, a small river, compared to what had once been a mighty flow.

The silence seemed deafening at first. Tara still felt herself rocking, as if the car still had forward momentum.

She looked over at Martin. He nodded at her. "We're here," he announced. He stood up, bending himself over the front roll bar to look down and around. "And he knows it."

WHILE MARTIN SEEMED to have an unnatural ability to descend along the rough animal track at the head of the cliff, Tara had to take her time, placing her boots carefully along the trail, making sure that she didn't either twist her ankle or fall to her death.

Fortunately, they didn't have to make it all the way to the bottom of the chasm. If they had, she would have insisted that they bring camping gear or something. As it was, she really wasn't looking forward to having to make it up that track after some sort of fight.

Martin led them to a wide meadow about halfway down the cliff that Tara hadn't seen from the top. It seemed like such a beautiful, peaceful place. The sun shone down on them cheerfully. Little white flowers danced at the ends of tall stalks. Tiny blue butterflies flew across the tops of them. The air smelled of rocks baked by the warm sunlight. The meadow itself was maybe about twenty feet across, ten wide. The back of was delaminated by the cliff face, just as the front was as well.

Tara would have loved to have stayed here. Maybe with a picnic or something.

Except for one thing.

The whitish boulders that she saw piled haphazardly roughly in the center of the meadow started moving.

The Riprap man rose, staring ominously at them.

Crap.

Tara and Martin weren't supposed to find him until later that evening, after the coven had gathered in Hallowed Ground.

Too late now.

TARA HAD A LITTLE DEFENSIVE MAGIC, merely a sort of bubble shield that she called up around herself. As for attacking, she knew that as long as she stayed in control of her familiars, they could do a lot of damage. However, she was afraid to send them into the fight. The Riprap man could easily wrest Soot and Teruko's loyalty from Tara, getting them to attack Martin instead.

At the moment, none of them needed to do much. The Riprap man and Martin circled each other. Tara found it difficult to watch, as neither of them had much of a human aspect anymore. Instead, it was like watching two monsters who were all too real face off.

Martin had grown white and pale, like a slug who lived underground. He'd also grown more slender and willowy, appearing as a living whip. He moved slowly as he faced off with his opponent, circling to the right, then to the left.

The Riprap man's physical body resembled the one Tara had always seen, made out of hard stone. Only this stone was eroded and rough. His face was obscured by the rock, his expression fixed in rage. Instead of deep blue, his eyes were now pits of darkness. He wore no trousers, not that he needed any, as he had nothing remaining of his gender.

The Riprap man roared his displeasure at Martin instead of taunting him with words. Tara wondered if he'd actually lost all language when he took on stone form, or at least the ability to form speech, given how frozen all of him now seemed. Martin hissed in return, like an overgrown snake. The sound chilled Tara to the quick, reminding her once again that she faced nothing human.

She still hesitated to send either Soot or Teruko forward, afraid she might distract Martin and not the Riprap man.

Suddenly, Martin tore forward. Tara wasn't certain what he was trying to do. Possibly knock over the Riprap man? That seemed foolish to her. He was too set and grounded to be blown to the side.

It proved to be a mistake, as the Riprap man managed to get ahold of one of Martin's arms and wouldn't let go.

The Riprap man swung Martin to the side, then swung a rocklike fist at his face, pounding him and knocking Martin's head back.

Where was the killer that Tara had been fearing? Should she send Soot in? Or Teruko, to get the Riprap man to let go of Martin?

Except that Martin wasn't trying to get away. He let himself be pummeled, again and again, his head jerking back as the Riprap man slammed his fist into Martin's face.

However, Martin wasn't bleeding. Not like how Tara had assumed a human would bleed. His face wasn't cut or bruised, either.

An eerie sound filled the quiet meadow.

Martin, laughing.

The Riprap man tried to strike Martin again, only this time, Martin dodged the blow. Then he grinned at the Riprap man, taking hold of the other's hand.

Tara wasn't certain what Martin was doing to the Riprap man. He appeared to be staring at him, staring him down.

No, wait.

Shrinking him down.

Martin's white skin started to bloat up while the Riprap man was disintegrating. Dust flaked off his flat cheeks. His physical form continued to shrink, until he was a good head shorter than Martin.

Seemed that Tara had made the right call, keeping Soot and Teruko beside her.

The Riprap man tried to let go of Martin's arm, only to have both his hands now caught. Martin held onto the Riprap man's forearms, like some sort of dancer. They started circling again, only much more slowly this time, shuffling to the side.

Tara swallowed hard when she saw Martin's jaw begin to distend. It was like watching an alien horror movie, only it was happening, right in front of her. Martin's face continued to stretch, his jaw growing wider, until it was at least ten inches across. The smell of rotten oranges washed over her, sickly sweet.

Martin suddenly lunged at the Riprap man. The Riprap man ducked, and Martin only managed to wrap his mouth across the top of the Riprap man's head, instead of his full face. Martin's bottom teeth were digging into the Riprap man's eyebrows, while his top teeth were firmly latched into the crown of the Riprap man's head.

A loud, grating howl echoed across the meadow. Tara knew it had been torn from the Riprap man's soul.

She wasn't about to send in Soot or Teruko at this point. Martin had things well in hand.

She also wouldn't allow herself to turn away. This battle had been her doing. She'd made the decision to end the life of the Riprap man before he destroyed all of Portland. She would see this through, even if the sight would live forever in her nightmares.

The Riprap man stumbled backwards one step, then another. Then he managed to find his feet. He picked up Martin and raced toward the edge of the meadow, ramming the other creature's back straight into the hard rock.

The impact jarred Martin's grip and the Riprap man was able to step away. He didn't try hitting Martin again. Instead, he looked up, as if calling for help.

Martin didn't see the danger quick enough. Neither did Tara.

Huge boulders came bounding down the hill, landing on Martin. They were each the size of a small car. Martin was quickly buried.

Martin screamed, a high-pitched wail.

The next rock that landed on the pile cut off the noise, suddenly.

But the Riprap man wasn't finished yet. He used his hands to start to compress the rocks, pushing them together, both physically as well as magically.

Tara didn't have to watch anymore. She raced away, heading back up the trail before the Riprap man could finish. However, she had no doubt of Martin's fate. He would be completely crushed by those great rocks, pulverized until nothing but a wet slick remained, all his bones broken. She could already hear the crunching sound, different than the sound of boulders grinding together.

Then the Riprap man would be coming after Tara. And she had nothing to either attack with or defend herself, not from that monster.

<hr>

TARA PANTED as she raced up the steep slope. She kept looking over her shoulder, waiting for a moving boulder to be rolling up behind her. Soot loaned her feet fleetness, as did her own terror. Sweat dripped down her forehead and pooled at the base of her spine. The sourness of her own fear left a bitter taste in her mouth.

There was nothing she could do to stop the physical form of the Riprap man. His mental presence was bad enough. The original plan had been to engage both, the coven keeping him distracted while Martin attacked.

She felt bad that Martin had been killed, though she knew in her heart that Martin had also been a killer his entire existence.

For now, she just had to survive.

Tara had taken her time when they'd been going down the steep path. It had taken them thirty minutes or so to reach the meadow. Due to the steep climb, she'd expected it to take her over an hour to get back up to the top.

However, even as winded as she was, her legs feeling rubbery and her insides loose and jelly-like, it took her about thirty minutes to climb back to the top.

The sight of the mud-covered Jeep filled her with relief. She could get there. She could escape. Martin had hidden the keys to the Jeep in the wheel well of the driver side front wheel, as it was much easier to let someone steal the car than to lose the keys in the bush. While Tara didn't have a driver's license, it couldn't be that hard to get herself out of here. Could it?

Tara couldn't help but scream when a nearby rock suddenly transformed itself into the Riprap man.

She still raced toward the car. If she could get it started, she might be able to get away.

The Riprap man came running after her. He didn't move as quickly as she could, even with her recent climb.

Tara raced around the rear of the car, leading him away from the front. While he lumbered around, coming after her, she pulled the keys out. Then she kept going, heading back across the small clearing they'd parked in what seemed like a lifetime ago.

The Riprap man roared his displeasure. He lifted his rocklike hands after her, making a punching motion with his fist.

Tara ducked to the side as a large rock flew past her head.

She whistled for Soot, who started running quick circles around the legs and feet of the Riprap man, forcing him to stop, the strong wind blowing him back.

Tara raced back toward the Jeep. Just before she got there, she heard a loud yelp.

The Riprap man had finally managed to get ahold of Soot. He lifted up the dog by the scruff of the neck, then tossed it over the cliff.

The wind came racing back, but Soot had lost some of his corporeal form.

Tara managed to start up the car, remembering that she needed to put on the brake before the engine would turn over.

The Riprap man roared again. This time, when she looked over, she saw that Teruko now crouched on his chest and clawed at his face, spitting hot coals into his eyes.

Tara spun the wheel and managed to get the car pointed in the right direction, down the forest trail. She couldn't take her eyes off the road as she bounced along. Grasses whipped against the edges of the Jeep. The bright sunlight blinded her as it flickered through the canopy.

She couldn't stop.

She kept feeling as though the road was trying to wrest control of the wheel from her hands. She fought it, fought to stay in control. She sent a quick prayer to Brigid, asking for the strength she needed to make it out of the woods. She also asked Hayyu the goddess of the western winds to blow her foes away from her path, while Samil needed to protect her and guard her soul.

Loud crashing came from behind her. No, it moved to the side, now.

When she glanced to her left, she saw the Riprap man was shouldering his way through the bramble and bushes.

He was trying to get in front of the car. If he made it, he would block her. Running into him would be like driving into a brick wall.

Soot suddenly flew out of the trees from in front of the Riprap man, knocking him back.

Then Soot appeared again beside Tara.

Teruko landed on his shoulders out of nowhere, causing him to fall back again.

Tara realized that she was drawing close to a small creek just ahead.

She called on Mulinohana. Though this wasn't his waterway, he could still help.

All the water in the small creek suddenly rose up, spinning like a hurricane. The Riprap man couldn't avoid the water, and ended up crashing into the middle of it. The water spun all around him, whipping him around.

Tara bounced off the smaller track and onto the larger service road. She kept looking over her shoulder, but she no longer heard him crashing through the underbrush.

Soon, she reached the narrow blacktop, shooting out of the darkness of the trees and into the sunlight. She took a shaky breath and kept going, pushing forward, going as quickly as she dared down the highway.

Would the Riprap man keep after her? Not now, she suspected. She would be safe, at least for a while.

Later tonight, though, would be another matter.

Tara slowly drove the Jeep back into the city. It was just after 1 PM. She had already pulled over once and left a message for Lucius, asking him to meet her at Hallowed Ground.

Tara didn't fall down on the ground and kiss the dirty sidewalk, though she considered it as she stepped out of the Jeep. Her legs were still jelly, this time, though, from having to drive for so long, concentrating on something so foreign to her.

At least she'd made it.

"You're sure he's gone?" Lucius said, appearing out of nowhere. "You're quite positive?"

Tara nodded, blinking her tired eyes. "As sure as I can be," she said. She shivered in the warm sunshine. How did people stand to drive such long distances? Though she'd been sitting for several hours, she was still completely exhausted.

"His family will not be pleased," Lucius said.

"He had a family?" Tara asked. They'd talked about that, hadn't they? Family of choice. Though he couldn't choose one. Would wear people down, eventually.

"His parents," Lucius said. He looked displeased. "How could he be dead? He was older than I was. Much older. I've known him for most of my life. How can he be gone? I would have expected him to outlive us all."

"The Riprap man was waiting for us," Tara said. "In the meadow. We thought we'd have to call him. We didn't."

Lucius nodded. "Well. It will be the last time that thing hurts one of ours," he said. He held out a hand to Tara, seeming impatient.

It took Tara a moment to realize that Lucius wanted the keys to the Jeep. She slowly handed them over to him.

"Where are you going?" Tara asked as Lucius climbed into the dirty vehicle.

"To get reinforcements," Lucius said. "I will be back by eight."

Tara nodded tiredly and watched the elegant man drive away, struck by the contrast between the rough and ready vehicle and the driver.

It took Tara three tries to open the door to Hallowed Ground.

Kaede came out of zir office immediately. "You need a bed," ze said, taking one look at Tara.

Tara nodded, though she doubted she would sleep. Or rather, that she would sleep without nightmares.

The crunching sound of bones being broken by rocks followed her all through her dreams.

SIX

TARA WAITED with Kaede at Hallowed Ground until close to 9 PM, but Lucius never returned. She'd called the rest of the coven, telling them that they didn't need to meet that evening. Kyle had made plans with her to meet the following evening, while Richard had asked to have lunch with her.

She never actually talked with Lucius. Had the Riprap man gotten him as well? It wasn't unusual for all calls to go straight through to his voicemail, as he rarely answered his phone. The being had a singular distaste for talking on the device, and only carried one for convenience.

Heartsore and still tired, Tara went home slowly. She slept better than she would have imagined. She managed to put off any nightmares until three AM, so managed to get a few hours of uninterrupted sleep.

Her morning class went better than she would have thought. Again, it struck her as so odd that everything else was so normal around her while she continued to look at every building she entered, making sure she knew where the exits were, what would be the best place to hide in case of a major earthquake.

Richard met her at a place that did all sorts of different veggie and meat bowls. Tara got a hearty bowl with a lot more carbs than she normally ate, just to build her system back up, a taco salad with black beans, rice, as well as spicy hamburger, sour cream, cheese, guacamole, and lots of fresh greens.

"You look better," Tara told Richard as he joined her at a table. He no longer looked as pasty, and his eyes appeared less haunted. He was in work clothes that day, so a nice gray shirt with thin white pinstripes. It made him look professorial, with his large aviator glasses and lanky black hair.

"You look like shit," Richard told her in return, with a grin to help soften the words. "No, seriously. Are you sleeping at all?"

"Some," Tara admitted. "It's been hard. I've been worried all the time, you know? And the fight yesterday..." Tara couldn't help but shudder.

"Do you need to talk about it?" Richard asked.

Tara shrugged. "It was bad," she said quietly. She gave him a brief outline of what had occurred.

"Didn't Lucius say that there might be someone else there? Who could possibly help?" Richard said.

"He did," Tara said, nodding. "I'm not sure if the person didn't show up because I escaped successfully, or if they hadn't been there."

"We'll have to ask. If we see him again," Richard said sourly.

"He never promised us that he'd be there for long," Tara said. "And I'm still just hoping he's all right. That nothing happened to him."

Richard nodded. He paused, obviously thinking.

"Spit it out," Tara said after a moment. "You obviously have something on your mind."

Richard grinned at her. "See? This is what I was thinking about. How well we know each other. How well we get along."

"We've always gotten along together well," Tara said. "That's why we're friends." A spike of fear raced through her core. He wasn't thinking about something else, was he?

"Well, we started off dating. We couldn't continue because we were of different religions," Richard said, grinning at her. "But since I've converted, do you think we could try again?"

Tara blinked, surprised but not. Richard was not the solitary type, despite his chosen profession. Though he claimed to be an introvert, he was the most extroverted introvert she'd ever met. He liked people, and talking with people, and hanging out with people. Tara did as well, but not to the same extent.

"So what do you think?" Richard said, keeping his smile firmly in place when she didn't reply immediately.

Tara shook her head. "You know that I adore you, and you're one of my best friends," she said.

"Keeping me in the friend zone," Richard said, nodding. "Any chance I could make my way out of there?"

Tara sighed. "I don't think so," she said after a moment.

"It's because I'm not a witch, I don't have magic, right?" Richard said, finally starting to sound bitter about the whole thing.

"That's a big part of it," Tara said. She shrugged. "But really, I don't think of you that way. I'm sorry."

"It's okay," Richard said. He gave her a brave smile. "I just thought I'd try my luck. You never know, right?"

"You don't know until you try, that's right," Tara said. She reached over and squeezed his arm. "I still enjoy your company, and wouldn't mind hanging out more."

Richard shook his head. "No. I'll need to put up more boundaries. If we aren't getting closer, I don't want to get closer as friends, if that makes sense." He reached over and squeezed her hand, releasing it quickly.

Tara got the hint and took her hand off his arm. She felt bad for hurting his feeling on the one hand. On the other, she couldn't hurt herself for him. That would never work either.

They gave each other sad smiles and finished their lunch. Richard promised to call her later, as well as to stay in the coven, at least for now.

Tara had been so happy with her group, her found family.

How did she prevent it from falling apart all around her?

KYLE STILL HADN'T HEARD from Lucius by the time he met up with Tara for dinner at his place. Though she'd moved out, he was still cooking at home more.

Kyle took Tara's coat and hung it in the closet just behind the front door. Tara looked around the familiar condo with curiosity. It had been a few months since she'd been there. She and Kyle still had the occasional movie night, but they'd fallen out of meeting regularly.

The kitchen, immediately to the left, seemed much the same, with stir fry sizzling on the stove and filling the air with the smell of ginger, lemon, and chicken. The rice cooker on the countertop was new, though.

Right in front of her was the living room, with its masculine, leather furniture. It was still in the same configuration, with the long brown couch facing the glass doors that led out to the patio, a small eating nook on the left, and the TV with the comfy chairs to the right.

In the far right corner, Tara saw that Kyle had increased the size of his altar. She didn't stare at it, though she was curious about the carved white statue that now sat prominently in the center of it.

Behind the altar was…something. Tara remembered that before, Kyle had a hidden set of shelves that she'd not really ever noticed. He'd protected it with a distraction spell so she wouldn't pay attention to it.

At that point, she hadn't been a strong enough witch to see through the spells Kyle had put up.

Now, though she still couldn't actually see the shelves themselves, at least she knew that something was there.

"You sense the shelves now, don't you?" Kyle asked as he stepped back into the kitchen, turning the heat back up on the stir fry and stirring as it sizzled back to life.

"I do," Tara said slowly. "I don't mean to pry," she added.

"No, I was curious if you'd finally gained the strength," he said. "I know you couldn't see them when you first passed in, to the circle of water. So I wasn't sure when you'd be able to."

Tara shrugged. "I haven't been studying," she said. "Not at all."

Kyle nodded. "I know," he said as he pulled the wok from the stove. "And we needed to talk about that."

Tara gave an expressive sigh.

"What is it?" Kyle asked. He held up a bottle of red wine, silently asking if she'd like a glass.

"Yes, please," Tara said. Though she rarely drank alcohol, a glass of wine actually sounded really good that evening.

Kyle poured them both a glass then continued serving, putting a large serving of rice in his dish, a smaller one in hers, then covering both with the stir fry. He carried them both to the eating nook. Tara followed, carrying the two glasses of wine and the bottle.

"To old friends," Kyle proposed lifting his glass in a toast.

Tara smiled at him. "To old friends," she added, though she felt deep in her gut that this old friend was also going to ask something of her, something she possibly wasn't going to be prepared for.

TARA PUSHED BACK her bowl and cradled her wine glass in her hands. "When did you become such a good cook?" she asked. The meal had been fantastic. Kyle had used fresh ginger to liven up the stir fry, as well as some lovely peppers to give it heat. The chicken had been marinated in the lemon juice before being cooked, so it had been nice and savory as well.

"I can follow a recipe, you know," Kyle told her with a grin. "Plus someone may have shown me a thing or two about herbs, you know."

"Yeah, but you were barely cooking when I was living here," Tara told him.

Kyle's grin widened. "Maybe I didn't want you to stay. I knew I'd have to kick you out of the nest sooner rather than later. And if I'd been cooking a lot, you wouldn't have wanted to go."

Tara had to nod. "True, that."

They cleaned up, the quiet falling between them happy and content. Tara almost was able to fully relax.

Almost. She knew that Kyle had something more to say, though. He was just softening her up with a good meal.

And it had worked. She joined him on the couch, looking out through the glass doors into the night.

"How is Soot doing?" Kyle asked. She had called the wind first out on his balcony.

"He's fine," Tara said. She'd been worried about him after his battle with the Riprap man, but he'd come racing to her when she'd finally managed to call him. Same with Teruko.

"Good," Kyle said. "It always surprised me, how you'd managed to tame a wind. And a fire elemental. As well as a water element."

"Yeah," Tara said. A year ago, she couldn't have even imagined doing such a thing. Now, Soot, Teruko, and even Mulinohana were such a part of her life, she couldn't imagine living without them.

"So that's kind of what I wanted to talk with you about," Kyle said.

Tara couldn't help but stiffen in fear. What was her good friend about to ask her?

"Now, I know you haven't been studying at all," Kyle said. "It's getting harder for you to do schooled witch spells, isn't it?"

Tara nodded. "It is," she said. She hadn't wanted to admit it to him. He was one of her best friends, and a schooled witch. He couldn't understand the way she worked with the elements, needing always to follow along the straight lines set out by the laws and lore.

"It's okay," Kyle said. "I'm still here to act as your conscious, whenever you start to abuse the natural magic."

"Thanks, I think," Tara said. She and Ginny tried to keep reign over their natural abilities whenever they were with the rest of the group.

"You're welcome," Kyle said. "Now, I know that Lucius has said that we've been thinking too small. It was why he wanted to try to mesh with the other covens."

"And you know how well that turned out," Tara said sourly. Aaloka, her former mentor, wouldn't even have tea with her anymore. While it had been a remarkable amount of power, the psychic and magical backlash had been severe. Tara and her group had suffered the least. Miss Lucy had let her know that her coven wasn't going to be able to do any magic for a month or more. Aaloka had hinted at the same for their coven.

"I hadn't meant to hurt anyone," Tara said. At least now they had a good idea why it was such a bad idea to try to bring the covens together. The chances of this sort of fallout were too high.

"I know," Kyle said. "Not just them, but Martin, as well."

"I've never seen Lucius so…distraught," Tara said. "He was really devastated that his friend had been killed."

Kyle gave her an odd look. "I'm not sure that was what was causing him so much grief," he said slowly. "I think that Lucius's pride was hurt as much as anything else."

"What do you mean?"

"He's proposed two solutions," Kyle said. "Neither of them have worked. He isn't mortal. He certainly never sees himself as fallible. Nonetheless, here is where we are."

Tara nodded. That actually made more sense. Lucius wasn't the kind to really care deeply for anyone other than himself.

"Do you know where he might be?" Tara said. She'd asked before, but thought there would be no harm in asking again.

Kyle pressed his lips together. "I may. But I wouldn't tell you, and I certainly wouldn't go there myself."

"Understood," Tara said. "It's just—I'm worried about him. It isn't like him to set an appointment and then not show up."

Kyle gave her a huge grin. "Unless it's to show up at eight PM some other night, and claiming that he meant that time all along."

"That would be exactly like him, wouldn't it? That the misunderstanding was all on our part," Tara said, smiling at Kyle.

"Exactly," Kyle said. He paused, then added, "I'm not worried about him. Not at this point. He's wily, and though he's upset, he wouldn't be stupid enough for the Riprap man to actually catch him. Not yet."

"Okay," Tara said, slightly less worried. "But that isn't the only reason you invited me over here and softened me up with such a good meal."

"No it isn't," Kyle replied, more serious than he'd been earlier. "As I said, you haven't been studying. I know that in order to pass within, to the next level, you're going to need to learn more lore."

Tara grimaced. "Yeah, I know. But do I really need to pass to the next circle? As I said, it's already harder for me to do those sorts of spell. Will learning more help?"

"It might," Kyle said. "And passing to the next level might help as well."

"But why?" Tara said. "Help with what?"

"The next level is the circle of earth," Kyle pointed out.

"And?" Tara prompted when he didn't continue.

"Maybe we've been thinking too big," Kyle said. "Asking other witches and old friends for help. What if the solution is right in front of us?"

Tara still wasn't sure what he meant.

"What if instead of a huge battle, it needs to be smaller? More intimate? Personal?"

Tara made a gesture, urging Kyle to get to the point.

"The Riprap man is associated with the earth, like you are associated with the water, right?" Kyle said. "What happens if we fight like with like?"

Tara still had no idea what her old friend was asking of her.

"What would happen if the next time you met, you had an actual earth elemental to fight against him?"

***

TARA STILL WASN'T sure what to do with Kyle's suggestion. It made sense in a way. Fight fire with fire, or earth with earth.

She was finally home, curled up on her bed with Soot and Teruko curled up around her. She couldn't ask them, couldn't really talk with them. They weren't that strong, couldn't really communicate with her, not with words. Sure, they still let her know things. But it wasn't human speech.

Mulinohana was her strongest familiar. He took on the form of a person, and could talk.

Ginny had told Tara long ago that part of the problem with hedgewitches and their magic was that it was individual. While the schooled witches magic was weaker, it was more predictable. Tara's magic generally worked about half of the time, and she had no idea how to make it more reliable.

So while Tara could ask Ginny about calling up an earth elemental, working with that type of familiar, she already knew that Ginny wouldn't have any experience with it. Tara already was different than any other witch Ginny had known, having a familiar from more than one element.

Instead, Tara made herself sit up in her bed. Teruko protested, as his purring had already started to fade away as the cat headed toward sleep. Soot just nodded and rolled over, slithering down to the foot of the bed, then laying there like a statue, ready to protect her.

Tara folded her legs under her and leaned against her headboard. She closed her eyes, holding her hands out in lotus pose, then took a deep breath.

She expected that she'd have to fight her tiredness, and would fall into sleep instead of a meditative state. But she found that her breathing smoothed out easily, her mind falling into her body, her thoughts sliding away.

It didn't take long for her to reach a state of altered consciousness. She concentrated on the sound of dripping water, that soft splash that a sink might make, the drips constant and reassuring.

The sound of a louder splash made Tara open her eyes. She stood near the headwaters of the Willamette river. Moss-covered rocks impeded the flow of the water, causing it to make a loud rushing sound. Mud felt cool under her bare toes, while the sunshine warmed her skin.

It didn't embarrass Tara to realize that she'd shown up naked. It wasn't as if Mulinohana were a human male. Plus, much of her craft was done better without the hindrance of clothing.

Still, Mulinohana gave her a bemused smile when he appeared beside her. He looked much as he always did, like a young Native American man in his twenties, wearing his long black hair in two braids that hung down past his shoulders. He was still clothed, wearing light-brown leather vest and no shirt, as well as jeans that had the knees artfully torn out. His bare feet and toes dug into the mud next to hers.

"Thank you for meeting me," Tara said. She paused a moment, breathing in the peace of this place.

"You are always welcome in my home," Mulinohana said. His words never sounded loud, and always seemed to have the hissing of rushing water behind them.

"Thank you also for the aid with the Riprap man," Tara said. She knew that the only reason she'd survived had been because of her familiars.

"That, too, was my pleasure," Mulinohana said. He turned serious dark eyes toward her. "I would not see you come to harm."

"Thank you," Tara said.

When they'd first bonded, Tara had asked him about the process that he'd used to create the Riprap man. It wasn't a spell that she wanted to experience, as it had greatly, though artificially, extended his life.

Fortunately, Mulinohana hadn't wanted to perform it with her. He'd only done it at the insistence of the Riprap man, plus the fact that while Mulinohana had realized that the Riprap man wasn't necessarily a water person, he hadn't at the time realized how much that mattered.

Tara told Mulinohana about her day. She hadn't planned on talking about Richard, but ended up telling the river spirit about him anyway.

"Do you suppose there's a way to give him magic?" Mulinohana asked.

Tara shuddered. "Possibly. But it would be wrong."

Mulinohana tilted his head to one side. "Why is that?"

"That isn't who Richard is," Tara explained.

"It isn't who you see him as, yes. Can you say for certain what is in his soul?" Mulinohana said. "You may want to talk to your friend Lucius about it. He may have some ideas."

Tara nodded. She'd mention it to Richard, then let him decide if he wanted to move ahead. She, however, would also have to make it clear to him that even if he suddenly developed magic, she wouldn't necessarily be interested in him.

Probably. She honestly couldn't say for certain.

"What else?" Mulinohana said. "Surely you didn't come to see me just because of a lover's tiff."

Tara opened her mouth then shut it again, not wanting to try to explain how she and Richard weren't lovers. Then she saw his sly smile, and realized that the river spirit was teasing her.

"Kyle had an idea," Tara said. "He suggested that we fight fire with fire, as it were. Since we know that the Riprap man is associated with earth, would it make sense for me to acquire an earth familiar?"

Tara wasn't prepared in the least for the sudden splash of water that splashed against her lower legs, soaking her from the knees down.

"Why would you come and ask that of me?" Mulinohana said.

Tara took a step back from his sudden rage.

"I am the most important element in your life," Mulinohana said, still angry. "No other familiar you call will be as strong or as willing as I am."

Tara hadn't realized that her water element might be this jealous. She regretted coming here. "I'm sorry," Tara said, trying to back-peddle. "I hadn't meant to insult you. I was coming here to consult you, to ask your wisdom about these things."

"I see," Mulinohana said, though he was barely mollified. "I think it's a dumb idea," he stated plainly.

"But wouldn't you like some help the next time we confront the Riprap man?" Tara asked.

"I need no help," Mulinohana said firmly. "None."

Tara realized that the water spirit would never be able to advise her on this topic. "That's good to know," she assured him. "I will call on you first for our next battle."

Mulinohana narrowed his eyes at her. "The Riprap man is more wily than you realize," he said. "You must take care. It might, maybe, make sense to have more power the next time you meet."

Tara nodded. She thought she understood what Mulinohana wasn't saying: That while he'd never condone Tara enlisting the help of an earth elemental, he still approved it in his own way.

"Thank you," Tara said. She turned to face the river again. Mulinohana stood silent beside her. The rushing water filled her head and carried her off to sleep, finally without nightmares or dreams.

SEVEN

The spring waters are rushing toward Vanport. I've already weakened the main waterway, meant to keep the waters from taking the town. Mulinohana is helping, adding to the mountain streams, pushing more force this way. The destruction will be spectacular! The power of the river will be remembered for always.

Wilson Evermore, Magician and Primary Initiate, 1948

TARA PUT her tablet down beside her on the porch swing, her head spinning. She'd been trying to stuff so much lore into her brain it actually hurt. Later that evening, Kyle was going to try to use the spell that would help her pass within, from one level to the next. However, she didn't know if she was ready, if she'd ever be ready.

She'd spent the morning working at the Y, and now had a few hours off before putting in more time at Hallowed Ground. Despite the terrible aftermath of trying to mesh the covens, both Sheila and Lucy continued to support Tara's work at the homeless shelter, at least for the time being, by supplying ingredients for Tara and her "teashop".

All Tara had ever wanted to do was to run her own teashop. The one at Hallowed Ground had just stoked that fire, rather than vanquished it. While making teas and sachets for the youth there, what she really wanted to do was to run a business. Feel like a success for a change.

Instead of always feeling as though she was behind in everything, part of the gig culture, working for other people and never for herself.

She might be able to take out a business loan. But that was iffy. She still had her college debt to pay off, would for another five years or more, and she was already approaching thirty.

Some year…

In the meanwhile, here she was studying again. The last few times she'd tried cramming for one of these exams she'd felt as though her brain had been put through a wringer. This time, it just felt like mush.

Was she getting too old for this?

She snorted to herself. Yup. Definitely too old for this saving the world shit. And it just didn't pay well.

She stood up and stretched for a few moments, wondering if she should go for a walk. Her phone rang.

"Hi, Mom," Tara said cheerfully. "What the news from the farm?"

While her parents had spent her childhood in the city of Menominee, Wisconsin, after she'd left home they'd sold the place and bought a hobby farm north of the city. She'd never suspected that her parents would end up being outdoorsy people, but they were.

Her mother launched into a long description of the garden, what she'd planted, what was still in seed pots. Tara grinned listening to her mother's stories. While Tara considered herself more of a city girl, she certainly appreciated a good garden.

As they finished up their call, Tara realized that yet again, she was facing never talking with her mom again. "You know how much I love you and Dad, right?"

"What's going on this time?" Mom asked sharply.

"What do you mean? Nothing's going on," Tara said.

"Three, maybe four times now, you've gotten morose and needed to tell me just how much you cared for me," Mom said. "It's been happening like clockwork. Right around the time of the equinox or the solstice."

"I can't really tell you about it," Tara said, not wanting to lie too much to her mother, but needing to for her own good. "Let's just say that my life gets really weird sometimes. And it worries me."

That, at least, was the truth. Here she was studying hard to be a stronger witch, to pass within in terms of the circles of power, and to call up an earth familiar so that she could fight someone called the Riprap man.

"You should come and see us, sometime," Mom said. "Soon." She paused, then added, "I could send you a ticket."

Tara knew that her parents didn't have that much money either. But they were at least better established than she was.

"I might take you up on that," Tara said.

"After the summer solstice?" Mom asked.

'That sounds wonderful," Tara said. Hopefully either she would have successfully fought off the Riprap man somehow before then.

Or the west coast would be in ruins.

"I do love you," Tara said.

"I know. I love you to. As does Daddy."

"Thanks, Mom. Bye!"

"Bye."

Tara held the phone in her hand and just looked at it for a while. While she enjoyed being an adult, sometimes she wished she could be a little girl again, let someone else take care of her for a while.

Honestly, that had been the most appealing part of Richard's offer. Not that she wanted a boyfriend or even a constant companion. Just someone to take care of her more often.

Then again, Kyle would cook for her anytime she asked. Ginny would make her teas as well as regale her with stories and make her laugh. Kaede made Tara think, as well as made her a better person. Richard was a dear friend who found things out for her. And Lucius— he brought a wonder to her life, showing her how much else was out in the world, waiting to be discovered.

Tara did have friends, good friends, and a good network.

Did she want more?

And would she be able to answer that by the time the next battle was over?

———

TARA STOOD with Kyle in Rose Park, up in the Rose District. They'd decided that it made more sense for them to do the ritual outside, and not on his balcony, as she'd been calling up earth powers.

It was near the park where Tara had first met Ginny, almost a year ago. Roses lined the edges of the park, as well as grew along the walkways. A few eager bushes had already started blooming, though most would wait until early summer before they'd show their true colors. The wind still carried the scent of sweet roses through the evening air.

Though Tara had thought about contacting the rest of the coven, this was really a private ceremony between her and Kyle. She wasn't about to try binding an earth spirit to her, not yet. This was just the passing within.

Tara and Kyle had already discussed the possibility that she might not be able to pass within, not yet. As she'd managed to call her other familiars before actually becoming that level of witch, Tara tried to reassure herself the it didn't matter if she succeeded or not.

And though she hadn't always been a good student, she had always tried her best, and maintained at least a B average all through school.

Not that an English degree had actually done her much good out here. She would have been much better at a technical school, particularly one that might offer something like a master gardener program.

She'd considered it, but what she still really wanted was to run her own teashop.

Kyle met her in the park, in the middle where all the pathways converged. She saw him walking toward her, then had to look again. For a moment, she thought that he was wearing judges robes. Instead, it was just a black jacket with four long panels hanging off the back, like a ribbon cloak. Fancy knotted frog closures, the kind that were used on old-fashioned uniforms, in black kept the front of the piece shut. Black braid decorated the collar and cuffs as well.

Kyle looked stern, as though he was waiting to pass judgement on her. And he was.

She followed him off the main gravel path, onto the grass nearby. The rose bushes on either side of them appeared to swell up, providing them with privacy. Kyle casually dropped a sachet on the ground. A silence rippled out of it, hiding their words as well.

"We have come here tonight to verify if you are ready to pass within, from the circle of water to the circle of earth," he intoned, his words solemn and clear. "Are you prepared?"

A part of Tara wanted to joke and reply, "As ready as I'll ever be."

But she knew that wouldn't be appropriate. Kyle was taking this seriously. She had to as well.

"I am," she said, holding herself straighter. She was glad that she'd worn something better than just a T-shirt with her jeans, though she doubted her nice, pink and white striped blouse would pass muster with Kyle's fashion sense.

"Then let us begin," Kyle said. "Tell me all the properties of *hyssopus officinalis*," he said.

Tara swallowed. She had a moment of anxiety. Would she remember anything that she'd just learned?

Then the moment passed and she started reeling off the practical, medicinal, culinary, and magical uses of common hyssop.

She could do this.

By the time Kyle asked his last question and told her that he considered himself satisfied, Tara felt completely wrung out. She felt as though her brain was leaking out of her ears. Her tongue had continually gotten twisted on the Latin names for things. Usually, she could figure out the uses, but she'd missed, more than once.

If she'd done this badly the first time, when Aaloka had been testing her, she wouldn't have passed at all. But Kyle appeared to take pity on her.

"You've acquired the minimum knowledge necessary for passing within," Kyle said. "Now, for the practical."

Tara blinked, confused. He hadn't named a plant. Practical uses for what?

It slowly dawned on her that he was telling her that she needed to perform some earth magic, before he'd try the spell that would pass her within.

"Right. Gotcha," Tara said.

"We can take a break," Kyle told her, his eyes narrowed.

"No, no, I'm fine," Tara lied. "Now, the practical." She thought for a moment. Earth was related to roots, as well as to sex. It was the root of all things. She didn't have to suddenly plow a furrow in the ground between them, though that would be fun.

Instead, Tara reached out and touched one of the nearby rose bushes. She twisted off a branch, ignoring the thorns that dug into her skin. She could heal herself later.

Instead, she held the bush up to Kyle. "Young," she said, touching the pale green leaves. This branch didn't have any buds on it yet. She cupped the bare stem between her palms, pressing her hands together, crushing the thorns into her skin, letting the rose feed from her own blood.

"Older," Tara said as she speeded up the branches inner systems. Buds started popping out at the ends of a few of the stems.

"Mature," Tara announced as the buds began to bloom. The heady scent of roses washed over her. The flowers were the same color as her fresh blood. They fed one another, her life essence seeping into the beauty that supported her soul.

"Aged," Tara finally said as the roses started to wilt, the petals shrinking as they turned black. Brilliant red hips formed where the roses had been. Tara could smell the sweet, almost tomato taste that they'd have when she used them for tea.

"Gone," Tara added as she pushed the branch all the way past maturity and into death. The leaves went from green, to bearing yellow spots, to blackened, finally drying up to dust. All the green left the stem itself. Even the thorns pushing into her palms turned brittle, snapping off, sticking deeply into her skin.

It was the cycle of life, going from a green growing thing into death, decaying so that something else could grow in its place. That was the lesson that Tara had taken from when she'd walked the circles, the old oak showing her the way to pass through the earth and beyond.

Tara released the now dead stalk and looked up at Kyle.

He held a questioning look on his face. "You're sure that's the way?" he asked her.

Tara blinked. She had always thought of that sort of magic as earth magic. "Yes?" she said, questioning herself now.

Kyle nodded. "That was very powerful magic," he said. "I don't believe it was earth magic, though."

"It is! It must be," Tara said. She'd explained to him about the tree who'd helped her.

He shook his head. "I think that's hedgewitch magic, not lore."

"What was I supposed to do instead? To show roots and a process?" Tara said, growing angry and frustrated. No one ever knew exactly what they'd be tested on, besides the various forms of magic.

"Oh, I don't know. Something simple. Like maybe changing water to wine or something," Kyle said.

His sarcasm didn't make sense to Tara. "What did I do wrong?" she asked simply. "Do you want me to do some other spell? I can try." Her exhaustion was filling her up now. She found it difficult to even stay standing up straight.

Kyle sighed. "I am willing to try to pass you within," he said, holding out his hands. "And while you're very powerful, I don't believe you're at the next level yet."

Tara bit back her frustration. If he'd just tell her what she needed to do, she'd do it!

But they didn't have a lot of time. She nearly reached for his hands, then paused, looking at her bloody palms.

"Just a moment," she said. She picked out the three thorns that had remained imbedded in her skin, the wiped the blood off on the grass nearby.

Kyle looked at her, alarmed. "What the hell did you do?" he asked. He grabbed her wrists and turned her palms up so that he could see.

"I fed the roses what they needed so that they could mature and die," Tara said. She looked back up at him. "Not part of the earth process?"

"No," Kyle said. He kept hold of her wrists, not allowing her to take his hands with her dirty ones.

Kyle called on Areebin first, the protector of souls, then Brigid, then finally Sammil.

The other two times that Kyle had cast the spell to pass Tara within, she'd felt a jolt, then everything cleared.

This time, the shock was clear and sharp, as if she'd just touched a live electric wire. However, instead of the world seeming clearer, she heard a loud buzzing in her head.

Kyle released her hands and stepped back, shaking his head.

"What was that?" Tara asked. She shook her head again. She felt even weaker than she had before.

"I think…I think that we shouldn't have done this at all," Kyle said. "This diminished your powers this time."

Tara nodded. She could tell that.

"It's like you stepped me back, away from the circles I'd already passed through," she said, the hissing noise inside her head turning into a loud roar, as though a waterfall had just sprung up a few feet away.

Kyle nodded. "That's exactly what it seems like," he said. "You've gone too far over into being a hedgewitch," he said. "The schooled witch part of you is leaving."

Tara sighed out loud. Great. This ritual was supposed to help her gain more power, not take away some of what she'd already had.

"What am I going to do now?" she said. She hated the plaintive note in her voice, but magic was really all she had at this point.

"You're going to call an earth elemental," Kyle said firmly. "If you can."

***

TARA SPENT the night sleeping restlessly. She kept dreaming that something was poking her in the back. Was it her powers trying to make their way back inside of her? She had no idea. Every time she turned around, there was nothing there.

Well, except for the one time when the dream turned nightmarish and the ghost of Martin started haunting her. He looked dark, while at the same time, she could see through him to the rock wall behind him, that still held an impression of his shadow. He'd become a simple ghoul, slobbering after whatever life she might grant him.

It was icky and she desperately needed a shower by the time she got up.

She spent the day volunteering at Hallowed Ground. It was good to be reminded that she still had a community. Service went well, and Kaede let her go early so that she might, maybe, perhaps, be able to catch up on her sleep.

At least that was what Tara told Kaede. In actuality, Tara had decided that she needed to see if she could call an earth element on her own.

She'd deeply shocked Kyle with the magic she'd performed the night before. She still wasn't certain why. Was it because she'd used her own blood to fuel the spell? That she'd brought a rose branch from young and growing to producing and then all the way into death? Or was it something else?

He hadn't been able to explain it, and she was still at a loss for what she should have done instead.

Tonight, it would just be her and the gentle earth. Or at least that was what she'd planned on. She didn't know if the Riprap man would show up if she was trying to call an earth spirit. She was tired of running from him, though.

She felt daring, trying this on her own. Maybe it was a dumb idea. Maybe it wasn't. She didn't know, and at this point, she was too tired to care.

Was this the essence of hedge magic?

Tara walked along the river, calling Mulinohana to her side as she ambled. He didn't ask her if she was sure of what she was doing, just walked beside her, lending her his great strength.

Would Mulinohana insure that whatever earth spirit she called would not be as strong as he was? Possibly. But she'd rather have him by her side than put any more of her friends in danger.

They reached a wide spot on the river walk. On the one side, a steep bank covered in blackberry bramble went down to the water's edge. On the other side, a beautiful fountain splashed.

Tara found herself drawn to the water. She didn't recall seeing this fountain before. It was made out of a polished, brownish-red stone that was speckled with white. The fountain itself was maybe five feet across. A single column rose in the center, fluted along the side. The water flowed out across a flat top with four carved channels in it, splashing down into the basin below.

The water felt cool and soft against Tara's fingers. Her palms had almost completely healed from the ordeal the night before—had some of it just been an illusion? That she hadn't even realized she'd been casting? Or had all of it been real?

Her palms suddenly tingled under the water from the fountain. Tara gasped. When she looked up, she realized that she wasn't in Portland anymore. Or at least not the physical space. Instead of buildings in the distance, all she saw was a wide open field, carpeted in lush summer grass, silvered by the full moon directly overhead. She heard the river behind her, the waters suddenly grown fierce and wild.

Mulinohana no longer stood beside her, but she still heard his voice in the splashing water. She washed her face in the fountain, the cool water tasting sweet on her lips.

Then she strode out into the field, ready to try her hand at the next calling.

***

Tara stood in the center of the open area. Trees loomed in the distance, cutting off the rest of the land. In the distance, she still heard the gushing fountain, as well as the rushing of the waters. The air smelled of sunbaked rocks, warm and earthy, remembering the brilliance of the sun from earlier that day.

"I call upon Sammil, the protector of the people, to watch over the rightness of my deeds. Brigid too, hear my prayer, defender of the earth. May the Old Mother moon light my path and keep me away from darkness, and may the wind goddesses Hayvu and Eural carry their righteousness to me."

Tara paused, considering what she needed to do next. She'd chosen a spot that was slightly more bare, where the earth wasn't completely covered in grass.

"I place my hand here," Tara said, easily kneeling and laying her palm against the cool dirt, "and I call to the firmament, to those spirits who are fundamental to us all. I have great work to do elsewhere. Hear my plea and rise to my cause."

Was that her imagination? Or had the ground just trembled?

Tara pressed her will down into the earth. She clenched her fingers in the dirt, trying to draw up a cohesive spirit.

She knew they were there, coursing through the earth like currents in a stream. She could feel the edges of them, but she didn't know how to pull one up or direct it.

"Oh powers of the earth!" Tara called. "I need your aid! Help me prevent the destruction of the west coast!"

A groaning filled the air.

That wasn't her imagination. The ground was truly shuddering.

Tara stayed where she was, kneeling with one hand placed on the earth.

A shadow rose up in front of her. It gained height quickly, growing from knee-height to far over her head.

It was changed into a grass-covered hill, then continued transforming as she watching, a head forming first, then the body slimming down, until there was a neck, arms, and a torso. It didn't bother rising up above that, or forming legs.

Tara swallowed against a suddenly dry throat.

She'd asked to speak to an earth elemental.

Seemed that someone, or some*thing*, had heard her plea.

EIGHT

The drowning of the city of Vanport was so very satisfying. It took less than two hours for the entire place to be wiped off the face of the earth. Nothing of it remains except the mighty river. However, I got too close to the destruction. I let myself be carried away in the celebration of the river. I cannot stay here. My physical body is not necessary for most of the work I do. I have learned how to travel far and do much without it. I will instead set it to live someplace else, someplace safe. Someplace far from the river, where the waters cannot find me. For I intend to live forever, as long as Portland maintains her shining light.

Wilson Evermore, Sole Initiate of the Mighty River and Destroyer of Vanport, 1948

TARA STOOD UP SLOWLY. Though she was tall, nearly six feet, the creature in front of her was easily twice her height. It had taken on a vaguely human shape in order to speak with her, though the face was covered in grass that shone in the light of the full moon. The air smelled of fresh dirt and grass.

If Tara was being fanciful, she'd say that the creature had grown bangs over its forehead, while keeping the rest of its hair cut short around its ears. Its cheeks were flat and it had a weak chin, reminding her of the Riprap man. Dark holes would do for eyes, as well as just a small bump that worked as a suggestion of a nose.

You ask for help, the creature said. The words didn't reach Tara's ears. Instead, they vibrated through her bones, as if she was listening to the language of earthquakes. Her breastbone tingled as the words passed through her.

"I do," Tara said. "What do you know of the Riprap man?"

Strong, the creature said. *Very strong.*

"Yes. He plans on sending powerful tremors through the earth, enough to destroy all the land along the west coast," Tara said.

The creature nodded, and waved its left hand.

Suddenly, a bas relief map of the west coast of the United States sprang up. Forests wound their way up and down the coast. The major cities were highlighted with bright red lights, while the mountains sprang up blue and cold.

Interesting, the creature said. Fault lines appeared in the map, cracking the earth apart. The city lights dimmed, then bled away. Mountains crumbled. The west half of the map disintegrated. Tara could see it falling into the sea after the earthquakes that the Riprap man would cause.

You want to stop it, the creature rumbled. *Why?*

Tara held herself steady, not taking a step back when the creatures eyes bored into her. "I want to prevent such a huge loss of human life," she said.

Even though the creature was not human, the shrug it gave was recognizable. *You are like ants. More will come.*

"But these lives will be lost. And you will lose many of your hills," she added. How did she impress upon the earth that humans were important?

You would battle instead, the creature said.

"Yes," Tara said when it appeared that it wanted her to answer. "I would stop the Riprap man. Prevent the huge earthquakes."

The creature nodded thoughtfully. *Let me show you.*

The original map fell away. Tara saw a representation of herself suddenly standing in that space. The rest of her coven also appeared. Soot was there, as were Teruko and Mulinohana. They all stood in an open field. Tara recognized the park, close to Hallowed Ground, tall, modern apartment buildings surrounding the small green square.

The Riprap man stood on the other side of the park, facing them. Behind him stood the witches he'd once bound. Tara could tell they were under his control, as they moved in a jerky fashion, and their stare was fixed.

Suddenly, a shape rose in front of the fighting Tara. She recognized it as the cousin of the creature she currently talked with. It had two same weird haircut, the same stocky build, but it also had legs. It was roughly the same height as she was, though twice as wide.

The Riprap man and the earth creature ran at each other. The clash was deafening. They tore at one another, great hunks of earth and rock flying. They both roared. Neither appeared to be able to get the upper hand.

And the ground started to tremble.

Tara and her friends tried to hold the very earth together as the Riprap man and the earth elemental fought. The coven of the Riprap man still worked with him, channeling their energy into the fault line.

Even before it happened, Tara knew the outcome.

The clash of the two earth elementals was going to be disastrous. Neither of them knew any other way of fighting, than to use and destroy the very earth they stood on.

The ground began to undulate, as though it was no longer solid but made of water. Tara felt sick to her stomach. Solid earth was *not* supposed to move that way. All around the battling witches she saw the nearby buildings start to fall.

Still the Riprap man and the earth element fought on. Their raging fueled the tremors, causing the land to tear itself apart.

It was too late. The Tara in the vision couldn't stop the two creatures. She destroyed Soot, Teruko, even Mulinohana in her attempts to separate the two fighters. Lucius died as well.

The Riprap man and the earth elemental fought on, raging out of the park and into the nearby street. Everywhere they went, destruction followed, a deep fault line that destabilized the earth.

They fought for two days, Tara saw. In the end, at least the earth elemental was successful, managing to smash the Riprap man into pieces.

However, half of the world had been destroyed in their wake.

When the battle was finally over, Tara turned from the terrible sight back to the earth creature in front of her. "Does it have to be that way?" she asked. "Is that the only outcome?"

The creature gave her that very human shrug again. *A chance. A very small chance it works another way.* The creature cocked its head to the left, looking at her. *Are you willing to take it?*

Tara took a deep breath, then let it out, shaking her head.

She hadn't realized how much damage an earth element might do. Particularly when faced with another one, like the Riprap man.

Wise, the creature said. It nodded. *Hope for you yet.*

With a sound like gentle wind blowing through newly fallen leaves, the creature dissolved back into the earth. Tara felt the ripples of its departure deep in the earth. The smell of daisies came to her, slightly sour but bright.

Tara paused for a moment, then she folded her hands in front of her in prayer and bowed her head. "Thank you for hearing my prayers, for coming to my call," she said loudly.

Then she turned and walked back toward the fountain.

Mulinohana no longer stood beside the fountain. She saw his watery face in the bowl, the water from the fountain splashing down on it.

"Did you get what you needed?" he asked.

Tara shook her head. Then shrugged. "Maybe," she said. "I know that I can't fight the Riprap man. Anything strong enough to defeat him will destroy too much. And the witches that he bound are being forced to work for him."

"What will you do?" Mulinohana said.

"I don't know," Tara said. "But I must find another way."

THE QUESTIONS that Tara had followed her into her dreams that night. She floated on a boat woven out of rose petals. She herself was tiny as well, the bank of the river towering over her head. Each thorn on the blackberry bramble was as long as her arm. She felt she could swim on the scent of the flowers.

Golden words appeared in the water, as if drawn there with fire. The wind kept tugging her this way and that, instead of giving her time to think or respond. She shivered as she tried to steer her tiny craft, but the twig she used for a rudder wasn't solid enough to resist the elements.

How was she going to stop the Riprap man? How could she defeat something so strong, without fighting him? When was he going to strike? She knew they were living on borrowed time at this point.

There had to be something she could do. But she kept going round and round in her boat, never getting anywhere. She felt as though she was circling the drain.

Finally, as dawn started to slide its light around the edges of her window shade, Tara had an idea.

At one point, the Riprap man had been the protector of Portland. He'd gone about it in a strange manner, killing witches and binding their souls to the bridges of Portland so that it wouldn't be flooded again. However, Tara had the impression from Mulinohana that the Riprap man had at one time cared greatly about the city.

Could he be made to care again?

Tara couldn't bind the Riprap man to herself. Even if she had the power, that was just delaying the inevitable problem that would occur when she died. He'd be cast free again and would cause more mischief.

Could she bind him to the city itself? Make him a protector again? Would that work? Could he be made to be a savior instead of a destructor?

Tara wasn't sure if it was possible to change the man's basic nature. He was a killer, had been one for well over a century, now. What sort of sacrifices would he demand in order to keep the city safe? Whose souls would he demand?

Though as usual, Tara had more questions than answers, for the first time in a long while, she felt as though she might be on the right path.

As Tara was walking toward her MAX stop, heading to the Y for her morning classes, a melodious voice asked her, "Must you really be so cheerful this early in the morning?"

Tara stopped and smiled at Lucius, who'd just appeared beside her. "I'm normally not this cheerful this early," she assured him jovially. "I just might, perhaps, have a plan."

Lucius was beautifully dressed as always, this time in a cream-colored shirt with wide blue stripes and gray trousers. His black leather boots shined as though they'd once been mirrors. He carried his cane with him. As Tara watched, he appeared to be leaning on it more he usually did.

"Does your plan perhaps *not* involve the death of all creatures on the west coast?" Lucius said.

Tara bobbed her head from side to side, as if thinking. "Perhaps," she said.

"Then why are you so cheerful?" Lucius asked.

"Why are you in such a bad mood? What happened? Where have you been for the last few days? We were worried about you," Tara said.

"I shall tell you my news in a bit," Lucius said sourly. "Though may I assure you that I believe I may have something of a plan as well."

"Good!" Tara said. "Do you want to hear what I've been up to lately?"

"May as well," Lucius said with a sigh. "as I'm assuming that I can't possibly dissuade you from going about your business today."

Tara shrugged. "I have a job," she said seriously. "I don't have enough money that I could just go gallivanting off whenever I feel like it. I need to work in order to make money so I can live."

Lucius nodded. "I've noticed that is a failing with most people. This need to make a living."

"Inconvenient for you, I know."

"Terribly so. But do tell me your adventures, then I'll tell you mine."

Tera told Lucius of her failure to pass within, how she felt as though Kyle's spell to move her to the next circle had actually removed some of her powers, so that she was no longer as advanced with it came to the circles of the schooled witches.

"Fascinating," was Lucius's comment. He actually did look rather interested in her account. "You aged a rose branch in your bare hands?"

Tara nodded, then shrugged. "Circle of life, you know? I figured that was what he was looking for, in terms of the circle of earth."

"I'm sure I wouldn't know," Lucius said. "Strange, though, that he wouldn't tell you ahead of time. Hadn't he prepared a wind for you that first time?"

"He had," Tara said, nodding. An uncomfortable thought occurred to her for the first time. "Wait. You don't think he weakened me on purpose?"

"No, that doesn't sound like our friend Kyle," Lucius said. "And I know he's still true. No, I think he didn't have anything in mind because he isn't ready to pass to that level yet himself."

Tara nodded, taking a deep breath. Yes, that might have been part of it Kyle was at the same level as she was, in the circle of water. He'd never stepped beyond.

Had it been wrong of them to assume that maybe he could? "Should I have worked with a stronger practitioner? Like Kaede?" Tara said. Though she didn't believe that Kaede knew the passing within spell. Maybe Kyle could teach it to zir…

"You need to ask one of your witches," Lucius said. "I wouldn't know." He paused, then added, "As for weakening you, is that really what happened? Or did Kyle clear the way for you?"

Before Tara could reply, Lucius held up his hand so she'd let him continue. "Are you now a stronger hedgewitch? Now that you aren't as tied down to those circles?"

"I don't know," Tara said. "I don't think that's what he meant to do, at any rate."

Then she thought for a moment. She'd never had such an easy time going into a projected plane before. That she'd traversed so easily with Mulinohana, walking beside the river one moment, then talking to an earth creature the next.

Maybe Kyle hadn't really weakened her after all.

"Was that all?" Lucius said as the MAX train finally pulled up to the station.

"Oh no, there's more, but you'll have to come with me to hear it," Tara told him with a grin.

"Very well," Lucius said.

While Tara was certain that Lucius wouldn't bother with anything so mundane as a ticket, she also assumed that he could turn away any of the transportation cops who might ask for one.

Lucius sat down on the plastic seat beside her with obvious distaste. At least the train smelled more like left over grape gum than the urine from a homeless person.

Tara told Lucius about the night before, and meeting with the earth creature. How it had convinced her that if they somehow managed to conjure a creature strong enough to destroy the Riprap man, it would still have disastrous consequences.

"I am impressed, my dear," Lucius said. "No, really," he assured her. "I have a suspicion of the nature of the creature you spoke with. It does not abide fools gladly. You do realize that you had as great a chance of being destroyed as of it speaking with you, yes?"

"No, I didn't know," Tara said, turning to look at Lucius. "It could have killed me?"

"Easily," he assured her. "But I'm glad it didn't. My adventures sound rather pale in comparison, now."

"I'd still like to hear," Tara assured him.

Lucius looked over at her with a wide grin. "I first tried talking with some of my other brethren. That…didn't go as well as planned." He grimaced and shifted awkwardly in his seat.

Tara's eyes went to his leg. Had Lucius been injured? Had he had some sort of battle with others of his kind?

When she looked back up at his eyes, he shook his head at her.

Seemed that she would never know the full story.

"Since they didn't seem inclined to help us, I went to meet with the other witches. The ones under the bridges. We may have become allies."

"LET me tell you about the other coven," Lucius said. They were sitting at Hallowed Ground, chairs pulled into a circle. He had assured them that they had one more night before the Riprap man would attack. He was waiting for the dark of the moon, which would occur the following evening.

The room was colder than usual. Tara sat with her coat pulled over her shoulders. They'd served some sort of cream sauce that night for service, and the smell of the butter and milk left a sour taste in her mouth. Ginny also seemed to feel the cold, and had two sweaters on. Kyle, Richard, and Kaede appeared to be comfortable in just T-shirts.

"I went to visit Dorothy first, as I felt she might be the most open to my suggestions," Lucius started. "And because I already knew her name," he added, nodding toward Richard.

"It appears that the Riprap man is using them to further his cause," Lucius said. "They are being trained to spread the tremors that he's started, send them out deep under the earth. Not all of them are in agreement with his plan. They know that if they do as he asks, they'll destroy much of the world above them. However, he'll also release his hold on them. They'll be free."

"Do they believe that he'll actually let them go?" Tara said. "Do they trust his word?"

"Not all of them," Lucius said. "Which is why he's had to work so hard at controlling them. If he could have, he would have initiated his plan long ago. He needs their help. So he's had to work at directing their will. He's planning on bringing all the bridges down, in addition to the general chaos."

Tara nodded. None of the bridges had been retrofit with enough earthquake resistant materials. Only the single port had been upgraded and would possibly survive.

"Fortunately, I have managed to bring them all over to my side," Lucius said with a very satisfied smile. "Our side, as it were. Once the battle is engaged, they will change the direction of their focus from spreading the Riprap man's chaos to stopping him."

"How can you guarantee that?" Kaede asked. "You've already said that they will be under his control."

"It's…complicated," Lucius said. His smug smile didn't decrease in the least. "But may I assure you, we have a good plan."

"And if ye fail, so will the world," Ginny said darkly.

"Believe me, I understand the risks, better than you lot," Lucius said, his manner growing colder. "I will not fail."

Tara glanced over at Kyle. He gave her a small nod. While she understood that part of it was Lucius's pride speaking, she also knew that the being would do everything in his power to succeed this time.

"So we have something of a plan," Tara said. "Or yet another plan. Where should we meet?"

"Where should the battle be joined?" Richard said. He seemed most determined of all of them.

"Here," Kaede said firmly. "It needs to be here. We can protect this spot the best."

"I'm not sure that's what we need," Kyle said slowly. "We need a place we can protect, yes. But we need to actually meet them in battle. They wouldn't be able to even come inside here."

Kaede looked unhappy, but nodded. Hallowed Ground was that protected at this point. Everyone felt it when they walked in. It was probably one of the safest places in the city.

"Do we want to meet at the park nearby?" Tara asked. "That was where the creature showed me we'd chosen for the battle. I mean, we *lost* there, but we were also following a different strategy. That way we'd be close to Hallowed Ground, but not actually on the premises."

"It is a wide open park," Ginny said. "But it's kind of sterile, you know? It isn't a real living space. Not green enough."

Tara found herself nodding. She never would have put it that way, but what Ginny said made sense. They needed someplace more green.

"But I don't want to leave the city limits," Tara said. "That won't work, not with our plans to try to bind the Riprap man."

"We need to be close to the river," Lucius said suddenly. "Near the foot of one of the bridges. That way, we can work better with the witches bound there."

"Mulinohana will be better able to aid us," Tara said. "And probably both Soot and Teruko as well."

"And my winds," Ginny said.

"How about Hayden island?" Richard suggested.

"No," Kyle said after a moment. "Not enough park. We need to be somewhere along the river front."

They finally settled on a park near the Hawthorne bridge. While there would be people around, they felt certain that they could hide themselves well enough.

The location selected, a plan in place, Tara and the others reluctantly said goodnight. None of them really wanted to leave. That would mean that the night was nearly over. The next day would come.

Whether they liked it or not, the next battle would be upon them.

However, Tara had had too many last days and nights. As she'd said before, she was getting too old to regularly do this saving the world shit.

She ended up walking out the door with Richard, who seemed determined to remain friendly with her. He offered to walk her up to the MAX station.

They shared a comfortable silence as they walked. It had rained earlier, and the air still smelled of wet blacktop. Streetlights reflected orange against the high clouds. Though the night was calm, Tara pulled her jacket more tightly around her.

"So we're doing it again," Richard said softly.

Tara nodded. "Hopefully this will be the final time," she said.

"I wanted you to know that I thought about what you said," Richard said after a few more moments of quiet. "About possibly approaching Lucius, seeing if there's some way for me to stop being so mundane, and maybe acquire some magic."

"As long as you still understand that even if you had magic, that wouldn't change my mind about dating you," Tara felt the need to say.

"I get that," Richard said. His eyes stared off into the far distance. "I really do. And I want you to understand that if I decide to go through with it, it isn't for you. I couldn't make that big of a decision based on someone else. It has to be about me, and what is right for me."

"Good," Tara said. She'd always respected Richard. His consideration made her like him even more.

"I still haven't made up my mind," Richard added after a moment. "I mean, I've already talked with Lucius about it. He said it may be possible, particularly since I've been so involved with the group already, and have an affinity towards, as he put it, the unseen arts."

"Really?" Tara said. She had no idea. "So it's possible?"

Richard hesitated, but then nodded. "It is. He couldn't guarantee it. All he could assure me was that it wouldn't be pleasant. And that I might go mad."

Tara nodded. That actually sounded about right. She'd heard stories in both of her covens about people not being able to handle the power once they discovered it. There wasn't anything anyone could do about it. They had to either come to grips with it themselves, or else, in this modern age, be thoroughly medicated so that they didn't have to deal with it.

"So I might pursue it. I might not," Richard warned.

Tara shook her head. "If we make it through tomorrow, you'll do it," she said.

"No, really, I haven't decided yet."

"Yes, you have," Tara said. "I do know you better than just about anyone else. If you've come far enough along that you're willing to talk with someone about it, it means you've made up your mind. Might not be willing to admit it yet. That's all."

Richard merely shrugged. "I really don't know," he said slowly. He sighed.

"What is it?" Tara asked.

"If I do take on any magic, any at all, I'll never have another Jeannie," he said all in a rush.

"Is there a Jeannie now?"

Richard shook his head. "But it's one of the considerations. Like you, I'm probably not going to want to date outside of my religion, as it were. Which means, if I pursue magic, I'm going to severely limit my dating pool." He paused for a moment. "I'm not like you. I need a partner. Someone to hang out with regularly. More regularly."

"Okay," Tara said, though she didn't really understand. She liked the amount of social interaction she currently had. Didn't need anymore.

"And that's why you were right, keeping us as friends," Richard said. "I get it now. It doesn't have to do with the magic. It's because socially, we'd both have to make a lot of compromises. I get it."

"Thank you," Tara said after a few moments. She'd been worried that he might try to press his luck, or that they'd be awkward together. She really did consider him a dear friend, and nothing more.

"Thank you for still being my friend," Richard said. He bumped shoulders with her. "I need this group as well," he continued. "Who else is going to give me such fascinating research to conduct?"

That made Tara grin. It appeared as though they were healing after all.

As the MAX drew up, Tara turned to Richard and said, "Just one other thing to consider when you're thinking about that dating pool. Most witches are still female. Being a straight male in such a pool may actually increase your chances."

She gave him a quick hug then boarded her train, leaving him still gaping.

NINE

Portland is my city. It holds my heart. I've looked over her, protected her, as well as cheered on her progress. However, I must admit that she has grown foreign to me. I am feeling old, suddenly. I watch the trees disappear, the hills sprouting houses instead. I still have the mighty work to do for Mulinohana, keeping the witches at bay, binding their hearts to the bridges so that Portland can continue to thrive. I find myself leaving the city regularly now, for the first time in decades. I've set my physical body in the hills east of the city. The area had been declared a wildlife refuge, so it won't be developed. The path to the meadow is difficult to access. None will threaten me there. I sit in the meadow and look out on the rocks, let the rain fall on my skin, watch the butterflies flit across the grass. Water flows far in the creek far below me. I can just hear the sound of it passing during the spring. I must admit, as much as the rushing sound soothes me, the cliffs that I watch bring me joy as well.

Wilson Evermore, Long-Standing Guardian and Ancient Soul, 1961

Tara woke early that morning, unable to sleep late.

Today was the day. She and the others would either bind the Riprap man, stop his plans from coming to fruition.

Or the entire west coast would be destroyed.

There still might be some damage. She and the other witches would do their part to keep it to a minimum.

Tara hugged Teruko to her chest for a moment, despite his protests. He wanted to always be the one to initiate contact. Normally she respected that, but this morning, she needed a bit more. He settled against her breasts after a moment, and started up a loud purr.

Soot lay down long her back, spine to spine, warming her up that way. She felt Mulinohana's presence as well, the sound of water splashing somewhere in the distance, like a comforting fountain.

Thus bolstered by her companions, Tara finally felt ready to face the day.

Her classes at the Y flew by that morning. She spent extra time praising the younger children. They would need this warm memory if the world went to hell that evening.

It surprised her that Lucius was waiting for her at her bus stop. "Is everything all right?" Tara asked as she came rushing up.

"You need to go teach because you need the money, correct?" Lucius said, studying her intently.

"True," Tara said. "Though I might teach anyway. I do enjoy it."

"Really?" Lucius said, surprised.

Tara smiled at him. "However, if money were no object, I'd like to open a teashop," she said quietly.

"That makes more sense," Lucius said. "Thank you."

He turned and started striding confidently down the sidewalk.

"See you tonight?" Tara called after him.

"Absolutely," Lucius assured her, waving his hand negligently, not bothering to turn around and look at her again.

Tara made her way into the bus and found a seat. The person in the seat in front of her was eating some sort of spicy potato chips, reminding her that dinner was still a few hours away. She sat on the hard seat and looked out the window. Everyone was going along their business, as usual. Just as she had been. No one knew what was coming.

Then again, life just happened that way. You never knew what was just around the corner. Whether it be the Riprap man or the love of your life.

Tara shook her head and realized that she'd fallen into a funk. The last time she'd thought the world was ending, she'd started making a lot of plans so she'd have something to look forward to, to keep her moving.

She needed to keep moving this time as well.

She pulled up her phone and started looking at real estate sites, searching for commercial space that might work as a teashop.

She was nowhere near being able to fulfill that dream.

But she recognized how important just having the dream was.

ALASKA and two of the other regulars were waiting for Tara when she reached Hallowed Ground. They were all standing in the industrial kitchen.

"The water's filled for you," Alaska told her. "The cups have been set out. We didn't want to touch your teas, though." She was in all black today, artfully torn and patched, her pale cheeks looking pinched.

"Tonight's the night, right?" Eric asked. He'd been one of her first clients. The calming teas she'd made for him had helped him get better grades in school. He'd grown less pale over the year, more sure of himself, though he was still shy around girls. Tara wondered sometimes if he really liked them, or if he was actually attracted to boys instead and was still figuring it out.

"What do you mean?" Tara asked. She didn't want to lie to them, but she didn't want to put them into harm's way.

"The next fight. It's on," Alaska said, trying to sound much fiercer than she looked.

Tara sighed. "It is," she said slowly. "And I expect you to be safely tucked away in your beds."

Shanice rolled her eyes. She had her hair done in tight braids across her skull, though she'd been threatening to shave it all off, as her feminism didn't have time for your style shit. "Uh huh. So that you can come by and tell us a nice bedtime tale? Not buying it."

"It's going to be dangerous," Tara warned. "And I can't afford to have my focus split, trying to protect you while at the same time defeat the bad guy."

The three looked at each other. "We get that. We really do," Eric said. He gave her an earnestly stubborn look. "But you can't keep us away. We'll stay back, out of trouble. You might need extra help, though. And so we'll be there. Whether you want us there or not."

Tara knew she couldn't argue them out of it. "Thank you," she said. "It does mean a lot to me that the community is so committed to helping each other. I hope we won't need your assistance. It is good to know it's there."

That made all three smile at her, though Eric still narrowed his eyes slightly, as if wondering if this was actually some sort of trick.

"So let's get this party rolling," Tara said, lifting up the curtain on the shelf that held her teas.

THE AFTERNOON PASSED QUICKLY. It seemed that most everyone in the neighborhood had to stop by for a quick hello that afternoon. Tara had faced the possibility of the world ending by herself before, or at the very least, her world. It was odd to have an entire support network to go through the rough times with her. But good.

After service that night, Tara and Kaede made their way to the riverside park, taking their time and walking through more than one neighborhood as they made their way. Several small groups of people from the neighborhood followed after them. Tara expected that once they arrived at the park, phone trees would be activated and a lot more people would just stop by.

Fortunately, the day had been sunny and nice. A refreshing breeze had picked up as evening had settled in. People rushed by in their cars, hurrying to get to their families. The air smelled of gas and hot sidewalk. It felt good to Tara to stretch her legs, even after working hard all day then standing through much of the evening meal.

"What does Portland mean to you?" Tara asked as they strolled.

Kaede gave her a quick smile. "I've always been attracted to the old buildings," ze said. "The Chinatown gate. The warehouses in the Pearl district. The craftsman houses out in the various neighborhoods. Portland has so many great old buildings downtown still. Like the courthouse. You know?"

"I do," Tara said. She planned on weaving those into the binding spell. Along with the parks and the waterways, which were her first love.

The park was mostly empty by the time they arrived, one last group just finishing up their collective meal. Kyle and Lucius had already staked out the area where the coven would be meeting, close enough to the water that Tara could smell it. Boats passed by as they watched, the sky darkening. The sound of cars passing far over their heads on Hawthorne led a steady beat to the night.

Tara felt the others join them. Even without being in a circle and directing their magic together, just their presence brought a certain hum to the air. In addition, she felt the rest of the community that had gathered, under the trees. They had kept their promise and had stayed far enough away that they weren't in immediate danger. It was still nice to know they were close by, and could be counted on if necessary.

Hopefully, it wouldn't be necessary.

Gracefully, the coven joined together. It was like winds melding. At one moment, they were each their own individual force. Then they braided together, their force multiplying one another.

Tara thanked the gods and goddesses for their protection, their love, their support. She asked for their aid before the great battle, to carry their truth to the four corners of the world, to save the people of the coast.

When Tara finished, she looked out over the river, feeling the deep currents in the waters. They ran like warm breezes over her skin, down to her fingers.

Then Tara pushed her senses under the earthy, searching for the currents there. She felt them as she had the night before, aware of their existence but no idea how to grasp onto them. They flowed through her fingers like sand. However, she could feel the spot on the earth where her friends stood behind her, prepared like she was.

They were ready. Or at least as ready as they would ever be.

After a final deep breath, Tara began her challenge.

———

THE GROUP HAD DEBATED how they'd draw the Riprap man to them. Tara had agreed to try Lucius's suggestion first: that she challenge the Riprap man individually.

It was a guy thing that Tara didn't really understand, but she was willing to try.

So Tara reached deep under the earth and sent out a quiet call. A loud one might bring tremors that she did not want.

I challenge the Riprap man.

It was a simple enough sentiment.

She would bet that no one else had ever done such a thing.

I challenge the Riprap man.

Though Tara didn't add the phrase, she still thought about double-dog daring him to show his face.

She felt a trembling in the distance, as if a warning light several miles away had just come on.

I challenge you.

With a great roar, the Riprap man appeared in front of Tera.

She examined him carefully. The body he projected was similar to his physical form. This shape was more manlike, more defined. He had blue eyes and a more human face. Like the first time she'd seen him, he was formally dressed in an old-fashioned brown wool suit and vest, a brilliant white shirt with a black string tie around his neck, and a bowler hat. The smell of wet ropes washed over her, a reminder of how he'd tried to kill her in the past.

Tara felt that she was underdressed suddenly, but she wasn't going to bother changing her appearance. She was wearing a comfortable gray men's T-shirt that fit her perfectly across her shoulders and chest, along with blue jeans and bright red sneakers.

While the Riprap man represented Portland's past, Tara represented the reality of Portland's present day. In addition, she felt that the community, stretched behind her, was really the future, of where the city needed to go.

"Surely you don't intend to actually fight me," the Riprap man said. "You and your little group aren't strong enough." His voice sounded rough, as if he hadn't been using it much lately.

Tara smiled at him. "No. I challenge you for control of the city," she said simply. "You've been the protector of Portland for an age. Time for you to let go and move on."

It was astonishing to her how wide the Riprap man's eyes grew. "You challenge me?" he asked, incredulous.

Yup. This obviously was the way to go.

Tara gave him her most impertinent grin. "I do. You don't seem very interested in protecting the place any more. Time to give it up, old man."

"You think you can do better?" the Riprap man sneered.

"I know we can," Tara said. "You intend to destroy the entire west coast. We want to save it."

The Riprap man scowled at her. "It's just you I want to stop. To blame. You ruined everything."

"So you're going to destroy the entire place, kill millions of lives, just to get even with me?" Tara said. "You're kidding, right? You know how ridiculous that sounds?"

"You broke my bonds," the Riprap man said. "You ripped apart my reason for being. It is only right that I should destroy everything you love."

"What if there's another way?" Tara asked.

"There is none," the Riprap man said. "Time for you to die."

Behind the Riprap man, the coven of witches who had all been bound to the bridges rose up.

The strength of the blast of power that struck Tara surprised her.

Weren't they supposed to be on her side?

She rallied her coven, keeping their power woven together. She didn't want to blast the witches in return. They needed them. Needed the binding they had to work against the Riprap man.

Tara turned her focus back to the enemy in front of her. He laughed and took a few more steps toward her.

The smell of wet ropes returned. Tara felt them sliding across her ankles. They'd bind her to the earth where she'd be helpless as the bridges tumbled and the waters rose.

No. She would not allow that.

She sent her own binding out to the Riprap man, her winds racing around him. She would not allow him to come closer. He couldn't reach her.

The Riprap man struggled. He seemed surprised by her strength.

He raised one hand behind him, making a gesture, asking for more.

The witches behind him complied. More power poured from them and into the Riprap man.

He moved one of his feet forward a few inches.

Tara risked looking behind her. What was happening? Why weren't they turning on him?

Lucius still stood there, a part of her coven, woven in with the rest.

However, his eyes had already turned back inside his head. Only the whites were showing. Tara felt his will seeping away. He was a drain on the group.

Instead of bringing the other witches to him, combining the covens, he was being taken over by them. And they were still too influenced by the Riprap man.

Tara didn't want to let Lucius go, release him from the circle of her coven.

She had no choice.

It was either weakening her group, or letting it get taken over from within. Tara released Lucius from the circle, sending him spinning away to the side.

Kaede immediately reached out to the community, drawing from their strength instead to bolster Tara and the others.

It wouldn't be enough. Tara could tell from the grin that the Riprap man gave her.

He was coming for her. Coming for her soul. And he'd take the city with him.

Tara pushed back again, drawing on everything she could. She took strength from the earth as well as the water. She would not go down easily. She pushed the Riprap man back another step, just through sheer force of will.

The witches behind him continued to pour strength into him, continued to bolster his attack.

The ground trembled under Tara's feet. She had to finish this. Soon. Or the Riprap man would end up tearing the world apart.

A warm blast of power nudged Tara's left side.

What was that? Was that Lucius?

Tara risked another look.

By releasing him from the coven, he'd been able to start working on his own again. He gave her a smile, then lifted his hands like an orchestra conductor.

The nature of the power pouring into the Riprap man changed in that instant.

Instead of supporting him, the magic of the witched began to tear at him, ripping away his strength.

The Riprap man tried taking another step forward Tara before he turned his head. Horror crossed his face as he realized what was happening.

The witches he'd bound were suddenly binding *him*.

Tara and her group added to the chains suddenly wrapping around the figure in front of her. They were huge boat chains, each link longer than her palm. Length after length of linked steel, passing around the Riprap man's body and then sinking into the rock.

The witches bound every single part of him, every rock, every muscles, every cell. He no longer had a heart that they could tug out and wrap chains around. Instead, they bound his will. It appeared to Tara like a core of steel, deep within the figure, unbending, but covered in rust and decay. The witches wrapped it in silken gauze woven from their will and desperation, soft but implacable.

The Riprap man roared and tried to escape. He flung himself down into the earth, only to be chased back above ground by the witches waiting for him there. He flew towards the water, intending to swim away.

Mulinohana rose like a water cyclone, unwilling to let him pass. The river spirit added his own fine lines of water binding the Riprap man's soul, blue and white ribbons added to the chains.

When the Riprap man tried to break free again, Ginny's winds, as well as Soot, kept him in place, not allowing him to step away. Even Teruko helped, setting up a terrible fire that the Riprap man had to turn away from.

And still the chains piled on, until the very figure was obscured by tons of metal links.

With a howl that came from his very soul, the Riprap man came to a stop before Tera. He dropped down onto his knees. Heavy links wrapped around his shoulders. Shackles now covered his wrists. He cried and moaned as he knelt there, his face aged, the stone pitted and flaking.

"I do not want to destroy you," Tara said, stepping forward. Or maybe gliding there, as it felt as though the power she directed lifted and carried her there. "But I will if I must."

The Riprap man raised his face toward her. "I have shown no mercy towards you or your kind. I do not expect any shown toward me."

"Why did you kill the witches?"

The Riprap man managed a minute shrug, the chains rattling. "The river directed me to, at first. They were not worthy of His attention."

"Who else is not worthy?" Tara asked.

"Those who would harm the bridges, hurt the city," the Riprap man said. "And those who have harmed me. Like you."

"Do you wish to become a protector again?" Tara said. That was the heart of the matter.

Miss Lucy was right, Tara might not have the will to actually kill the Riprap man, despite how he'd been brought low before her.

"No," the Riprap man said. "I will not lie to you. I cannot merely live for the city anymore."

Tara thought she understood. She'd seen the wilderness the Riprap man had chosen for placing his physical body. "What if you were to protect not just the city, but all her lands? The trees and forests surrounding her? The waters and the mountains?"

"I would still deal harshly with those who would mean the land harm," the Riprap man warned. "Their souls would still be mine."

Tara wondered if that was good enough.

The witches who had been bound by the Riprap man, who held him now in chains, came forward. "And those who would remain, who would not choose to pass on, we would also judge," they said in unison, a ghostly Greek chorus in the night. "So it would not just be his singular judgement of who posed a threat and who did not."

Tara liked that better. While she trusted that the Riprap man might exaggerate the harm that someone might pose, the witches more level heads. It wouldn't be judge, jury, and executioner, all wrapped into one warped soul.

"Would you be bound under those terms?" Tara asked.

The Riprap man nodded finally. "I would," he said. "For as long as my strength holds me. I would still protect the brilliant pearl of Portland, as well as her lands, from all who would do her harm."

"Thank you," Tara said. She reached for the chains still binding the Riprap man and started adding the places and things of Portland that were dear to her to each link. After she imbued a link, it would pass out of view and into the very body of the Riprap man itself.

The smell of the roses in the city, so sweet and pervasive. Especially the scent of the pioneer roses, that you could track from blocks away. As well as the smell of wet pavement and new concrete, the scent of old bricks and newly waxed floors. Coffee roasting, and fresh rosemary.

The sound of the river in the morning, gently slapping against an empty rowboat tied to a pier. Crickets and frogs sounding off in the mornings and evening, the loud call of a kingfisher as it dove into the water, the industrial sounds of the bees in the blackberry bramble. How the cars swished in the rain, the lonely sound of the train whistle, the chugging of a semi up the steep hills.

Tara thought of all the historic buildings, how long they'd stood, the marble and stone solid against the weather. The beautiful craftsman homes, with their leaded windows and individual designs. The wood that covered them, painted all different colors. The incredible backyards that many of them still had, with mature trees and amazing flowers.

She added in the surrounding wilderness. The feel of the bark of the pine trees, rough under her palms. The prick of the rose thorns. How soft the rain felt when it came in the spring, the chill of the winter that sank into your bones. Soft springy grass under her feet, along with the hardness of boulders and the steepness of cliffs.

The city held all the flavors she loved. Coffee sweetened with honey. Tea with dried blackberries and peppermint leaves. The yeasty sourdough that came from the bakeries in the Pearl District. The way a good steak tasted charbroiled when you went camping. Freshly picked blueberries. Cream and cheese from local cows.

Tara tried to wrap all the feelings and love she had for her city into the binding. She knew it wasn't enough. Just her memories weren't enough.

So Tara reached out to the community who waited under the trees, asking for their impressions of Portland, to help bind the Riprap man completely.

Wave upon wave of sights, smells, tastes, sounds, as well as the feel of so many things came through Tara, wrapping gently around the Riprap man, tying him firmly to all the good things. The warmth and love of the people, not just the places.

By the time they were finished, the Riprap man had changed. He still had the outward appearance of an old fashioned gentleman. However, the skin of his face had changed, as had his body.

Instead of being made of stone, he now appeared to be flesh and blood. But a modern twist had been added.

Tattoos blossomed across all of his skin. Brilliantly colored scenes of the city intermingled with the rivers, waterfalls, forests and mountains nearby. His entire body was now one singular painting set deep into his flesh. The tattoos flowed up his neck, down across the backs of his hands, and everywhere else.

The Riprap man staggered up to his feet, swayed for a moment, then he found his strength and stood proud and tall.

Tara could feel the way he reached his roots down, into the very land itself, feeling the firmament on which the city had been built. His gaze reached up to the underbelly of the bridge they stood beside, then past it, to the clouds. He looked all around himself, turning a small circle.

"This is…different," he said slowly.

His voice sounded much more melodic than Tara had ever heard it. She still caught the scent of wet ropes, but also of spring roses.

For the first time, the Riprap man gave Tara a real smile. "I could get used to this," he said softly. He banished his hat and jacket. A much younger man suddenly stood there, almost modern looking. "You can call me Wilson." he said. "Wilson Evermore."

"I am pleased to meet you, Wilson Evermore," Tara said. She strode forward and held out her hand.

Wilson paused for a moment, then reached out and shook it firmly. "No one has addressed me by that name in over a century," he said softly. "Thank you."

Tara nodded. He'd lost his name so long ago. What sort of man, being, protector, would it describe now?

The coven of witches that the Riprap man had once bound started drifting forward. One by one they touched him. Some of them disappeared slowly, leaving their long stasis and traveling forward to whatever the next place was for them.

Others, though, touched him and suddenly took on a stronger form. Some of the ink flowed out from Wilson, wrapping around their skin. They took on purpose and place beyond the bridges where they'd been bound, five witches in all.

It was a formidable force, Tara recognized. Instead of threatening each other, they could now all work together.

A community.

She felt her own coven form around her, stepping forward to see what they'd created. Ginny's winds appeared to be celebrating, dancing from one end of the line to the other. Kaede held out zir hands in welcome. Tara understood that ze was opening up Hallowed Ground to them, whenever they needed a respite. Kyle bowed to them, and she heard him pledging his use of law to uphold their decisions and to protect the lands as well. Richard vowed to answer any questions they may have, research whatever it was they needed.

Lucius granted them the ability to call on him if there was ever a great need.

The people behind them also stepped forward, pledging to do their part, to further the effects of the protectors. To heal Portland as much as was in their ability.

Tara finally spoke again. "Thank you, thank you, thank you. I cannot express how much joy this brings me."

Wilson gave her a huge smile. "I'll be seeing you," he said before he faded away with the other witches.

Tara couldn't help but grin. Finally, she'd be looking forward to his visits.

As well as the rest of her much more peaceful life.

"It wouldn't be that difficult," Lucius assured Tara.

She looked around the empty space, dubious.

For the past week, since the final battle, Lucius had been insistent that Tara accompany him to various commercial sites available for rent, trying to find the location for her eventual teashop.

Lucius had promised that he would loan Tara the money to start up her shop for as long as she needed it. It seemed like such a large outlay to her, as well as a huge project. And what if she failed?

But Lucius wouldn't hear any of her excuses, and just dragged her to the next location.

Tara just wasn't sure she was ready for this. Though as Lucius had pointed out, if not now, then when?

The most recent shop he'd brought her to might actually work. It was zoned for commercial and had been a retail shop at one point. A built-in counter was on the left, a few feet from the door. Wide windows looked out on a street. As it was near a university, there would be plenty of foot traffic.

Tara had determined that she wouldn't cook on the premises, and instead, would just sell others' goods. She already had the contact information from a number of different suppliers.

The amount of the loan worried Tara the most. Not just for renting the location, but for fixing it up, buying all her supplies, doing advertising, hiring staff. Kyle had assured her that Lucius would keep his word, and would never hound her for the remainder of it. The amount of interest was miniscule as well. And the contracts would have provisions for if Tara got behind in her payments, allowing her to step out of her obligations gracefully.

At least she'd gotten Lucius to agree that she needed to start small. At first, he'd been taking her to huge restaurant spaces, with over two thousand square feet of space. Finally they'd started visiting much smaller locations, more like two hundred sqaure feet. And he'd had to learn about locations as well. Putting up a shop out in the middle of the a suburban shopping mall, while she could charge a lot for her teas, wouldn't be right for the type of shop she had in mind.

This place, though…Tara turned silently in the space. She could already see the clean white chairs and tables that would take up most of the floor. There would be a corner over there for kids, with lower tables and maybe a basket of toys or games. Power strips would have to be added along the walls, so students could come in and work. She'd have to set hours, so that students didn't hog the tables but would willingly pay "table rent" as it were. One of the things that Richard had suggested was setting up the WiFi so that the password changed after someone had used it for a couple of hours.

Lucius stood there like a proud papa. "This is the longest you've spent in any place I've taken you," he said when she finally looked over at him. "Dare I hope that you might decide to take a chance on this?"

Tara sighed. It still seemed like so much. But she wasn't afraid of hard work.

Her mom and dad had also offered to help. As they'd grown so handy over the last decade or so, she knew that she could rely on them, and they'd actually be a help when they came out to visit.

Plus, she had a community now. So many of the teens from Hallowed Ground would be fighting for a chance to work in her teashop. They run fliers for her, spread the word to all their friends. They'd be there for whatever needed doing.

Tara looked around the empty space again. So much potential. So much hope.

If she was only willing to take the chance.

"Shall we?" Lucius said, a big grin on his face.

"I'm still not sure what you're getting out of this deal," Tara said, even as her heart was already starting to settle into this new space.

"I will not be with your coven for that much longer," Lucius said seriously. "You've done the most important, incredible work. Much more than I've ever thought humans could achieve, particularly in such a short amount of time."

"Thank you, I think," Tara said.

"You gave me a space," Lucius said. "I truly appreciate that, more than you know. I wasn't drifting, my kind don't drift or have the need to 'find ourselves' as you so quaintly put it. But we do need to pause now and again, dip our toes back in the stream of life before moving on. You gave me that experience."

"You're welcome," Tara said. She thought she understood. Lucius was as close to an immortal being as she'd ever met. It made sense that he'd float away from society now and again, then get closer for a time.

"So I wanted to return the favor," Lucius said. "Give you your own space. See what other amazing antics you might get up to with a modicum of support."

"I appreciate it," Tara said.

"But?" Lucius said with a heavy sigh.

"So," Tara said, "I'd like to take you up on your offer."

"Really?" Lucius said, sounding amazed and pleased.

"Really," Tara said.

It was time for her to have her own space to protect, to grow, to love.

RICHARD DECIDED to pass on Lucius's offer of seeing if he could pick up some magic. It was too big of a leap for him, to give up being fully mundane and possibly become something else. The risks were too great as well.

The following week, he also started dating someone new. He said he'd just needed a push, and thanked Tara once again for turning him down.

Kyle shyly showed up at the coven's next picnic with a date, a tall black man who had a ready smile and a hearty laugh. Tara had never seen Kyle be physical with anyone before, and was fascinated with them holding hands. She hoped it would work out for them.

Ginny turned out to be Tara's first hire for the teashop. Like Tara, she had a knack for creating the perfect, bespoke tea for a customer. She also had a better knack for hiring people than Tara did, so the teashop was quickly staffed with the perfect combination of people.

Tara still volunteered at Hallowed Ground, though she cut down the hours. Kaede found other people to man Tara's "teashop" in the community center, an older couple who were great with the teens, and able to give them what they needed, even if there was no longer any magic involved.

The tea shop, which Tara had very imaginatively called, "Tara's Teashop" had been open for three months before Wilson found the shop.

He looked much younger than the last time Tara had seen him. He still wore a long-sleeved shirt, despite the summer heat. But he also wore shorts and sandals, showing off muscular, tattooed legs. The colors of his tattoos were still amazing, as if they were all brand new.

Tara took one look at Wilson and reached for the purple heather, adding it to wild mint and tossing in a sprig of lemon thyme. She steeped it, then served it over ice for him, with a splash of lemonade and a hibiscus vinegar shrub.

"Thank you," Wilson said, raising his glass to her. He sipped it, then his eyes grew wide in surprise. "That's lovely," he said. He smiled, then added, "It tastes like a wonderful combination of old and new."

"Good," Tara said. She was about to step out from behind the counter to talk with him when one of the staff called her name.

When she turned back, Wilson was gone.

No matter. She knew that he'd blessed her shop, blessed her place, just as he was doing for every place he traveled to.

There were a lot of places for him to go to. The witches, as well.

Tara went back to work, content for the first time in a very long time.

The future was finally truly bright, not just for her, but for the region and everyone she loved as well.

EPILOGUE

After living in the city for so long, it's strangely freeing to be able to just wander. To go to the countryside, be in the foothills and forests that I adore, then travel back to concrete and lights. Portland continues to thrive. Not everyone can see it, but I can sense the glimmer of a greater plan. The community will come together, not in the short term but generally, overall. The witches I work with ensure that the right people are starting to find their places. The crowning moment of glory won't come for a few generations. Ah, but then? Such a bright light will shine from this small city, over the entire world. And though I will do my part, and will have to work hard, I will continue to bless the name of my benefactress who has put me on the right path finally: Tara.

Wilson Evermore, Protector of the Greater Portlandia and the Former Riprap Man

ABOUT THE AUTHOR

Leah Cutter writes page-turning fiction in exotic locations, such as a magical New Orleans, the ancient Orient, Hungary, the Oregon coast, rural Kentucky, Seattle, Minneapolis, and many others.

She writes literary, fantasy, mystery, science fiction, and horror fiction. Her short fiction has been published in magazines like *Alfred Hitchcock's Mystery Magazine* and *Talebones*, anthologies like Fiction River, and on the web. Her long fiction has been published both by New York publishers as well as small presses.

Find Leah's books on Knotted Road Press at (www.KnottedRoadPress.com)

Follow her blog at www.LeahCutter.com.

Reviews

It's true. Reviews help me sell more books. If you've enjoyed this story, please consider leaving a review of it on your favorite site.

Come someplace new...

Are you a traveler? Do you enjoy exploring strange new worlds, new cultures, new people?

Journey into the various lands envisioned by Leah Cutter.

Sign up for my newsletter and I'll start you on your travels with a free copy of my book, *The Island Sampler*.

I will never spam you or use your email for nefarious purposes. You can also unsubscribe at any time.

http://www.LeahCutter.com/newsletter/

ABOUT KNOTTED ROAD PRESS

Knotted Road Press fiction specializes in dynamic writing set in mysterious, exotic locations.

Knotted Road Press non-fiction publishes autobiographies, business books, cookbooks, and how-to books with unique voices.

Knotted Road Press creates DRM-free ebooks as well as high-quality print books for readers around the world.

With authors in a variety of genres including literary, poetry, mystery, fantasy, and science fiction, Knotted Road Press has something for everyone.

Knotted Road Press
www.KnottedRoadPress.com